Praise for *What the Dead Leave Behind*

"Naturally I always gravitate toward any book set in old New York, and this one exceeded expectations. It has everything one could expect from a historical mystery: set against the blizzard of '88, a smart heroine pits her wits against an evil stepmother out to destroy her."
—Rhys Bowen, *New York Times* bestselling author of the Molly Murphy and Royal Spyness mysteries

"Simpson's debut, first in a planned series, features complex characters, a vivid look at old New York in the late 1800s, and a mystery with a twist." —*Kirkus Reviews*

"Launching an atmospheric new series set in Gilded Age New York, Simpson incorporates historical events and figures to add verisimilitude to this tension-filled story. For mystery readers who appreciate period detail, including fans of Anne Perry's Thomas and Charlotte Pitt mysteries."
—*Library Journal* (starred review)

"This is a story to savor . . . Prudence is a stubborn, quick-witted American heroine who will remind readers of Tasha Alexander's Lady Emily Ashton and Deanna Raybourn's Lady Julia Grey."
—*Booklist*

"Richly plotted . . . Simpson anchors an appealing detective duo in a colorful and well-researched depiction of period settings and personalities."—*Publishers Weekly*

Books by Rosemary Simpson

WHAT THE DEAD LEAVE BEHIND

LIES THAT COMFORT AND BETRAY

Published by Kensington Publishing Corporation

WHAT THE DEAD LEAVE BEHIND

ROSEMARY SIMPSON

KENSINGTON BOOKS
http://www.kensingtonbooks.com

KENSINGTON BOOKS are published by

Kensington Publishing Corp.
119 West 40th Street
New York, NY 10018

All Kensington titles, imprints, and distributed lines are available at special quantity discounts for bulk purchases for sales promotion, premiums, fund-raising, educational, or institutional use.

Special book excerpts or customized printings can also be created to fit specific needs. For details, write or phone the office of the Kensington Sales Manager: Kensington Publishing Corp., 119 West 40th Street, New York, NY 10018. Attn. Sales Department. Phone: 1-800-221-2647.

Kensington and the K logo Reg. U.S. Pat. & TM Off.

First Kensington Hardcover Edition: May 2017

eISBN-13: 978-1-4967-0910-3
eISBN-10: 1-4967-0910-1

ISBN-13: 978-1-4967-0909-7
ISBN-10: 1-4967-0909-8
First Kensington Trade Paperback Printing: January 2018

10 9 8 7 6 5 4 3 2 1

To Marie McCormack Brady, whose lifelong love of New York City knew no bounds.

CHAPTER 1

March 12, 1888
New York City

Sunday's heavy rain turned to icy sleet and then snow after midnight, blanketing the sleeping city in layers of white that whirled into drifts and billows as the wind picked up. In the dark hours before dawn an unexpected spring snowstorm turned into a killing blizzard, the worst New York City had ever known.

The blizzard howled its way across Manhattan early Monday morning. Most of the city's inhabitants stayed home; the wind was strong, the ice slippery, and the snow so blinding that familiar stoops and sidewalks were too treacherous to risk. People who out of curiosity opened their front doors had to struggle to close them again against the howling gusts. New Yorkers turned up their gas furnaces, checked basement coal bins, fretted over the size of backyard woodpiles.

Despite the dangers of the storm, there were those who worried that if they didn't show up for work, there wouldn't be any work to show up for. Times had been bad after the war; jobs were scarce, hard to find and keep. Too many husbands and fathers lived in fear of being fired; for every man earning a weekly wage, another was ready to step into his shoes. Daily help, mostly women, lived hand to mouth; to lose a day's pay was to upset an already precarious balance. Empty bellies had to be filled no matter how treacherous the weather.

Easter was only three weeks away, they told themselves. How bad could a spring snowstorm get? How long could it last? Who'd ever heard of anyone freezing to death in mid-March? Few of the foolhardy who ventured out from their brownstones and apartments in the general direction of their places of employment got where they were attempting to go. Two hundred of those who did not turn back disappeared, not to be found again until the snow melted around their upthrust, desperate arms.

As Monday morning wore on, trains from the suburbs ground to a halt in monstrously tall drifts; the city's horse-drawn delivery wagons and hansom cabs failed to appear on snow-blocked streets. In front of every apartment building supers and doormen shoveled as fast as they could, but the wind and the snow beat them back into lobbies and foyers where they stomped their feet, gulped hot coffee, and warned the building's tenants against going out into the storm.

Already the phenomenon was earning itself nicknames. The Great Blizzard. The Storm of the Century. The Great White Hurricane.

Under any name, it brought death in its wake.

Wrapped in a fringed paisley shawl, Prudence MacKenzie stood at her bedroom window and tried to pick out where she had last seen the cobblestones of Fifth Avenue before the entire street disappeared under a blanket of white. All day long she had felt herself drawn to peer out through one or another of the mansion's windows, searching for a figure struggling through the impenetrable white. Charles had said he would be bringing the final copies of their marriage settlement documents today, just as soon as Roscoe Conkling, her late father's friend and lawyer, declared them fully in compliance with the Judge's will.

No carriage could have made it through the icy, snow-clogged streets, but Charles was a man of his word and nearly as stubborn as the notoriously immovable Conkling. Prudence could envision both men arguing their way out of their warm, safe offices into a storm that neither would admit was stronger than either of them.

By late Monday afternoon she'd worried herself into exhaustion and fallen asleep fully clothed when she lay down on her bed to stretch out for a moment. She dreamed of Charles until another howling blast of wind hurled itself against the corner of the brownstone and woke her up.

In her dream Charles had been a figure barely discernible through fiercely waving veils of snow, a living sculpture of ice struggling blindly up Broadway from Wall Street, calling out to her.

The nightmare part of the dream had been that she couldn't answer him.

New York's fifty-eight-year-old ex-senator, Roscoe Conkling, was pleading a case that Monday morning. Flamboyant, indefatigable, and commanding enormous fees, he mushed his way two and a half miles down Broadway from his apartment in the Hoffman House Hotel to the United Bank Building at the corner of Broadway and Wall Street where he received one of the few telephone calls completed in Manhattan that day. Telephone, telegraph, and electric poles were already toppling down into the streets, blocking access, spitting and sparking until the cold, wet snow shorted out the lines. The judge before whom Conkling was to appear was snowbound at his home. Court had been canceled.

Resigning himself to being stuck in the office, Conkling waded through the paperwork that was so much a part of every lawyer's life. This morning it was the last of the trust documents that his late friend, Judge Thomas MacKenzie, had had him draw up to safeguard the considerable fortune he had bequeathed to his beloved daughter by his first marriage.

Prudence, whose mother died when her only child was six years old, was two weeks away from becoming Mrs. Charles Linwood. Before that happened, Conkling had to be certain her interests were as well protected as the Judge had wanted. Not that Charles Linwood showed any trace of being the type of husband more enamored of his wife's fortune than the person of the lady herself. Far from it.

The Judge had been delighted when Linwood asked for Prudence's hand. Charles had gone from Harvard straight into his family's law firm where he'd proved himself as adept at drawing up finely crafted wills and contracts as he was persuasive before a jury. Already a skilled lawyer with a bright future, Charles Linwood loved Prudence MacKenzie in the honest, gentlemanly fashion every father wished for his daughter. The man could be trusted to care for his young bride and make her happy in her new life.

It was a perfect match.

The afternoon was turning shadowy despite the whiteness of the mesmerizing snow. Prudence lit the gas lamps on her bedside tables, listening for a few moments to their reassuring hiss, drinking in the comforting light. She had been awake most of the previous night, ever since the storm began to blow in earnest. Regardless of the weather, she had seldom slept through the hours of darkness since her father's death barely three months ago.

She had been given drops to dull the immediate agony of loss, but as the weeks of mourning wore on, a furious itching began to interrupt her sleep at night. She'd wake up to the bite of her fingernails scratching and digging at the thin, dry skin of her arms and legs. If she didn't stop herself soon enough, rings of dried blood showed reddish brown beneath her nails in the morning. She'd open her eyes, light the gas lamps, then reach for whichever book she was currently reading. She would still be awake at dawn.

And always there was the aching longing for her father, the memory of standing at the gate of the family crypt, hearing the creak and clang of wrought iron shutting him in forever.

Prudence unbuttoned the left sleeve of her black mourning gown, pushed it above the elbow, and examined the skin, bending to hold the arm under the soft yellow glow of one of the lamps. The scratches that had so recently been an angry red had faded into the faintest of tracks, as if she'd absentmindedly run the tip of a folded ivory fan along the length of her arm. The itching was less, almost unnoticeable, tamed and soothed by the face cream she'd rubbed into the sore skin morning and evening. Something else, too.

The cup of boiled milk brought up to her from the kitchen every evening had sat undrunk on the mantel for hours again last night, an ugly, wrinkled skin formed across its surface. It was after she'd stopped drinking the nightly milk that she noticed the itching no longer tortured her, that when she woke in the night, it was with a clear head. Despite the fatigue of too little sleep, she now felt restless where for a while she had been so lethargic that it was all she could do to get through the day.

The first time she left the milk undrunk, her stepmother, Victoria, folded her lips in tightly, made an odd clicking sound deep in her throat, but said nothing except to remind her stepdaughter that it wasn't the only thing Prudence had forgotten to do recently.

"You haven't been yourself since the Judge's funeral," Victoria insisted. "I worry about you. Grief has been known to do strange things to a woman's delicate sensibilities."

It wasn't grief that was destroying Prudence, deep though that was. It was the laudanum she had been given to help her through the mourning and soften the pain of loss. Prudence recognized its effects, but not its dangers. Not until it was almost too late.

When her mother's pain had grown too excruciating to be borne, the only thing that eased it was the tincture of opium commonly sold as laudanum. She'd seen Sarah MacKenzie claw fretfully at the thin skin of her chest, drops of blood staining her nightgown. Not everyone who took laudanum suffered from itching, but those who did often scratched themselves raw.

One day Prudence had touched a finger to the spoon lying on her mother's bedside table and then licked the bitter drop from her skin. Her father knew what she had done the moment he saw the grimace on her face and the telltale brown smear on her fingertip.

"Promise me you'll never taste Mama's medicine again, Prudence. It's only for very sick people, and my precious little girl isn't sick, is she?"

She had promised.

Then years later the father she adored died and she found herself alone with a stepmother she despised and distrusted and an uncle by marriage who made her skin crawl every time he looked at her. Her world fell apart, and so did Prudence. Laudanum was prescribed. Nearly three months of what were supposed to be only a few drops a day had brought her perilously close to the cliff of ladylike addiction. She remembered the worried frown on Dr. Worthington's face when he took the brown glass bottle with its tight-fitting cork out of his leather satchel.

"Not too much," he cautioned. "I would limit the dosage to five drops at a time, and no more frequently than once or twice a day."

Stepmother Victoria had taken the bottle from the doctor's hand with ill-concealed relish.

"She's not to dose herself, Mrs. MacKenzie."

"Of course not, Doctor."

"Accidents have been known to happen."

Barely ten years older than her stepdaughter, Victoria was now a widow whose much older husband died less than two years after pronouncing the marriage vows. By the terms of the Judge's will, this relative stranger had immediately upon his death become the trustee of her nineteen-year-old stepdaughter's inheritance and the arbiter of her every daily activity. But the legal loophole of Prudence's fast-approaching wedding would force Victoria to relinquish the control she obviously enjoyed. The mask behind which lay another Victoria was slipping; power once seized is never given up without a fight.

Prudence was counting the days until she would pass from the guardianship of a stepmother to the protection of a husband, slipped along with the signatures on her marriage contract, her future safely, predictably, and comfortably arranged by the father who was no longer here to care for her himself. The Judge had built high legal fences around his only child so no one could take away what was rightfully hers, had foreseen all eventualities. Or had he?

Two weeks after Dr. Worthington gave the first bottle of laudanum to Victoria MacKenzie, Prudence's stepmother declared Prudence capable of measuring out her own doses. After all, she wasn't a child any longer. Victoria handed over the brown bottle with a smile of encouragement, a pat on the hand, and a promise that when that bottle was empty another would be obtained.

Prudence hardly noticed that the doses she gave herself gradually grew larger. Five drops, then six, then seven. Laudanum numbed the agony of losing a parent, flattened out emotional peaks and valleys, made it possible to sleep. And really, it was only drops.

Charles worried, she knew he did, though he said nothing.

Not until the bedtime milk began appearing did she begin to wonder how much laudanum she was actually ingesting every day, how much was being given to her in addition to what she prepared for herself. And why? The wedding was so close. Victoria would be leaving the house that would then become Charles and Prudence's first home together. The Judge had bought his second wife an apartment in the Dakota before he died. As always, he'd seen to everything.

Or had he? Prudence was convinced that Victoria MacKenzie never did anything that would not benefit her, never moved a muscle unless it was to her advantage. She wondered if all stepdaughters disliked their father's new wives, if perhaps she should be less wary of Victoria. The Judge had taught his daughter to be fair, to consider an argument from every side. But where Victoria was concerned, there were questions, always questions. Never answers.

Now that the laudanum fog had dissipated, Prudence's unease about her stepmother was fast becoming something stronger than disquiet or simple anxiety. It was suspicion tinged with apprehension, a feeling that Victoria was determined to shape Prudence's future in a way the Judge would never have countenanced. Was there some hidden menace in the wording of her father's will that not even Charles had spied out? No matter how hard Prudence tried to figure out her stepmother's intentions, Victoria was always one step ahead. What could Victoria possibly gain if Prudence became one of those sad women whose pathetic lives were lived inside a brown glass bottle?

It was only when she tried to deny herself that Prudence discovered how very deep, dark, and comforting was the well down which she had begun to slide. No one had forced her to seek solace in laudanum. A trusted family doctor had provided a time-proven remedy, but cautiously, and she had taken it willingly. Drop by drop, until finally she knew it was time to stop. Some women carried tiny vials of the bitter potion with them everywhere they went and appeared none the worse for it. She did not think she could be one of them; the urge to feel the powerful warmth spreading through her body was too strong, too compelling.

She could not bear it if Charles broke his discreet silence, if he were finally driven to ask about the laudanum. And worst of all, what would her father say if he knew?

Since the night she had first denied herself the laudanum-laced milk, Prudence had resolutely refused what her body craved. She made sure Victoria saw her mix five drops of dark brown liquid into her coffee at the breakfast table and six drops into her afternoon tea, but she knew herself to be finally free of the drug. She replaced the laudanum in the bottles Victoria gave her with strong unsweetened tea nearly as bitter as the tincture of opium. It wasn't difficult to feign a moue of dislike as she drank it down. Victoria always smiled when Prudence shuddered at the sharp afterbite. To do any good, medicine had to taste bad. Everyone knew that.

The question she could not answer was why it was so important to continue to pretend she was taking Dr. Worthington's laudanum, why she emptied her nightly cup of milk out the window, why she didn't say a word to anyone about what she suspected her stepmother had tried to do to her.

Two more weeks. Then she'd be with Charles as his wife. Safe.

Last night, sometime between midnight and dawn, while the storm was gathering strength, Prudence had carried the teacup of tepid milk with its calming dose of laudanum to the window against whose glass panes snow had already mounded. She had eased the window frame open, gasped delightedly at the touch of icy flakes on her fingertips, then watched the milk freeze as it flew through the wind, as it became one with the snow and fell harmlessly into the street below. Every refusal was a victory.

She was not naturally a secretive person, nor one given to fanciful delusions. Her father had trained her to see life as realistically as intelligence and a tender heart could bear.

But there was something about Victoria that was deeply disturbing, even frightening.

Two more weeks. Then she'd be safe.

*   *   *

With his desktop clear for a change, Conkling ate the last two apples in the bowl of fruit that was normally replenished every morning by the very competent secretary he'd occasionally caught in the act of eating chocolates at his desk. Sure enough, there was a half-full box of cherry cordials in one of Josiah's drawers. Roscoe scribbled an IOU, dropped it into the now-empty container of candy, and gave himself a mental reminder to replace what he'd eaten.

Conkling was an anomaly among his peers. Far more athletic than most men in their late fifties, he rarely drank alcohol to excess and did not smoke. He sported a full, bushy beard and decked himself out in bright waistcoats and cravats that never allowed his six-foot-three-inch frame to blend into a crowd. People who disliked him called him a peacock and names so foully descriptive they were unprintable.

Roscoe's chief vice was women, the lovely creatures. Every one of New York's seven newspapers had scrupulously dissected his long and scandalous liaison with Kate Chase. Her father had been Lincoln's Secretary of the Treasury, then Chief Justice of the Supreme Court; she had married the governor of Rhode Island. Politics and illicit love always made good copy.

As much as Roscoe enjoyed reading about himself, it was the possibility of a dangerous or even fatal encounter with a husband that added that certain *je ne sais quoi* to every affair. He thrived on risk; every new adventure made the blood run faster through his veins. The taste of the chocolate cherry cordials on his tongue the day of the blizzard was nearly as sensuous as the first encounter with a new woman.

It was getting darker. Still midafternoon, but definitely darker. And there seemed to be something wrong with the gas lamps that usually lit up Broadway like a string of yellow pearls. The wind blew steadily between the buildings, and the snow never stopped falling. He'd thought to wait out the storm, confident it couldn't continue so violently for more than a few hours, but there hadn't been any letup. He'd sent the MacKenzie trust papers down to the Linwood office on the floor below hours ago. It wouldn't surprise him if young Charles had already taken them to Prudence. Maybe it was time to think about leaving. While he still could.

"Mr. Conkling. I thought I saw your light on. Almost everyone who managed to make it in today has already left." Charles Linwood stood in the doorway, bundled against the weather in thick coat, muffler, and tall top hat. One hand held a pair of gloves, the other a heavy briefcase. "My father talked me out of trying to take the MacKenzie trust papers to Prudence until tomorrow when all of this will have blown through. I'm sure he was right, though I wish I'd been able to get a message to her. It's too late now. The snow doesn't seem to be lessening, so I'm leaving. What about you?"

"I'll keep you company if you're going toward Union Square."

"I am, and I'm hoping to find a hansom cab somewhere along Broadway."

"I haven't seen any kind of vehicle in the last few hours. Not a cab or a carriage in sight."

"It wasn't too bad early this morning. I'm sure some of the sidewalks have been shoveled by now."

"The snow's still coming down too heavily to be able to see very much." Conkling turned from the window.

"If the drifts are too high, we can always stop at one of the hotels along the way."

"I hope Prudence didn't try to go out today."

"She's much too sensible for that." Charles Linwood smiled as he said it. He was immensely fond of Prudence MacKenzie, and looking forward to their marriage. They'd always gotten along so well as friends that it was inconceivable they wouldn't grow even closer as husband and wife.

Conkling reached for his coat. "Losing her father was a terrible blow. The Judge was a good friend; he sent Jay Gould along to me, and Mr. Edison. They were among my first clients when I came back to the city. I miss Thomas MacKenzie like a brother."

"He and my father practiced summation speeches on one another when they were just starting out. My deepest regret is that I won't have the honor of knowing the Judge as a father-in-law, but I'm sure Prudence and I will want to welcome you often as a guest in our home."

"And I'll be more than happy to come. Has Mrs. MacKenzie begun to move her things out yet?"

"She says she plans to be gone by the time we get back from Saratoga Springs."

"Not France or Italy?"

"Perhaps next year. Prudence is still very fragile. I asked where she would most like to spend our honeymoon, and she chose Saratoga. The Judge took her to the Grand Union Hotel every summer for years."

"And so that's where you'll also be staying?"

"I don't think she'd be content anywhere else."

"I wish you both great happiness, Charles."

"Thank you, sir."

"When you get back, when you have time, we should sit down together. The Judge was meticulous in seeing to his affairs, but there are sealed envelopes he gave me that are not to be opened until after the marriage has taken place."

"I didn't know that."

"No reason why you should. I haven't said anything to Prudence, either. My instructions were to see to them within the first month after the wedding. The Judge smiled when he handed them to me, so I don't suppose there's anything much to be concerned about. It may just be his way of ensuring that you both receive whatever fatherly advice he wanted to give you."

"The will was a bit unusual." Charles Linwood hesitated. Until he became Prudence's husband, he was too much the gentleman to feel entirely comfortable discussing the fortune bequeathed to her by her father.

"In the normal way of things, it might have been expected that the family home would go to the widow, at least for the remainder of her lifetime," Conkling agreed. "But Mrs. MacKenzie has only lived there for the two years of her marriage to the Judge. She doesn't have the ties to it that Prudence does. Thomas was the soul of discretion. It was no secret to him that his daughter didn't have the same warm feelings for Victoria that he did. He provided very well for his widow, just not perhaps exactly in the way she might have been expecting."

And that, Roscoe Conkling's headshake seemed to say, was his last word on the subject. For the moment, at least. Until after Saratoga. After the wedding. After this damned blizzard that looked like it was capable of blowing them over as soon as they stepped out of the building.

People likened these streets to canyons; they funneled wind and rain and now snow down narrow walled passages that increased velocity and turned harmless raindrops and snowflakes into missiles that stung the skin and made the eyes water.

"Are you ready?" Conkling asked.

"As I'll ever be," laughed Charles.

Even before they managed to make it onto the sidewalk, both men realized it was going to be worse than either of them had imagined.

CHAPTER 2

As Conkling and Linwood pushed open the doors of the United Bank Building, the force of the wind threw them back into the vestibule. Conkling thought he would have been slammed against the marble floor if Linwood had not grabbed his arm and held on to him as the two men struggled to regain their footing. Snow swirled into the lobby, making the expensive Italian marble as slippery and dangerous as the icy street outside.

"I'm not sure we're going to make it up Broadway after all," Linwood said, one gloved hand holding on to the handle of the door that had almost flattened him. "We might be better off spending the night here, Mr. Conkling."

From behind them came a shout, then the sound of rapidly approaching footsteps. "I thought I heard voices. I stopped by your office because I knew you'd come in today, Mr. Conkling, but you'd already left." William Sulzer, whose office was down the hall from Conkling's, had been in such a hurry that he'd left his coat unbuttoned and carried his wool scarf in his hand. "I hoped I'd catch up with you."

"It's very bad out there, William." Charles took a few cautious steps across the slick wet marble floor.

"Nonsense," scoffed Conkling. "We may have some difficulty making our way along the sidewalk, but once we get around the corner we'll find a hansom cab. We're going toward Union Square, William."

"Perfect. I'll join you, if I may."

It was on the tip of Linwood's tongue to tell both of his fellow lawyers they were as mad as the Hatter in the Alice story Prudence loved to quote to him. She'd told him more than once there was a model for every one of Mr. Carroll's odd characters in their own immediate social circle. He certainly felt as though the blizzard raging outside had frozen them in Alice's upside-down world. No place to go and no way to get there.

Conkling and Sulzer peered out the doors, bickering amiably about whether they should walk to the corner of Wall Street and Broadway in search of a hansom, or strike out through the drifts in the direction of Union Square and keep going until a cab came along. New York City was famous for its sturdy horses; you saw them all the time in winter, nostrils steaming clouds of vapor as they slogged along under the protection of heavy canvas or plaid wool blankets. The snow might be too thick at the moment to be able to make them out, but there would definitely be horse-drawn hansoms out there somewhere.

"Charles, are you with us?"

"William, I'm not sure we should attempt this. It's getting darker and colder by the minute."

Roscoe Conkling flashed a challenging smile at the much younger men. "Two miles to Union Square, gentlemen. Forty-five minutes more or less. An easy late-afternoon stroll." He could already imagine captivating an audience with the tale of how he'd conquered the elements when lesser men had surrendered. He pushed open the heavy outer door and disappeared through a curtain of white.

"We can't lose sight of him." William Sulzer slammed his way out into the snow. "Mr. Conkling, we're coming. Stand still until we get to you," he shouted.

If he caught a catarrh from the wind whipping around his head, Charles knew that Prudence would have words to say about being careless with his health this close to the wedding. But if he didn't follow Conkling and Sulzer into the storm, he'd never live it down. The story would be told and laughed over in every law office in the city. On the whole, he'd rather take his chances with Prudence. "I'm coming," he yelled over the wind that bellowed as loudly as one of the new steam-engined trains rushing through the city.

The three men trudged off together toward Trinity Church, though they could barely make out its impressive gothic revival bulk. The tall cross-topped spire that usually dominated the skyline had disappeared. They saw nothing but blinding whiteness, heard nothing but the howl of the blizzard roaring down the city's canyons. By the time they reached their first destination, where Wall Street met Broadway, they knew there would be no long line of hansom cabs lined up waiting for passengers, patient horses munching contentedly in their nosebags.

Snowdrifts had piled up against the massive arched doors of Trinity Church; in places the wind scoured the sidewalk almost clean, only to dump impenetrable snow mountains higher than the top of a tall man's head farther on. Broadway stretched before them in glorious emptiness. Landmarks were unrecognizable; utility poles had toppled into and across the street like a bizarre forest of branchless young pines in a tangle of snapping, buzzing wires.

Roscoe Conkling led the way, his tall, athletic body moving like an upright white polar bear along the ice floes of Broadway. His luxuriant beard froze stiff on his chest; icicles glittered, melted under his breath, dripped, and reformed almost immediately. Snowflakes hung from his eyebrows, piled up on his eyelashes, clung to his hat and the fabric of his coat. He should have been as frozen as the landscape around him, but he wasn't; the energy it took to keep moving generated a heat that defied nature. Charles Linwood and William Sulzer, struggling along behind and occasionally beside him, told themselves it was their duty to see the older man to warmth and safety, to continue on as long as he did. They had to match Conkling step for step.

They almost didn't believe their eyes when a hansom cab pulled up beside them, the horse stomping its great hooves as billows of steam surged from its nostrils. The driver had swaddled himself hat to boots in blankets so all they saw of his face was a pair of dark eyes peering down at them.

"How much to the New York Club at Madison Square?" shouted Conkling.

The driver of the hansom cab looked at the three swells as if calculating the price of their fur-collared coats and beaver hats, gazed for a few moments at the empty stretch of Broadway that lay ahead, turned to peer behind through the snow as if searching for another vehicle. "Fifty bucks," he growled. "Take it or leave it."

Sulzer was already reaching for the carriage door when Conkling raised his cane and brought it down so hard against the wheel of the cab that they could all hear the crack of split wood. By the time he'd finished cursing the man for his thievery and the bastardy of his lineage, the driver had whipped up his horse and disappeared into heavy whirls of falling snow.

Linwood stood thunderstruck and speechless. Not a one of the three of them couldn't have afforded the exorbitant demand; highway robbery though it be, they could have been out of the icy wind and on their way up Broadway in relative comfort and security. Conkling must think he was invulnerable, some sort of physical marvel who could triumph over the worst challenges of God and nature.

"Mr. Conkling, I think we'd do well to turn in at Astor House," Sulzer said. "It's not much farther. I know we can make it that far. I'm not sure we'd be wise to try to continue on to Madison or Union Square." His breath froze into vapor as he spoke. "I realize that's what we set out to do, but an army in the field that doesn't take note of its battleground and revise its plans accordingly is an army that's condemned itself to losing the fight."

Conkling hadn't donned a uniform during the war, but as a member of Congress, he'd been more than familiar with the successes and failures of its campaigns. All Sulzer got for his clever attempt at rationalizing retreat was a stare and a noise that might have been a clearing of Conkling's throat or another outburst of muttered imprecations.

Everything was losing color now as the sky continued to darken. What little light remained reflected palely back from the whiteness beneath their feet. The world around them turned black and white and gray on every side, with only here and there the pale yellow glow of a gas lamp that had somehow, miraculously, remained lit.

Conkling stepped off the curb into the street, pushing his way out into the middle of what had been a busy thoroughfare twenty-four hours ago. The wind blew harder out there, but without the changeability and violent gusts that came from hurling itself through the New York canyons. It was a good strategy, though there was nothing to break a man's fall or support his weight when he needed to rest. When he looked behind him, he saw Linwood propping up the more slender Sulzer, as though the younger man no longer had the strength to battle the force of the wind on his own. Sulzer's coat bore thick patches of snow and hung crookedly from his shoulders. How many times had he fallen and gotten up again?

Off in the distance could be glimpsed the lights of Astor House, six stories tall, once the most famous hotel in the city, now eclipsed by half a dozen other temples of luxury, including the Fifth Avenue Hotel on Madison Square. There were bound to be other refugees from the blizzard gathered in its dining rooms, bars, and celebrated rotunda, probably most of the staff of the *New York Herald* covering the storm of the century from the newspaper's offices a few steps away. The three of them might be alone on Broadway at the moment, but they wouldn't be alone for long. Comradeship, warmth, and whiskey beckoned to them. Every labored footfall brought them closer.

He couldn't reach his pocket watch, but Charles Linwood thought they must have been walking for at least an hour, several times what it would have taken to cover the seven or eight blocks from their offices to the Astor House on a sunny day. He'd done it last week in less than ten or fifteen minutes.

"I'm going to stop," William Sulzer declared. "I don't think I can go any farther." His breath was coming in short, wheezy gulps of air that sounded like a faulty bellows failing to blow a dying fire into life again. His walk had become a stagger; he'd lost his briefcase in one of the drifts into which he'd stumbled, and he clung to Linwood's arm as if it were the only thing holding him up. "You'd both do well to do the same. I'd rather spend the night in a chair in the Astor House bar or lobby than be found frozen stiff and stubborn in the street tomorrow morning."

They had reached the Astor House's entrance, warm yellow gaslight streaming out onto the sidewalk between Greek Doric columns. A cluster of the hotel's uniformed staff stood just inside the doors, and beyond them stretched a sea of men who had reached their offices that morning but were now stranded. Strains of music poured out as one of the porters cracked open a door to welcome them in. Gusts of laughter, the clink of bottles against glasses, the heavy smoke of dozens of cigars. The famously stiff and proper Astor House wore for this Monday night only the relaxed and welcoming joviality of a neighborhood saloon.

"Mr. Conkling?"

"I don't blame you, William. I don't blame you at all. I absolve you of responsibility for my safety. When reporters for the New York newspapers ask how it could be that a man of fifty-eight full years of life could best a stripling only halfway through his twenties, I trust you'll tell the unvarnished truth. The man of the hour was Roscoe Conkling." The ex-senator could almost see the headline of the story that would ensure his place as the talk and the toast of New York City.

"Mr. Conkling, there are already so many tales told of your exploits that one more will scarcely make a difference."

Sulzer tipped his top hat, its well-brushed beaver skin barely visible under the snow that had fallen on it. He raised his frozen eyebrows at Linwood, who shrugged resignedly, let go his companion's arm, and stretched out his gloved hand. The two young lawyers shook as solemnly as if they were about to argue a case against each other, then Sulzer turned into the porticoed entrance of Astor House.

Moments later, following on Conkling's heels, Linwood continued the long trek to Madison Square. Two more miles up Broadway. At least another two hours, Linwood thought, even without Sulzer to slow them down. The trek that Conkling called a brisk one-hour walk between office and apartment would end up taking them three times that to complete.

Prudence would simply have to understand that it was beyond the realm of conscience to allow the Judge's close friend to totter off alone into the snowy night.

This stretch of Broadway, usually bustling with people and carriages, was nearly as deserted as the area down by Wall Street and Trinity Church. Occasionally a bundled-up figure darted out into the snow carrying a shovel, dug frantically for a few minutes at the nearly impassable banks piled up before every doorway, then disappeared again into the warmth and security of office or apartment building. The hansom cabs and their sturdy horses had retreated to warm stables, drivers rolled in blankets and bedded down outside the stalls. As soon as the streets were clear enough to get out again, they'd be carrying gentlemen from the hotels where they'd found shelter back to their homes. At a nice price, to be sure. Nobody thought it possible that the storm could rage unchecked through much of Tuesday.

Prudence drew long royal blue velvet drapes over lace curtains, closing off the outside world, its unpredicted storm and unknowable future. No point continuing to peer out through the thick flakes for Charles. He might be stubborn, but he was also sensible. Too sensible to stagger along icy, windy streets to keep a promise that wasn't even that important. Two weeks until they married, plenty of time to write her name on the documents Charles and Conkling would have gone over with the proverbial fine-toothed comb.

She had pretended to be indisposed when the gong rang for dinner. Victoria had come looking for her, but Prudence had pleaded a headache and asked for a tray to be sent up later. She'd eaten the food, then poured the wine and the coffee out the window to join last night's milk. She would go to bed early, she told her stepmother. She was feeling so sleepy.

Victoria's smug smile as she left her stepdaughter's room had enraged Prudence, but there was nothing she could say against it, nothing she could do. She needed to talk to Charles, needed to share her suspicions and her fears. In the meantime, she had to sit out the storm as best and as safely as she could. If that meant hiding herself in her bedroom, then so be it. Being alone was infinitely preferable to having to exchange stiff excuses for conversation with Victoria and her brother. Donald Morley made her stomach churn with the force of some unnameable menace. His sister, her late father's widow, was an unknown quantity who had lately frightened her beyond all reason. She would avoid them both until Charles came to rescue her.

Still with the shawl around her shoulders, Prudence crawled back into the four-poster bed where she had slept since her fifth birthday, smiling as books tumbled against one another. She'd always fallen asleep in a nest of words, one hand resting on a beloved favorite, the other curled into the pages of one of her father's legal treatises or the latest volume from Mr. Henry James or the exciting Mr. Stevenson.

It struck her quite suddenly that her new husband might not want to have to reach his bride by crawling over her drawbridge of sharp-cornered tomes. She pushed away the thought on the same breath as it occurred to her, then, for reassurance, reached out for the small studio portrait of Charles Montgomery Linwood that had been a Christmas gift. Charles was clean-shaven, as had been Prudence's father. She thought it made a man look neater and less fearsome not to be peering out at the world through tangles of curly beard hairs that too frequently bore evidence of their owner's most recent meal.

Charles was a lawyer, of course, a partner in his father's office, destined for Prudence ever since Judge MacKenzie and his long-ago law partner agreed that a match between their offspring was to everyone's advantage. Charles had not objected; neither had Prudence. They had expected to marry, expected to fall in love. And so they had. He was thirteen years older than she, exactly the right number. She'd known him since babyhood, and if there wasn't a burning passion between them, there was the comforting warmth and ease of long familiarity.

The wedding was to be a small, private affair; Judge Thomas Pickering MacKenzie had been dead less than three months. If his most recent will had not stipulated that his daughter was to marry her fiancé within ninety days of his death, Prudence would have waited for the full year of mourning to be over. Charles wouldn't have opposed her. But her father had toyed with his final testament as frequently as some men bought new cravats. It amused him to tinker with codicils, to mention deserving servants by name, to strike out old friends as they predeceased him, to add conditions that sometimes verged on the absurd. His marriage to Victoria had necessitated major changes, but the habitual fiddling and tweaking had soon made the new document as long and complex as the one it replaced. The last version contained the stipulation about his daughter's marriage, naming Charles Linwood as the fiancé to which it applied.

To avoid saddling his future son-in-law with a possible conflict of interest, Judge MacKenzie turned all of his legal affairs over to his longtime friend, the ex-senator from New York. Roscoe Conkling was as adept in the fine points of the law and as maddeningly precise and bullish in the defense of a client as the Judge. Unlike his far less flamboyant friend, however, Conkling turned down President Garfield's offer of a judgeship. Twenty years in Washington had been enough; when he quit, he quit.

"If you don't think being an Associate Justice of the Supreme Court of the United States is as political as it gets, you don't know the first thing about government," he explained when he refused the appointment. "Garfield invited me to stop by the White House for a visit. I wrote him back that I was too damn busy. He knew why. Hell of a way to die though, poor bastard."

She should have studied the entire will herself, from the part about being of sound mind to the distinctive and wonderfully scrawled signature, but Prudence had been too dazed immediately after her father's death, too deep in grief and despair to be logical. Too lost in laudanum. No one expected the Judge's heart to give out when it did; his docket had been full for months to come. She wouldn't think of that now; she couldn't. Just allowing her father's name to creep into her mind made her crave the blessed oblivion of the laudanum.

"Small amounts for a few weeks or a month or two won't hurt," Dr. Worthington promised. "Sometimes that's all that's needed to help someone through the worst of the grieving, my dear Prudence."

He'd delivered her, closed her mother's eyes, diagnosed and treated every childhood ailment, and scolded her father regularly for the number of cigars he smoked and the prodigious amount of fine French brandy he managed to consume each day. Dr. Peter Worthington had seen the good that laudanum could do and he'd also attended soldiers whose worst war wound was not from a shell or a Minié ball, but from the liquid in the brown glass bottles that brought relief and unbearable pain seemingly at the same time. No one quite understood laudanum; nearly everyone who had ever dosed himself with it craved another swallow, then another and another and another.

Charles interpreted her father's will as only a fellow lawyer could, and if its provisions hadn't alarmed him, and she didn't think they had, then surely there was nothing to worry about. Nothing except that the training her father had given her screamed in her head now that she was beginning to think clearly again.

The Judge had delighted in treating her as the son he'd never had, as heir and lawyer-to-be. Together they had shared long evenings poring over case histories, discussing and debating the fine points of the arguments that had been made before Judge MacKenzie's bench. Prudence had the makings of a great lawyer who, because she was a woman, would never be admitted to the bar. Even knowing how limited her future must be, she'd reveled in the challenge of it all, in the prickling dance of her stimulated brain. They'd had a wonderful life together, Thomas Pickering MacKenzie and his daughter.

Until Victoria. Dear Victoria. So sweet, so tender.

Prudence hated her.

From the very beginning Victoria had tried to drive a wedge between the Judge and his daughter, inexorably determined to pry them apart. It began with the marriage itself. Victoria persuaded Thomas MacKenzie to exchange vows in a city registry office without his daughter in attendance. It had been like a knife cutting out Prudence's heart.

"I have a surprise for you, Prudence," he had said one morning two years ago. "I hope it will make you happy and ease the loneliness I know you've felt."

When she asked him what the surprise was, he only smiled. Sadly, resignedly, not at all like a groom about to claim his bride. Prudence hadn't suspected a thing.

The woman she met for the first time that afternoon was already her stepmother, the so-called wedding picture, taken days later, as much a sham as the marriage.

And it never got any better.

When the Judge wasn't there, Victoria alternately ignored or belittled her stepdaughter. Nothing Prudence said or did was right. Her clothes were unfashionable and unbecoming, her few friends unwelcome. Prudence withdrew into herself, stayed as far away from Victoria as she could, found solace in the books she read and the four-poster bed that gradually became her fortress. Invitations dwindled and then stopped. Victoria declined them all, only informing Prudence of what she had done when it was too late to reconsider.

Victoria became another woman altogether when the Judge was witness to how she treated his daughter. *Butter wouldn't melt in her mouth* was the saying; Prudence had never fully understood what it meant until she saw Victoria at work. So innocent, so sincere, so fawning in the attention she lavished on the motherless girl, so sure that Prudence would never complain to her father about how she was treated when he was in court.

And she didn't. Even after she was certain that Victoria's dislike had turned into a spiteful malevolence, Prudence said nothing. She believed her father loved his new wife. Why else would he have married her? No matter how malicious Victoria became, she would not risk the Judge's happiness by telling tales.

She thought now it had been a terrible mistake, one she would regret to her dying day.

Divorce was rare, but it did happen. If the Judge had remarried because he believed Prudence needed a mother, she should have found the courage to tell him he had made a singularly bad choice. He might have decided to free himself from Victoria, and that would have made all the difference. Thomas MacKenzie's last two years of life had been as much torture for him as they were for his daughter. Because she hadn't dared tell him the truth.

Victoria had ruined two lives.

Prudence hated her stepmother. And she would never forgive her.

For almost another full hour Conkling and Linwood struggled through the snow with hardly a word said between them. The closer they got to Union Square, the more Linwood became convinced that he wouldn't be able to continue much beyond Grace Church. Surely its doors would be open to anyone foolish enough to have allowed himself to be trapped in the city. He heard the sound of footsteps crunching through the snow behind him, and wondered if William Sulzer had changed his mind and left Astor House after warming up a bit. When he turned to wave to him, he glimpsed a figure that was too bulky to be the very tall, very slender Sulzer.

Up ahead, Roscoe Conkling was almost out of sight, already crossing into Union Park, his long legs striding through what looked to be drifts taller than any they'd encountered so far. Charles saw him turn and raise an arm, beckoning him to hurry and catch up, signaling he was continuing on. For a moment, with Grace Church less than a hundred yards away, Linwood was sorely tempted to forget about Conkling and his stubborn determination to get back to his club off Madison Square tonight. But the worry of leaving the ex-senator alone in what was still a dangerous blizzard nagged at him. What if he fell and was unable to extricate himself from a snowbank? He'd die there, suffocated, frozen. Such an ignominious ending for so distinguished a career.

Reluctantly, but worried now that Conkling had gotten too far ahead of him to be easily caught up, Linwood tried to make better time along the icy street, weaving between snowdrifts and solid objects. The wind hurled rubbish bins along the sidewalks, lifted baby carriages parked overnight on front stoops into the air, blew the overhanging canvas awnings off shop windows. Sometimes he sank up to his shoulders in an unexpectedly deep drift, clawing at whatever debris he could reach to help push and pull himself out. He could no longer hear Conkling, who couldn't be more than five or ten minutes ahead of him, probably fighting mountains of snow piled up in Union Park. Barely half a mile to go. They were almost there.

He thought he could still hear someone behind him, someone following along rather closely, but in no particular hurry. He turned around to catch another look at the man, but could make out nothing and no one through the thickly falling snow.

Somehow Linwood reached a tree-sheltered bench on the edge of Union Park, a bench miraculously outlined as such, beckoning whitely to him through the darkness. He hadn't even realized that he'd kept hold of his leather briefcase, but now he used it to brush mounds of snow from the wood and metal seat. If he could just sit down for a few moments, he knew he'd be able to push on fast enough to join Conkling before he reached the lights of the New York Club.

There was something menacing about being so absolutely alone, even in a place he knew very well in daylight. He told himself he'd count slowly to twenty, then get up and get going again. Willing his eyes open the whole time he was counting, he could feel a terrible lethargy creeping over him. He didn't dare risk falling asleep.

When the blow struck Charles Linwood on the back of his head, he fell forward without a sound. A hand reached for his briefcase, then rifled his leather wallet from the inside pocket of his suit jacket. With no identification, the body would remain unclaimed a little longer, the inquiry less urgent. The tree branch that had been used to crack his skull was tossed atop the body, a few others added, as if the weight of the snow had caused them to fall at precisely the moment when their unlucky victim sat beneath them.

Within minutes Linwood was no more than another hard-to-discern shape rapidly disappearing under what was likely to be two more feet of snow before morning.

An hour after Linwood died, Conkling staggered into Madison Square. He had floundered in the deep snowdrifts of Union Square Park longer than a lesser man would have been able to endure, battling his way along what he thought must be pathways beneath his frozen feet, swinging his arms to keep his balance and the blood moving through his body, utterly determined that nothing as impersonal as an act of nature would defeat him. Linwood might have given up and sought refuge in Grace Church, the last place he'd glimpsed him through the white, but Roscoe Conkling never, never surrendered, so matter how dire the situation.

He thought later that he might actually have been only semiconscious for the last several blocks of his journey because all he could remember of it afterward was the crackling of his frozen beard against the snow every time he fell and the agony of feet that pained and burned unmercifully. He made it across Madison Square and nearly to the door of the New York Club before collapsing one last time.

A porter half carried, half dragged him the rest of the way.

CHAPTER 3

The *Herald* listed Charles Linwood among the two hundred metropolitan victims of the Great Blizzard, many of them found buried in snowdrifts that paralyzed the city. One by one the dead were discovered, their stories pieced together from what could be surmised by where they fell and what grief-stricken friends and relatives could tell reporters. New Yorkers read the newspapers, shook their heads over the sadness of it all, and as the piles of snow began to melt, gradually forgot the fate of strangers they did not know and got on with the business of daily living. Easter came early this year, on April 1; it would be just three short weeks after the storm.

"I don't know how it happened," Roscoe Conkling said. He held Prudence MacKenzie's hands lightly but firmly in his own. "I've thought about nothing else for the past four days, but all I can recall is struggling our way up Broadway together, then gradually getting separated. I know I fell into huge drifts in Union Square. I remember seeing the lights of the Fifth Avenue Hotel and knowing that Madison Square had to be right in front of me. By that time I was stumbling and falling every few steps. If the doorman at the New York Club hadn't happened to be looking toward the park, he wouldn't have seen me."

"They think Charles sat down on a bench to rest, and a limb fell on him." Victoria MacKenzie touched a small lace-edged handkerchief to her eyes. "We didn't begin to worry until Wednesday night. He hadn't sent word."

"He would have wanted me to know he was all right," Prudence said quietly. Her voice sounded flat and muted, as though she were not fully aware of having spoken. "He would have sent someone to inquire about us. Or come himself. That's how I realized something was wrong." She eased her hands from Roscoe's, folding them in her lap.

Eyes on her stepdaughter, Victoria continued the story. "Mr. Sulzer called on us. He said the first thing he did when he was able to leave Astor House on Tuesday was check to make sure that you and Charles had made it through to the New York Club. The doorman there told him he'd pulled you in out of the night, but that he hadn't seen anyone else. They might not have found Charles as quickly as they did if they hadn't known he was missing. A policeman called on Charles's father after they located him."

"I was in court Tuesday," Roscoe said. "It never occurred to me that Charles had not gotten through safely. I thought he'd stopped at Grace Church. I looked back and saw him wave at me; he was gesturing toward the church. I could just make out the steeple."

"The funeral will be next Wednesday," Victoria said.

"I shall be there," promised Roscoe. He watched closely as Prudence sat without moving, eyes downcast, fingers still and white against the black silk of her dress. *Laudanum,* he thought, *that damn Worthington has given her more laudanum.* "I wonder if I might have a few moments alone with Prudence."

Victoria pursed her lips and made an odd clicking sound deep in her throat. She let you know without saying a word when she heartily disapproved of what you'd done or asked her to do.

"I'll order tea," she said, getting gracefully to her feet. "And perhaps my brother will join us."

By which she informed Roscoe that he was not the only man in the house, though he could not for the life of him remember how Mrs. MacKenzie's brother spent his days. Couldn't even remember the fellow's name, for that matter.

"Prudence, I need to talk to you," he said as soon as the parlor door clicked shut. "Charles's death changes things. Do you understand what I mean?"

"He won't be here to marry me." She sounded as though she were reciting a lesson learned at school.

Odd way to put it, Roscoe thought. He reached for Prudence's hands, held them more tightly than before, gave them a little shake as if she were asleep and he wanted to wake her up.

Her eyes flashed briefly in comprehension before they fell again to her lap. The muscles of her face slackened and drooped.

My God, he thought angrily, *the damn quack has her doped to the gills.* "Prudence," he said forcefully, willing her to listen to him, to answer his questions. "When was the last time you took the laudanum?"

"I can't remember. Victoria knows."

"How many drops does your stepmother give you at a time?"

"Four or five, I think. Perhaps ten. You should ask Dr. Worthington."

"You can be sure of that. Prudence, you need to listen to me and remember what I say. Can you do that? Will you?"

No answer, but the long white fingers twitched. She had heard him.

"I don't want you to take any more laudanum. I don't want you to drink anything at all that Mrs. MacKenzie prepares for you. I'll speak to her, but she may not listen to me. Can you remember that you're not to swallow anything you're handed, anything that seems to have been fixed only for you? Can you remember that?"

"Why, Mr. Conkling?"

He thought he saw the Prudence who had sat devouring the law at her father's feet trying valiantly to swim up from the laudanum depths where sounds were hard to discern and sights were hazy. "Why, Mr. Conkling?" she asked again.

Perhaps if I give her something or someone to fight against. The Judge had never been more alive than when he had a cause to champion or a despairing client to defend. "We have work to do, Prudence. You and I have important work to do. Together. But you can't do it if you allow your senses to be dulled by laudanum.

"No matter what Dr. Worthington told you, no matter that half the girls and women you know keep a brown bottle on their bedside tables, laudanum is not your friend. It's your enemy, Prudence. It weakens you. You know how your father felt about weak men; he despised them. This is something you'll have to do alone, my dear child, without help from anyone else. Come to my office after the funeral. Come alone. Don't tell Victoria where you're going. Will you remember what I've said?"

"Yes, I'll remember." The pupils of her eyes were pinpoints of black nearly lost in a sea of gray. "I'm very tired, Mr. Conkling, and I know about laudanum. Dr. Worthington gave it to me when my father died. I stopped taking it for a while. Now Charles." She wanted to tell him that she couldn't remember pouring that first spoonful after Charles's death had been confirmed, but laudanum confused everything. She thought she recalled Victoria's cold blue eyes staring into her own, the touch of Victoria's hand as she guided the silver teaspoon toward Prudence's lips. Her stepmother had murmured something soothing, and then had come the blessed oblivion of sleep. Laudanum could make it possible never to feel pain, to live life in a dream.

If she had been a man, Conkling would have said she'd been at the brandy a little unwisely. Her speech was slurred; she

seemed to be making a great effort just to stay awake and follow what he was saying.

"I am so very sorry, Prudence. Did you love him very
much?" Keep her talking, keep her struggling to make sense of
what had happened.

"Not so very much. But Charles was always kind, always
thoughtful. I can't remember a time when we didn't know one
another."

"You were going to live here together," he said, standing and
bringing Prudence also to her feet. He walked her to the tall
windows that looked out onto Fifth Avenue. When she nodded
her head, he pulled back the heavy crimson drapes, flooding the
room with bright spring sunshine. Horse-drawn sleighs skimmed
their way along the still-snow-packed street, messenger boys had
donned skates, crews of laborers were creating mountains of
white with every scoop of their shovels. New Yorkers smiled
and laughed as they linked arms and made sliding progress toward home or work or recreation; they'd survived, the city had
survived. Life was worth living again.

"If I open the window, you'll be able to hear the sleigh
bells," he said.

"I wish you wouldn't, Mr. Conkling." Victoria MacKenzie
gave orders under the guise of suggestion, but the whip in her
voice was unmistakable. She'd opened the parlor door without
making a sound.

A man's voice echoed her remark. "I'm afraid I have to agree
with my sister. I've just come from that delightful scene you're
looking at, and I'm quite chilled, thank you very much."

"You remember my brother, Donald, Mr. Conkling? I believe you met here once before, but that was some time ago.
Business, I think. You had stopped by to bring the Judge some
papers."

"I'm sure a gentleman as well-known as Mr. Conkling can't
be expected to remember the name of every man whose hand
he's shaken, Victoria. Donald Morley, at your service, sir."

"Of course, Mr. Morley. I do remember you. Quite well, actually."

There was no way to avoid the outthrust hand, but Victoria's brother was right about one thing. Roscoe Conkling had shaken so many hands in the course of his political life that one more scarcely made a difference. He detected a heartiness about Morley's grip that screamed falsity.

"Donald, will you close the drapes again, please. I think the light may give Prudence a headache. Come, my dear, sit down beside me. Colleen will bring tea in a few minutes." Victoria steered her stepdaughter away from Conkling's side and across the intricate pattern of a crimson Turkish carpet to an upholstered sofa in the style of Louis XV, all fluid lines, gilded wood, and delicately curved legs. It served to remind the two men that these ladies perched like blackbirds on its cushions were to be treated with delicacy and care. They appeared just as lovely, just as fragile as the furniture on which they sat.

"Victoria tells me that Mr. Linwood's funeral is to be on Wednesday." Morley waited for Conkling to be seated before ensconcing himself comfortably in one of the armchairs that flanked the fireplace. "I'm sure most of the snow will be gone by then. It's already begun to melt in many places."

"I saw merchants piling wood in the drifts in front of their stores and then lighting fires to melt the snow so customers can get from the roadway to the sidewalk." Conkling said. "Some of the streets look like they have rivers running down them."

"I'm curious, sir, if you don't mind my asking. We read the interview you gave the *Herald* on Wednesday. Have you suffered no ill effects from your ordeal?" Morley took a pipe from his jacket pocket, glanced at his sister, then abruptly put it away. "I'm sure I would have come down with the pneumonia or worse."

Conkling looked at his deceased friend's heavyset brother-in-law as if taking his measure. Donald Morley was younger than Roscoe Conkling by a good twenty years or so and at least half a head shorter, but he carried the hard, round, protuberant belly of a man overly fond of the pleasures of the table. The pattern of broken red threads across his cheeks and nose branded him a heavy drinker.

"I box nearly every day, Mr. Morley. I neither drink much alcohol nor indulge in tobacco. In fact, I think I can boast that I am fitter than most men of my age and profession. Lawyering can be as injurious to the health as lack of gainful employment or sloth."

Courtroom expert that he was, Roscoe waited for Morley to bluster and overtalk himself. But he didn't. He reacted not one whit to what was clearly as close to an insult as Conkling would allow himself in front of the ladies. Mrs. MacKenzie's brother smiled with no real warmth, then clasped his hands together in anticipation as the parlor maid carried in a heavily laden tray.

"Lemon or milk, Mr. Conkling?" asked Victoria.

"I'm not taking any calls this morning," Conkling told his secretary.

"None at all, sir?"

"None. Sign for anything that gets delivered and otherwise make excuses for me."

"Are you all right, Mr. Conkling?" Josiah Gregory had been with his employer during the last bad days in Washington, D.C., and throughout the painful process of sifting through the accumulated books, papers, and memorabilia of a political lifetime. He'd stood by him loyally during the Kate Chase scandal, when one or another newspaper excoriated him every day for weeks on end. He'd spent long idle months cataloging Roscoe's letters and speeches, and then done his best to make the first rented law office on Nassau Street reflect the ex-senator's importance. In all that time he hadn't seen him look as pale and weary as he did today. It must be the effects of the blizzard.

"Of course I'm all right, Josiah. Why wouldn't I be?"

"You almost died Monday night, sir. You were out in the

wind and the snow for more than three hours, up to your neck in the drifts in Union Park and then again in Madison Park. Mr. Linwood did succumb, and so did a good many others, from what I've read in the papers."

"But I didn't die, and I'm not going to die. Not right now, and not for years to come. I've made up my mind about death; I'm not ready for it." Conkling could feel drops of perspiration on his forehead. The damn office was always too hot. The outside temperature had gone back to something close to what was normal for mid-March, and the snow was melting. It was time to open windows, not keep them closed like some pestilential sickroom.

"I'll bring you coffee, sir."

"Bring the pot. I'll serve myself as I work."

Josiah made fresh coffee, set out cup and saucer, found an unopened box of English digestive biscuits. When he carried the tray into the inner office, he lingered for as long as he could, doing aimless bits of rearranging and straightening. Finally, when there was nothing else to fuss over, he closed the door behind him and sat down heavily at his desk, determined to puzzle out what his employer was up to now.

He'd left Mr. Conkling staring at a stack of letter paper piled neatly before him, the lid off his inkwell, pen in hand. Either he couldn't think of how to begin whatever it was he intended to write, or he'd dozed off sitting up. Which was patently ridiculous because Roscoe Conkling had more energy than any two men put together. Something was wrong, something was finally wrong with the legendarily healthy and athletic former senator. Except for coming down with some sort of lung congestion from fighting through the blizzard like one of those Eskimo natives up there in Seward's Ice Box, Josiah Gregory had no idea what it could be.

Conkling was two thirds of the way through his written account of the Great Blizzard and his trek through the storm-ravaged city when he heard the front door of his office suite open, then close. Tumblers turned and clicked in the lock. He'd forgotten that Josiah only worked until noon on Saturdays. Funny, he'd never asked him what he did on his Saturday afternoons off. Did he go walking in Central Park or duck into one of the vaudeville palaces in the theater district?

Vulgar comedy somehow didn't seem to suit Josiah's rigid personality. Conkling tried to imagine him at one of the Gilbert and Sullivan operas, something like the one he'd seen three years ago at the Fifth Avenue Theatre. What was the name of it? Something odd that started with an M. That actress Geraldine Ulmar played a heroine with a ridiculous name. Yum-Yum. That was it. *The Mikado.*

Mental stimulation was every bit as important as physical training. Conkling believed that as strongly as he believed in the Constitution, so while he shadowboxed around his office to work the stiffness out of his muscles from sitting too long at his desk, he cataloged the list of women he had known. In the Biblical sense. Other than his wife, of course. In order, he challenged himself, leaving no one out, all while humming what he could remember of the music that was the best part of *The Mikado.*

He refused to pay attention to the sweat coursing down his face, ignored the sudden sharp twinges in his head, the pain hammering in his right ear. He lifted his arms up even though they felt like sticks of heavy firewood nailed to his shoulders. *Dance on the balls of your feet. Keep the heels up. Jab. Jab again. Right, left, right, left again with a hook to it.* In the end, ten minutes was all he could manage.

Coffee. He gulped down the dregs of Josiah's thick brew, reminding himself that the remedy for illness was hard work. He'd pulled out of weak spells before, but not by giving up and crawling away into a bed to be hovered over by some ugly nurse.

He sat down at his desk again, reached for his pen. Reminded himself why he'd decided to make detailed notes of that terrible walk up Broadway when the newspapers had already interviewed him and printed the story. *His* story. He hadn't mentioned Linwood or Sulzer to the reporter. He'd told the Roscoe Conkling story because that was what people wanted to read about. He was a celebrity; he'd been written about enough in the past to know what sold papers.

But two nights ago he'd awakened in a cold sweat from a nightmare that stayed with him all that day. Conkling had known fear before, but nothing like the heart-pounding terror that had repeated itself last night. Twice now, something or someone had invaded his sleep to bring him a message. He was as convinced of that as he was certain that consulting one of New York's many mediums was a remedy of last resort. He'd scoffed publicly at the claims of spiritualists who maintained that nightmares were the efforts of the dead to communicate with the living. The newspapers would have a field day with him if he were discovered at a séance or a reading. Which he would be. Anyone who thought he could conceal any titillating tidbit of his life's story from the press was a fool.

He didn't need an intermediary to the spirit world. If a damned spirit was so intent on dragging him through the blizzard again to get in touch with him, have at it!

He'd reached the point in his narrative where he'd started across Union Square. This was where twice now dreaming had turned into nightmare. Why? What was there about this moment that was so different from the hours of cold struggle that had preceded it? Wide awake from the coffee and the shadowboxing, Conkling willed himself back into the events of five days ago, concentrating as hard on what needed to be accurately remembered as on any speech he'd ever prepared for a jury.

Every gut instinct he trusted as a lawyer told him he was walking toward an unsuspected crime that demanded to be solved, approaching a place where motive and opportunity waited teasingly just beyond his waking reach. Hence the nightmares.

In his mind's eye he saw Charles Linwood struggling along behind him. Sulzer had remained at Astor House. Or had he? Conkling's pen scratched furiously across the paper. He was positive now. Just before he entered Union Square he'd turned around and seen someone else fighting through the drifts behind Linwood; he'd barely been able to make out a dark outline through the falling snow, but he was convinced it was there.

Had Sulzer had second thoughts, left Astor House, tried to catch up, then given in to fatigue and fear a second time? Had he experienced a soldier's guilt because he'd gone after Linwood but hadn't been able to save him? Decided not to mention that abortive attempt that ended in ignominious retreat? Chosen to save his reputation by pretending it never happened? Assumed no one at Astor House would have remarked his temporary absence? And where was Sulzer now? He was sure he hadn't been back to his office just down the hall since the blizzard. Victoria said Sulzer had come to call on them, but Conkling had been too concerned over Prudence to pay much attention to whatever else she had told him.

Of course there was always the possibility that the man battling his way along Broadway behind Charles had been someone else. Not Sulzer at all. No, that didn't make sense. Where had he come from? Where had he gone to? Why hadn't he rushed to tell his tale and see his name in print the way hundreds of his fellow New Yorkers had done?

Scratching away on his thick letter paper, Conkling wrote what he knew to be true and what he had observed. Nothing more, nothing less. If necessary, he could always go back and add to what he was recording today. He reread the notes he'd made about Linwood and Sulzer. That same lawyer's gut instinct he'd trusted all his life told him that this was where the heart of the mystery lay. But what was it?

He really didn't feel well at all. It was only one o'clock, but he'd finished writing. He'd done the best he could. Not a full day's work, but if a secretary could work half a day on Saturday, why not the man who paid his salary? He'd walk up Broadway again, all the way to the New York Club, retrace the route he'd taken on Monday evening. Why not? The exercise would strengthen his legs, the spring air was chilly but eminently breathable, and from what he'd observed, hansom cab drivers were still trying to extort highly inflated fares from their passengers. No, he'd definitely walk.

And maybe he'd tease out that bit of memory that wasn't quite sure about the identity of the figure he'd glimpsed struggling along behind poor Charles Linwood through the snow just south of Union Square.

Maybe the exercise and the effort of remembering would let him sleep without dreaming tonight. Would be enough to hold the nightmare at bay until the mystery chose to reveal itself.

CHAPTER 4

Charles Linwood was interred in his family's crypt nine days after he died in Union Square Park. Curiously, the well-respected mortuary firm of Warneke and Sons stored Linwood's body just as it had been delivered to them for two full days without beginning to prepare it for visitation and preservation. Then Charles's father requested a private viewing of his son. Warneke Sr. had to make a decision.

The wound on the back of the late Mr. Linwood's head had not been what killed him, but it had been brutal enough to render him unconscious. The blizzard did the rest. Bits and pieces of bark and snow-soaked wood embedded in the dead man's skull were enough to satisfy the New York City Police Department, but Maurice Warneke had examined and prepared hundreds of bodies for burial. He wasn't convinced that one or more falling tree limbs could do the kind of damage he would have to repair or disguise before Linwood could lie in his open casket.

Warneke had seen head wounds made by falling down stairs and by being pushed down stairs. He had filled in the deep grooves where a fireplace poker or a brass-tipped cane battered fragile bone. He had worked and sighed over the bodies of women beaten to death by the fists of their husbands. The mortician knew the marks of willful violence and the signs of accidental trauma. He wondered who hated young Linwood so viciously that he snuck up behind him in the midst of a blizzard and knocked him unconscious into the snow. Where he froze to death.

Warneke had no evidence to support his suspicion. Nothing but years and years of commiserating with the dead, of listening to the stories their silent bodies told, of doing the best he could to restore them to something like wholeness before they were lowered into darkness. He might be wrong. The tree limbs might have fallen with the force of a human arm, might have been driven by the wind to angle into the most vulnerable part of the dead man's skull. At least one blow had struck precisely where neck joined head to spine.

No one else seemed in any doubt. So be it. Nothing would bring the young man back to the life he should have lived. His father wanted to sit beside his son, look at the calm face of a soul gone peacefully to its rest, be able to reassure the corpse's mother that all was well, that their child was with God. So Maurice Warneke picked out the pieces of bark with his best tweezers, washed the blood from the wound, and combed Charles's hair into the style he wore in the photograph supplied by his father. He brushed some color onto his cheeks, pegged his mouth shut, drained his blood, pumped his body full of preservative fluids, and let it go. Decision made.

Everybody died. Justice was a myth. Consolation was the best that could be hoped for.

Charles's casket was taken directly from Warneke's premises to Trinity Church, where it lay open for an hour before the service began. Mourners who would ordinarily have come to the Linwood home to pay their respects had been unable to negotiate many of the residential streets in the days immediately following the storm. Now they stood for a few silent moments looking down at the young man's perfectly composed face before whispering the ritual phrases of condolence to his parents and his fiancée.

Geoffrey Hunter was one of the last mourners to enter the church; he'd only made it in time by the happy accident of being able to step into a hansom cab in front of the Fifth Avenue Hotel moments after its previous occupant descended. He and Charles had been classmates at both Phillips Academy and Harvard, friends since the day nine-year-old Geoffrey arrived at Phillips five months after the war ended. He was the only Southerner to enroll that year.

As he stood in the central aisle of Trinity Church waiting to pay his respects to the body of his dead friend, Geoffrey remembered their long-ago first meeting. Neither he nor Charles had ever forgotten it. *Do you remember?* How many times had they laughed together over Geoffrey's bravado and Charles's ability to lie with absolute conviction?

Both boys had known from an early age that a certain kind of harassment had to be met head-on if life was going to be worth living. It didn't matter where you were when the incident occurred. You dealt with it.

"Hey, Reb," someone hissed during morning prayers.

Without missing a beat of the Our Father, Geoffrey stood up. Before any of the boys around him realized what he meant to do, he laid the hisser out flat with a tight fist and a protruding middle finger knuckle. Stepping smoothly back into his place he kept on praying. Not a single one of the teachers saw what happened. Charles Linwood, whose delicate good looks and curly blond hair made him the butt of many a bully's cruel joke, told the headmaster that he'd been right next to the new boy throughout the morning service. He'd swear on the Bible that Geoffrey hadn't budged, certainly hadn't left his place to bloody anyone's nose.

By the end of the day the headmaster knew he'd been bested

by two students who shouldn't even have liked each other, let alone become allies. One of them was a New Yorker whose lawyer father had championed the Abolitionist cause, the other the scion of a defeated Southern clan whose wealth had once rested on the backs of its hundreds of slaves. With nothing in common except their loneliness, Charles and Geoffrey quickly and permanently became the best of friends.

Being a pragmatist, the headmaster got even by watching their every move until they graduated, making their lives a living hell for the smallest infraction. The boys counted him a worthy opponent, one of the more intriguing challenges of the school.

As Geoffrey's turn came to bid his friend a final good-bye, he leaned over the casket and unobtrusively slid a playing card into the pocket of Charles's frock coat. The ace of spades, highest card in the deck, their secret sign to one another that a prank was about to be played, a girl's defenses had been breached, the head of school had left himself open yet again to student satire.

The ace of spades was also a warning against danger as well as a good luck piece. Neither of them ever went anywhere without that special card in an easy-to-reach pocket. Charles had taken his card out and laid it on the bar the last time they'd had drinks together. *Do you remember?* What had they been talking about? His soon-to-be wife, of course. Charles had had little else on his mind these last few months. As if wrestling with a premonition, he'd slid his ace of spades toward his friend.

"I may need your help, Geoffrey," he'd said.

"You know I'll come running whenever I see this." Geoffrey had raised his glass. A toast, a promise, a salute to his friend's new happiness, an end to his loneliness.

Where had that card gone after Charles repocketed it? The undertaker who prepared and dressed the body wouldn't have known its importance. He would have discarded it, perhaps without mentioning it to the grieving family. Perhaps only Geoffrey knew that Charles could not be buried or trundled into the Linwood vault without a brand-new ace of spades in his pocket. Just in case there were games to be played wherever he'd gone or dangers to brave with his lucky card.

Sleep well, Charles, Geoffrey thought. *And when you wake up and feel the card in your pocket, spare a smile for the comrade you left behind, your other half who will miss you every day of his life.* Geoffrey and Charles had known from their first meeting that they were brothers in spirit if not by blood; nothing had come between them in all of the years they had known one another to weaken that bond.

I'm burying a part of myself that I'll never be able to reclaim, Geoffrey mused. He wasn't sure he believed in an afterlife, but it helped assuage the pain to imagine his friend opening his eyes in some other world, knowing immediately who had placed the playing card in his pocket, taking the first steps into eternity not quite alone.

As he turned from the casket, as he embraced the man who rose from his pew to receive the loving warmth of his son's closest friend, Geoffrey's eyes fell on a slender figure draped in the black widow's weeds to which she was entitled as fiancée if not yet wife. Prudence was her name, though he had never actually met her. Strange, that, when he and Charles had been so close.

For someone who had not been formally introduced, he knew a great deal about Prudence MacKenzie. Knew that she was frighteningly intelligent for a woman, that her father had indulged her to the point of teaching her the law as if she were a son. There was a stepmother who had somehow contrived—Charles's word—to marry the Judge and outlive him into a happy and wealthy widowhood. Prudence didn't like her stepmother, and there was something worrying about laudanum. He couldn't quite remember exactly what that was. Charles had been concerned, though, concerned enough to mention it over a casual drink and a cigar in the Gentlemen's Smoker of the Fifth Avenue Hotel.

"You must meet Prudence when this is over," Charles's father whispered, following the direction of Geoffrey's gaze. "Charles was certain you would like one another."

He thought she inclined her head the merest fraction of an inch, as if she had recognized him, knew him to be the friend about whom she had heard so much. But he could have been mistaken. It might have been a breath of air wisping against the mourning veil.

"There's something else, Geoffrey," Mr. Linwood continued, his voice pitched so low that Hunter had to strain to make out what he was saying.

"What is that, sir?"

"Are you still living at the Fifth Avenue Hotel?"

"I am."

"Then with your permission, I'll call on you tomorrow morning. Early. Before breakfast. And please don't mention my visit to anyone."

"Can you tell me what it's about, Mr. Linwood?"

Charles's father hesitated. He looked into the dark eyes of his son's best friend and made up his mind. "I saw you place the card in Charles's pocket. That was well done, Geoffrey."

"It goes all the way back to early days at Phillips Academy. It was the way we communicated with each other."

"Charles trusted you like no other. You were the brother he never had."

"And he was mine, Mr. Linwood."

"He died with the ace of spades clutched in his hand, Geoffrey. Somehow he found the strength to reach into his pocket and pull it out. The police said it had frozen to his fingers."

Whatever else Charles's father had been about to say was cut off by the rolling peal of Trinity Church's pipe organ. The service was about to begin.

Geoffrey heard hardly a word of the eulogy preached in honor of Charles Linwood. All of his attention was focused on a mental image of his friend's hand curled tightly around a wet and wrinkled ace of spades. Charles's last conscious act meant something. What message was he sending to the only person he could be certain would understand its urgency?

Geoffrey worried the mystery like a dog a bone, but he got nowhere. The Pinkerton training clicked in, as it always did when there was a puzzle to solve. More information; he needed more information. And until he got it, presumably tomorrow morning from Charles's father, he was only muddying the waters. *Think clearly and don't speculate in a vacuum,* he reminded himself.

In the meantime, the best thing Geoffrey could do was extend his condolences to the bereaved fiancée. A few moments of conversation could reveal a great deal about someone, and after today it would be difficult if not impossible for him to see Prudence MacKenzie socially. She and her stepmother were already in mourning for the Judge. Charles's death had now doubly excluded her from New York society for at least another year. Some women seldom if ever left their homes during those initial twelve months, preferring a kind of living death to the condemnation of their neighbors.

If Charles expected his friend to safeguard Miss MacKenzie and come to her aid when she needed assistance, Geoffrey had to manage an introduction. Right now Prudence MacKenzie's part in all of this was as much a mystery as why a branch had chosen to fall from its tree at precisely the moment Charles opted to sit beneath it.

Try though he might, Geoffrey hadn't been able to get the coincidence out of his mind. He didn't like coincidences, didn't usually believe in them.

He decided he'd think about the meaning of the ace of spades and the coincidence of the curious twist of fate later, after the funeral.

They extolled the virtues and talents of Charles Linwood, then closed him into his expensive, satin-lined box, and carried him down the aisle of Trinity Church to one of Warneke's best funeral carriages. The interment was to be private, so leavetakings at the church portico were prolonged and tearful.

His duty paid to Charles's parents, Geoffrey Hunter looked around him one last time, thinking to find Charles's Prudence and extend his condolences, but he couldn't pick her out of the crowd of veiled, black-clad women. Moving through the mourners, he saw faces he recognized from his days at Phillips Academy and later at Harvard. Nods were exchanged, handshakes given, promises made to get together soon. They were all strangers; the only one Geoffrey had cherished from those long-ago days was gone.

He murmured his good-byes, edging away from the church steps. One final searching perusal of his fellow mourners. This time he caught the gleam of pale eyes fixed on him from beneath a widow's veil thrown back over a small, brimmed bonnet. She'd been watching him as he made his way through the crowd; he was easily one of the tallest men there. The intensity of her stare bore into him like pinpoints of gray fire. It was the face of the fiancée whose likeness Charles had carried in his watch case. The gray eyes whose piercing clarity his friend had described so many times. Soft gray eyes that turned to steel when she was angry. *Yes,* Charles had laughed, *she does have a temper. So did her father, the Judge.*

Prudence MacKenzie stood ramrod straight between a slightly older woman dressed in widow's full mourning and a man whose heavy facial features had twisted themselves into a mask of angry frustration. Geoffrey immediately knew who they must be. The stepmother and her brother, about whom Charles had at first shaken his head, then chided himself for speaking. It didn't do to wash dirty family linen in public, even if the public were one's best friend and the family hadn't been married into yet.

The stepmother held tightly to one of Prudence's arms. Geoffrey could see her lips moving as she leaned toward Prudence, who shook her head and tried unsuccessfully to wrench her arm free. The black veil cascaded down, hiding the young woman's face, but not before the gray eyes shot one last look of entreaty across the crowd. The heavyset uncle by marriage took the other arm, and the threesome began moving toward the line of waiting carriages, Prudence plainly being unceremoniously hustled along.

Geoffrey acted. Didn't stop to consider what he was doing or why, just moved quickly and efficiently to cut them off.

"My very dear Miss MacKenzie," he said smoothly, lifting his top hat politely, reaching out to clasp her hand in both of his. For a moment, Geoffrey thought the ploy might not work, then the stepmother's brother let loose Prudence's right arm and she seemed to fold herself toward him. The small gloved hand gripped his so tightly, he couldn't have shaken it loose if he had wanted to.

"How very kind of you," she murmured.

"Mrs. Linwood is asking particularly that you share their carriage."

"Miss MacKenzie will not be going to the cemetery," the woman beside her declared.

"I mustn't disappoint Charles's mother, Victoria. Not today of all days." Prudence's voice was low, but insistent.

"My compliments, madam. Sir. Allow me to present myself. I'm Geoffrey Hunter. I would have had the honor of being Charles's best man."

A sob came from behind Prudence's black veil. Somehow, in the polite confusion of introductions, she managed to free herself, so that before anyone was aware of it, she had wound both hands around Geoffrey's arm. Seconds later they were moving together toward where the Linwood parents were being helped into their carriage.

"Is she watching us?" Prudence didn't dare look.

"They've turned away. Toward their own carriage. Will they follow?"

"Probably. She's determined not to let me out of her sight."

"This way then." Geoffrey snapped open a black umbrella against the first patterings of spring rain. All around them other umbrellas bloomed until the steps of Trinity Church and the row of carriages appeared as islands in a sea of bobbing black circles. "If they look for you, they won't be able to tell us from everyone else. Around to the side door."

They picked their way along the sidewalk in the crowd of other mourners, eyes cast down to find and keep their footing between half-melted drifts of snow. It took only a few minutes to reach one of the church's small side doors, but to Prudence it seemed like forever. Not until she stood in the dimness of the still-emptying sanctuary did she feel safe.

"We'll give them until we hear the last carriage leave," Geoffrey Hunter said, "then we'll go out through the door that opens onto the old graveyard. I'm sure the path has been shoveled but there's still so much snow piled up alongside that no one will notice us."

"That was cleverly done." Roscoe Conkling stepped from behind one of Trinity's fluted stone columns, his voice pitched low enough to reach them but not an inch beyond. "My compliments, Geoffrey."

"Mr. Conkling." Geoffrey's eyes never stopped sweeping the aisles and pews of the church.

Tears of impotent rage still glittered on Prudence's lashes, but her lips were set in a grimly determined line. She had flung back the face veil so that it hung slightly askew from the hat pinned above coils of light brown hair.

"I wasn't quite sure how you were going to manage it, but once I saw Geoffrey begin to move in your direction, I knew that whatever the plan was, it would succeed." Roscoe smiled at her, then turned to Geoffrey. "I asked Prudence to come to my office after the funeral, and not to let her stepmother know we were meeting. You do know one another, don't you?"

"I'm Prudence MacKenzie," she said formally, as if Geoffrey

did not already know. "I'm grateful for your help. It means a great deal to me."

Geoffrey bowed over her hand. "Charles spoke of you often, Miss MacKenzie. Always with great admiration. Allow me to express my condolences on your loss."

"Thank you."

"I'm afraid you give me too much credit, Mr. Conkling. There was no plan, at least not on my part. I just didn't like seeing Miss MacKenzie being bullied. Charles wouldn't have liked it either. So I acted on the impulse of the moment, hoping I was right to do so."

"It was the absolutely correct thing to do, Mr. Hunter," Prudence said. "I knew who you were. Charles had a photograph of the two of you together at Harvard. You're both wearing white sweaters with an enormous letter H on the front."

"We were barely nineteen or twenty years old when that was taken. It was the day of the first Harvard-Yale football game. No idea how to go about it, but we both played just the same. It's already become a tradition, you know, the Harvard-Yale game."

"Who won?" Prudence asked.

"We did. Harvard. Though I have no clue how we managed it. Charles and I were so badly beaten up, we swore off football then and there. Harvard hasn't won against Yale since."

"What did you put in the casket? I saw you slip something out of your pocket when you leaned over."

"It was a playing card."

"The ace of spades. Charles told me it was your secret signal to one another."

"We were like brothers."

"He told me that, too. He told me so many stories about the two of you that I can't feel we're strangers."

Prudence laughed, a tinkling sound like silver bells; her gray eyes flashed a bit of green. She was really quite a beautiful young woman at that moment, somber in the flowing black veils and skirts of mourning, but with a glint of brightness as of sunlight breaking through dark clouds.

Not yet, Geoffrey decided. He wouldn't tell her yet that Charles had died with that special, precious card in his hand.

"Is it safe to leave now? Geoffrey, will you take a look?" Conkling asked.

"The funeral procession is gone, and I think the last of the mourners hurried off as soon as it began to rain." Geoffrey stepped out into Trinity Church's venerable cemetery, scanning its pathways and headstones. "The sky is clearing, at least for the moment."

"Let's go then. Prudence, my dear, take my arm. It's just a few steps to my office."

She hesitated. "Mr. Hunter, will you come with us?"

"I don't like to intrude."

"Please."

"You did a number of commissions for Charles and his father, didn't you, Geoffrey?" Conkling asked.

"I did, sir."

"It may be that Miss MacKenzie will also need your services."

Geoffrey Hunter's face froze into the impassive mask of a professional man of secrets. It changed him. The intensely dark hair and eyebrows communicated threat, an implacable menace strong enough to warn off any adversary. His jaw tightened, the strong, even lines of mouth and slightly arched nose became more pronounced; the eyes that were a warm brown in sunlight deepened to black. He was as tall as Conkling, well over six feet, but he seemed to gain inches by the sheer force of what he willed himself to become.

Prudence lowered her veil and glided past Charles's best friend. She held tightly to Conkling's arm as the trio approached the United Bank Building, intensely aware of the protective bulk of a man she had not known until an hour ago. A man whose presence seemed so right and inevitable that she did not think to question it.

"I'll have Josiah make coffee," Roscoe said as he settled Prudence into the office's most comfortable chair. "I think we could all do with a bit of restorative."

Prudence looked up, half-removed gloves forgotten, the quick movement of her head like the questioning stare of a startled doe.

"It's not quite that bad, my dear," Conkling reassured her. "But it's not entirely good news either."

CHAPTER 5

"I'd like you to stay, Josiah," Roscoe Conkling directed. "It may be wise, under the somewhat unusual circumstances, to have a record of what is said here today, even if only for ourselves. Do you have any objection to my secretary's presence, Prudence?"

"None at all." She smiled warmly at the small, immaculately dressed man who had spent more than half his life seeing to Mr. Conkling's lawyerly needs and staunchly defending him against criticism.

Unlike his employer, Josiah Gregory always looked slightly unwell, as if he were courting a fever or skirting consumption. Yet he prided himself on never missing a day's work. He kept chocolates in his desk, combed and brilliantined his thinning brown hair over the top of his balding skull, and took Pitman shorthand notes faster and more accurately than any agency-referred expert. He wore dark gray suits, embroidered waistcoats, stiff collared white shirts, and a massive gold pocket watch whose heavy chain and fob were his only jewelry. He wasn't married, and never mentioned parents, siblings, or cousins. Josiah's entire life circled around Roscoe as reliably as a small planet orbited the constant sun.

Thomas Pickering MacKenzie's will lay atop four neatly stacked dark brown cardboard folders, each of which was tied with a strip of black silk ribbon. "All of your father's directives," Conkling explained, one hand atop the paper remains of a life. "Notes, initial drafts, executed documents, everything that came into this office pertaining to the Judge. Josiah also made copies of anything that left."

"Haven't I seen everything, Mr. Conkling? I remember the will being read and then later both you and Charles explaining some of it to me."

"Exactly how much do you remember, Prudence?"

She had taken off her damp hat and veil so that her soft brown hair gleamed with gold highlights in the flattering glow of the office's three oil lamps. Electricity was leaping into businesses as fast as wires could be strung, but women who caught a glimpse of themselves in its stark brightness quickly avowed they preferred candles or oil.

"The important points, of course. My father made sure I knew how to craft a will and Charles insisted I be clear on the essentials." Prudence glanced at Geoffrey Hunter's unreadable face, down at her hands lying clasped in her lap, up again at Josiah as if he could or would come to her aid. When it became obvious that she was floundering, Conkling took pity on her.

"I think you believe you remember, Prudence, but I'm not sure you actually do."

"The laudanum," she whispered. "No matter how hard I tried to concentrate, the laudanum got in the way. I couldn't remember what my father had spent hours teaching me."

"The laudanum," Conkling confirmed. "I don't think Dr. Worthington meant you any harm; in fact I know him well enough to be certain he didn't. He saw a young woman who had just lost her only living parent and he wanted to give you the gift of some relief from the pain you were suffering. A very temporary respite. He never intended it to be anything else."

"Victoria."

"What about your stepmother?"

"I wept so much those first few days. I went into my father's study and threw things. Books from the shelves, papers from his desk, the cigars he kept in a box above the fireplace. I was like one of those madwomen you read about, screaming and destroying whatever falls into their hands. I remember feeling I had to break something or I would lose my mind. I made it easy for her. How else could she control me except with the laudanum Dr. Worthington gave her?"

"She was warned. I know he lectured her. He cautions all his patients."

"I wasn't supposed to dose myself. I remember him telling her that, warning her that accidents had been known to happen with laudanum. A few days later she gave me the bottle and told me to measure out whatever I needed. She never said a word when the bottle was empty, never asked how much I was taking. She handed me another one of those corked brown bottles and said I shouldn't worry about running out. There would always be more."

Josiah's pencil stopped moving when Prudence fell silent. Neither Conkling nor Geoffrey Hunter said a word. The minutes ticked by, each second loudly punctuated by the Ansonia Parisian Mantel clock that Gregory wound once every eight days.

"I think Victoria wanted to make me so dependent on laudanum, I wouldn't be able to think for myself. And she very nearly did," Prudence finally said, pale skin flushed with the embarrassment of being forced to reveal something so personal and so discomforting. "I don't know what her motive was, but she almost succeeded. It was a near thing. A very near thing.

Once I realized what was happening to me, I began to refuse the drinks Victoria prepared, and then I stopped taking any laudanum at all. And when I did, when I wasn't sleepy and confused all the time, I began to be afraid of her, afraid of Victoria. I can't tell you exactly what I feared, but I let her think I was still taking the laudanum. I even filled the bottles with strong tea and counted out the drops in front of her. The day of the blizzard I remember looking out the window at the snow and deciding to talk to Charles about my suspicions. I felt so strong.

"But then he died. I stopped fighting and started giving in again until Mr. Conkling came last Friday. I remember you telling me we had work to do together, important work. We stood by the window looking out at Fifth Avenue until Victoria and Donald came into the room and ordered the curtains closed. You told me to come to your office after the funeral. I knew you meant more than that because of what you said about my father despising weakness." Her eyes sought and held Conkling's; strength seemed to flow from the tall, garishly vested, full bearded former senator into the slight, black-clad child-woman who sat the width of a desk away from him. "I'm grateful to Mr. Hunter for helping me after the funeral, but I promise you, Mr. Conkling, I would have gotten here somehow even without his assistance. I may have shown weakness these past few months, but I really am my father's daughter. Tell me again what the will says. I give you my word I'll understand every line, every provision, every codicil."

There was another long silence, broken this time by the soft waterfall sound of coffee being poured, of silver spoons clinking lightly against china cups. Josiah sat down again and picked up his shorthand notebook.

"We'll address the major issues first," Conkling said. Shocked beyond words at what Prudence accused her stepmother of doing, he needed time to consider the implications. Over his years in Congress and now in the private practice of the law, he'd met human wickedness in so many of its manifestations that he'd thought nothing could surprise him. He'd been wrong. *Cui bono? Who benefits?* He needed time to think this through, to decide whether the woman he had always thought of as merely venal was truly evil. And what he was going to do about it if she were. In the meantime, Prudence was waiting, clearheaded and determined. He owed it to the Judge to explain her new situation and to make it as palatable as possible.

"I beg your pardon, sir." The secretary cleared his throat.

"What is it, Josiah?"

"Mrs. MacKenzie, sir. Since she is a named inheritor, should she not be present?"

"It may be custom, but there is no binding legal requirement." Conkling rattled the papers he held as if he would use them to rap someone's knuckles. "The Judge's will was properly probated at the time of his death. If certain of its provisions are nullified now and others come into force due to changed circumstances, that may leave various bequests and their administration open to some interpretation. Let her get her own lawyer." One hand flew to his chest, as if to push more air into his lungs. His face went suddenly red and every breath he struggled to take became a wheeze.

Hunter was pounding on Conkling's back before Josiah could reach him. Within moments Roscoe's face, what could be seen of it above the bushy black beard, returned to its normal color, and his breathing eased.

"Perhaps we should do this another time?" Prudence had seen her father fight for breath in the last few days before his death.

"No, no, I'm perfectly all right."

"If I may be permitted, sir, your chest doesn't sound at all good."

"Are you a doctor now, Josiah? I wasn't aware you'd been admitted to medical school along with every other half-wit who can pay the fees. I may have taken a bit of a chill last Monday, but it's nothing to be concerned about. Now, if we can all take our seats again, I'd like to begin. Prudence needs to know how her life will be changing.

"Your father, my dear, much as I admired him and counted him a close friend, wasn't always as judicious and farseeing in his private life as he was on the bench. After his marriage to Victoria, he rewrote large portions of his will; I argued with him as a friend, but as his lawyer I was bound to do as he asked. I'm sorry, Prudence."

"I don't understand, Mr. Conkling."

"Your father didn't expect to die before you and Charles were married."

"What difference could that make?"

"It's all in the wording. When he appointed Charles Linwood trustee of your estate, he was very precise. He identified him by his relationship to you as your husband and he specified Linwood, and no other, by name. He knew Charles would never do anything without consulting you, that you would, in effect, be your own trustee."

"Are you also a lawyer, Mr. Hunter?" Prudence asked. She had caught his swift glance, read comprehension and concern in the dark eyes.

"I am, Miss MacKenzie. Among other professions at which I've tried my hand."

"Good." She opened the black purse that was too small to hold more than a handkerchief, smelling salts, and a few coins. She handed him a greenback, smiling when he folded it into one of the pockets of his vest. "Do you agree to represent me at law?" she asked formally.

"I do," Hunter replied. "It shall be my honor and my pleasure." He bowed over her ungloved hand. "A contract now exists between us. As does confidentiality. Your interests are mine."

"I hope this doesn't mean you've fired me, Prudence," teased Conkling.

"If one lawyer is a good thing, then logic dictates that two must be better." She'd heard her father say that one lawyer spawned a host of others like rats in a sewer. Nobody liked or trusted lawyers, but nobody could do without them, either. It was the great triumph of the profession to make themselves indispensable.

"As I was saying, every time the Judge specified Charles Linwood by name and identified him as your husband, he automatically invalidated that clause should Linwood die before the marriage. Which he did. The problem is in one of the final codicils your father added shortly before he died."

"Which states?"

"He came to see me here at the office, Prudence. With Mrs. MacKenzie. Do you remember, Josiah?"

"I do, sir. I had to add it to the will that very afternoon so it could be signed and witnessed before they left. Mrs. MacKenzie was very determined about that."

"And the Judge?" Hunter asked.

Josiah shrugged. "He seemed willing to go along with what she wanted."

"The codicil states that if Charles Linwood is unable, for any reason, to fulfill any of the offices or duties specifically given or assigned to him, then the offices and duties pass immediately to Mrs. Victoria Morley MacKenzie. When Charles died in Union Park, she became the sole trustee of your entire estate, Prudence."

"Until my thirtieth birthday?"

"Until your thirtieth birthday. I am named as advisor to the trust, but I am not a trustee. Which means that I can and must continue to counsel your stepmother on financial and other matters, but she is not in any way obliged to heed or follow my advice."

"The house?"

"Was to have gone to you and Charles upon your marriage, but now it's essentially hers, along with everything else. Furniture, carriages, horses, investments, funds on deposit in banks." Conkling saw her reach for the ebony mourning brooch that he knew contained miniatures of her parents and locks of their hair. "Even your late mother's jewelry, Prudence. Everything that is held in trust for you is under her control for the next eleven years."

"Including me."

"Including you."

"I don't suppose there is any way to break the will, to invalidate the codicil?"

"I drew it up, Prudence. Your father dictated some of the wording. The two best legal minds in New York City wrote as watertight a document as I've ever seen. We boxed you in. I'm so sorry, my child."

"What did the widow inherit in her own right, Mr. Conkling?"

"You're quite right to ask, Geoffrey. I should have summarized the Judge's wishes more completely than I did. He left half of his estate in trust to his widow, Victoria, with the proviso that upon her death, what remained should pass to Prudence. The other half he placed in trust for his daughter, naming Victoria sole trustee until Prudence's marriage to Charles Linwood, at which time Linwood was to become trustee until Prudence attained the age of thirty and was of proven mental competence."

"He didn't believe I could manage my own life." There was no trace of tears or the mawkish sentimentality fueled by laudanum in Prudence's voice. It snapped with anger and something else, something last heard when her father had delivered judgments from the bench. Implacability. She had pronounced her own verdict and there would be no appeal.

"I asked him, whenever Victoria was not at his side, what he meant by tying you up so tightly and putting the reins in Victoria's hands. He would never answer. Told me to mind my own business or he'd find someone else to represent him. Said he trusted Charles to see to your welfare. He left envelopes to be delivered after the marriage. One for Charles, one for you, Prudence."

"Where are they?"

"Here." Conkling pointed to one of the heavy cardboard folders.

Wordlessly, Prudence held out her hand. Conkling shook his head. Gave the folder to his secretary.

"Josiah, read the addresses on the envelopes, please."

"Yes, Mr. Conkling." He held the first envelope close to one of the oil lamps. The handwriting on it was thin and spidery, as if penned by someone whose hand was unsteady. "'To Prudence MacKenzie Linwood, wife of Charles Montgomery Linwood,'" he read.

"Such a person does not exist. Will never exist." With a flick of the wrist, Conkling dismissed her. "And the second one?"

"'To Charles Montgomery Linwood, husband of Prudence MacKenzie Linwood.'"

"That person does not exist either."

Conkling nodded his head. Josiah, who was well schooled in the lawyer's ways, rose from his chair and placed both envelopes on the coals burning brightly in the center of the office fireplace. Flames licked eagerly at the new fuel. The envelopes flared, crackled, then dissolved into black ash. In the few moments before their complete destruction, as the pages within uncurled, lines of the same shaky handwriting could be glimpsed. But not deciphered. Whatever the Judge had wanted to tell his married daughter and her husband was gone forever. As completely as if the words had never been written.

No one moved. No one spoke. Josiah stood beside the fireplace until the last flake of ash collapsed on itself.

"I don't know what he wrote, Prudence. I haven't the slightest notion of what might have been on his mind. He was already ill, but he managed to bring me the envelopes shortly after the day he and Victoria came to arrange for that special codicil. He was alone and he'd come by hansom cab. I looked out the window and saw it waiting below, saw him helped inside by the driver. I wondered why he hadn't used his own carriage; it seemed unlike him. The next time I saw your father was when Worthington sent to tell me he was on his deathbed. I don't know what Thomas was thinking, but there was no final request I could fulfill. He was already unconscious when I got to the house."

"I remember." With a last anguished glance at the fireplace, Prudence straightened her back, sitting as upright in her chair as a schoolgirl called to the headmistress's office. "Nothing has changed," she said. "Nothing has changed."

"Expectations have changed, and that may be the most important thing to have resulted from Charles's unfortunate and unexpected demise." Conkling's eyes sparkled the way they always did when he was about to take on a case that no one else thought he could win. "Do you see where I'm going, Prudence?"

Puzzled, she shook her head. She knew he was hinting that the Judge had somehow managed to circumvent the woman who seemed to have controlled the last months of his life, but Prudence could not untangle Victoria's web enough to see a way out of it. "Explain, please," she asked, embarrassed not to know the answer.

"Victoria's initial expectation was that she would be the trustee of your estate for only the months between your father's death and your marriage, and he had stipulated that one was to follow closely upon the other. Three months. I thought that odd, but I assumed he did it purposely in order to allow Victoria her freedom and to ensure that you were safely and legally in Charles's care. Victoria was to move into the apartment he had secured for her at the Dakota, and you and Charles were to have the house. But there was one other codicil that Victoria didn't know about. The Judge added it on the day he brought me the envelopes, and from the look on Victoria's face when the will was read, he never informed her of what he'd done."

Conkling stood up and moved from behind his desk to the fireplace where the envelopes and their secrets had burned. He held out his hands to warm them, then turned to face his audience, very much like an actor about to deliver the climactic lines of a scene.

"If you died before you married Charles Linwood, the fifty percent of the Judge's estate intended to come to you in trust would go to the four charities named in his will. Since that did not happen, the alternative clause is activated. The charities also benefit if you die before you reach the age of thirty. Neither you nor Victoria can name new beneficiaries. You either live to enjoy the fruits of the trust or everything contained in the trust passes out of the family. Victoria, in turn, may not name a beneficiary for what she has inherited from the Judge. She has the use of his wealth for her lifetime, but everything she possesses at the time of her death reverts either to your trust, to you yourself if you are past the age of thirty and mentally competent, to any heirs of your body, or to the named charities."

"None of this seemed important when the will was read. Even afterward, when you and Charles explained it to me. I understood that Victoria would administer the trust and be my legal guardian until Charles and I married. But then I would be free of her. Nothing else made much of an impression, I'm afraid."

"No one, certainly not Charles himself, thought he would die when he did. It was the one contingency the Judge did not envision. That's what I meant when I said he was not as farseeing in his private life as he was on the bench. No one expects a healthy young man in his early thirties to freeze to death in a blizzard, but it happened. I asked your father, just once, what he envisaged for you if Linwood were not here. He flew into a rage, as though simply asking the question were tempting the Fates. You remember how precise he always was in his speech? That day he sputtered like a Roman candle. I could hardly understand him. He had a plan, you see, and it was inconceivable that anything, human or divine, could possibly interfere with it."

"It's in Mrs. MacKenzie's best interests that Miss MacKenzie live a happy and healthy life for the next eleven years. If, that is, she wants to enjoy the income from both fortunes." Geoffrey Hunter's comment was frankly speculative.

"She does, Mr. Hunter. Have no doubt about it. My stepmother brought nothing but her body to that marriage."

"Prudence!"

"My father would say the same, if he were here, Mr. Conkling. And probably in far more explicit terms."

"He was a true gentleman in speech and manners, Prudence."

"He taught me law the same way the students at Harvard are now taught. Case law, Mr. Conkling. One on one and face to face with one of the bench's great jurists. I learned human nature along with the law. Victoria is a greedy woman. She dislikes me as much as I despise her, but she needs me. Mr. Hunter is right. She has to have a stepdaughter who is both healthy and happy. How else can she maintain the place in society that marriage to my father brought her? She can't drain the trust dry;

that would be malfeasance. But she can live very, very well on it, and as long as both of us are seen to benefit, as long as she appears to be a loving and responsible guardian, no one will question what she does or how she does it."

"There's no oversight at all?" asked Hunter.

"The bank has its officers, of course," replied Conkling, "and they'll monitor what flows in and out. Strictly for their own purposes, however. They have no power to refuse a transaction. Even to question it. Fraud is one of the more difficult crimes to prove."

"How well did Charles understand the provisions of the Judge's will?" Geoffrey asked. "Did he go over them in detail with you, Mr. Conkling?"

"Charles was as good a young lawyer as you're likely to find anywhere." Conkling stroked his beard while he debated whether to say something that would sound like a criticism of the dead man. "The only thing I can fault him for was a certain reticence about discussing all of the will's provisions before his marriage to Miss MacKenzie took place."

"Charles was the consummate gentleman," Prudence said.

"He was, my dear. He knew what had to be done and what his role would be in the management of your trust, but he felt it was indelicate and indiscreet to probe too deeply before he became your husband. After all, nothing about the will could be changed. It was just a question of implementation."

"I'm meeting with Charles's father early tomorrow morning," Geoffrey interrupted. "At his request."

Neither Conkling nor Prudence could find the words to ask him why.

"He told me something at the funeral I didn't know before. When they found Charles in Union Square Park, he was holding an ace of spades in his hand. From what his father hinted, it had to have been the same card he always carried in his pocket.

Like this one." Geoffrey laid a playing card on Conkling's desk. An ace of spades worn around the edges with frequent handling, its large black center spade rubbed to gray by time and fingertips. "The one I placed in his coffin this morning was from a new deck."

"What does it mean, Mr. Hunter?"

"The card itself means danger, Miss MacKenzie, though I don't know why Charles had it in his hand. There wasn't time at the church to ask Mr. Linwood any questions. As I said, he's calling on me tomorrow morning."

"I want to be there. I think I have a right to know what he tells you."

"It may not be anything, Miss MacKenzie," Geoffrey said. "I imagine there are things too painful for Charles's mother to hear. She's not a strong woman. Mr. Linwood may just want to talk about his son with someone else who knew and loved him."

"You and I both know it's more than that. Charles was sending you a message, Mr. Hunter."

"I think you should leave it at that for the moment, Prudence." Conkling squared the corners of the stack of papers lying before him. "Let Mr. Hunter meet with Charles's father as planned. Mr. Linwood is more likely to be forthcoming if he doesn't have to worry about upsetting you."

"And you have hired me to represent you," Geoffrey reminded her with a smile.

"I want to know everything he says to you. I don't want anything to be kept hidden from me."

"You have my word, Miss MacKenzie."

"We were talking about the will, and Prudence's stepmother," Conkling reminded them. "At the moment, Prudence's most important problem is what to do about Victoria's hold on her inheritance."

Prudence wrenched her mind back from contemplation of

Charles's hand outstretched in the snow, the ace of spades dark against the white. Mr. Conkling was right. Until Hunter found out what Charles's father wanted to talk to him about, there was no point speculating. She had a more immediate, more pressing problem, and the afternoon was wearing on. She could imagine Victoria pacing furiously in the parlor, enraged that her stepdaughter had eluded her. Something had occurred to her just before Geoffrey Hunter's revelation sidetracked the conversation, something the Judge had been very vehement about.

"Mr. Conkling, does the codicil say anything about the moral turpitude of the trustee? I seem to remember my father telling me that some such language should be a part of every legal situation where control of one person is placed in the hands of another." Prudence smiled at him when Conkling handed her the document to read for herself. It meant she was whole again, her father's daughter again, free of the taint that haunted every laudanum addict. Tears flooded her eyes; she passed the Judge's will to Geoffrey Hunter.

"Here it is." Hunter paged immediately to the codicil that Victoria had insisted upon, the one in which she was named sole trustee of her stepdaughter's fortune. "You were right, Prudence. The trustee is described as being an individual free of moral turpitude. The implication is clear. If Victoria is guilty of evil intent where you or anyone else is concerned, she can be removed as trustee. The catch is that intent may be the hardest thing in the world to prove."

"He slipped it past her, Prudence." Conkling pressed one hand to his right ear; it felt as if an insect were burrowing along the canal. "You were wrong. He did trust that you would be able to manage your own life. For some reason we don't know yet, the Judge couldn't openly challenge Victoria. So he did it by the back door. He left you a clue, my dear. He knew you would remember what he'd taught you. He wagered your freedom on your ability to find out whatever Victoria has to be hiding. It's not a bet he expected to lose."

No one spoke for a moment. The next move was up to Prudence.

"That's the motive for the laudanum, that's why Victoria was so generous with it, why she encouraged me to ignore Dr. Worthington's warnings about taking too much. Laudanum makes the brain flaccid, dulls curiosity because there's no energy to ask questions, no interest in finding answers The women who carry those tiny brown bottles around in their reticules have no more willpower than some of the unfortunate war veterans no one wants to talk about. Every family has someone nodding away his or her life in a quiet upstairs bedroom. My father taught me about powers of attorney, about petitions to declare someone incompetent. That's what Victoria planned for me, Mr. Conkling. A very long, very slow decline until just past my thirtieth birthday. After that, who knows?

"You said you've tried your hand at many professions, Mr. Hunter."

"I'm a curious man, Miss MacKenzie."

"He was a Pinkerton, Prudence."

"Not for very long, Mr. Conkling."

"Long enough. He made some very sensitive inquiries for Charles. Especially for one client who didn't wish his name mentioned."

"May I ask what the result was?" Prudence turned to look directly at the man she had known for only a few hours. He met her eyes steadily, as if he already knew what she was about to ask of him.

"Charles was pleased. His client was ecstatic. Or so I'm told. The client paid very well. Promptly and without demur. Always the best indication of success."

"I want to know who Victoria Morley was before she married my father. Where and when she was born, who her family is, her education or lack of it, what her brother does and why he sticks to her side like an overfed dog. We'll need the name of every man who courted her, every woman who might have been jealous of her. Where her money came from before she married my father. How much of it there was, how she spent it. I want to know everything about her, Mr. Hunter. Everything."

"So do I, Miss MacKenzie. So do I."

CHAPTER 6

The rain had stopped and the skies cleared to a bright spring blue by the time Geoffrey Hunter handed Prudence into a hansom cab outside the United Bank Building at the corner of Wall Street and Broadway.

She paused in the lobby, looking around her as if trying to capture those last few moments before Charles, William Sulzer, and Roscoe Conkling plunged out into the fierce winds and blinding snow of what people were already calling the Great Blizzard. Just nine days ago. This morning she had seen the cheerful yellow of early daffodils breaking through what remained of the snow in the Trinity Church graveyard; now the afternoon breeze was light and playful. Almost impossible to believe that Charles, young and strong, had not survived that walk up Broadway.

"I won't contact you directly, Miss MacKenzie," Hunter said. "I'll send word via Mr. Conkling's office."

"When?"

He shrugged his shoulders. "I don't want to make promises I can't keep. I'll start with the obvious. Your father's death certificate and their marriage license. Both are on file at the City Records Office. Anything else you can find will help. Letters, your father's diary, if he kept one, financial records."

"Mr. Conkling has copies of the bank holdings."

"Household accounts are more what I had in mind. The Judge's personal expenditures. Your stepmother's also. Any regular payments that would indicate MacKenzie funds were being used to support someone or several someones outside the immediate household."

Blackmail? The word breathed itself in Prudence's mind like the unforeseen answer to a baffling case history. *Blackmail?* Was Hunter suggesting that the Judge was being blackmailed? That knowledge of that blackmail was what had given Victoria MacKenzie the strange power she seemed to have held over him? No, she refused to consider it. As a practicing lawyer, her father had rarely lost a case; as a judge, he'd never been overturned. Victoria was young and beautiful; the Judge had been lonely for many years when they met. Prudence could forgive that in some respects he was a man like any other. But his professional life was a model of probity. To believe anything else was to desecrate his memory. *Victoria,* she reminded herself. *Concentrate on finding something in Victoria's past that will prove her guilty of moral turpitude.*

"Be careful." Geoffrey nodded to the driver, watched the hansom cab edge its way out into the traffic surging around this busy section of Lower Manhattan. She was long out of hearing when he repeated, "Be very careful, Prudence."

The man who opened the door to her had joined the MacKenzie household as underbutler shortly before the Judge's death. He was of medium height and muscular, with thick brown hair turning gray above oddly flat ears, ice-cold eyes more yellow than brown, and lips so thin they were like pencil lines drawn onto his face. Even though it had been more than four months, Prudence hadn't gotten used either to Obediah Jackson's looks or to the sneer she read in his eyes after Victoria dismissed Ian Cameron and installed Jackson in his place as butler.

"Prudence, my dear, we were so worried when you didn't arrive at the cemetery." Victoria stood at the parlor door like a headmistress about to deliver a punishment. "Jackson, take Miss MacKenzie's coat."

Prudence repressed a shudder as Jackson helped her off with her coat. She missed Cameron, who'd been the Judge's valet and then his butler since before Prudence was born. In all those years he'd never failed to see her out or welcome her home.

The worst part of the abrupt dismissal that Victoria termed a well-deserved retirement was that it had happened so quickly, without warning or explanation, another event Prudence only vaguely remembered from the dark, laudanum-drenched weeks immediately after the Judge's death. Cameron was gone before Prudence knew he had been relieved of his position. No chance to ask what his plans were, no opportunity to say good-bye to the man she had thought of as a second father. *Where was he?*

Ask few questions, answer none. It had been one of her father's favorite maxims, Prudence reminded herself. Now that she had the promise of Geoffrey Hunter's help, she'd find Cameron without Victoria's knowledge. It would be another of the small victories over her stepmother that were going to count for so much in the coming days.

"I think it best you join me in the parlor, Prudence. Jackson, tell Colleen to bring tea." Victoria's back was eloquently stiff; her silk skirts rustled like leaves in an autumn wind.

Ask few questions, answer none, she repeated to herself as she followed Victoria into the parlor, removing the pins from her hat and hair, wrapping the black mourning veil into a neat package, seating herself without waiting for her stepmother to choose her place for her. *Never put yourself into a situation where someone else can give you orders you have to follow.* Another of the Judge's maxims. She could hear them coursing through her brain one after the other, her father's mellow voice as clear in her mind as if he were standing beside her.

"Donald and I were worried about you, Prudence," Victoria said again.

Prudence had planned this conversation during the ride up Fifth Avenue, rehearsing what she would say, imagining how Victoria would respond. Then Jackson's cold stare had momentarily unsettled her, sending a shiver of apprehension along her spine. She needed time to pull herself together, to find that determined self who had hired an ex-Pinkerton to investigate the woman sitting opposite her.

"I really must insist that you tell me where you went." When she was angry, a thin white line pierced the sharp flare of Victoria's nostrils.

If she were a horse, thought Prudence, *she would have snorted.*

"As you can see, I'm quite all right. But I do appreciate your concern." She removed her gloves one finger at a time, smoothing, pressing, and folding them, laying them atop the narrow black silk purse she had already placed on the table. Playing for time.

Colleen came quietly into the room, balancing a heavy silver tea tray with apparent ease. She laid it on a small mahogany sideboard, then stepped aside and looked to her mistress for further instructions.

"We'll serve ourselves," Victoria snapped.

Colleen bobbed a perfect curtsy. "Yes, madam." She closed the parlor door behind her with only the slight snick of the latch sliding into its faceplate.

"I'll take milk and sugar this afternoon," Prudence announced, pouring a dollop of milk into a gold-rimmed cup, adding the fragrant tea and a small sugar cube. "And the sandwiches look delicious." Protocol dictated that she wait for Victoria to pour, but she was determined to do every little unexpected thing she could to annoy her stepmother. Crack Victoria's outer shell, and the woman who hadn't dared show her true self to the Judge might emerge.

Teacup in hand, Prudence strolled slowly toward the mantel, where a small studio portrait of the Judge in his judicial robes sat beside a picture taken on the occasion of his second wedding. Victoria looked very beautiful, certainly not much older than the new stepdaughter posed woodenly beside the groom. Donald Morley, who had given his sister away, seemed less repulsive and more sober than usual. This was the picture Geoffrey Hunter would need when he made his inquiries: clear, full face, easily identifiable likenesses no one could mistake. The mantel was crowded with silver framed pictures; more photos stood on nearly every tabletop in the room. But only one included the Judge, his second wife, and his brother-in-law; that would have to be the one she smuggled out of the house.

"Victoria, Jackson needs the key to the study." Donald Morley stood in the doorway, one hand curled around the knob. Behind him loomed Jackson's squat bulk. "Prudence. I didn't see you standing there. Where on earth did you go? Is that tea and sandwiches?" He crossed to the table, telling Jackson over his shoulder that he'd ring for him. Within moments he was sipping tea and munching contentedly on sandwiches and cake.

"Sit down, Prudence," ordered Victoria. "You're pacing like one of those lions in the Central Park Zoo."

"It would be much more convenient if you'd allow me to have a copy made," mused Donald around a mouthful of crumbs. "Jackson says that particular door is the only one not to have a key on the butler's master ring. One of your late husband's many idiosyncrasies, my dear sister."

She would have to ask. *Ask few questions, answer none.* Prudence had to know. But she kept her back to him so Donald couldn't read her face, pretending interest in the slightly dusty leaves of the enormously ugly aspidistra plant that was slowly dying in a too-dim corner far from the front windows. "Why do you need the key to my father's study, Donald?"

No answer. No sound except the slurp of tea and the crunch of thinly sliced cucumbers between crustless triangles of buttered bread. Prudence waited. She wouldn't repeat herself. *The only way to make people listen to you is never to repeat yourself.* Another of the Judge's maxims. She thought she heard Victoria start to make that familiar clicking noise in her throat that signaled annoyance, but Donald was too quick for her.

"Charles won't be needing it now, will he? I'm sorry, Prudence, but that's the truth of the situation, and the sooner you face up to it, the better. I thought—that is, your stepmother and I decided there was no point letting the room gather dust, as it were."

"You haven't been in there in weeks," Victoria said primly. "Really not since those dreadful days just after Thomas passed away. I was heartbroken, of course, and you didn't make my grief any easier to bear, Prudence. Not with all of that shouting and crying and flinging about of books. Now that poor Charles is dead, too, there's no reason to keep things as they were. Jackson and one of the maids will box up the Judge's law books. I'll leave it to Mr. Conkling to suggest a suitable law school or library to which to donate them. Donald has made do with that small dressing room just off his bedroom, but there really is no more reason to deprive him of a decent study where he can see to his business affairs and smoke his pipe in peace."

A fait accompli, then. Just like the removal from the house of the loyal and beloved butler who had helped her through the scrapes of childhood and kept a gimlet eye on her transition into young womanhood. She would find out where Cameron had gone, and she would not allow the room that was more her father's than any other spot in the house to be desecrated by the likes of Donald Morley. If she was Victoria's financial prisoner for the indefinite future, she was also the only thing that stood between her stepmother and the loss to charity of half of the Judge's fortune. She had to find out exactly what her place was in this new threesome created by Charles's death.

"Donald is *not* to have my father's study."

For a moment the only sound in the room was the faint hiss of the warming candle under the silver teapot of extra water. Not even the crunch of cucumber sandwiches. For once, Donald Morley had heard something that froze his jaws in midchew.

"That's not your decision to make, Prudence." Victoria recovered more quickly than her brother. "I'm willing to forgive a certain amount of questionable behavior today, given the circumstances. Funerals can be very upsetting. You've suffered two terrible losses. But there are limits, my dear. And you are rapidly approaching them."

"Donald is *not* to have my father's study." She had no weapon except the strength of her own will in this first battle, this urgently important decision of who was to occupy Thomas MacKenzie's library. The instinct that her father always said was a lawyer's best friend suddenly told her that Victoria was not as sure of herself as she sounded. She didn't know where or with whom her stepdaughter had spent most of the afternoon, or why she had so obviously evaded telling her. Prudence was more certain than ever that Victoria had something to hide, perhaps many somethings, and that the threat of discovery might be the only leverage she had.

She had to trust Hunter to ferret out Victoria's past, whatever it was, but for now Victoria had to be led to believe that Prudence knew or suspected something the Judge's widow had been at great pains to conceal. That same lawyer's instinct told her to take advantage of every little weakness, to feign a strength she wasn't sure she possessed. Not to falter, not to break. Victoria intended to control and manipulate her stepdaughter through the use of laudanum; believing her plan was working might buy Prudence the precious time she needed.

"I plan to inventory my father's private papers. His letters, especially the ones he wrote to my mother. His study wasn't just a law library, you know. It was where he could retreat from the rest of the world, where he could write the history of our family, where he confided his most private thoughts to his diary. As his daughter, those papers belong to *me* now."

She set down her teacup. Not a drop had been drunk. If Victoria really was secretly dosing her with more laudanum than Dr. Worthington had advised, she would fear an overdose if Prudence grew so addicted that she managed to buy her own supply. She had to confirm what she suspected.

From the pocket in her skirt designed for a handkerchief and a vial of smelling salts Prudence brought out one of the small brown bottles that could be bought at any pharmacy, bottles made expressly for a lady to carry on her exhausting social rounds. The distinctive odor of alcohol and honey was released into the room as she removed the cork. Ladies preferred the bitter laudanum dissolved in something sweet. "Family papers can reveal so much. Don't you agree, Victoria?"

Moving surprisingly quickly for the size of his belly, Donald snatched the small brown bottle from Prudence's hand, recorked it, and dropped the offending object into his coat pocket. "You buried someone very dear to you today," he said unctuously. "It's understandable that you should be upset. But to lie to us, Prudence! To pretend that you were going to accompany the Linwoods to the cemetery and then to steal away like some wanton girl of the streets just to find a pharmacy where no one would know you! Sensible people know when enough is enough!"

"I don't take many extra drops of laudanum, Donald," Prudence said. "Just occasionally, or when a nervous headache becomes too painful." She remembered Roscoe Conkling's warning. Her father's will could not be broken by any ordinary challenge of a disgruntled beneficiary, but malfeasance, though hard to prove, was grounds no judge would ignore. And Prudence's death by overdose would mean the loss of a great deal of money.

Morley stared at her as if he weren't quite sure who she was, then turned to his sister. "Victoria, I can wait until Prudence has gone through her father's papers. I've made do for the past two years with that little dressing room, and I imagine I can survive for a few more weeks there. She can take her time about it." He reached out clumsily, folding Prudence into a brief, avuncular embrace.

"I believe I'll go lie down for a while," Prudence said, pulling away from him.

"I'll send Colleen up to you when it's time to dress for dinner." Victoria's voice was as brittle as ice. She wasn't exactly sure what had happened, only that the stepdaughter she had dismissed as not worth worrying about had unexpectedly developed a backbone.

Prudence nodded, but said nothing. She felt Donald's eyes boring into her as he opened the parlor door and stood aside. He smelled of whiskey and pipe tobacco, expensive whiskey now, a cheaper corn sweetness when he had first come to live with his sister and the Judge. Prudence forced herself not to wrinkle up her nose as she brushed past him, as she stepped carefully into the hall.

"Donald, close that door and come over here."

She heard Victoria's peevish command and the sound of the parlor door closing. Heard angry hissing and the muted sounds of an argument. Victoria hadn't conceded yet, hadn't agreed to give Prudence access to her late husband's study. For once, brother and sister did not seem to be agreeing on something. Prudence wondered why, but she didn't have time to linger.

She dared a quick look behind her, held both hands against her skirts to keep them from rustling. She could hear the murmur of voices, but no matter how hard she concentrated, she could not make out what they were saying. She dared not approach the door too closely, nor could she stay where she was in the empty hall. There was no telling when Jackson would come back. Donald had said he would ring for him, but a good butler had the ability to sense his master's wishes before they could be expressed.

The key. Prudence moved as quickly as she dared down the wide central hall of the house, stopping when she reached the heavy oak door through which she had entered and left so many times. There had been three keys to the Judge's study, one of which he kept on a thin gold chain threaded through a buttonhole of his vest. The second key lay upstairs in Prudence's jewel case, hidden under the black velvet on which nestled her mother's pearls. She reached behind the heavy coatrack that was as tall as the front door, found the shallow niche that had been whittled out of one of its upright posts. Within seconds she was inside her father's study, the door safely locked behind her, the third key buried in her pocket.

The key that Jackson didn't have could only be the one the Judge habitually carried, and if Donald hadn't been able to give it to him, then Victoria had it. Not on her person, but somewhere in the satin-draped bedroom that Prudence privately thought was the epitome of overblown bad taste. The pink of the drapes was too deep, too much of the furniture had been decorated with bright gold leaf, there were mirrors everywhere you turned, and the air behind the always-closed windows reeked of the heavy, cloying perfume that was her stepmother's signature fragrance.

As she turned from the door and walked toward her father's great mahogany desk, Prudence sensed his presence in the room, smelled the warm leather and ink scent that always surrounded him, caught a whiff of the fine imported cigars he loved. Once, a very daring young lady, she had begged to be allowed to puff on the burning tobacco that men seemed to enjoy so much. An indulgent father, he had allowed it, and then hadn't so much as chuckled while she choked and coughed and waved her hands around to dispel the awful smoke.

She had been angry with him in Roscoe Conkling's office, angry because he had claimed to love her, had defied convention to educate her in the law. Had then weighed and found her unworthy to stand on her own. Had given over control of her trust to a husband she would never marry, and then to a woman she despised. It was as if Prudence had been examined and found lacking in some fundamental way she could neither identify nor understand. The choice of Charles she was prepared to forgive. The Judge had believed that Charles's character was too honest to allow him to touch a cent of his wife's fortune without her consent. But Victoria? Victoria?

She seated herself in her father's leather armchair. Someone had dusted and polished the desktop, the bookshelves, the tables that sat beside the wing chairs placed close enough to the fireplace for warmth and light. Someone had cleared away whatever papers had been left stacked for the Judge's attention when he was forced to take to his bed. She wondered how much had been hidden from sight in drawers, how much tossed into the fire. There were no ashes in the grate; fresh logs had been laid but not lit.

This was what she wanted. If she could have this room and this desk, this link to her father, she would be able to withstand whatever pressures Victoria brought to bear on her. She could be strong in this study, could resist the lure of laudanum here, could envision herself the fulfillment of what the Judge had begun to create. What had Donald said? That he could wait a few more weeks for her to go through her father's papers? He had given in so quickly. Why? And would Victoria also decide to placate her stepdaughter, even temporarily? She wondered how long they would argue.

She heard a cautious but insistent scratching at the door. A short flutter of soft knocks, then the scratching again.

"Miss Prudence. Miss Prudence."

She sped to the study door, unlocked it, opened it just a crack.

"Miss Prudence, the mistress rang for me to take away the tea things. I thought you should know."

"How did you . . . ?"

"I dust and polish that old coatrack, Miss Prudence. I found the key a long time ago, but I never said a word. The Judge was good to me."

Prudence stood frozen in the hallway, the study door locked again, the key in her hand.

"Give it to me, Miss Prudence. I'll put it back. You may need it."

"I don't want Mr. Morley in my father's study, Colleen. Ever. I don't think I could bear it. And I don't want him or my stepmother to know that I have my own key."

"You'll think of something, Miss Prudence. Your daddy used to tell all of us that you were the smartest thing he'd ever seen, for not being a boy."

The Judge's daughter spun on her heel and was up the broad, curving staircase before Colleen slid the key back into its hiding place. The maid thought she heard something that was very like the strangling noises the Judge used to make when he was too angry to speak. Everyone who worked for him learned to scatter and hide when that deep chest rumbling began.

I am my father's daughter, Prudence repeated to herself over and over again. Her boots beat a tattoo on the Turkish carpets where as a girl she had stretched out on a pile of cushions to read and dream of a future wondrous beyond imagining. *I am my father's daughter, I am my father's daughter.*

If Geoffrey Hunter couldn't find out who Victoria was, she

would. She'd tear her father's study apart until she found what she knew must be hidden there. *I am my father's daughter.*

She wouldn't give Victoria the gentleman's courtesy of a formal challenge. Ambush was a far more effective tactic. Gentlemanly attitudes toward war had been the South's undoing. They were lovely and romantic and fit for the court of King Arthur, but in the real world of the late nineteenth century, they weren't worth a fiddler's damn.

CHAPTER 7

"Donald has been very generous, Prudence." Victoria unlocked the door to her late husband's study with the key that still hung from the thin gold chain he had worn across his vest. "He's very fond of you and he only wants what's best; there are times when he simply must stand in for your father."

"I don't take additional laudanum very often, Victoria."

"You frightened both of us. I won't ask you again what pharmacy you bought it from yesterday, but you have to know how dangerous it can be to buy from an unknown source. There's no telling what might have been in the mixture."

Victoria withdrew the key from the lock and when Prudence reached for it, shook her head. "You might misplace it," she said, turning abruptly, heels tapping along the polished wood floor of the hallway.

Only when Victoria had disappeared into the parlor did Prudence enter the study and close the door behind her. She didn't dare lock it; that risk would have to be run late at night, when the house slept. If there were private papers hidden somewhere in this room, she would search for them when she could be sure of not being interrupted.

Geoffrey Hunter had mentioned a diary, household accounts, letters. Victoria was not a stupid woman; she would have gone through her husband's papers before anyone else could get to them. Prudence wouldn't put it past her to have ransacked the Judge's desk while he lay ill and dying in his bedroom on the second floor. No, she wouldn't have ransacked his desk; she would have gone through it drawer by drawer, meticulously replacing the contents exactly how and where she found them. Just in case. In case he recovered. In case he persuaded Cameron to help him downstairs despite the doctor's orders to remain in bed. Victoria was not the type of woman to take chances. As far as Prudence could tell, she had made not a single mistake since marrying the Judge. Not one.

"Miss Prudence." Colleen carried two heavy cardboard letter cases into the room. "Mrs. MacKenzie said I was to take these back up to the attic again when you finish with them. I'm supposed to tell you she's ordered more from the stationer."

"You can put them on the table, Colleen."

The long library table stood beneath a broad expanse of windows overlooking the garden. When the heavy dark green drapes were drawn back, light poured over whatever was laid out there for study. The Judge had used it to organize a case, moving around evidence reports, witness statements, his own notes, and even newspaper clippings according to some unfathomable logic of his own. He had taught his daughter that every case was different, and that therefore each one had its own interrelated structure of irrefutable facts. It was up to the investigator hidden inside every good lawyer to find and apply the principles that would validate his conclusions and strengthen his argument. What might look to the uneducated eye like a random collection of odds and ends was actually an exercise in shifting patterns.

"There are papers inside these cases," Prudence said, hearing the rustle within.

"Yes, miss."

"Thank you, Colleen."

"Is there anything else, miss?"

"You've already taken one big chance for me, Colleen. Mrs. MacKenzie won't forgive you for not telling her about the key hidden in the hall coatrack. You could lose your position over that if she finds out."

"She won't, Miss Prudence. Nobody dusts that rack except me."

"There is one other thing, Colleen."

"I can do it, miss, whatever it is." Excitement reddened the maid's cheeks and made her blue eyes sparkle. Like most parlor maids, she'd been chosen as much for her looks as for her skills.

"A gentleman who works for Mr. Conkling, the Judge's lawyer, is working for me now." Prudence thought a more detailed explanation would be confusing. "I need a way to receive messages from him without Mrs. MacKenzie knowing, so I gave him two names. Yours and James Kincaid's. I couldn't think of anyone else I can trust."

"Mr. Kincaid is the safest, miss. Nobody goes out to the stables and carriage house except him. He could easily bring a message to the kitchen when he comes in for a meal or a cup of tea. If he gave it to me, I could get it to you and no one the wiser."

"I think you have the makings of a Pinkerton, Colleen. That's exactly what Mr. Hunter told me would work best."

"A Pinkerton, miss?"

"Mr. Hunter is a former Pinkerton."

"Cook sends hot tea to Mr. Kincaid sometimes. I can be the one to take it out. They'll just think down in the kitchen that I'm sweet on him."

"He's twice your age!"

"A coachman is a good catch, miss, and Mr. Kincaid's a favorite with all the maids."

"I hope there's a message for me this morning, Colleen."

"Not to worry, Miss Prudence. I'll see to it Mr. Kincaid is warned what to expect."

The first cardboard letter case held only a scant handful of documents. Prudence placed them one by one on the table, lining them up precisely. She recognized the handwriting immediately, the heavy black ink her father had always used, the thick letter paper that had the look and feel of vellum. *My most darling Sarah,* she read. Tears filled her eyes. She counted ten letters, and knew immediately that if the Judge had written ten letters to his wife, he had written hundreds. *Cameron would know,* she thought. *Cameron would know if my father boxed up his letters to my mother before he married Victoria.* Boxed them up in heavy cardboard letter cases to preserve them.

Victoria burned them, she thought. *She left only these few so I would think my father had destroyed what he thought too private and too tender to share.* Each letter began with the same words: *My most darling Sarah.* But these letters might have been written by a fond brother sending household instructions home to his sister. There were requests to tell his valet to ready a certain suit which he must have for court, inquiries about a favorite horse discovered to have a split hoof just before the Judge left for Philadelphia, reminders that his prize roses would need careful pruning in the heat of summer, questions about the various dinners and evening galas which his darling Sarah had had to attend without him. The letters were chatty, but oddly impersonal, as if each one had been written in a hurry, almost as an afterthought to a more ardent missive that had already been sent.

This was not the deeply enamored husband who had bought a bucolic country home in the hills of Staten Island so his consumptive wife could breathe fresh, clean air. Be distracted from her illness by the elegant white-clad cricketers and lawn tennis players at the Staten Island Cricket and Tennis Club. Prudence remembered her father telling her about those few years when it had still been possible to hope that Sarah would recover. She wasn't poor, malnourished, living cheek to jowl in a tenement flophouse; she was surrounded by the best and most constant care the Judge's considerable wealth could obtain. Neither husband nor wife gave in to despair, not even when she lay dying and he knelt beside her bed aching to breathe for her.

He wrote her every day, sometimes several times a day, and sped those letters by messenger across the harbor when they were separated, Sarah in the many-windowed summer house he had built for her atop a wooded hill, Thomas in the law courts that occupied his mind and kept him sane. *You can read them when you're older,* he had told Prudence, *when you know what love is and how glorious and painful it can be.* Ten letters to a wife he adored? Ten letters over the course of a passionate marriage that lasted eight years? Never. Not possible.

And where were Sarah's letters to her husband? She had lain on a daybed in the shade of the house's wide white porch, reading, napping, and writing. *Your mother wrote poems,* the Judge had told Prudence, *and the most beautiful letters imaginable.* Those, too, he put aside for her to read when she got older. But he waited too long. Victoria captured him when Prudence was not quite seventeen; life in the mansion on Fifth Avenue had never been the same. Wherever the Judge stored his letters to Sarah and hers to him, they had not survived Victoria.

The second letter case contained what seemed to be the contents of a desk drawer, a jumble of notes, fading photographs, unopened invitations, and what looked like bills from a tailor. They were many times folded and creased, with here and there a stain of spilled brandy or coffee, such an unsorted miscellany that Prudence was hard put to believe the mess had really been her father's. The Judge was conscientious about record keeping; he said no man could be a good lawyer who didn't respect minutiae. He would never have allowed this accumulation of detritus in his immaculate and well-organized desk. Where had it come from? What did it mean?

When she read Donald's name on one of the bills, she knew that Victoria and her brother had lied to her. Sometime during the past three months, Donald had usurped her father's desk long enough to fill a drawer with his leavings. Which Victoria then unceremoniously dumped into one of the letter cases Colleen brought from the attic.

But that didn't make sense. Charles was to have moved into the Judge's library when the newly wedded couple got back from their honeymoon in Saratoga. That had been the plan. Why would Donald have taken temporary possession of the Judge's office? Unless he had intended it to be permanent. Which made even less sense. And even more confusing, why would he or Victoria have tried to conceal what he'd done, tried to remove all traces of his presence? It was almost as puzzling as learning that Charles had died with the ace of spades in his hand.

Prudence heard the longcase clock in the hallway strike the hour. Mr. Linwood should have arrived at Geoffrey Hunter's suite in the Fifth Avenue Hotel by now. She pictured the two men drinking coffee together, exchanging stories about Charles, allowing an atmosphere of trust to build between them. She thought Mr. Hunter would wait patiently until Charles's father was ready to talk about whatever was disturbing him. Something to do with the card; it had to be that. Was it a clue to a case Charles was handling? He hadn't mentioned anything out of the ordinary to her, and he knew how much she enjoyed conundrums of the law.

Enough. Geoffrey would send word as soon as he had anything to tell her, and Colleen would make sure she got the message. In the meantime, she had work to do here in the study. One by one Prudence examined each of the items Donald had carelessly left behind, returning each to the letter case when she was satisfied it could not answer her questions. The suspicion that Victoria and her brother were concealing vitally important secrets about themselves was stronger than ever. There were no answers here, but it gave her hope that Donald was slipshod enough to have made other mistakes.

The black silk ribbon was worn and frayed; Prudence retied and knotted it as tightly as she could, careful to leave no trace that the contents of the letter case had received any but the most cursory of examinations.

She read each of the ten letters the Judge had written to his wife, reread some passages. Not until a tear splashed on to the back of her hand did she realize she was weeping, mourning the loss of all the letters that had been stolen from her, that by rights should have been hers to treasure, that would have kept alive the love her parents shared. Reverently, because unrevealing though they were, they were all she had, she put the letters in order by date, placed a piece of clean white paper in between each of them to keep the ink from bleeding through, and returned them to the letter case.

The table shone empty in the late-morning light, its polished cherry surface gleaming and bare. Was this a portent of what she would find in her father's study? In his desk? Bits and pieces that Victoria had decided were not important enough to destroy?

She tried to go back through the hours and days and weeks after her father's death, tried to remember the daily life of the house after its master left it. How had Victoria spent those first days of widowhood? Had servants cleared out her father's clothing after the funeral? Had Victoria closed up the study because the room was supposed to become Charles's private domain after the wedding? Closed it up and locked it after stripping it of everything that could possibly be of value? She couldn't remember. She had fallen into the deep and comforting embrace of laudanum, been led into a drowsy world that seemed made of the softest of feathers so that escape was impossible. Even if she had wanted to. Which she didn't think she had.

Prudence settled herself deeper into her father's chair, placed both her forearms on the desktop as she had seen him do many times in a courtroom when he poised himself to listen intently to the questions and answers of the drama playing out below his bench. *Listen, really listen to what is being said. You never know when something vital will slip out.* She would listen to herself, would examine whatever there was to hear, would search her dulled brain for whatever it might have absorbed but never probed. *Always begin with the obvious, start with what you're tempted to ignore.*

Victoria claimed she had wanted to summon Dr. Worthington when the Judge first fell ill, but he scoffed at the idea and refused to allow it. He had a history of dyspepsia, he reminded her. Peter Worthington would scold and fuss, mix him an unpalatable and hideously smelly drink, prohibit cigars and brandy for a week, then collect a fat fee for what he'd done innumerable times before. Victoria should tell Cook to put a spoonful of baking soda into some warm water and be done with it.

He got better at first, the nausea and pains in his upper abdomen easing on a diet of boiled milk and dry water biscuits straight from the barrel. The day after he pronounced himself cured, he had a second attack, longer and more severe than the first. This time the Judge sent for Dr. Worthington. Prudence had sat so quietly in her dead mother's dressing room that neither man suspected the connecting door between the two rooms was cracked. She hadn't trusted either her father or Victoria to tell her the truth about his condition.

"Judge, I've known and treated you for more than twenty-five years. You're not getting any younger. Neither am I, for that matter."

"You have a case to make, Peter. Make it and be done."

"Not to put too fine a point on it, Thomas, you have a young wife. Young and very beautiful, if you will allow the compliment. An older man with a much younger wife needs to see to himself more carefully than he's often prepared to admit. If you understand what I'm saying."

"You're as good as a lawyer at implying much and stating nothing. Victoria's age and our marital status have nothing to do with this fire in my gut and the urge to empty myself even when there's nothing left inside me to get rid of."

"I see." Perhaps if Peter Worthington hadn't known Thomas MacKenzie for a quarter of a century, didn't count him as much a friend as a patient, he would have asked the obvious question. But looking at the wan face on the pillow, taking in the fiercely proud and stubbornly set jaw, he knew the Judge would count it an unconscionable invasion of his privacy and refuse to answer.

He suspected his aging friend had fallen foolish victim to one of the hundreds of patent nostrums advertised to improve male performance; the best he could do under the circumstances was warn him off. The Judge was far from stupid, although as vulnerable as any man to certain weaknesses; he'd have to accept that with years came certain unmentionable dysfunctions. Sad, but true. And nothing to be done but accept the new limitations.

"I would get rid of any patent medicines you may be taking, Thomas. No matter how beneficial they promise to be. Walk to the office instead of taking the carriage or a hansom cab. Restrict your consumption of brandy and cigars. You'll be as right as rain in a week or two."

In the end, it was Dr. Worthington himself who provided the blueprint for the Judge's demise. How fortuitous. Many of the male enhancement tonics contained arsenic, which had long been used in the treatment of syphilis. The police and the press had dubbed it *inheritance powder*.

Buy a bottle of the strongest tonic, boil it down to increase the concentration of arsenic, add the resulting syrup to the heart-regulating concoctions prescribed by the Judge's physician, and wait for the poison to quietly do its deadly work.

The Judge was possessed of a young and beautiful wife; it was only natural that he would dose himself with whatever nostrum promised him the staying power of a younger man. Dr. Worthington had warned his patient against the patent medicines. He wouldn't question the inevitable result. The plan was foolproof.

The hand that laced the Judge's heart medicine with arsenic did not hesitate.

Two weeks later the Judge was dead.

"His heart gave out," Dr. Worthington told the widow and daughter. "It happens to men of his age, and he hadn't been well recently."

"Not for months, actually, though he wouldn't admit it, wouldn't allow me to send for you until it was too late," sobbed Victoria. "He knew, Doctor, he knew what was coming."

Peter Worthington doubted that very much, though he seldom bothered to contradict grieving relatives. They rarely heard what he had to say, and usually resented any implication that the corpse brought it on himself. What puzzled him about the Judge's death was not the fact of his heart giving out, but the suddenness of it. Usually there were warning signs aplenty.

Shortness of breath, numbness in the extremities, a tinge of blue beneath the fingernails, the pallid complexion and dark circles under the eyes of someone whose blood isn't circulating the way it should.

But aside from the dyspepsia and what Worthington suspected the Judge had done to keep his so much younger wife happy and satisfied, Thomas MacKenzie had been in good health. In fact, he and his friend Roscoe Conkling were the same age. Conkling's robust physique and enormous energy were envied by some, resented by others. In that, as in his far too blatant affairs with attractive women of all ages, he was a figure of controversy and a boon to the muckrakers. Yet the conservative judge died and the flamboyant Conkling seemed to remain close to his prime long after he should have conceded gracefully to the constrictions of advancing years.

Victoria would recover; she was the type of woman who rebounded from the worst of tragedies. It was Prudence who worried Dr. Worthington. She had that air of disengagement often worn by ladies who faded away in their beds and on their couches until they breathed a last quiet sigh and were gone. As if life had grown too much for them to bear and the alternative too attractive to resist. Laudanum could help, but it could also be risky. Still, he had no other balm to offer.

He warned Victoria about the dangers of overdosing and hoped he had done the right thing.

As if she were reliving the moment, Prudence saw Victoria sobbing, heard Dr. Worthington confirm what everyone in the house already suspected. The Judge had suffered a massive and fatal heart attack. Then she floated through the wake and the funeral, glided above the heads of the mourners who came to express their condolences, hung weightless over the open casket in which her father's body lay. Not his body. Him. Thomas Pickering MacKenzie, sleeping beneath her gaze until some magic word or potion should awaken him. She couldn't separate what was dream from what was reality, what was true memory from what might have been.

And finally she understood that she would never be able to force back what the laudanum had muffled in grayness so she could bear it. What was gone was lost forever.

CHAPTER 8

James Kincaid took the team of prize grays to be reshod later that morning, after confirming with Mrs. MacKenzie and Mr. Morley that the carriage would not be needed until the afternoon.

"There's been no throwing of shoes yet," he explained, "but they're almost due for a change and Smoker's gait is off. I noticed it the last time we took them out. No point waiting for the worst to happen. Cobblestones are the hardest surface in the world for horseshoes; they wear down the nails faster than anything else."

Donald Morley knew nothing about fine horses, but it was the mark of a gentleman to be knowledgeable about the steeds he owned, so he nodded his head sagely and gave permission for Kincaid to drive the team to the farrier's. James had been prepared to explain that while the farrier usually came to the MacKenzie stable to trim and shoe the grays' hooves, he'd lately taken to requiring his clients to bring the animals to him, and since he was the best at his craft, they did. It turned out that Mr. Morley's ignorance was so profound, the explanation was unnecessary.

*   *   *

"Shall I come back for you, miss?" James Kincaid reined in the grays at the entrance to the United Bank Building on Wall Street where Roscoe Conkling's office was located.

"I don't think we'd better risk it, and I'm not sure how long I'll be," Prudence told him. "I'll take a hansom cab home."

"Mrs. MacKenzie won't like that." Kincaid smiled at the thought of her discomfiture. He'd been in the Judge's service for more than twenty years, ever since he'd been hired on as a stableboy. He'd driven Prudence's mother all over Staten Island when it was thought the fresh air would do her good. Might cure her. He didn't like the woman who'd replaced her, and he didn't always care who knew it. "Mr. Conkling uses a cabbie named Danny Dennis. He's the best in the city. Josiah can get him for you. Don't forget to ask for him by name. You can trust Danny to take you wherever you want to go."

Kincaid waited until Miss Prudence disappeared into the bank's lobby before moving away from the curb. Something was going on that he didn't understand yet, but he hadn't hesitated for a second when he'd been handed a note to pass along to Colleen. Whatever Miss Prudence needed was what he was prepared to help her get. Especially if it meant putting one over on Mrs. MacKenzie and Mr. Morley. They weren't quality; he felt it in his bones, the same way he recognized the truth of good bloodlines in the animals he drove.

The grays didn't need their hooves attended to, but since he was the one who kept the stable account book, he'd also be the one to fiddle with the numbers.

"This is the card Charles was holding," Geoffrey Hunter said. The piece of pasteboard was wrinkled, ripped along the edges, mottled with melted snow, and stained with dirt and something darker that he didn't tell Prudence was probably dried blood.

"Where did Mr. Linwood get it?" Prudence asked. She wanted to touch the object that had been so important to Charles, but she was afraid that if she did, she would begin to weep with the sadness of it all. She would wear black for many months to come, but she was determined not to sink down again into the helplessness of laudanum-laced grief.

"You would expect the police to have viewed it as evidence, but they didn't," Hunter explained. "The body was taken to Bellevue along with so many others who had died in the blizzard that not much individual attention was paid to the victims. The deaths were all presumed to be accidental, and that's the way they were treated. Only cursory examinations. No autopsies. People flocked to Bellevue in search of their missing relatives, and as soon as a body could be identified, it was released to the next of kin or a mortuary parlor. We only know Charles was holding it in his hand because the policeman who notified Mr. Linwood of his son's death retrieved it. He thought it might mean something to a relative and was afraid it would be thrown away by one of the Bellevue attendants."

"Mr. Linwood isn't satisfied that his son's death *was* accidental," Roscoe Conkling declared. "He doesn't know what it was, but he doesn't believe the word *accidental* fits what happened."

"How can he know that?"

"He can't. No one can, Prudence," Conkling replied. "But someone like Hunter will come as close to the truth as it's possible to get without actually having been there."

"Is that what Mr. Linwood asked you to do, Mr. Hunter? Find out the truth of Charles's death?"

"His firm has hired me a number of times in the past. I told him this wouldn't be one of those cases." Geoffrey's strong fist closed over the ace of spades. "I told him I'd do this because Charles was asking me to take it on." He opened his fist. "You were right, Miss MacKenzie, when you said Charles was sending me a message. I just have to figure out what it is."

"Not alone, Mr. Hunter. I've read about Kate Warne."

"She's been dead for twenty years, Miss MacKenzie. Very

few women have followed in her footsteps, even though Allan Pinkerton did create a division of female detectives in his agency."

"But there have been some. She wasn't the only female spy during the war, and she hasn't been the only woman detective since then. You know that's true."

"There have been a few women making a name for themselves in detection," he conceded. "But not many."

"Perhaps that's because no one is willing to give them the opportunity." Prudence turned to her late father's lawyer, the man who was very nearly an uncle to her. She was counting on his support, on his love of womankind in general, and his passion for women who had made names for themselves before taking up with him. "Don't you think that's the reason, Mr. Conkling? Not because a woman isn't intelligent or cunning enough to probe the depths of a mystery, but because no one is willing to give her a chance?"

"What are you proposing, Miss MacKenzie?"

Geoffrey Hunter's question was simple and straightforward. Her answer needed to be equally as frank.

"I'm proposing that you and I become partners, Mr. Hunter, that you share with me and I with you whatever information we find. Two minds are better than one. You may well understand what puzzles me, and I the same for you. We reached an understanding about my stepmother, about finding out everything there is to know about her. Now Charles is asking us to do the same for him, but for a different reason."

"What would that reason be, Miss MacKenzie?"

"What his father suspects. Why he came to you in the first place. If that tree branch didn't fall on Charles all by itself, with only the wind for accomplice, then someone picked it up and used it to kill him. Deliberately. Knowing full well the police would assume he was another victim of the blizzard." Prudence had phrased it as succinctly as she could. Now she waited for a reaction.

Conkling chuckled. "I think she's got you, Hunter," he said.

Geoffrey Hunter reached out his right hand. "I believe partners shake on a deal," he said.

Prudence MacKenzie stripped off her black glove and for the first time in her life touched the flesh of a man who wasn't a member of her family.

The Warneke and Sons funeral home was quiet and smelled of lilies. In silence, Maurice Warneke led Geoffrey Hunter and Prudence MacKenzie past parlors being readied for afternoon and evening visitations to an office whose door he unlocked and held open for his guests. He wondered if this was the call he had been waiting for, though he'd said nothing to Charles Linwood's father about his suspicions.

"I read about Mr. Conkling's walk up Broadway. He's lucky to have survived it," Warneke began. "The note his secretary sent said you had questions about the late Charles Linwood. How can I help you?"

"Miss MacKenzie was Mr. Linwood's fiancée," Hunter explained.

"My condolences, Miss MacKenzie." Maurice Warneke doubted the young woman remembered him, though he had spoken briefly to her before the funeral service. He had caught a faint whiff of bitter laudanum, not from her breath, but as if she had spilled a few drops of the liquid on the black mourning veil covering her face. Odd, but nothing about the conduct of the bereaved surprised him. Except now, when she raised the mourning veil and looked at him with steady determination and not a trace of female weakness.

"You prepared the body yourself?" Hunter asked.

"I did."

"Is that usual?"

"I have a young man who normally does the preliminary work, if that's what you mean. But I chose to take care of Mr. Linwood myself."

"Why was that?"

"Sometimes when the death is a violent one, special skills are required if the body is to be viewed by relatives."

"And that was so in Charles Linwood's case?"

"His head was badly battered."

"By the tree limb that fell on him?"

Warneke looked intently at Hunter, assessing the former Pinkerton operative he knew had investigated cases for the Linwood law firm. Hunter had the look of a stalker about him. Appropriate, given his name. He glanced at Prudence MacKenzie, sitting rigidly alert in her chair. She hadn't said a word so far, but from the look on her face, she was prepared to hear what he had to tell. These two people might be the only individuals who ever came to inquire about the late Charles Linwood. Maurice Warneke decided it was time to break his silence.

"It might not have fallen," he said. There. He could tell by Miss MacKenzie's quick, indrawn breath that the statement had not been entirely unexpected.

"I think that requires some explanation," she finally said.

"It was the spot where the tree limb hit, and the amount of force it took to drive as much bark into the wound as I picked out." Warneke raised a hand to his own head. "Right here, just where the back of the neck meets the spine." He turned and then bent his head forward and to one side to show the exposure.

"He must have been wearing a hat and scarf. He couldn't have gotten as far up Broadway as he did if his head had been uncovered." Miss MacKenzie's voice was steady. No trace of choked-back tears.

"It wasn't," Warneke agreed. "I suspect that when he sat down, he was readjusting the scarf, perhaps taking off the hat momentarily to brush some of the snow off it. The timing of the tree limb was fortuitous."

"But not accidental," Hunter said. He looked briefly at Miss

MacKenzie as if in apology for exposing her to the details he knew would follow.

Warneke stood up and moved to behind the chair in which he had been sitting. He took a black umbrella from its stand against the wall and raised it above his head, holding it as though it were a branch attached to a tree. "This is how the limb would fall if the weight of the snow snapped it off," he said, bringing the umbrella straight down. "Even allowing for the wind, there wouldn't have been enough sideways force to make the wounds I saw. However, if the branch were held and swung thusly, it could easily have smashed into the base of the young man's skull." He swung the umbrella with a strong backhanded heave whose force whistled through the still air. Repeated the movement. "There's no other way he could have sustained the injuries he did in precisely that spot at the base of his neck. I've tried every type of blow I could think of. This is the only one that matches."

"So he *was* murdered," Prudence breathed.

"Perhaps."

"Yet you said nothing to the police?" Hunter questioned.

"What I just showed you isn't proof. Doesn't even come close to being proof. It could be argued that the wind gusted at precisely the moment the tree decided to release its limb, that the gust picked up the branch and hurled it against Linwood with the same type of accuracy that a human being could achieve. He was robbed and left to freeze to death, his assailant long gone and perhaps dead himself shortly afterward. The body was taken to the city morgue before being brought here to me. Released as an accident victim. Death by mischance is what they call it. The doctor who examined the young man when he was carried into the morgue called him a victim of the storm; the police had no qualms, and his family wanted him buried quietly, respectfully. I did the best I could for him and for them. I knew my questions would have no answers. What was the point in asking them?"

"Have you seen this kind of thing before?" Prudence asked.

"A murder gone unpunished, you mean?"

"Gone unsuspected."

"Ask any undertaker. We've all had our doubts at one time or another."

"Was there only the one blow?" Hunter brought them back to the matter at hand.

"Hard to tell. Definitely one blow that was particularly vicious and caused him to fall forward. If there were another, or even two more, the murderer would have had to step around the bench and strike him across the back of the neck and skull as he lay on the ground. The wound was examined while the body was in the morgue; it was probed, given a preliminary cleaning, and pronounced accidental. After that, the morgue attendants weren't too careful about preserving whatever evidence might have remained."

"Have you ever seen anything like this before?" Geoffrey Hunter took the battered ace of spades from his pocket and laid it on Warneke's desk. "The policeman who informed Mr. Linwood of his son's death took it from his hand. He thought it might have some meaning for the family and he was afraid a Bellevue attendant might throw it away."

"Charles's wallet and briefcase weren't found," Prudence added. "He was only identified fairly quickly because he was known to be missing."

"Could the card have been placed in his hand by someone else?" Warneke asked.

"You mean by whoever assaulted him?"

"It's not unknown for a revenge killing to be marked by the gang that's ordered it."

"My fiancé's legal practice wasn't a source of danger," Prudence explained. "Was it, Mr. Hunter?"

"Not as far as I know. The cases I investigated for him were far from being the type you read about in the headlines."

"That does explain one thing, then," Warneke said. "Why he'd taken the glove off his right hand. I assume Mr. Linwood carried the card somewhere on his person. In a pocket perhaps? If someone else didn't put it into his hand, he must have reached for it himself."

"As he lay dying, Mr. Warneke. That's how important it was to him. We believe he was trying to send us a message."

"I'm so sorry, Miss MacKenzie," Warneke said. He handed the card back to Geoffrey Hunter. "I can only tell you what I observed when I prepared Mr. Linwood for burial."

"There's nothing else you can tell us?"

"He was a young man in the best of health. He should have lived a long life."

"I thought my father would live longer than he did," Prudence said quietly, as if thinking of one recent death led her inevitably to remember another.

"I remember the Judge," Maurice Warneke said.

Geoffrey Hunter had stood up. Now he sat down again. "Did you prepare his body, too, Mr. Warneke? It would have been about three months ago. Between Christmas and New Year's." Again he glanced apologetically at Prudence, but he needn't have worried. There were lines of sadness carved on her lovely face, but overlaid by the clenched muscles of stern control. He had the strange idea that if he hadn't asked the question, she might have. Suddenly the need to know more about Victoria MacKenzie grew more urgent.

"In the Judge's case, my assistant and I washed and dressed the body and then placed it in the casket. He stayed in his own home until it was time to transport the remains to the church and then on to the graveyard."

"And was there anything unusual about my father's body, Mr. Warneke?" Only Prudence MacKenzie's tightly clasped hands indicated what it had cost her to ask the question.

"I was given to understand that he had suffered for some time from an increasingly debilitating weakness of the heart. He had the blueness around the fingertips and lips that one often sees when the heart is unable to function well. The death certificate was in order, and a doctor had been in attendance, so there didn't seem to be anything amiss that I could discern."

Warneke was taking great care with how he phrased his answers.

"But there's a reason why you particularly remember the Judge?"

"He was a very well-known man, Mr. Hunter, often in the newspapers. His wife had begun to make her mark in society."

"Do you always know this much about the people you bury?"

"Part of what we do is advise families on the most suitable services for the departed, tailored to the appropriate station in life. We assisted with Judge MacKenzie's first wife, so we naturally assumed we would be serving the family again. There's a certain comfort and trust in familiarity."

"I don't remember much about what happened in the hours and days immediately after my father's death, Mr. Warneke. By the time I was able to ask, I was told it would be better to remember him as he had been in life. I accepted that idea. Then. Now I want answers."

"I don't wish to cause you undue pain, Miss MacKenzie. Or to reawaken your grief."

"I want the truth, Mr. Warneke. You may be one of the very few people who can at least give us some clues as to what that might be." Prudence leaned forward and placed one hand on his desk. "Please."

"You must stop me if it becomes too much to bear." Warneke thought he'd never dealt with a daughter as brave as this one.

"I shall. But I must hear whatever you can tell me."

"Was there anything unusual about Judge MacKenzie's death?" Hunter asked. "Anything that made you question what you saw?"

"Usually, in a household that large, there is someone who will see to the washing and the clothing of the deceased. It's felt that hands that served the departed in life bring some personal solicitude to the tasks that must be done. Very often it's one or more of the older servants, the cook or the housekeeper. Those are the women most likely to have been with the family for a number of years. We usually take over once the intimacies have been completed. In Judge MacKenzie's case, the body lay unattended in a darkened room until we arrived. Nothing had been done, nothing had been prepared. There is always at least one candle burning, but he lay in utter blackness."

"I don't remember anything after Dr. Worthington closed his eyes," Prudence said.

"You had been put to bed before my assistant and I arrived. I understand Dr. Worthington administered laudanum and advised that you continue to be dosed with it at least until the funeral was over. Mrs. MacKenzie was bearing up very courageously; her brother was there to assist and support her. I was told he lived in the house."

"Donald Morley," Hunter contributed.

"Yes. Mr. Morley served as intermediary between me and my staff and Mrs. MacKenzie. As I say, she was dealing with her loss very bravely, but she naturally avoided company as much as possible. At one point, she took refuge in her husband's study. That's where I found her when I went to report that we had coffined and laid him out in the large parlor so there would be room for everyone who was expected to pay respects."

"Did you go into my father's study?"

"Yes."

"What was Mrs. MacKenzie doing when you came into the room?" Allan Pinkerton had insisted that all of his operatives establish a base of facts at the beginning of every case.

"It was a very cold evening. The fire had been built up and she was standing in front of it warming her hands." Warneke paused, cleared his throat. "She was also throwing papers into the fire. By the amount of black ash I could see drifting over the logs, I surmised that she'd burned a great many papers. She was very angry that I'd come in unannounced. I apologized, told her what I'd come to report, and took my leave."

"Anything else?" Prudence's question pleaded for more information.

"The death certificate had been signed by Dr. Worthington. He's not the kind of physician who makes mistakes."

"But something was wrong or you wouldn't have remembered so many details," she insisted. "You must tell me."

"It's difficult to pinpoint exactly what it was. All I can really say is that the Judge's home didn't *feel* like a house of mourning, despite the fact that his body lay in the parlor. With true loss it's as though the loved ones left behind are walking through waves of rough water; they hold themselves erect and push on ahead, but their hearts aren't in it. They want nothing more than to sink into the ocean with their departed and give up the struggle. Of course most of them don't. A very few will never recover, but almost everyone else gradually finds peace and acceptance. I never saw or spoke to you that day, Miss MacKenzie, but what I sensed in the widow and her brother was an *absence* of feeling, a blankness of spirit that I hope never to encounter again." He paused. "None of the Christmas decorations, including the tree, had been taken down."

"Nothing else?"

"Mr. Hunter, if you're asking what I think you are, all I can say is that everything I've told you is speculation. You'll have to give it whatever weight you think it deserves. I look death in the face every day of my life. I know what to expect in almost every instance. When I see something I don't anticipate, I look more closely. But I keep my doubts to myself unless they become certainties. I found Charles Linwood's death to be deeply disturbing. Judge MacKenzie's fingers and lips showed the blueness of heart failure, but a man's heart can give out for many reasons. I'm truly sorry for both your losses, Miss MacKenzie."

Maurice Warneke stood up and ushered his guests from his office. As he opened the funeral parlor's massive front doors and bowed his respects, he summed up what he knew to be true and the creed by which he lived.

"Once they are in their graves, the dead can no longer speak to us. I don't believe in ghostly communication, but I do think that what has been left behind can bear eloquent witness. If we know how to listen."

CHAPTER 9

"There's something I must do by myself, Mr. Hunter," Prudence said.

They were moving slowly down Fifth Avenue in the hansom cab that had taken them from Conkling's office to the mortuary parlor of Warneke and Sons. It was nearly noon. The streets of Lower Manhattan were crowded with carriages and cabs carrying the city's elite to the fashionable restaurants and hotel dining rooms where as much business was done as in any of its office buildings.

"Can I be of any help?" asked Hunter.

"I'll meet you again at Mr. Conkling's in two hours."

"Are you all right, Miss MacKenzie?"

"I wasn't sure until I had listened to everything Mr. Warneke told us," she answered quietly. "I thought perhaps I was imagining things about Victoria that couldn't possibly be true. But I know differently now, and I won't ever be the weakling she thought to make me become when she handed me the laudanum and told me to dose myself. I don't know how she did it, but she killed my father, Mr. Hunter."

"Even Warneke wouldn't go that far, Miss MacKenzie.

What he described was a callous, unfeeling woman, but not a murderess."

"If she let him die through neglect or if she ruined his life somehow so that the will to live was sucked out of him, she's guilty of his death. That may not be the law's definition of murder, but it's mine."

"I wish you'd tell me what you're planning to do."

"I'm not going to confront my stepmother and accuse her of causing my father's death, if that's what you're afraid of. It's too soon for that. Mr. Warneke said suspicions are not evidence, and he's right. I'm going to try to gather more information, but I have to do it alone. I have to prove to myself that I *can* do it. It's important to me, Mr. Hunter."

She's going to question Worthington, Geoffrey Hunter thought. He'd never known a doctor who would admit to having made a wrong diagnosis. Admitting to error wasn't in their lexicon.

"Two hours, Miss MacKenzie."

"I won't need any more time than that." Prudence smiled confidently at him as Hunter helped her out of the cab in front of the Fifth Avenue mansion where she and Charles Linwood should have begun a new life together. She had never known any other home but this one, yet as he watched her walk up the marble steps and disappear through the massive front door, he could not help but wonder how safe this sanctuary really was.

The dining room was empty, the long, polished mahogany table bare of dishes, silverware, and crystal.

"Mrs. MacKenzie is having a tray in her room, miss. Shall I tell Cook you'll do the same?" The tone of Jackson's voice left no room for any other arrangement.

"I'm going out again," Prudence informed him. "No need to disturb Mrs. MacKenzie. I'll look in on her before I leave," she lied. "Where is Mr. Morley?"

"He left about an hour ago, miss. Said he'd be home for dinner."

They were making it easy for her, Prudence thought as she climbed the staircase to her bedroom on the second floor. With any luck at all she'd be gone before that toady Jackson realized that she was coming and going without her stepmother's knowledge or approval. She pictured Victoria lurking in her heavily scented boudoir like a black widow spider sitting invitingly at the center of her web, waiting for some careless bit of succulent life to wander into the sticky strands from which there was no escape. Prudence smiled to herself as she moved silently down the carpeted hallway, wondering if spiders ever got trapped in their own webs.

When she left the house twenty minutes later, Prudence had exchanged the heavy black veils and skirts of full mourning for a day costume of dark gray skirt, jacket, and matching hat that might have been suitable for a young working woman of good family and limited income. A closer look would reveal that the gray wool was too fine and far too expensive for a lady who had to earn her own bread, but it was the best Prudence had been able to do. No one intercepted her as she eased open the heavy front door. Minutes later she blended into the foot traffic of Fifth Avenue, one more dark figure hurrying along the street.

As she wove her way up the avenue, she realized this was the first time in her life she'd gone out entirely alone, no lady of her family or acquaintance to accompany her, no gentleman to protect her, no coachman to drive her wherever she chose to go. Not even a maid for the most basic of proprieties. It was liberating, exciting, and just the slightest bit frightening.

She had been to Dr. Worthington's home and office twice before, the first time when, as a very small child, she had fallen on a piece of glass that cut open the palm of her hand. Cameron had scooped her up in his arms and run the three blocks to the doctor's office. She had been older the second time. James had driven her in the coach, her father sitting by her side holding her tightly in his arms while she sobbed hysterically. She remembered with perfect clarity every turn of the coach, every building sliding by the open window. She had no idea what had brought on the attack of hysteria; neither her father nor the doctor ever mentioned it to her again.

She retraced on foot that long-ago coach ride, Dr. Worthington's address memorized and also written down for good measure. If necessary, she could ask someone to direct her; she wouldn't be defeated by a simple thing like city streets that all looked the same. A discreet brass rectangle identified Peter Worthington's consulting room, though nothing else about the brownstone that was very much like her own indicated that business of any kind might be conducted there. She climbed the steps, rang the bell. When a maid wearing a crisp white apron opened the door, she congratulated herself on having taken the first step to independence.

"I want to know what caused my father's death," Prudence said baldly. She had taken the seat offered her, refused tea, and waited impatiently for Dr. Worthington to finish with another patient. Now that he was facing her across his consulting desk, she was determined not to waste another moment on social niceties. She wanted truthful, honest answers, and she was prepared to stay right where she was for as long as it took to get them.

"I wish I knew all of it, my dear, but I don't. I can only give you what is a medically sound diagnosis. I did not live his daily life alongside him, and sometimes that is the only way to fully explain why a person remains healthy or dies." Peter Worthington wasn't sure when he had begun to expect this visit; he only knew that the something pricking at him must have communicated itself to the Judge's daughter. How else to explain her presence and her question? "Do you understand what I mean by that, Prudence?"

"I'm not a child any longer."

"I didn't mean to insinuate you were. I only want to be sure you understand that there are many factors affecting a life in addition to what is written on the death certificate." He waited, and when she nodded that she understood, or at least accepted what he had said, he sighed deeply. "Your father's death was caused by the sudden failure of his heart to beat. It simply stopped. I doubt he felt anything but a single sharp pain and perhaps a feeling of bewilderment. *How could this be happening to me?* he must have thought. Patients who have survived their heart attacks all tell me that is what ran through their minds as they fell. Their last conscious thoughts were not of family, not of business, not even of a particularly beloved dog. Just a sense of surprise, astonishment, shock at the suddenness, and fear of the finality of what they were experiencing. I tell you this as comfort, the only comfort I can offer. He went very quickly."

"That's what you wrote and signed your name to on the death certificate. But as you said, there are many factors that take a life. I want to know what these might have been in my father's case."

"He drank far too much French brandy and smoked too many cigars. Every time he had to order a man's life strangled out of him by the rope or curtailed by prison bars, a piece of your father was cut out and thrown away. He worried that some among them might not be guilty of the crimes proven against them. We talked about it."

"So did we. In the evening, when he taught me the law, he also reminded me over and over again of the price an honest lawyer pays. Of the doubts that plague a good judge. Over brandy and cigars for him, weak tea and later on sherry for me. But brandy, cigars, and the law didn't kill him, Dr. Worthington. You and I both know that."

"He married a much younger woman, Prudence."

"He didn't die of an excess of marital obligation. I lived in the same house with them. I sat in their company day after day for the two years of their marriage. There was no affection between them, though it took me months to realize it. I had believed he was lonely for a woman the way only a man who has been happily married can be. But whatever he thought he had found in Victoria turned out to be nothing at all. When Donald Morley moved in, which was almost immediately, the four of us might have been living in a hotel. We met in the dining room for meals, sat in stiff silence in the parlor, nodded politely when we passed on the stairs."

"A life may seem to be composed of many parts, but they all fit together when you examine it closely. Every piece is joined to every other piece; it's a jigsaw puzzle whose separate bits can only go one way. So all of what a person is might be what destroys him. Sometimes the dying is just the acknowledgment of everything that's gone before."

"You won't name it, will you?"

"I can't, Prudence. I'm a medical man. I can observe, but I cannot speculate."

It wasn't the clear-cut answer she had come for, but she sensed it was all she would get. The absence of the word she feared might be as telling as if Peter Worthington had pronounced it. He denied nothing. He simply refused to go any further than his signature on the Judge's death certificate allowed. So be it.

Maurice Warneke had said much the same thing when he talked about lack of evidence. He had been willing to entertain the possibility that Charles had been murdered because that death had been so violent and so unexpected, but he had drawn back from suggesting that the Judge's death had been anything but natural. Unmourned by his widow perhaps, but not murder.

Geoffrey Hunter had cautioned her against telling anyone about their visit to Warneke and Sons, and so Prudence left Dr. Worthington's office without sharing the undertaker's observations about Victoria's unwidowlike behavior. She didn't think it would have made much difference. Peter Worthington regretted the loss of his friend, but he would not have welcomed the unsubstantiated conjectures of a man whose clients were already dead when they came to him.

As she walked to Roscoe Conkling's office through the rush of midday crowds, Prudence decided that nothing and no one would prevent her from finding out the truth of her father's death. Of Charles's puzzling and entirely too coincidental accident. She wouldn't live with the niggling finger of doubt scratching at her as insistently as the laudanum once had, with the urge to look over her shoulder at odd moments as if a threat loomed just behind her. She would not spend the rest of her life pretending to welcome Donald Morley's presence in the house and Victoria's reign as stepmother.

The idea that her father may have been murdered by his own wife strained credulity and challenged the ordinariness of everyday life, but it was the damnable logic of the suggestion that was drumming away at her.

What if he didn't die of natural heart failure? What if he were given something that stopped his heart from beating? Something that left no trace, that fooled even the doctor who tended him? What if?

The first attempt came three blocks from Dr. Worthington's office.

As Prudence paused before crossing the street, the driver of a hansom cab whipped up his horses to barrel around the corner and into the traffic along Fifth Avenue. Prudence felt herself teeter on the curb. She stepped backward, startled by the pounding of hooves as the cab veered closer to the small knot of pedestrians waiting for it to go by. Another cab slotted itself behind the first one, taking advantage of the leader's luck in the dangerous game of taking the corner too fast.

Something, a cane perhaps, prodded the back of her legs so hard, they buckled. She screamed, windmilling her arms to regain her balance. She felt her knees collapse, her upper body sway backward, then begin to fall forward between the charging hansom cabs.

"Steady, miss." Two men, one on either side of her, reached for an arm at the same moment and held her upright. "You don't want to be in too much of a hurry along here," one of them said, letting go her arm and touching his hat politely. "It's dangerous."

"Are you all right?" asked the other man, ready to be on his way now that the vehicles had swept by and the crossing was clear.

"I am," she replied, settling her hat and her skirts with trembling hands. She looked behind and to both sides for the person whose cane had caused her to lose her footing, but the crowd was thick and impatient to move on. No one looked either apologetic or embarrassed to have bumped into her. "Thank you very much."

A moment later she was being pushed across the street in the midst of a hurrying Fifth Avenue crowd, her rescuers striding rapidly along in front of her. A woman beside her patted her lightly on the arm. "The same thing happened to me once," she said. "I had new boots on and the pavement was slippery. Are you sure you're all right?"

"I felt something shoved against the back of my legs," Prudence said. "I'm sure I did. Was there anyone with a cane or an umbrella standing close to me?"

The woman looked at her curiously. "I didn't see anyone bump into you with a cane or an umbrella, miss. You just lost your balance for a moment," she said, leaning closer to whisper, "and perhaps you've got your stays laced too tightly." She smiled conspiratorially, then walked on.

Too surprised to argue, Prudence stopped to study the display in a store window, staring at the bonnets arranged attractively in tiers, trying to seem interested in them. She watched her reflection in the glass, but saw no one lingering suspiciously behind her, recognized no one hurrying by. When she could trust her legs, and her hands no longer trembled, she moved out onto the busy sidewalk again.

I'm imagining things, she told herself as she walked quickly toward the safety of Roscoe Conkling's office, debating whether she should mention the incident to Geoffrey Hunter. *That woman said there wasn't anyone near me with a cane or an umbrella, and she must be right. She would have seen or felt something herself in that crush of people. Mr. Warneke and his speculations have me spooked. I'm expecting murderers where there are only accidents.*

By the time she reached the United Bank Building, she had convinced herself that nothing untoward had happened. She had also decided she would tell no one of the embarrassing incident. Empty-headed women with nothing much to do chattered on about the inconsequential events of their daily lives; Prudence was determined not to be one of them.

"The Dakota? What can we find out there?" Prudence asked between bites of a delicious and unpronounceable almond-topped German pastry filled with vanilla custard and thick cream.

Josiah Gregory had insisted on providing her with fresh coffee and pastries from the bakery two doors down from the United Bank Building as soon as he heard she'd gone straight from Fifth Avenue to Dr. Worthington's consulting office.

"You can't go for hours and hours without food, Miss Prudence," he'd scolded. "This is called *bienenstich*. Bee sting cake, though I have no idea why."

"Don't fight him," Roscoe Conkling advised. "It won't do you any good."

"I thought the marriage license would give us Victoria's date and place of birth and her address in February of 1886, when they married, but it doesn't," Geoffrey Hunter reported. "Donald Morley is one of the witnesses, but the other signature is illegible."

New York State had only very recently begun to require centralized record keeping of births, deaths, and marriages. Licenses seemed to follow no set pattern; the information requested was minimal at best.

With no other promising avenues to pursue, Hunter had decided to visit the Dakota, where, according to the Judge's will, an apartment had been obtained for Victoria. No lease or purchase contract had been found among Thomas MacKenzie's papers; Victoria almost certainly had a copy, but Roscoe had no logical or legal grounds to demand to see it. The longer their fledgling investigation remained unknown to Prudence's stepmother, the better.

"I'm not sure exactly what we're looking for, Miss MacKenzie," he confessed, "but I'd like to believe we'll recognize it if we find it."

"I'm coming with you," Prudence told him.

"I wouldn't have gone without you," he answered gallantly.

"Be that as it may." Comfortably revived with *bienenstich* and coffee, Prudence was eager to be on their way. The more she thought about her near stumble on Fifth Avenue, the more certain she became that there was nothing suspicious about it. She'd made the right choice when she decided not to mention it.

"Take these," Josiah Gregory said, handing her a small leather briefcase, one of his stenographer's pads, and several sharpened pencils. "If anyone asks, Mr. Hunter can say you're a secretary from our office, sent along to take notes."

"I don't think I could fool anyone who knows anything about . . . what is it called?"

"Stenography," Josiah said. "Just make tight scribbles across the page and pretend you know what you're doing. Stenography is a mystery to the uninitiated. All you have to do is *look* as though you work in an office. I think you've done an admirable job at that, Miss MacKenzie. I almost didn't recognize you."

"I'll take that as a compliment, Josiah, though I really wasn't trying to disguise myself. I just knew that a woman in deep mourning walking along the street might attract attention. We're supposed to be prostrate with grief, you know." She felt herself flush as she realized what she'd said. "I didn't mean that the way it sounded," she floundered.

Conkling knew, and so did Josiah, that Prudence's marriage would have been a union of friendship and convenience, not great passion, though there was no disgrace in that at all. It was difficult to feign a broken heart when the heart had not been a major player in the drama.

"Shall we go?" Geoffrey suggested. "I told Danny Dennis we'd be needing him again this afternoon. He'll take us up to the Dakota and bring us back when we're finished there."

"I'm going to want to hear what you find out," Conkling said. "But in the meantime I have a case to get ready for tomorrow morning. If you'll clear this food off my desk, Josiah, we can get on with it."

"I think we're being asked to leave, Miss MacKenzie," Hunter said.

Standing in solitary grandeur at the corner of 72nd Street and Central Park West, the Dakota had only been completed four years ago. Wealthy and socially prominent New Yorkers were gradually moving uptown; the Dakota's sixty-five apartments, no two of which were alike, ranged from a comfortable pied-à-terre to a spectacular and palatial home nine floors above the busy, noisy streets of the city. The entire structure had been built around a spacious courtyard into which carriages passed under a portico, but from the street it was like a child's elaborate sandcastle, all pitched gables, carved arches, windowed dormers, and fanciful carvings. The Dakota wasn't Geoffrey Hunter's style at all, but then he wasn't really a New Yorker.

"Mr. Conkling appreciates your making time to see me today, Mrs. Markham." Hunter bowed over the concierge's hand, his dark good looks and expensive suit giving him every right in the world to be here in New York City's most-sought-after new address. "Our stenographer, Miss Carson," he said, introducing his silent companion.

"Everyone knows Mr. Conkling," Mrs. Markham answered, ushering them into her private sitting room. "I was thrilled to read about his adventure during the blizzard. And so sorry that poor young Mr. Linwood came to such a tragic end."

"We were all touched and saddened by his loss." Hunter let silence hover over them, waiting for the right moment to ask his questions.

"Mr. Gregory said there would have to be some changes now that Mr. Linwood has passed on and Miss MacKenzie is in mourning."

He could hear the tremolo of curiosity in Mrs. Markham's voice. He thought she must very seldom come this close to the private lives of the Dakota's residents, most of whom would not bother making the effort to remember her name. Yet it was she who oversaw the smooth functioning of every one of the building's departments, she who made sure the residents were never bothered with worrisome details that could interrupt the comfortable flow of their daily lives. Invisible, she was invisible. But once in a very long while, like today, someone needed something from her that was not in the ordinary way of things.

From his leather briefcase Hunter pulled out a document case. He handed it to Prudence, who untied the silk ribbons holding it closed and flicked through the contents as if searching for something in particular. "Mrs. MacKenzie, a widow now, must of necessity concern herself with young Miss MacKenzie, of whom she is very fond."

"Poor girl. To lose her fiancé so close to the wedding. I read in the *Herald* that he stopped to rest and was killed by a falling tree limb. How very terrible for her."

"Very. So you understand that Mrs. MacKenzie will remain in

the family home now. She will not be moving into the Dakota after all."

"And you are acting on her behalf?"

"Mr. Conkling is the family attorney. I am associated with his office."

"I see."

"The problem, Mrs. Markham, is that neither Mr. Conkling nor his secretary, Mr. Gregory, nor I have ever seen the apartment. We have no way of knowing what work may have been done in the months between the Judge's death and Mr. Linwood's accident. I regret to have to confide to you that bills have come to Mr. Conkling's office that he is reluctant to pay without some verification of what they entail. Mrs. MacKenzie is not a woman of business, as you may imagine, and she is very preoccupied at the moment with the care of her stepdaughter."

"I'm not sure how I can help you, Mr. Hunter."

"I hardly know how to ask it, but I'm afraid I must. I should like to inspect the apartment so that I can report back to Mr. Conkling. Miss Carson will accompany us to take notes. Mr. Conkling would have come himself, of course, but just between us, and you mustn't breathe a word to anyone, he is ever so slightly feeling the effects of that horrible afternoon."

He could tell from the gleam in her eyes that the Dakota's concierge was weighing the value of the information he had just given her, trying to decide where the sharing of it would do her the most good.

"I'll take you up myself," she declared, rising to her feet, jingling the ring of master keys hanging from her belt.

"And one other thing, if I may. I should like to see the bill of sale, please. We have a copy with the Judge's papers, of course, but given the circumstances, Mr. Conkling would like me to verify the original signatures."

"I didn't know what you might need, so I took out Mrs. MacKenzie's entire file this morning. I'm afraid it's a bit bulky."

Without a moment's hesitation, Mrs. Markham handed it to Prudence, then turned and led the way to the bank of elevators that would take them to the fifth-floor corner apartment that a loving husband had secured for his widow. "I do so regret losing Mrs. MacKenzie as a resident again. She was always a lovely lady, such a pleasure to serve." Should she mention that she had been privileged to be a witness at Mrs. MacKenzie's marriage? Perhaps not. The whole thing had had a furtive air about it, and the gratuity she had been given had been far in excess of what might have been expected for a few minutes in a crowded downtown office decorated only with a soiled American flag. She'd used her left hand to write her signature, which was embarrassing because it made her name impossible to read. But Mrs. MacKenzie had insisted. No explanation, just a fat sheaf of bills that bought her silence then and was still buying it today.

As unobtrusively as possible, Prudence handed Geoffrey the Dakota file, which he slipped into his briefcase, wondering as he fastened the straps if he had heard Mrs. Markham correctly. It sounded as though she were speaking of Victoria MacKenzie with some degree of familiarity, as a former resident of the Dakota. *Again? Was that the word she used?* If that were true, there would be a copy of the earlier lease in the file. Whose name would they find on it? He needed to get himself and Prudence out of the building without going back to the concierge's parlor, without giving her the opportunity to remember that he hadn't returned her documents file. Later, a few days from now, after they'd had a chance to examine its contents, Josiah Gregory could be dispatched with the file, a bouquet of flowers, and Geoffrey's heartfelt apologies for having forgotten to return it before he left.

"This is one of our larger apartments," Mrs. Markham explained.

Geoffrey and Prudence walked quickly from one room to the next, each more opulently European than the previous one. Shining parquet floors. Marble mantel fireplaces. A silk walled boudoir rivaling anything Geoffrey had seen in France. And from the windows that ran the length of the forty-foot drawing room, views of Central Park that took the breath away. But empty. Not a stick of furniture, nothing left behind by workmen planning to return.

If Victoria had intended to place her own stamp on this apartment, she hadn't begun to do it in the months between the Judge's death and the demise of her future son-in-law. Strange. Geoffrey would have thought she would be eager to make her preparations for leaving the Fifth Avenue mansion that would go to the married couple. Plunging into the maelstrom of redecorating should have been a welcome distraction from the loss of the husband she was presumed to have loved. Hunter had expected to find renovations that had been halted when Linwood died and Victoria's plans changed, but they should have been very nearly complete by that time, two weeks before the wedding. Yet here was proof that nothing had been done. Very strange.

Geoffrey didn't dare catch Prudence's eye, but he could sense that she was also puzzled, was asking herself the same questions. He pulled his watch from a vest pocket.

"Mrs. Markham, I'm sorry. I didn't realize how quickly the time was passing. Mr. Conkling is waiting for us back at the office. We have a deposition to take and I'm afraid the individuals involved are due there at any moment. We'll need Miss Carson's skills. Please do excuse us. I apologize for the haste, but we must be going. I shall be sure to tell Mr. Conkling how very hospitable you've been, and I do hope you won't mention to Mrs. MacKenzie anything about those tradesmen's accounts. It's obvious there's been some mistake. Mr. Conkling will see to untangling whatever mess someone has managed to create. We won't bother either of the late Judge's dear ladies. They have quite enough to bear as it is."

Prudence and Geoffrey caught one last telling glimpse of the very cooperative Mrs. Markham as they turned briefly before leaving the luxurious apartment where no one lived. The concierge was standing in front of the Central Park facing windows, keys dangling from her hand, mesmerized by the glitter of the spring sun on the waters of the lake. She would return to the real world and her duties in a moment, but for as long as it took to imagine it, she was seeing herself as someone else.

Geoffrey understood and he pitied her. It was hard to live with dreams that were shattered every time you opened your eyes in the morning. Hard to think about what might have been.

"You've answered one question, Geoffrey, and raised a host of others. I thought I knew Thomas as well as anyone and better than most, but I knew nothing about this. Nothing. It makes me wonder what else he was hiding."

Victoria Morley had lived at the Dakota for a full year before she married the Judge. The lease lay on Roscoe Conkling's desk, Thomas MacKenzie's bold signature scrawled across the bottom of the page in thick black ink. The Judge had pledged financial responsibility for the considerable rent, but the lease itself was clearly in Victoria Morley's name.

"I thought you'd want to see these," Geoffrey said, indicating the pile of papers he and Prudence had brought back from the Dakota.

"Josiah will make copies of everything. We'll have them compared and witnessed, so there's no doubt the copies are true and authentic."

"I'll need to hire at least two temporary clerks to do the copying," Josiah said. He had already contacted the agency, but Mr. Conkling liked to believe that nothing was done in his office without his express permission.

"Hire as many as you need. We have to get the file back to the Markham woman before she begins to suspect she's done something very stupid. Something that could cost her her job. She won't dare say a word. Rich people don't like to think their secrets will be shared."

"We've stumbled into the hive of what may be a particularly nasty queen bee, Roscoe." Geoffrey had been flattered when Conkling urged the younger man to call him by his first name. It wasn't an invitation he extended to everyone.

"I've just realized I don't know Victoria at all, Prudence. Not at all." Conkling piled the Dakota papers into his secretary's outstretched arms, then sat down heavily behind his desk, one hand pressed to the side of his head as if bearing down on an incipient ache. "I remember the day the Judge told me he was getting married again. Frankly, I couldn't believe it. I hadn't met her; I don't think too many of his friends even knew she existed. Later, afterward, we deluded ourselves into thinking that surely it hadn't happened as quickly as we thought, surely Thomas had introduced her to some of us. But now that I take a hard look backward, I'm not sure that's right. I think it very possible we deceived ourselves because our friend Thomas MacKenzie deserved happiness and we refused to see anything else for him."

"Danny Dennis says if you're going to get home before dark, it's best to start now, Miss Prudence," Josiah interrupted.

"Thank you. I wish I didn't have to go, Mr. Conkling."

"Do you want me to arrange somewhere else for you to stay, Prudence? I have any number of respectable clients who would be only too happy to offer you their hospitality."

"Do you mean am I afraid?"

"It's nothing to be ashamed of, under the circumstances."

"I'm angry, Mr. Conkling. I tried to explain to Mr. Hunter what anger does to me, but I don't know that I was able to make it clear. My father had a temper, too, you know. He rarely showed it on the bench and he never erupted at someone who couldn't fight back. One of the servants, for example. But I heard stories about him, usually by listening when I wasn't supposed to. Kincaid, the coachman, could curl your hair with what he witnessed. Cameron, who was our butler for years, matched him story for story. They were proud to work for a man who stood up for himself and others, who wouldn't be bullied or manipulated, who let everyone within reach of his voice know exactly how he felt. That's one of the reasons I don't understand why he capitulated to Victoria. It doesn't make sense. But no, I'm not afraid of her, Mr. Conkling. I've discovered how very much my father's daughter I am."

"You'll need to be careful, Miss MacKenzie. Watch what you do and say. Remember they'll be keeping as close and suspicious an eye on you as you on them." Geoffrey Hunter thought there was real danger lurking in the MacKenzie mansion, but he hadn't figured out the form it would take. Physically, Prudence was untouchable. Alive, she was worth a fortune to her stepmother; dead, she decreased Victoria's wealth by half. The laudanum had been a clever ploy to control her, but it hadn't worked. Once Victoria and her brother realized they'd been duped, they'd try something else. That's what had Hunter worried.

"I'm going to search that house from the attic to the basement," Prudence declared. "Every room, every hallway, every drawer in every piece of furniture. There won't be any secrets by the time I finish."

"Be careful," Hunter warned again.

"I'm remembering what you've been telling me all day, Mr. Hunter. Suspicions without proof are like water running through a sieve."

"I couldn't build a case on what you found out," Conkling said. "And believe me, I've argued and won on threads so thin, they were almost invisible."

"We'll get the evidence," Prudence promised. She wanted to tell them she'd do her best to be as brave as they believed her to be, but she choked back the words. It was all about putting up a spirited front now, about stoking the anger she had felt burning away her fears. Nothing was certain except that she was no longer alone. The Judge was dead, but between them, Josiah Gregory and Roscoe Conkling almost filled his shoes. Charles was gone, but into his place had stepped Geoffrey Hunter, a man unlike any she had ever met.

Prudence would enlist Colleen's help tonight and then she would sleep. Tomorrow, rested and wary, she would begin the search for what would bring down Victoria.

"Do you have that picture Prudence got for you?" Conkling asked when Josiah had escorted the Judge's daughter out of the office and down to the hansom cab that was waiting to take her home.

"I do." Hunter placed the photograph and its silver frame on Conkling's desk. He had located a photographer who promised he knew a process that could produce copies without a negative. Once the copies were made, Prudence would smuggle the original back onto the MacKenzie parlor mantel.

"All you have to do is look at the expression on Prudence's face to know she's unhappy. Miserable, I'd say, but determined for her father's sake to feign happiness about this second marriage. She may not understand why the Judge feels he needs a new wife, but she loves him enough to pretend that all will be well between her and her new stepmother."

Conkling was right. The Prudence in the wedding photograph and the Prudence who had listened dry-eyed to Maurice Warneke's vivid description of Charles Linwood's head wound were not the same person. Entirely on her own she had questioned Dr. Peter Worthington as skillfully as Hunter himself could have managed and she'd played the role of stenographer well enough to fool the Dakota's shrewd concierge. Prudence was the only one of them who could search the Fifth Avenue mansion for the information Geoffrey had asked her to find; she would beard Victoria in her own den. Alone.

Once Prudence returned to the mansion, she would have to resume full mourning, every step she took encumbered by heavy black silk skirts. She would become a virtual prisoner of her home, since any sortie outside the Fifth Avenue mansion would cause comment, attract unwanted attention, fuel gossip that was bound to get back to Victoria. She had managed to disguise herself and elude her stepmother today, but her luck would not hold forever. Colleen and James Kincaid were her conduits to Conkling and Hunter, but they would have to be especially cautious. Victoria MacKenzie had already rid herself of her late husband's housekeeper and devoted butler.

"What will you do next?" Conkling rubbed the side of his face until the skin reddened above his beard.

"I need to trace Victoria Morley backward. From the Dakota to wherever she met the Judge. Having a name is almost never enough; being able to show a likeness makes all the difference."

"Have you considered going back to the Pinkerton Detective Agency now that Allan is dead?"

Conkling threw you off with his abrupt changes of topic and questions that demanded direct answers. It was a tactic he'd cultivated in the years when he was teaching himself to be the best lawyer of his generation.

"What brought that up?" Geoffrey was very transparently stalling for time.

"I understand that Robert and William are just as dedicated as their father, but a little more inclined to let bygones be bygones."

"We parted amicably."

"That's not exactly what I heard."

"We agreed not to get in each other's way."

"A bit closer to the truth. Have you? Thought about becoming a Pinkerton again?"

"I'd be lying if I said I haven't. They're the very best to be had anywhere in the world. Allan created something entirely new when he built his agency. No one disputes that. But he didn't tolerate dissent, which he defined as anything that even vaguely resembled the desire for discussion. In the end, I couldn't stomach being told what to do and how to do it every minute of my working day. Which was every minute of my life. When you signed up with Allan Pinkerton, when you became a Pinkerton, you were expected to give up everything else. I couldn't worship the Pinkerton god long enough to get used to it. But I have nothing against Robert and William, and they have nothing against me."

"Are you sure of that?"

"If you mean, have I been in touch with them since Allan died? Yes. Yes, I have. I went to his funeral. I paid my respects. The man saved my life once, but the price he asked me to pay was too high. Being his sons, Robert and William understood."

"I'm glad. Prudence will need you. She'll need someone who sees her as something more than a client. I've been having nightmares about this case, Geoffrey. As if there's some very fundamental evil waiting to spring out and overwhelm us. Not us. Prudence. We can walk away. She can't." Conkling rubbed the side of his head again. He had no patience with any part of his body that did not perform the way he expected it to. "To tell the truth, the nightmares aren't just about Prudence. I see Charles Linwood struggling up Broadway in the snow every time I close my eyes. Despite what you told me Maurice Warneke said, I don't know how his death could be anything except an accident, but I can't seem to shake it off." He cupped his hand over the bothersome ear, as if the heat from his palm would ease it.

"Are you all right? Shall I call Josiah?"

"Don't set the watchdog on me just yet."

"We need to prove that Victoria was the Judge's mistress before he married her." Hunter brought the focus of the conversation back to the main thrust of the investigation. Charles Linwood was still an everyday presence for him, too, but he told himself they might never know the truth of his friend's death. Destroying Victoria's hold over Prudence MacKenzie was much more possible.

"Why does any man marry his mistress?" Conkling had never even considered formalizing any of his many liaisons.

"Because he has to?"

"Because she has something on him so potentially damaging that he dare not refuse her."

"Unless he's already married."

"Which Thomas wasn't. Sarah died when Prudence was no more than six or seven years old. 1875, I think. Ask Josiah to check the date. He didn't marry Victoria until February of 1886. Eleven years a widower."

"What made him decide he needed a wife again after all that time?" Geoffrey thought he already knew the answer, but he wanted to hear it from Conkling.

"Perhaps it was Victoria who decided he needed a wife."

"And then he died. Less than two years later."

"Under circumstances I now find very odd. Suspicious circumstances. My poor friend."

"You don't know that yet."

"Yes, I do. And so do you. Peter Worthington thinks like a doctor, you and I reason like lawyers. Thomas Pickering MacKenzie was murdered."

Chapter 10

There were two places in the house Prudence was determined to explore without Victoria's knowledge: the attic and her father's bedroom. Both were locked.

"Can you get the keys, Colleen?"

"What are you looking for, Miss Prudence?" The hairbrush in Colleen's hand remained suspended above Prudence's unbound hair; the question had startled her, coming out of nowhere like that.

"You don't have to go into either place with me. Just get the keys. I'd have to explain myself to Mrs. Barstow, and I'd rather not do that. She might refuse to give them to me. At any rate she'd be sure to tell my stepmother, and I don't want Mrs. MacKenzie to know where I've been."

"She's bound to find out, miss. She knows everything that goes on in this house."

"How?"

"How, miss?"

"How does Mrs. MacKenzie know everything? Only if someone tells her. If you wanted to keep a secret, Colleen, who would you be sure not to tell?"

"Not to tell, miss?"

"Who would be most likely not to keep your confidence?"

She thought for a moment, then brought the hairbrush down through Prudence's hair with a brisk, determined stroke. "That would be Mrs. Barstow herself, Miss Prudence. Mrs. Dailey was a lovely woman, housekeeper when I first came. She knew I missed my mother something fierce, and she'd let me have a bit of a cry now and then and never scolded me for it. Told me to drink a cup of tea and look forward to my next day off when I could visit with her. Mrs. Barstow came with the second Mrs. MacKenzie. Not to say anything critical because she's the first one up and dressed in the morning and the last to put out her light, but Mrs. Barstow is a cold woman. Not cruel, just without a drop of good warm blood running through her veins. Ice water, if you ask me."

"I don't want you to do anything that will get you in trouble, Colleen."

"I think I know a way, miss." Colleen's deft fingers worked Prudence's long hair into the poufed upswept twist that framed her face in soft waves. "Mrs. MacKenzie told me to take the letter cases back up to the attic when you finished with them. I can tell Mrs. Barstow that you're done and ask for the key to put them away. The only thing she's always looking for someone else to do in this house is climb stairs. She'll let me go up to the attic on my own. I can leave the door unlocked. And I don't think she'll bother saying anything to Mrs. MacKenzie since I'll only be doing what she told me to."

"Won't she find out? I'll have no key to lock it when I leave."

"You could say you forgot to put some of the letters back in the case, couldn't you? Then I'd have to go up again. This time I'd lock the door behind me. Nobody ever goes into the attic unless they have to."

"I don't know, Colleen."

"Leave it to me, miss."

*   *   *

Colleen might not have done it if Mrs. Barstow had shown half the understanding to the maids as the housekeeper she'd replaced. Not that Mrs. Dailey hadn't been strict. She had. But she'd also had a heart in her, and she'd comforted many a homesick kitchen girl and maid. They worked all the harder for her because of it. Colleen herself hadn't known Mrs. Dailey all that well; she'd only been in the house for six months when the Judge married again and his housekeeper retired. Young to retire, Colleen had thought at the time, never having known a working woman who didn't keep on working until she dropped in her tracks. But the rich had different ideas about things, and if Mrs. Dailey was lucky enough to be one of the very few that a family pensioned off, then good luck to her.

Mrs. Barstow shook the staff up and made sure they came down standing. She found fault with everything they did, even to the way the maids' caps sat on their heads. Cook had always seen to her own domain, but the new Mrs. MacKenzie made it clear there would be no autonomy in the kitchen. Cook and her helpers were firmly under the housekeeper's thumb, as were the young male servants and the bootboy. Cameron had been heard to say that it was an odd way to run a household, but now Cameron was gone, too. There was a streak of Irish mischief in Colleen, always had been, which was probably why Mrs. Barstow rode her so hard. And why Colleen was willing to help Miss Prudence. She flat-out didn't like the woman who ruled her days, so if she could nip at her heels a bit without her ever knowing it, so much the better.

"I've these two cases to take back up to the attic." Colleen held the awkward cardboard cases as though they were almost too heavy a load to carry. "Mrs. MacKenzie's orders."

"I know what the mistress told you," snapped Mrs. Barstow. She didn't like being asked for anything, especially by a maid who had the temerity to knock on her parlor door and interrupt her midmorning sit-down.

"I should take them up now, if you don't mind. I've the parlors to see to and the young miss wants the Judge's books dusted as well."

Colleen shifted from foot to foot, as if her legs hurt just to be standing there with the cases in her arms. If Mrs. Barstow decided to lead the way up three flights to the narrow uncarpeted staircase leading to the attic, she wouldn't be able to leave the door unlocked for Miss Prudence. She concentrated on those stairs, willing the housekeeper to think about them also. There were days when Mrs. Barstow's knees clicked as loudly as a cricket's chirp every time she took a step. Colleen prayed this was one of those days.

"Mind you bring this key right back to me," the housekeeper said, struggling to unlock the heavy chatelaine hanging from her waist. Keys to every room in the house were on that ring, duplicates to the ones held by the mistress and many she wouldn't bother carrying. Keys to storage cabinets, silver and china cupboards, to the attic and the cellar. There were rooms that were unlocked to be dusted and swept, then locked again when the maid finished with them. The Judge's study. His bedroom.

Colleen reached out while Mrs. Barstow's swollen fingers were still fumbling with the clasps and chains from which the keys dangled; the housekeeper handed her the entire ring, then sat rubbing her hands as though she'd just come inside on an icy winter's day. She had arthritis; most women who spent their lives in service developed the distinctive painful knots and knuckle knobs. Mrs. Barstow was tight-lipped about her past, but Colleen figured she must have put in her time as a maid like the rest of them before working her way up to the cushy post of housekeeper with all of its privileges and customary benefits. A special cut of chop from the butcher, just for her. A cup of tea made from the mistress's expensive best imported China leaf. The dregs of a decanted bottle of sherry. Housekeepers could live very well.

"I'll bring this right back," Colleen promised. She was out of the housekeeper's parlor and halfway up the basement stairs before the woman could think to tell her to take the attic key off the chatelaine. There was nothing wrong with Colleen's young fingers.

She sped up to the second floor on the uncarpeted back stairs, her indoor boots making hardly a sound. They were soft-soled leather, the better not to disturb the family with her comings and goings. She paused at the door into the second-floor hall, pushed it open without making a sound, stepped through, and then stood frozen in place, listening for approaching footsteps. Nothing. Not a sound. Nobody in sight.

She laid the letter cases down on the Turkish carpet runner that further muted sound, and in less than a minute had unlocked the door to the Judge's bedroom and scampered into the back staircase again. If anyone chanced to try the knob, which she knew was unlikely, they would assume that Clara, the new German girl who was both upstairs and downstairs maid, had not pulled it securely closed behind her the last time she dusted and polished in there. Or that she had been interrupted and was coming back. Clara herself wouldn't dare report it to Mrs. Barstow.

The attic staircase was as narrow as a coffin, the door barely wide enough to slide a piece of unwanted furniture through without scraping off the finish. Colleen set the letter cases where Mrs. MacKenzie had told her to, on top of a closed roll-top desk that looked as though it might once have been part of an office. Not grand enough for the Judge's private library, but sturdy and workmanlike. Maybe the first desk he'd used when he'd opened up his law practice as a young man. Kept for sentimental reasons.

She couldn't stand there wondering and making up stories to answer the questions bouncing around inside her head. Trying to be as quiet as she could, because the attic staircase was at an angle to the hallway that led to the servants' bedrooms up under the eaves, Colleen closed the door behind her. Just in case someone passing by should happen to glance her way, she inserted the key into the lock, pretended to turn it, then came down the staircase with Mrs. Barstow's chatelaine swinging ostentatiously from her hand.

She'd done it!

Prudence had to get into the attic during the day, when the servants would be about their duties in other parts of the house. Nighttime was out of the question; no matter how quiet she tried to be, she wouldn't be able to silence her footsteps or conceal the sounds of searching. The servants' bedrooms were too close to the attic staircase. So it had to be during the day.

With any luck at all, Victoria would have afternoon callers today, ladies stopping by to leave their cards, others arriving with the intention of staying for the allowable thirty minutes before moving on to another social call. Prudence would not be expected to receive them. Victoria, however, knew the delicious details of poor Charles Linwood's death, and although still in mourning herself for the Judge, she had let it be known that she was receiving again. Only close friends, of course.

There was so much to discuss. How long would Prudence mourn dear Charles before coming back into society? So many things had changed since the war, so many customs modified or even done away with entirely because there had simply been too many killed, too many young men who would never come home to wives, mothers, and fiancées. What on earth had possessed Charles to go out into the blizzard like that? So many questions to ask, so many stories to tell. Everyone in New York City had become an expert on the Great Blizzard, everyone would tell his own adventures over and over until even the storyteller grew bored. But that hadn't happened yet; it was too soon. And so when the weather turned springlike again, the social rituals resumed, none pursued more eagerly than the formal afternoon call.

Prudence was counting on a flock of chattering ladies to keep her stepmother occupied, and since Donald could not take refuge in the Judge's study, he was almost certain to be out of the house. Etiquette prescribed that a caller take her leave soon after another caller arrived, but New Yorkers did not always observe English etiquette to the letter, especially when there was so much to talk about. Prudence sent word she had a headache and would therefore have luncheon on a tray, then kept her bedroom door cracked as the hours crawled slowly by. One did not pay or receive calls until well past the midday meal.

She wasn't disappointed. At precisely two o'clock, the earliest possible hour to call without giving serious offense, the first of the afternoon's ladies was ushered into the parlor. It was as though a jolt of that new electricity had been sent throughout the house. Tea had to be brewed, small cakes and crust-trimmed tiny sandwiches arranged on silver platters, carried into the parlor, served, and replenished. God help the manservant or maid who spilled a drop or allowed a crumb to slide onto a guest's clothing; Mrs. Barstow would have words to say about anything so untoward. The staff would be far too busy attending to Mrs. MacKenzie's callers to notice any unusual movement upstairs.

As soon as she closed the attic door behind her, Prudence realized that one visit might not be enough. The vast attic stretched across the entire width of the house and for half its length, a cavernous storage area dimly lit by small dormer windows, peopled by ghostly sheet-draped mounds of furniture of all shapes and sizes, trunks piled one atop the other, and heaven only knew what else. Closer to the door were the larger and more recently discarded items, many of them unprotected by the ubiquitous white sheets, including the rolltop desk on which Colleen had placed the letter cases.

Where to start? And what was she looking for? She could have thrown up her hands and shrieked or stamped a foot in frustration, but she dared not make an unnecessary sound. *Think*. She had to think logically. Had to organize this search as though it were germane to a case, as though she were building an evidentiary structure to be laid before a jury. *Let's hide something, Prudence,* her father's voice whispered. *Close your eyes and count to ten. Then see if you can find it.* How many times had they played the game together, the Judge delighting in trying to baffle her? She'd eventually gotten very good at reading his mind. She forced her breathing to slow down, forced her eyes to stop darting from side to side and into the far distance, counted very slowly to ten, clenched and unclenched her fingers.

Except for the rolltop desk, whatever was closest to the door had probably been ordered put there by Victoria and no doubt been thoroughly examined before being carried into the oblivion of the attic. Just like the letter cases that had told her nothing. Therefore, the logical place to start was as deep into the space as she could penetrate.

Someone had been charged with seeing that dirt and dust did not accumulate up here, that spiders were not allowed to spin their webs, that mice would be trapped before they could multiply and forage under the sheets. A narrow passage led the length of the attic, just wide enough for one person to pass along, but nothing caught at her skirts or crunched underfoot as Prudence made her way toward the farthest dormer window.

Care had been taken to arrange methodically what were objects that had been important to someone; these were not the hoarded and broken bits that filled most attics, items a family should have consigned to the rubbish bin but somehow never did. This attic was meant to be visited, meant to be someone's treasure trove. Yet Prudence realized with a start that even as a lively, curious child, she had never set foot in this part of the house. Strange. So strange. Had there been orders to keep her out? Or had she simply never explored this far up? Privacy was a virtue inculcated into her for as long as she could remember.

The servants' quarters were private to them and strictly off-limits to an inquisitive little girl. Was that the answer? Had she never climbed the last set of stairs because good manners forbade it? Could it be that simple?

She ran her hand over what she thought must be a narrow armoire. The sheet draping it slid to the floor. Rosewood, beautiful, gleaming rosewood inlaid with rare woods of every imaginable color, decorated with swirled flower petals made of mother–of-pearl. A lady's armoire of many small drawers, it stood chin high, as perfectly preserved and fragrant as the day it was made. Instinctively, before she opened a single drawer, she knew it had belonged to her mother, knew that the Judge had placed it here because he could not bear to look upon it every day for all of the long years he had been without her. Prudence had never seen anything as beautifully delicate, as perfectly conceived for a lady's treasures, as this slender rosewood armoire.

Which drawer to open first? Would it be empty? Would all of them be as empty as a daughter's life without her mother? *I have to know. I have to know.* She thought she had forgotten her mother's perfume, but the fragrance that poured from the open drawer was as comforting and as familiar as if she had smelled it only yesterday. Jasmine and sandalwood, the faintest hint of lilac and perhaps a very old heirloom rose.

When her hand closed around a packet of letters tied with a satin hair ribbon, Prudence knew she had found the first of many missing pieces of herself.

CHAPTER 11

Time was running out. It would soon be too late in the afternoon for calls to be paid. When the last visitor left, quiet would descend on the house. Someone, perhaps Victoria herself, would come to Prudence's bedroom to inquire after her headache, ask if she felt well enough to dress for dinner. She had barely another hour, no more.

As Prudence opened the attic door, she heard the murmur of ladies' voices in the entrance hall, Jackson answering a question, the sound of the front door opening, then closing again. She knew the butler would remain in the hallway until he was certain no one else would be leaving immediately. She didn't dare a chance encounter. She eased the attic door closed, stood with her back leaning against its solid wood, willed herself not to panic. Five more minutes and she should be able to get safely down to the second floor.

The rolltop desk was within arm's reach, and as she laid a hand on its scarred surface, she suddenly remembered creeping over her father's feet in and out of the magical cave where he pretended not to see her. She couldn't have been more than three or four years old the first time she'd discovered the wonders of that desk, especially the banks of tiny drawers hidden behind the rolltop. Try though she might, she couldn't remember where the desk had sat, whether it had been in an office somewhere or downstairs in this very house.

She remembered seeing men carry in massive pieces of dark, highly polished furniture, easing them carefully through the front door, being cautioned by Cameron to mind they not scratch anything. So it must have been here. It seemed to her that those same men hauled other, smaller pieces of furniture up the staircase, probably all the way to the attic. The rolltop desk had been replaced by something much finer, much grander, much more suited to the dignity of a judge. Had she heard someone make that remark? *He's a judge now, isn't he?*

The desk did have a slightly battered look to it, as if a young lawyer had dropped hot cigar ashes here and there, worried the nib of his pen until it dripped ink, absentmindedly scratched the letters that proclaimed his profession with the same sharp penknife he'd used to open his mail. Prudence gave a short, quick tug; the rolltop disappeared without a sound, scrolled into its hiding place. There had to be at least a dozen small drawers, probably as many letter slots, taller vertical slots for documents, even a pipe rack that she remembered her father allowing her to fill with the thin Cuban cigars he liked to smoke. One by one she opened the drawers. All empty. Not even the smallest bit of paper in any of the cubbyholes or the faintest trace of tobacco where the cigars had once stood. Nothing. An emptiness that spoke of finality. She closed the rolltop. Turned to leave.

And then recalled what had so delighted her child's imagination, the secret her father had shared with her and no one else. *Our secret,* he had whispered, forefinger stretched across his lips. *Cross your heart and hope to die.* It hadn't seemed a prediction in those days, just a string of words you chanted whenever you made a promise, a hasty sign sketched on your chest. Dropping to her knees, Prudence inched her way under the desk, feeling with her fingers for the outline of the hidden drawer. She had put the cracked ball from her set of jacks into that drawer one day. Had she left it there? She couldn't remember the last time she played here or even how old she had been. Everything changed when her mother got sick. *Mama went to heaven.* Died of consumption. Coughed until her lungs bled, burned with afternoon fevers that radiated heat and turned cool cloths warm within minutes. Some doctors believed it ran in families.

Nothing. Her hand, her fingers found nothing that felt like the thin edge of a wooden ruler. Only a few inches long, with a round depression at one end. You pushed against that shallow concavity and the drawer popped open. Or did it slide? She'd been too delighted every time it opened to notice. *Don't give up, never give up,* her father had urged. A child's fingers were so much smaller than an adult's, the nails shorter. She tapped very lightly, barely touching the wooden surface with her fingertips, as if her woman's hand had shrunk to the size of a girl's. As if a cat's paw were softly patting the delicate skin of her cheek to wake her up. Eyes closed, fingertips grown exquisitely sensitive, she tapped and patted again and again.

And almost missed it. Almost missed the tiny ridge that then abruptly seemed familiar.

Seconds later the drawer slid open, raining down a shower of old dust. She felt inside for the cracked ball and felt something else. Her forefinger traced the outline of a leather-bound notebook scarcely larger than her outstretched hand, wedged so tightly in that small space that at first she couldn't get her fingers far enough around it to pull it out. She took one of the ebony combs from her upswept hair, slid the teeth beneath the small book, lifted, and pried until she felt it move. She couldn't see what she was doing, could only judge success by what her fingers told her. The leather cover had adhered to the drawer in which it had lain for who knew how long, but as she continued to work the comb along its length, she could feel it loosening, could finally hear the sucking sound of leather coming loose from wood. Moments later she was on her feet again, the secret drawer closed, the leather notebook shoved down into the stack of letters. The only pocket in the skirt she wore today wasn't large enough to hold it. She patted her hair into place, slid the ebony comb back where it belonged, and tried to look as though her head ached.

She had one more place to search.

"I do hope dear Prudence doesn't go into a decline. Her mother was never strong, you know, and she's very much like Sarah." Annabelle North sipped her tea, though she preferred a light China blend to whatever it was Victoria's cook had brewed. India, probably. "Sarah and I were great friends, and of course Brantly and Prudence have known one another since they were children, although he is four years older than she."

For any other woman in society, that would have been declaration enough of a mother's intentions, but Annabelle wasn't sure Victoria was quite like the other women of her acquaintance. Nothing she could put her finger on, just a vague sense that the Judge's widow was not entirely at her ease. Which she should have been, especially here in her own home.

Annabelle had been raised in society, had debuted in society, married, and lived her entire life in society. Knowing what to do and what to say no longer required any thought at all. One simply *was*. And that was the crux of what was bothering her. Victoria MacKenzie *wasn't*. The only thing Annabelle could think of was that Prudence's stepmother must have a past. Which seemed utterly absurd. The Judge would never have married a woman about whom the slightest whiff of scandal could be detected. It was really very troubling, this slight uneasiness. She resolutely put it aside. Brantly was her youngest child and would require a mother's extra attention to get him suitably married. The sooner the better. He had developed some habits that were better not to think about.

"It's very kind of you to inquire about her, Mrs. North."

"Dr. Worthington is seeing to her, I presume."

"He has said that we have only to send for him, no matter the hour." Victoria heard the lovely bongs of the longcase clock in the entrance hall. Another fifteen or twenty minutes and Annabelle North would have to leave. A call could last no more than half an hour at the absolute most. Only very close friends or family members were permitted to stay longer.

"Don't be tempted to skimp on the laudanum, Mrs. MacKenzie. Young girls are all at sixes and sevens even without the double tragedy that Prudence has had to bear."

"She's very brave."

"Of course she is. She's her father's daughter. And I'm sure you set her a good example, bearing your own grief as well as you do. We older women have a duty to teach the next generation. Thank you, I believe I will take a bit more tea. It's quite delicious. You must tell me the name of the blend."

Victoria was sorely tempted to pour the newly refreshed pot of extremely hot tea into Annabelle North's ample lap and watch her scramble frantically to try to save the mauve silk dress that would certainly be ruined no matter what she did. Twenty more minutes at the outside. She could put up with anything for twenty minutes.

The Judge's suite of rooms on the second floor looked out over Fifth Avenue. Bedroom, dressing room, private bath, smoking parlor that he had also used as a small study, each connecting one with the other, but with only two doors that gave onto the hallway. A door into the bedroom, another into the dressing room, the latter used almost exclusively by his valet. Adjoining the Judge's bedroom was first wife Sarah's bedroom, her sitting room, dressing room, and private bath facing the gardens. The entire U-shaped north wing of the second floor had been theirs alone. No one except the maid who cleaned the rooms and the housekeeper who unlocked the doors for her went there anymore. It was as though death had never left.

The doorknob to the Judge's bedchamber turned easily in Prudence's hand. Silently. Curtains and drapes covered every window from ceiling to floor, shutting out light, sound, and fresh air. The room smelled of nothing in particular, but of everything that had happened within its walls. An acrid miasma of uncorked medicine bottles, the smell of flesh that had begun to rot too soon, of teeth that no longer chewed food, of breath grown fetid somewhere deep in the lungs. Urine, feces, blood. Faint traces, but enough to call up vivid pictures of the Judge's last few weeks. Prudence had sat by his bed all day and half the night, leaving it only when she collapsed from exhaustion and had to be helped to her room. By Victoria. By Donald. Undressed and tucked into bed by Colleen, who then sat to keep watch over her as she had watched over the Judge.

The bed was stripped of its sheets after the body had been placed into its mahogany coffin. Then remade, the dark gray satin coverlet drawn up over the pillows, smoothed free of wrinkles, tugged down tightly at the corners. As if a dying man had never struggled under its weight, never grown thin and weak and pallid in the cold, dark weeks between the beginning and the end of December. The book he had been reading when he could still read lay on a bedside table, fringed bookmark imprisoned on the last page he had been able to absorb. Empty water pitcher and glass, a pair of reading glasses he was usually too vain to wear, a candle in case he woke in the night and didn't want to fiddle with the oil lamp.

So sterile now, where once there had been a forest of brown bottles vying for every inch of available space, sticky spoons cradled in stained glasses until a maid took them away. Prudence could just make out shapes in the dim light. She pulled back one set of drapes the width of her hand, enough to see, not enough to be seen from the street. She was thinking of every possibility now, as alert and cautious as a fox on the hunt.

I have to be able to come back. I need more time. She went from her father's bedroom into his dressing room, where armoires lined two walls and a narrow bed allowed his valet to nap while waiting for the Judge to come home from a late-night engagement. Or keep vigil when he fell ill. The drawers were still full of his neatly folded clothing, his suits and shirts hung perfectly pressed from padded hangers, his judicial robes occupying a special place of their own. Shoes polished and fitted with shoe trees to hold their shape. Gold cuff links, diamond tie tacks and clasps, the ring marking him as a Harvard man, his thick gold wedding band. He had been buried without the rings he wore every day, as if someone decided they were worth too much to hide in the dirt. And Prudence had never noticed, never really looked at the empty hands tucked along the length of his body.

The smoking room smelled of his cigars. The desk at which he wrote private letters and sipped brandy when he couldn't sleep looked newly polished, the books kept there because they were his favorites piled more neatly than any dedicated reader could manage. His shaving cup and razor strop, hairbrush and comb, toothbrush and powder remained in the bathroom as though waiting for him to return at any minute and pick them up. The bathtub sparkled, towels hung ruler straight, the dressing gown on the back of the door seemed to hold the shape of his body.

On an impulse, Prudence walked quickly back to the room where her father had died, to the door that she knew opened into her mother's bedroom. *Privacy is as important to a marriage as love.* Where had she heard that? Had her father said it in one of their late-night conversations, perhaps soon after she and Charles had become engaged? Or had it been her gentle mother, trying desperately to tell her too-young daughter all of the things that a mother should be able to reveal to her child grown into a woman? She'd have to try to remember later, when there was time.

Sarah MacKenzie's bedroom smelled of the same perfume that drifted out of the drawer of the armoire Prudence had found in the attic. Sandalwood, jasmine, lilac, roses. Victoria had never lived in these rooms. She had her own suite in the south wing of the second floor. At her request or by the Judge's decree? More questions. More questions than answers.

And here, too, it was as though Sarah had stepped out for an afternoon ride in Central Park. Everything was spotlessly clean, well ordered, the furniture polished, the fireplace grate blacked and restocked with kindling and logs of apple wood.

With one huge difference. Every drawer was empty, nothing hung in the armoires, there were no personal items in the bathroom. It was like a hotel suite before the guest arrives, before the staff fills the vases with flowers, arranges fresh fruit in tastefully placed baskets, sets out dishes of fine chocolates and cracked nuts, ices a bottle of French champagne, and places two crystal goblets within easy reach. Someone had tried to erase her mother, had emptied these rooms of the woman who once lived in them.

Prudence had to get back into the hallway. Back to her room. She hadn't heard the longcase clock strike the hour, but she knew that too much time had passed. Knew that the last caller must surely have left by now.

"Someone has been very careless with her keys," Victoria said. She stood motionless at the head of the wide staircase connecting the first and second floors.

How long has she been standing there? Can she see what I'm holding in my left hand, what I'm hiding in the folds of my skirt?

"The door was open," Prudence said. "I haven't set foot in my father's rooms since he died."

"I ordered his rooms locked. To protect his privacy during our period of mourning."

"The door was open," Prudence repeated.

"So you said. I wonder why."

* * *

German Clara cleaned each of the gaslight wall fixtures in Miss Prudence's room once a week, climbing atop a small step stool to remove the etched glass bulbs, which had to be washed free of soot in warm, soapy water. Each wall fixture was taken apart, cleaned, dried, polished, and put back together before the next one could be worked on. It wouldn't do for a member of the family to enter a room where all of the gaslight fixtures lay about in pieces.

Trimming the wicks was the hardest part. A wick had to be twisted between the fingers into a tight, upright position so as to cast a warm, amber glow around the room as the gas burned steadily at its tip. Too loose and the wick would quickly consume itself. Too tight and there wouldn't be enough air circulating through the strands to keep the flame alive. German Clara devoutly wished Mrs. MacKenzie would see fit to have those new electric lights installed, at least in the hallways.

Miss Prudence must have stayed up late, as usual. The reservoirs in the lamps that sat on her bedside and dressing tables were nearly empty, their glass chimneys even more smudged with soot than the glass bulbs of the wall sconces. Clara left the door to Miss Prudence's room open behind her when she went down to the basement to fetch more fuel. She didn't notice someone waiting in the corridor for her to disappear down the servants' staircase.

Untwisting the tighly furled wicks was the work of a moment, as was locating and blocking the tip of the gas nipple with rolled-up pellets of paper that would eventually burn through, leaving clear passage for the later gas that would find no flame and slowly fill the room with its deadly vapors. The knob that turned the gas flow on and off was easily adjusted with a small screwdriver. In the closed position it felt tight now, but once opened and then closed again, the valve would not reseat itself as it had been designed to do. A very small amount of gas would continue to leak into the room, but there would be no hissing sound to warn of its passage. It would be enough, over the course of a normal night, to send a sleeper into an eternal slumber.

The last thing to do was polish the brass housings so no fingerprints betrayed the tampering. German Clara would never leave a smudged fixture behind her.

CHAPTER 12

It was Josiah Gregory who arranged for Geoffrey Hunter to interview the Judge's longtime butler and the housekeeper who had retired within months of the second MacKenzie marriage. Without Victoria's knowledge, Thomas MacKenzie had settled a generous sum of money on Kathleen Dailey. "She was devoted to Sarah MacKenzie, cared for her night and day after Dr. Worthington diagnosed the consumption."

He handed Hunter a piece of paper with Mrs. Dailey's address written in a neat secretarial hand. "Just across the new bridge," he said. "She bought herself a house along the shore there. Ten bedrooms on the two upper floors; parlors, a library, music room, and kitchen on the ground floor. Land and houses hadn't gotten as expensive as they are now in Brooklyn; nobody was quite sure how popular the bridge would be. The Judge advised her on the purchase; he had a nose for things like that. Mrs. Dailey always said that if she'd inherited money at a young age she could have become as rich a millionaire as Hetty Green. She has nine paying guests, retired butlers and housekeepers like herself, what you'd call the upper crust of the servant class. She had us out for tea not long after her boarders moved in. I tell you, Mr. Hunter, I've never sat at table with a group that had better manners than those ladies and gentlemen. Quite a sight it is."

"You wouldn't happen to know Cameron's whereabouts also?"

"Ian Cameron went straight from Fifth Avenue to Mrs. Dailey's. She'd told him to come to her if something went wrong. When Mrs. MacKenzie informed him he was being replaced, that's exactly what he did."

Roscoe Conkling's secretary was as good as any Pinkerton operative Geoffrey had ever partnered. He'd known before being asked that Cameron's whereabouts would be important, and he'd made a point of finding out where the butler had gone. Probably got the whole story of his dismissal direct from Cameron's own lips.

"I took the liberty of telling Mrs. Dailey to expect you, sir."

The same way that Josiah arranged Conkling's life for him, he'd anticipated Hunter's needs. It reminded Geoffrey of the way things had been run in his father's household all those many years ago, before the war destroyed so much, before he'd had to be sent away to school. Anticipation was everything; the master and mistress should never have to ask for anything. Painful memories. He pushed them into the farthest recesses of his mind where they usually dwelt, and resolutely turned his attention back to the household he would visit in Brooklyn.

"Mr. Conkling isn't in today?" It was unlike Roscoe not to invite him into his office, no matter how busy he was.

"He's in court." A pained look twisted the lower part of Josiah's face, as though he were a child trying very hard not to cry. "I told him to ask for a continuance, but he wouldn't do it. There is no one on the face of God's green earth more stubborn than Roscoe Conkling. No one." His voice quavered, then steadied again. "He's not well, Mr. Hunter. I know he's not well, though he refuses to admit it."

"What's wrong?"

"He won't tell me. Won't utter a word of complaint. But I see him cupping his hand against the side of his head and rubbing the way you do when something hurts. I would swear he's been running a fever off and on for days now. He didn't look at all like his usual self on Saturday; I hoped he'd have the common sense to climb into his bed and stay there until this morning. But he didn't. He was at Delmonico's until all hours Saturday night, and then he got the wild notion to take the train up to Utica. I can't imagine Mrs. Conkling being all that glad to see him. He was back at the New York Club this morning and in court with his client right on time. But he has a look about him I've never seen before, not in all the years I've worked for him."

"What kind of look?"

Josiah hesitated, then cleared his throat. "Fragile, Mr. Hunter. He looks fragile. You know how someone gets when he reaches a certain age? Well, that's how Mr. Conkling seems to me. His eyes look like he's gone from fifty-eight to seventy-eight in a couple of weeks. Like he's seeing his own end, and it isn't as far in the future as it ought to be."

"I'll come back here after I've been to Brooklyn. Court should be over for the day by then."

"Maybe he'll listen to you."

"I doubt it." Geoffrey smiled reassuringly at Conkling's worried secretary. "You may be concerned about nothing, you know. Roscoe has sailed through more crises in one lifetime than anyone else I can think of. He's never down for long."

Josiah Gregory didn't contradict him.

The bridge to Brooklyn had opened five years ago, but it seemed so much a part of the landscape now that hardly anyone could remember what the East River looked like without it. The bridge was a spectacle, and a spectacle had promoted it. P.T. Barnum paraded twenty-one of his circus elephants across the world's longest suspension span to reassure the public of its safety; if Jumbo and his companions didn't cause it to collapse, nothing would. All you had to do was come to the circus to see the size of the elephants for yourself. Every performance sold out. Brooklyn's days as a hard to reach and sparsely populated haven in the countryside were numbered.

Mansions were being built all along the shore where Mrs. Dailey had found her boardinghouse. Manhattan's wealthy families had also discovered Brooklyn. The driver of the hansom cab Josiah had hired for Geoffrey was more than happy to put a nosebag on his horse and turn his face toward the cool breeze coming off the Hudson River. The blue water sparkled and danced under the spring sun, pleasure boats glided past with white sails stretched to the full, steamers made their way toward the docks that were busy night and day, ferries chugged back and forth to Staten Island and the Jersey shore. The hard, competitive core of the country's banking and investment houses in Lower Manhattan seemed a world away.

The only thing missing, Geoffrey thought, was Prudence MacKenzie. He would have liked to have her by his side, but the searches she was doing in the MacKenzie mansion on Fifth Avenue were invaluable. No one else could do them. They also couldn't risk raising any suspicions where Victoria was concerned.

"Hard to believe, isn't it?" commented the driver of the hansom cab.

"What's that?"

"Two weeks ago today. The wind was blowing so strong and the snow coming down so thick, nobody could make it across that bridge. It was iced over so bad, a horse couldn't keep his footing and a man would be bound to break a leg."

The high arc of the bridge soared into the sky, its stone towers and Gothic arches etched against the blue. Vertical steel cables looked as finely spun and perfectly designed as spider webbing. Some said it was the most beautiful bridge in the world. People had started calling it the Brooklyn Bridge despite at least two other names. Brooklyn Bridge had a nice, short ring to it.

"There was a picture in the *Herald* of an ice crossing in the river."

"Didn't last long. Broke up and trapped some people until they could jump back to shore."

"You were out in the blizzard?"

"Not me. I wasn't crazy enough to chance losing Mr. Washington here." The driver gestured toward his enormous white horse. "Named him that on account of what he looks like when he rolls back his lip. Biggest yellow teeth you ever saw. No, I didn't take the cab out, but I've heard stories from drivers who did. You wouldn't believe what some people were up to, you just wouldn't believe it."

"I'd like to hear some of those stories sometime."

"I've driven you before, Mr. Hunter, but I don't think Josiah Gregory took the time to do a proper introduction. Daniel Dennis is the name. Danny for short. I'm easy to find. Just leave word for me with Josiah. Mr. Conkling's been a regular ever since he came back to the city. Mr. Washington and I are on call, so to speak, though Mr. Conkling does like to walk. More than any other man I've ever met. Or you can send a messenger down to my stand at the corner of Broadway and Wall Street. Any of the drivers around there can tell you where I am."

"I'm pleased to make your acquaintance, Danny Dennis." Hunter held out his hand.

"Always a pleasure to meet a gentleman like yourself, sir." Dennis shook hands, then touched one finger to his tall hat. "Give my regards to Mrs. Dailey, if you will. A fine lady, very fine."

"Should I even ask how you happen to know her?" Hansom cab drivers knew more about who did what in New York City

than some of the newspaper reporters. Anybody who thought
he could remain anonymous in one of their cabs was fooling
himself. Conversations funneled their way up through the trap
door above the passengers' heads directly into the ears of their
drivers, as tantalizing as steam from a pushcart vendor's pan of
sausages.

"Drove Mr. Gregory and Mr. Conkling out here when she
first set up the boardinghouse. Made me a cup of good Irish tea
and sat me down in the kitchen to drink it. Very lovely lady.
Josiah knows he can trust Mr. Conkling's clients to Danny Dennis.
Mr. Washington and I always get them where they need to go."

"I'll remember that."

He left Dennis currying Mr. Washington and flicking bits of
mud off his harness. This road along the shore was still largely
unpaved, bordered on one side by the swift flowing waters of
the Hudson River and on the other by houses set well back in
large, heavily treed lots.

An immaculate white sign hung in front of Mrs. Dailey's
boardinghouse, discreetly indicating rooms to let to gentlefolk.
Not a single weed on the green lawn. Not a wilted or dead flower
bending over in the beds that lined the walk. Not a stray branch
growing beyond its allotted curve in any of the hedges flowing
gracefully out and down from the wide porches. This was clearly
the abode of a meticulously neat and well organized clientele.
He wondered if a stray dust mote ever had time to land on a
polished surface. Decided it wouldn't dare, and smiled to himself as he lifted the gleaming brass door knocker.

"I wondered if you'd come today," said the tall, dignified
woman who welcomed him with an appraising eye. Mrs. Dailey took Geoffrey's hat and ushered him into a parlor filled
with tightly tufted velvet chairs, fringed lamps, paisley patterned silk table scarves, small tables atop spindly legs, and a
forest of very healthy plants. The Judge's former housekeeper
rarely discarded anything.

He'd scarcely had time for more than a quick glance around and the briefest of pleasantries before a gentleman with the posture of a brigadier carried a silver tray of tea and cakes into the room, setting it down on one of the larger tables as if he knew exactly where it should go. As of course he did.

"Mr. Cameron is joining us. Josiah said you would have questions that it might take the two of us to answer to your satisfaction. Such a lovely boy, that Josiah." Mrs. Dailey poured and handed cups around; placed a selection of frosted cakes on tiny, flowered china plates; held out delicate, lace-edged linen napkins. When she raised her eyes to meet Geoffrey's gaze, there was a snap to the look she gave him. "Miss Prudence doesn't deserve what's happened to her. Miss Sarah would turn over in her grave if I didn't help her child. Mr. Cameron?"

"I worked for the Judge for more than thirty years, and before that for his uncle. I was born into service in the MacKenzie family, and if that woman hadn't come along, I'd still be there." Ian Cameron's voice was low in pitch and volume, every word pronounced with the educated accent he had learned growing up in a MacKenzie household. Slender and as perfectly groomed as any of the gentlemen he had served, he was the epitome of butler, as though the word had been coined to describe no one else. "Miss Prudence needs looking after. Miss Sarah loved that child to death and the Judge did the best he could for as long as he could, but it's not enough. There's a cloud moving in that's threatening to swallow her up, and I won't let that happen. You ask your questions, Mr. Hunter, as many as you want. I'll tell you everything I know."

"She came out of nowhere." Mrs. Dailey sat with clenched hands, determined to hold her anger in check until she'd given over every useful bit of information she could remember.

"Everybody comes from somewhere, Kathleen," interrupted Cameron.

"I remember the first time the Judge brought her to the house."

Neither the former butler nor the retired housekeeper seemed able to pronounce Victoria's name. It was as if they had decided she had no right to be called MacKenzie, and Victoria was too intimate.

"That was a few days before they married. There never was an engagement announcement." A trace of Ireland crept into Mrs. Dailey's diction. "She didn't like me on sight. I could tell. I knew my days were numbered. And sure enough, it was less than a month later that I found out I was being retired."

"Did she tell you herself?" It was the first question Geoffrey had asked.

"No. She left it to the Judge. He called me into his study, his library, he called it, and asked me to sit down. I hadn't sat in his presence since Miss Sarah died. He poured me a sherry, and a whiskey for himself, then he told me that in accordance with the late Mrs. MacKenzie's wishes, he was making it possible for me to retire. I nearly fainted when he told me how much money Miss Sarah had supposedly left for me. It was a reward for all my years of service, but one I'd heard not a single word about until that moment. I didn't ask any questions; I didn't have to. I knew what had happened as sure as if I'd been a fly on the wall.

"If it had been left to *her*, I'd have been out on the street with one suitcase and an old umbrella in my hand. But the Judge wouldn't stand for that. He couldn't refuse her, though I'll never understand why, but he did what he could to soften the blow. He knew I'd lived my life for him and for Miss Sarah and Miss Prudence, and he calculated that what I'd given away he'd give back to me. This house and the chance to start a new life, an independent life. Josiah, bless his heart, he was the one who brought me out here, who found the house and knew it was going to be put up for sale. Someone had died, and the heirs didn't want it. Mr. Conkling made the offer and negotiated the contract, and all I had to do was drive across the bridge and step through my very own front door. That was a little more than two years ago now. I miss not seeing Miss Prudence every day, but I'm truly happy with my family of gentlefolk."

Geoffrey turned to Ian Cameron. "Your name doesn't appear in the Judge's will, Mr. Cameron."

"The Judge didn't intend for me to have to fight over what he wanted to give me, and I know for a fact he didn't trust the former Miss Morley. So we rode down to Mr. Conkling's office one day and he signed over some stock to me. Josiah had all of the paperwork ready and he was one of the witnesses. The Judge made a deposit at the First National Bank of New York in my name; he said the worst thing an investor could do was have to sell his stock because he needed walking around money. So he took good care of me, too, Mr. Hunter. And I don't think she knows about it to this day."

"The Judge kept secrets from Mrs. MacKenzie? If I understand correctly, that's what both of you are telling me."

"Not only did he keep secrets from her, Mr. Hunter, he hardly talked to her at all. He'd keep a conversation going at the dinner table, and he knew all the right things to say whenever anyone else was around or they went out socially for an evening. But he'd close his mouth tighter than a fist when it was just the two of them."

"How do you know that, Mr. Cameron?"

"What I said about when it was just the two of them? You know people never see their servants, Mr. Hunter, and a good butler learns early on to make himself unnoticeable. Many a time I'd come into the parlor to bring a nightcap or see to the fire or inquire if there were any special orders for that night or the next morning. And there they'd be, the two of them alone, not speaking, him reading his newspaper, she staring into space or reading one of those trashy novels she was always buying. If Mr. Morley was there, he and his sister might be talking or playing cards, but the Judge was as silent as a stone statue. He wasn't rude, and I never heard an argument; he just disengaged himself from her as though she'd turned invisible."

"Her rooms were at the opposite end of the second-floor hallway from his." As far as Kathleen Dailey was concerned, a couple's sleeping arrangements either supported a happy marriage or sounded its death knell. "Miss Sarah's rooms stayed untouched, not a thing moved or packed away since she died. There's a connecting door between her bedroom and the Judge's, but there was never a key in the lock. Never." She wiped a tear from her eye with a fine lawn handkerchief. "He put the second one as far away from him as he could, and when the brother moved in, he had to go up to the third floor where the guest rooms are."

"When was that? When did Donald Morley become a member of the household?"

"Right after they married. They didn't go on a honeymoon trip, then or later, and it seems to me that Mr. Morley was up there on the third floor almost from the beginning."

"What about Miss Prudence?"

"She has her own rooms on the second floor, but they're on the front side of the house, facing Fifth Avenue. Even when she was a little girl she loved to curl up on the cushions of her window seat and watch the people and the carriages going by. The second Mrs. MacKenzie has bigger rooms, but they face the gardens and the stable out back."

"The Judge paid the bills when she redecorated, but I can't recall a single time when he asked to see what she'd done. I'd dress him sometimes in the evening, when his valet had a day off or was under the weather. She never came into his dressing room and he never went to hers. Unnatural, if you ask me. Miss Sarah liked to pick out his cuff links, and sometimes she'd drink a glass of champagne and chatter on about where they were going while I brushed him down. They were always finding excuses to be in one another's company."

"I've kept this close to hand for nearly four years now," Kathleen Dailey said, taking a calling card out of her pocket. "I couldn't ask the Judge about it, and then when he retired me, I thought about showing it to Josiah or Mr. Conkling, but that didn't seem right either. I told myself, *Kathleen*, I said, *you'll know when the time is ripe and you'll recognize who's meant to find out what it means.* That's what I've told myself every single day since I found this lying underneath the Judge's desk in his study. I could have put it with his papers, or maybe in the drawer where he kept the cards people left when they came calling, but I didn't. I knew it didn't belong there, and I knew it was too important to take a chance on never seeing it again." She handed the card to Geoffrey as ceremoniously as if it were the sacred Host on a gold paten.

It was one of the Judge's own cards, his name and title engraved in Gothic script on an expensive card stock that only the wealthy could afford. Nothing else. Geoffrey turned it over and saw one word. *McGlory.* Written in that thick black ink that could only have flowed from the nib of the Judge's favorite pen. Thomas MacKenzie's handwriting was as distinctive as everything else about him. *McGlory.* A fine spray of minuscule black ink spots rayed out from the name. He'd borne down heavily as he wrote, either in anger or determination, enough to splay open the delicate nib. *McGlory.*

"You don't have to be Irish to know that name, Mr. Hunter. McGlory's Armory Hall on Hester Street. The Irish gangs used to hang out there; now every pimp, pickpocket, and murdering thug in the city calls it home. I've nephews who know no better and couldn't be bothered to do an honest day's work. All you need is money in your pocket; McGlory will sell you anything from rotgut whiskey to women. Whenever some newspaper reporter decides to write an article on the depravity of New York City, you can be sure he'll devote at least half the story to Billy McGlory."

"Why would the Judge have written Billy McGlory's name on the back of his visiting card?"

"I've my suspicions, but no, I won't tell you what they are. You need to come to them on your own."

"Mr. Cameron?"

"Don't go to McGlory's alone, Mr. Hunter. That's the best advice I can give."

CHAPTER 13

Don't go to McGlory's alone.

Geoffrey Hunter knew of only one person in New York City who didn't fear the notorious saloonkeeper, one individual out of its million and a half inhabitants who could call on McGlory day or night and be made welcome. No questions asked. There'd been a time a few years back when the names Billy McGlory and Ned Hayes had been linked together in every newspaper you picked up. Not the best publicity for a New York City police detective. Hayes had been allowed to resign without any charges brought against him after the McGlory debacle, but he was ruined nonetheless.

Geoffrey hadn't seen Ned Hayes in over a year, but he had no trouble finding him. Josiah confirmed that the former policeman hadn't moved from the Lower Manhattan brownstone where he had lived alone since the end of the war.

"Ned's mother didn't come back after the surrender; I don't know that she's even still alive. Other than her relatives, he doesn't have any family. Once he was forced out of the police department, he cut off all contact with everybody he'd worked with. Except you. Tyrus is still with him, of course."

Geoffrey didn't ask how Josiah gathered the information he carried around at his fingertips. Conkling's secretary was a force unto himself, with contacts reaching out through all levels of New York social life and across all geographical boundaries.

"He's not doing well, Mr. Hunter. I hear he's taking opium by needle now. Which means he doesn't have much time left. What he did for McGlory is what's making it possible for him to get what he needs, a clean product that won't poison him outright until the day or night he decides to take too much. I'll miss him. He's a fine man. What happened to him shouldn't happen to a dog."

"We had drinks together in the Fifth Avenue Hotel bar. At least a year ago. Maybe a few months more than a year. He didn't look bad that day. Drank champagne instead of whiskey, which for Ned is like drinking nothing at all. He wanted to talk about the South."

"He loves it and he hates it. I'm not telling tales out of school. I heard him say so many a time."

"He thought because of my background I'd understand how you could be so divided about your birthplace, about the society in which you should have been proud to grow up. Lord help us, he sounded that day like he'd never left South Carolina. More than one head turned when they heard the accent. The war's been over for more than twenty years, but people haven't forgotten. It'll take at least another generation for that to happen."

"North Carolina, Mr. Hunter?"

"You can hear it?"

"Just once in a while. Like now. Mr. Hayes will be glad to see you, grateful for the chance to help out, but I thought you should be warned. He might not look like you expect him to, as you remember him."

"I appreciate the warning, Josiah." Hunter changed the subject. "You were worried about Mr. Conkling the last time I was here. I hope he's doing better."

"He's made up his mind. He won't listen to me. He's in court every day, all day long, at Delmonico's every night. Won't even discuss seeing a doctor about the pain I know he's trying to rub out of his head. It's like he's rushing toward something, but I don't know what it is." Josiah's eyes were bright with the unshed tears he didn't try to conceal from Geoffrey. "He's added a codicil to his will. That's all I can say. I can't tell you what it is."

"You're the last person I expected to see, and the only one I'd put up with. Welcome, Geoff, welcome." Ned Hayes was formally and immaculately dressed, fawn trousers creased, white shirt starched, velvet burgundy smoking jacket the perfect foil for his blond good looks. The pale silvery gold curls showed no trace of gray, he was clean-shaven and only slightly flushed, but the once-muscular body had grown far too slender. The pinpoint pupils of his blue eyes told his friend everything he needed to know.

"I'm here to get your help, Ned."

"You have it."

"Don't you want to know why? Or what I'm asking?"

"It won't make any difference. You know that." Hayes poured Kentucky bourbon for both of them, adding an infinitesimal splash of water. "Best whiskey there is."

The room in which Hayes and Hunter sat was exactly as Ned's mother had decorated it before the war began, precisely as she had left it when she took her sixteen-year-old son south in 1862. His father had not changed it, nor had the son. Twenty-six years later, Elizabeth Lee Hayes would have recognized every chair, every bibelot, every antimacassar, even the weave of the Aubusson carpet. Furnishings that were faded and a bit shabby, but still showing the quality she had prized. No dust anywhere, just the wear of empty years passing.

Anything new would be as jarring in this parlor as Ned himself, his clothes too fresh, too fashionable, his meticulous grooming sharp against the washed-out background in which he sat.

He'd been a misfit in the Confederate Army, an oddity in the New York City Police Department, an outcast from the joys of ordinary, everyday life. Ned Hayes had never fit in anywhere, not from the moment of his birth. Was it any wonder he was hastening his death, albeit quietly, without fuss, simply doping himself gradually into oblivion?

"What can you tell me about Billy McGlory, Ned? That I haven't read in one of the newspapers." The bourbon *was* good.

"He fancies himself a dandy. Medium height, very slender, always wears a diamond stickpin and gold cuff links. Tall silk hat. Carries a cane that I know for a fact is a weapon, and sports a mustache he keeps waxed and trimmed so there's never a hair out of place. Almost certainly a murderer, in the sense of personally dispatching whoever got in his way before he could afford to hire goons to do it for him. Born and grew up in Five Points. Ran with the Irish gangs in his younger days. Richer than any legitimate tavern owner could ever be. When I saved his life, he decided he was beholden to me. We get along quite well. I like his style and his audacity and he likes the fact that I never tell him anything but the truth. Why do you ask?"

"I have a case."

"Are you with the Pinkertons again?"

"No. I have no quarrel with Robert and William, and they offered to rehire me after Allan died, but working for somebody else doesn't sit well with me anymore. When you work for the Pinkerton National Detective Agency, you *are* a Pinkerton. There's no other way to describe what's expected of you."

"You seemed to thrive on it once."

"I was younger. I needed to learn."

"So you served an apprenticeship under the great Allan Pinkerton."

"That's one way of putting it."

"And now you have your own agency?"

"Yes, and no. Do you remember Charlie Linwood?"

"I read about what happened to him in the *Herald*. Hard to

believe." Ned sipped at his bourbon, put the glass down with the precision of a man who knows he needs to take extra care with his movements. "Very hard to believe."

"You wouldn't think so if you'd been out in that blizzard yourself."

"You were telling me about the agency you may or may not have."

"Charlie was bound and determined to make an honest, hardworking Yankee out of me."

"Waste of time."

"Be that as it may. I wasn't sure what I wanted to do after I left the Pinkertons, after that quarrel Allan never forgave. I took a suite at the Fifth Avenue Hotel and settled in to being a gentleman of leisure."

"And you were bored before a week was out."

"You know me too well, Ned."

"We're cut from the same bolt of cloth."

"The only time I really came alive was when Charles threw me a case. They were always what he referred to as *extremely delicate*. Which invariably meant that a wealthy gentleman had been doing things it were better he not do or a lady's spotless reputation was about to be revealed for the stained garment it was."

"No murders? It takes a murder to season a good detective."

"There were murders." Hunter took a small leather notebook from his jacket pocket, uncapped a gold-cased pen, and scribbled a name. He handed the paper to Hayes, then sat back in his chair to await the reaction.

"This was your doing?"

"I'm sworn not to speak about it. Ever. But yes, whatever little justice resulted from his not going to trial was mine to claim."

"I'm impressed, Geoff. I think even old Allan would approve of the way that was handled."

"As I said, I have a case and I need your help." He handed the visiting card to Ned, who nodded his head at the two names on it. *Thomas Pickering MacKenzie* embossed in Gothic script on one side, the single slash of *McGlory* in black ink on the other. "You're not surprised?"

"To find a well-known judge and one of New York City's most notorious criminals paired together? No, I'm not surprised. Billy McGlory has more public officials on his payroll than even he can count. He's been left alone so far, but his luck won't hold forever. There's a tidal wave of reform gathering strength, and when it rolls over places like McGlory's Armory Hall, it will wash them away in a howling hurricane of righteousness. Temporarily. McGlory and others like him will have to disappear for a while, until the ministers wear themselves out. Two, maybe three or four more years. That's all he's got until it breaks. He's never been a stupid man. He's making his preparations; he knows what's coming is inevitable."

"Can you get me to him?"

"Why?"

"I have to ask him a question."

"It would be safer if you'd let me ask it for you."

"I need to see the expression on his face when he answers."

"*If* he answers."

"I have a gut feeling about this, Ned. He'll answer. He won't be able not to. Why would the Judge write McGlory's name on his visiting card? That's what I have to find out."

"You're sure it's his handwriting?"

"Everything else may be murky and hidden, but his handwriting and the ink he always used are distinctive. The woman who found the card and gave it to me wouldn't make a mistake about that. There's also a daughter. She confirmed it."

"I think you've arrived at the heart of the matter, Geoffrey. *Cherchez la femme.*"

"I don't have to look for her. She's my client."

"All the better."

"Charlie Linwood was her fiancé. The judge whose card you're holding was her father."

"*Was* her father?"

"His heart gave out right after Christmas."

"I don't think I was reading the newspapers around that time. I must have missed the obituary."

"The daughter's name is Prudence. In the space of a few months she lost both father and fiancé. She's a very wealthy young woman. Except that her father placed everything into a trust that's administered by a stepmother."

"This is sounding more and more like an evil stepmother fairy tale."

"Victoria MacKenzie is barely ten years older than Prudence. She was the Judge's second wife."

"How long did this second marriage last?" Ned Hayes reached for his glass, one finger sliding around the rim of the heavy crystal tumbler before he drew back his hand, the bourbon left untasted.

"Two years."

"Very nice. Very nice indeed. I wonder how Victoria did it."

"Did what?"

"Killed him. Murdered her dear old rich husband. Got him out of the way. *After* convincing him to rewrite his will. How much of his estate came to her directly?"

"A very substantial portion. But it's also in a trust."

"Then she wasn't as clever as she thought she was. Or perhaps he was simply more stubborn. The only thing you don't know is how McGlory fits in. Am I right?"

"There's a lot I don't know, Ned. The few facts I *am* sure of are parts of a puzzle that won't lock together until the missing pieces are found." He hesitated. "You're not the only one who thinks there's something too convenient about the Judge's death, but there isn't any proof. Right now we're concentrating on finding out whatever we can about the stepmother's background to force her out of the role of trustee. She had to have been holding something over the Judge, something that would destroy his reputation and force him off the bench. It makes sense that she's dirty, too. She blackmailed him into marrying her. But murder?"

"I think we're in for a long night, Geoffrey. There's no point going to Armory Hall until ten or eleven o'clock." Hayes stood up and walked to the fireplace. Pulled the bell cord that hung to one side. "I'll have Tyrus bring us coffee and sandwiches. You might as well start at the beginning and tell me everything."

"It's the largest concert saloon and dance hall in the city," Billy McGlory boasted. One foot on the bar's brass foot railing, diamond stickpin flashing brilliance every time he moved, sporting a patterned silk vest as green as the hills of Ireland, the owner of Armory Hall looked out over a sea of hard-drinking, hard-living customers and smiled. He could calculate to the penny the profits he'd make on any one night just by doing a quick count of the house. Average for a weekday evening, he decided. "Keep the champagne coming," he told the bartender, then led the way down the length of the bar, past the tables grouped around the dance floor where couples at all levels of sobriety clung and steered one another about. Two men together was the specialty of the house. On the second floor of the Armory ran a wide balcony open to the dance floor below for the orchestra, studded on two sides with doors to private assignation rooms and larger parlors where more guests could be accommodated. It was said that you could buy anyone and anything at Billy McGlory's once you paid the fifteen cent general admission price.

McGlory led them up a broad staircase to the second floor, then to a door he unlocked with a key hanging from his gold watch chain. "We won't be disturbed here, gentlemen. And it should be relatively quiet tonight. No cancan dancers, no boxing matches, no beauty contests. No special show." He stood aside, waiting for Ned and Hunter to precede him, leaving the door open for the waiter who was coming up the stairs behind them carrying champagne and crystal glasses.

The room was both a parlor and an office. A round oak poker table and chairs stood to one side, a cluster of black leather easy chairs and small tables to the other. A fire had been lit earlier in the evening; gas lamps flickered on the walls. Wallpaper and carpeting were deep burgundy; all of the wood gleamed with fresh, fragrant polish. Billy McGlory's private retreat had been furnished with the best that a lot of money could buy.

"Did Ned tell you what he did for me, Mr. Hunter?"

The champagne glasses were full; a second uncorked bottle sat in ice beside the first one. French champagne. Billy Mc-Glory served himself only the best; his customers made do with what they could afford.

"Not the details."

"I took a knife in the gut. Most men don't recover from that. But most men aren't lucky enough to have Ned Hayes drag them off the street like he did me. I was being stitched up and hidden before the fighting stopped and the arrests started. No doctor, either. He carried me to a conjure woman who sewed me up like a purse, dowsed me in a potion that burned like fire, and prayed spells over me that no white person has ever heard before. I healed, I healed up as good as I ever was, and when I could get back out onto the street, I took care of what needed to be done."

"I think you embroider that story a little bit more every time you tell it, Billy." Ned turned to Geoffrey Hunter. "Even Mama Oshia couldn't have saved him if the knife had gone in just a few inches over. The fellow who stabbed him wasn't good at what he was doing."

"And won't have the opportunity to get any better." Mc-Glory smiled, a charming, winsome Irish smile that made him look like a mustachioed altar boy. "The New York City Police Department didn't like it too much that one of their own detectives crossed over to the other side, so to speak. Not that they all don't have their hands out every week, regular as clockwork. But this time a reporter saw what happened and made it his business to follow up. Got the whole story and printed it before I could convince him otherwise. The mayor yanked Ned's badge before the ink was dry on the presses."

"I told Billy if it hadn't been that, they would have gotten me with something else. I don't seem to be the kind of man who fits well into a uniform. I'm told I wasn't the sort of officer who was a credit to the Confederacy, and even when I traded in my nightstick for a detective's badge I wasn't able to squeeze myself into the police mold. I couldn't let a man die when I knew he could be saved. It didn't matter who or what he was. That's what they couldn't forgive me for."

"I pay my debts, Mr. Hunter. Whatever else they say about Billy McGlory, anybody who knows me will tell you I pay my debts."

"Not too much longer, Billy. It won't be too much longer. Throw me the biggest damn wake New York City has ever seen and we'll be square."

McGlory shook his head, then crossed himself, Catholic enough to believe that heaven might listen and answer a prayer, even from the likes of him.

"Show him the card, Geoff."

McGlory read both sides, smiled as if he'd been expecting something like this, then held it to his nose for a moment. "I thought her scent might be on it," he said. "She's one of the ones who doesn't know the meaning of the word *enough*. Always greedy. Grabbing with both fists. Holding on. Too much perfume, too much champagne when she drank, too many lies told to too many men." He handed back the card. "I'm surprised this got past her. And I'll be sorry to my dying day that she got it out of me."

"Something about Judge MacKenzie?"

"I'd had too much to drink. And the woman knew how to wring a man dry. Body and soul. Dry as a bone. She was like one of those snakes that coil themselves around you and squeeze until there's nothing left. I didn't even remember that I'd talked until much later. The Judge knew she had to have gotten the information from me or someone close to me. It was too late to stop her by then; she'd gotten what she wanted. But at least he knew the truth of it. When he asked me, I told him."

"His daughter wants me to find out whatever I can." Hunter thought he could guess what Prudence should never have to know about her father.

"That would be the child who was left motherless when the Judge's first wife died. A man loses more than a warm spot in bed when his woman passes over."

"What did you have on him?"

"He and a lot of other people lost all their railroad stocks in the Panic of '73. After Jay Cooke declared bankruptcy that September, the railroads started failing so fast, you couldn't keep up with them. The stock wasn't worth the paper it was printed on. When he needed cash money, he didn't have anything left to liquidate."

"He had other investments, other properties."

"What he had, Mr. Hunter, was a wife who'd been diagnosed with consumption. He'd bought land on Staten Island to build her a house, then overnight his capital was gone. He needed money to save Miss MacKenzie's mother. The New York Stock Exchange was closed for almost two weeks. Nobody was buying anything, even if you had something to sell. He was a desperate man. And it just so happened I needed a big favor. In a hurry. We got a case moved into his court; I paid him what he needed to build that house and my man went free. The Judge never sold his Staten Island house, even after his wife died. You could say it was his conscience, a reminder to him of how far a man would go when he didn't seem to have any other choice. You don't need to know any more than that."

Hunter took from his inner breast pocket a copy of the wedding photograph Prudence had smuggled out of the house. He held it out to McGlory, who took it, grimaced, then passed it along to Ned.

"She's a beautiful woman," Ned said quietly. "To be a snake, I mean." He handed the photo back to McGlory.

"The name she was using at the time was Ronnie, short for Veronica. I didn't hire her, so she wasn't one of my regulars. She had class, a lot of class. You could tell it just by looking at her. I don't think she came in here more than five or six times, all told. I could tell she was trouble, but she *was* beautiful. You're right about that, Ned."

"I think she came after you deliberately, Mr. McGlory. I think she knew you had judges on your payroll. All she needed was the right information about one of them."

"She never came back after that night I shot my mouth off. I never saw her here again."

"How did she know who to target, Geoff?"

"Mr. McGlory has a history of passing unscathed through the New York City court system. All she had to do was go to the *Herald*'s morgue and read back copies of the newspapers. It wouldn't have been difficult. She was looking for a McGlory henchman who should have been convicted, but wasn't. And a judge who was spending a lot of money. Put the two together and take a chance. She won the toss."

"She blackmailed him. That's why the Judge married her." Ned's blue eyes sparkled like an excited child's, the pupils slightly larger than before. He'd need something soon, but for the moment, the opium hunger was gnawing at his vitals a little less viciously than usual.

"I think we'll find that Veronica, or Victoria, whatever her real name is, had one goal in mind from the beginning. She wanted respectability, money, and a place in New York society. The only way she could get them was through marriage, so she studied the market, singled out her prey, and pounced. I don't know where the brother figures in, but we'll find out."

"She never came in alone. There was always a man with her. Heavyset. The kind you'd expect to have to pay extra for his whore. The one in the picture."

"He's calling himself Donald Morley now."

"Doesn't sound familiar. If she gave me a last name, I don't remember it."

"You did a good thing tonight, Billy."

"I pay my debts, Ned."

CHAPTER 14

There were always errands to be run, but most of the time it was the footman or the bootboy who set off down Fifth Avenue to deliver a message or make an urgent purchase. It was considered unsuitable for a female servant, particularly one of the younger ones, to be out on the street alone. You never knew who might want to take advantage, even in as elegant a residential neighborhood as where Judge MacKenzie had built his unostentatious brownstone. Four stories tall, with classic Greek columned portico and tall, narrow windows, it sat squarely and solidly on its oversized lot, the ivy that had reminded Sarah of the green hills of Staten Island allowed to climb freely on all of its walls.

It was still early, that narrow hour of grace between the end of breakfast and the resumption of every day's endless chores. The servants had been up since five, working quietly in the downstairs rooms while the family slept. Before the bedroom bells began to ring insistently, the staff caught its collective breath, ate Cook's first hearty meal of the day, and scattered to enjoy the only moments of privacy they were likely to have before bedtime.

Colleen slipped out of the service entrance at the rear of the mansion, where a cobbled courtyard stretched between stables and carriage house to the kitchen entryway and the delivery chutes for coal and wood. A high wall to one side of the space enclosed Sarah MacKenzie's small city garden, as perfectly trimmed and planted in the years after her death as though its mistress were still there to stroll the narrow paths.

She didn't think anyone had seen her. She'd oiled the kitchen door so it didn't make a sound when she opened or closed it, but Colleen was uneasy nonetheless. She'd had the oddest feeling the last day or so that someone was watching her. All the time. Saying nothing, doing nothing. Just watching. Yet no matter how many times she stopped what she was doing to spin around and catch the watcher in the act, there was never anyone there. Nerves, she decided. Miss Prudence's case of nerves had passed itself on to her.

She wished she had time to stop by the stable before she left; James Kincaid was as calm and reassuring a presence as the large, docile horses he groomed and drove. They'd talked about Miss Prudence over the cups of tea Colleen brought out to him, and reluctantly agreed that it would be easier and safer if it were Colleen who carried most messages from their young mistress to Mr. Hunter. "I'm sorry it has to be you, lass," he'd said, reminding her that he could still pass on a note or a message coming in the other direction, "but a horse doesn't need the farrier but a few times a year." They both knew that if Victoria MacKenzie called for her carriage and Kincaid wasn't there to drive her, he'd be shown the door without delay or discussion.

Colleen had Miss Prudence's note slipped between the palm of her hand and her glove. Invisible. Impossible to drop. Four blocks north to the Fifth Avenue Hotel between 23rd and 24th Streets where Mr. Hunter lived in a suite on the third-floor front. She'd been there and back twice before, safely out of the house, safely back in again. Together she and Miss Prudence had thought of the perfect excuse for being out. Just in case she got caught.

"You can say that I gave you permission to go to mass at Saint Patrick's Cathedral. To pray for your mother, who's ill."

"It's too far away, Miss Prudence. All the way up to Fifty-first Street."

"Isn't there anything closer?"

"Saint Anselm's. It's small and just off Twenty-second. But if anyone sees what direction I'm going or coming back from, it would make sense."

"All right then. Saint Anselm's."

"I can say she took a bad fall and injured her back. They're not sure she'll walk again. So that's what I'm praying for."

She set her face in the doleful look she'd practiced in the small mirror hanging above her washstand, wrapped her shawl around her shoulders, then set off walking as quickly as she could without breaking into a run. Speed attracted notice. All she wanted was to get to the Fifth Avenue Hotel as fast as she could, place Miss Prudence's note in Mr. Hunter's hand, and return safely to her dusting and polishing.

Colleen wasn't sure what exactly was wrong in the MacKenzie house; she just knew in the marrow of her Irish bones that there had been a great sadness there. And a great evil. The presences had never left. She could feel them sometimes in the night, when even though she was exhausted from all she'd had to do during the day, she woke in a wintry cold bed and could not lull herself back to sleep.

There, just ahead, rose the gleaming white marble of the Fifth Avenue Hotel. It dwarfed everything around it, reduced Colleen to the stature of one of the little people who caused so much trouble in Ireland. She scurried past the doorman and the bellboys, a familiar figure to them now, streaked through the lobby, and disappeared into the stairway to the third floor. She didn't think she'd been followed, but she stood for a long two minutes in the third-floor corridor waiting for someone else to emerge from the stairwell. No one. Only then did she move to ring the bell of Mr. Hunter's suite.

"What do you have for me today, Colleen?" Geoffrey Hunter stepped out into the hallway as he ushered Prudence's messenger into the suite. He stood listening for footsteps, gauging the emptiness in both directions. Nothing. No one. Satisfied, he stepped back inside and closed the door.

"Just this, sir." Colleen pulled out the folded note she'd been tempted to read but hadn't. She handed it to Mr. Hunter, her fingers trembling.

"There's nothing to be afraid of, Colleen. Miss MacKenzie and I won't let anything happen to you."

"I know, sir. But—"

"But what?"

"I'm not good at keeping secrets, sir. Cook says she can tell when I'm trying to hide something just by looking at me."

He laughed then, but it was a reassuring sound, not at all like the threatening mockery she heard so often in the MacKenzie household. Mr. Morley, Mrs. Barstow, Mr. Jackson, they all laughed with the same sharp edge that made her uneasy. Colleen watched Mr. Hunter scribble an answer to Miss Prudence, then fold the hotel stationery in half and seal it into a hotel envelope.

"Looks official, doesn't it?" he commented, writing *Miss Prudence MacKenzie* on the outside of the envelope in a measured, clerkly script. "Give this to her as soon as you can. Try to do it without anyone noticing, but if you sense that someone is watching, don't bother to hide anything. That's the worst thing you can do. It confirms suspicions. Just hand over the envelope and go on about your business. Do you know what to say if someone asks why you're carrying messages to her?"

"No, sir. We didn't plan for that. Just that she gave me permission to go to mass."

"Say that on your way back from church, I met you in the

street and asked you to deliver this note. I was in a hurry, and I gave you a quarter to run the errand for me." He put the envelope and the coin into her outstretched hand, pressed her fingers around them, and smiled again. "Nothing to worry about, Colleen. Even if someone were to read the letter, it's all open and aboveboard. Miss Prudence will understand what I mean; she knows to read between the lines. You'd better be on your way now. You don't want to be out of the house too long."

"There's something else, sir." Miss Prudence had made her promise not to mention the gas incident to Mr. Hunter, but Colleen had fretted over it every step of the way to the Fifth Avenue Hotel. If she didn't say something now and anything happened to Miss Prudence, she'd never forgive herself.

"What is it, Colleen?" Hunter drew the maid back from the door he'd been about to open, seated her at the table where he had been drinking his morning coffee when she arrived. Tears stood in her bright blue eyes; she bit at her lip to keep them from falling.

"Miss Prudence made me swear not to tell you."

"Then I think you'd better. If it's that important, I won't be able to help unless I know what the problem is. Don't you agree?"

Colleen nodded, miserably aware that Miss Prudence was going to be furious.

"All right, then. Start at the beginning." He took a clean white handkerchief from his jacket pocket and handed it to Prudence's servant.

"Miss Prudence had a terrible headache when she woke up on Saturday morning."

"Is she all right now?"

"Yes, sir. But Miss Prudence hasn't had headaches since she stopped dosing herself with laudanum. That's why I thought of the gas. It's always leaking down in the tenements, you see. Babies and old people die of it all the time. They sleep more than them what goes out to work and they don't know what's happening to them. The ones who don't die are damaged in the head; they're never the same again."

"Take your time, Colleen. Tell me exactly what happened. Don't leave anything out." Hunter reached for his half-filled coffee cup, then changed his mind. He was likely to crush the china into shards if Colleen confirmed what he now suspected.

"When I brought Miss Prudence's tray up to her on Saturday morning, the room was cold. She'd opened the window during the night, she said, because she woke up and there was a funny smell, as if the gas were still on. She got up and checked it, but the knob was as closed as could be. I felt it myself, right away, but it wasn't loose, and the lamps were all as tight as a drum. German Clara had cleaned everything the day before. She's the upstairs maid, sir. We call her German Clara because her English isn't very good."

"So you and Miss Prudence checked the gaslights on the wall and the lamps, too."

"Yes, sir. She got out of bed and stood right next to me while I fiddled with the knobs."

"Had she turned the gaslights on the night before?"

"Only one, sir, and just for a few minutes. She likes the lamplight better."

"How many wall fixtures are in that room?"

"Two, sir. One just inside the door, the other on the wall opposite."

"And which one had she turned on?"

"The one by the door just as you come into the room. She turned it off as soon as she lit a lamp."

"Did you smell gas, Colleen?"

"I'm not sure, sir. With the window open it was hard to tell. So when German Clara came upstairs to make the bed, I made her show me how she'd cleaned the gaslights. There was nothing wrong with them, sir, nothing I could find, anyway. I told her to leave Miss Prudence's window open to air out the room, and she did. Every time I got the chance that morning, I stuck my head in the door."

"Did you tell Miss Prudence what you suspected, that there'd been a gas leak?"

"I did, sir. She didn't say a word, just put her hand over her mouth, like this." Colleen mimicked the gesture. "She was thinking, sir, I could tell by the look on her face. That's when we checked the gaslight she'd turned on. I swear to you, sir, I couldn't feel anything loose or not catching."

"Tell me what happened next."

"Mrs. MacKenzie and Mr. Morley went out for a drive after luncheon. Miss Prudence said she was tired and would lie down for a nap. So I went up to check on her as soon as I could. She was standing on her dressing table chair, using her metal nail file on one of the gaslights. She had the strangest look on her face. She reminded me of the Judge when he'd had a bad day in court. We all knew to stay out of his way."

"Did she explain what she was doing?"

"I asked her, sir, didn't I?"

"And what did she say?"

" 'Be careful, Colleen. Someone's watching.' She wouldn't say much else, except that I wasn't to tell anyone about the gas, but I knew right away someone needed to know. She thinks she's fixed whatever was done to that gaslight, but it wasn't just the one; she had both fixtures opened up and she'd been at the valves with her nail file, so it couldn't have been an accident if both valves stuck. What if that's not the end of it? What if someone is trying to harm her, Mr. Hunter? What if he tries again?"

"Are you sure German Clara didn't unseat the valves when she was cleaning?"

"Miss Prudence sent me downstairs to fetch Clara. She knew what she was being suspected of because I'd already made her show me how she cleaned the gaslights. She was scared to death, Mr. Hunter. I'd swear on my granny's grave she didn't tamper with those valves, not even accidentally. Miss Prudence gave her a quarter and told her not to say anything to anyone."

"What about the next day?"

"I don't think Miss Prudence slept a wink Saturday. From what I could see when I went to help her dress on Sunday morning, she'd been awake all night. With the gaslights on and the window cracked. Sitting there waiting to open it wider as soon as she smelled something. There's a bad presence in that house, sir. I was thinking about it on my way here. I don't know who or what it is causing the trouble, but I know it's there."

"Do you have the sight?"

"My granny did. She could look in a person's face and name the day of his death."

"That's a terrible gift."

"I don't have it, Mr. Hunter. All I can tell you is that someone tampered with the gaslights in Miss Prudence's room, and it wasn't German Clara."

"I want you to tell Miss Prudence I pried the gas story out of you despite yourself, and that she's to be very careful. Make sure she understands that I'm certain there will be another attempt."

"Do you really think someone is trying to harm her?"

"Yes, Colleen, I do. And it's up to us to make sure that doesn't happen. I think she's safe from the gas. Whoever tampered with the valves has to believe his plan didn't work. He won't try the same thing twice. It will be something different next time, and it won't be right away. He'll want to lull Miss Prudence into feeling she's safe before he strikes again."

"How long, Mr. Hunter?"

"I don't know, Colleen. I haven't the sight either." He stood in the doorway to his suite watching her until she reached the stairwell, then with a final reassuring nod, stepped inside.

Colleen hid the envelope in the pocket of her black skirt, took the stairs down to the lobby quickly but carefully. Her leather boots could slip on wet marble. She didn't know when the staff mopped these spotless floors, but she didn't dare risk a fall. No one seemed to notice her as she wove her way through the sitting areas of the lobby, half-hidden behind towering potted plants and high-backed leather chairs designed as much for privacy as comfort. The doorman spared her a quick, dismissive glance, then turned his attention back to the hotel's paying guests.

Even at this early morning hour, Fifth Avenue was a busy thoroughfare, horse-drawn vehicles of all kinds in the roadway, newsboys and crossing sweepers darting from one side of the street to the other through piles of fly-ridden dung and puddles of reeking urine. There were few girls or women on the sidewalks, no ladies at all. Colleen felt eyes on her back as she scurried along, staying as close to shop fronts as she dared. Just a few more blocks to go.

This area of New York City was relatively safe, though no street was entirely free of pickpockets and casual whores. Hotels and businesses hired private security firms to ensure that their customers and clients would be free from harassment both inside and outside their premises, but the most wily of the city's petty criminals were expert at evading notice. At least the physical assaults that were common on the Lower East Side seldom happened in the more rarified atmosphere of Fifth Avenue.

By the time she could see the ivy-covered walls of the MacKenzie mansion, Colleen had nearly conquered her fears. No one had accosted her, she hadn't been greeted by anyone who knew her by sight, and now she doubted that her absence had even been noticed. All she had to do was slip back into the house through the basement entrance, hang her shawl in the servants' coatroom, and take the letter up to Miss Prudence.

The quarter Mr. Hunter had given her would go into the box where she saved her wages. It wasn't much, but she never tired of counting the coins. They represented a future that was bound to be better than the past.

*   *   *

Keys were what Prudence needed, and keys were what she had asked Colleen to find for her. Now a dozen keys of all sizes lay on top of her dressing table, most of them retrieved from drawers in the servants' hall where odds and ends were tossed until someone in authority decided what to do with them. None of them was tagged, and she suspected they had been presumed lost at some point, perhaps replaced before they turned up under a carpet or behind a piece of furniture. Servants found with keys in their possession were often accused of contemplating theft and unceremoniously turned out without a reference. The safest thing to do was let a key lie and risk being scolded for carelessness or toss the dangerous object in among others just like it. What she had to do now was fit these keys to the locks she wanted to open and hope that some of them would be a match.

She sorted them into three piles. The larger, heavier keys were clearly to doors leading to the outside, to the cellars or the attic. Slightly smaller keys with decorated bows or shanks she thought must be to parlors and bedrooms. The three smallest keys would fit desk drawers or jewelry cases; they were thin and half the length of a finger. She wrapped several keys of the same type into a handkerchief, folding carefully so they wouldn't make a metallic sound against each other. She hated the idea of sneaking around her own home trying keys in doors that should have been open to her without question. She tore pieces of paper from her journal, one for each key she hoped to identify, and added a pencil nub to the pile.

Before she left her room, Prudence checked once more the corner of the wardrobe where she'd hidden the letters found in her mother's rosewood chest of drawers. She had scattered them among birthday or holiday cards and letters received over the years from her father and from friends. Her hope was that anyone rifling through her old writing case would be looking for a packet set apart from the rest, would only glance casually at what seemed carelessly tossed together. She had taken the leather cover off the journal wedged in the hidden drawer of the rolltop desk and painstakingly separated its pages, inserting them into a battered copy of *Uncle Tom's Cabin*. Slipped the novel into a small bookcase amongst old schoolbooks and other volumes the Judge had given her over the years. As soon as Geoffrey Hunter sent word of where and how they could meet, she would smuggle both letters and journal pages out of the house.

The strands of hair she had affixed to the gaslights with her saliva were still in place, invisible unless you knew to look for them. She might not be able to stop anyone from tampering with the gas, but at least she would know when it happened. Despite having extracted a promise of silence from Colleen, Prudence fully expected her maid to say something to Geoffrey Hunter. In fact, she was counting on it.

Now for the keys.

"Something's wrong upstairs, apart from the usual," Cook said, rubbing mutton fat into her sore, reddened knuckles. She lowered her voice and leaned closer to Colleen. "Mr. Jackson has had a scowl on his face all day long. German Clara is on her way out, mark my words. Mrs. Barstow says she's tired of yelling at her all the time. Doesn't do much good to yell if the poor girl doesn't understand much English in the first place, I say."

"She's cried every night since she got here. Her room is next to mine. I can hear her through the walls."

"Best to let her go then. Maybe she can find something with her own kind."

"She's a hard worker, I'll say that for her. Once Clara understands what you want her to do, she goes right at it. Will they hire someone else in her place, do you think? I can't do all the maiding by myself, not and see to Miss Prudence, too."

"There's no telling what Mrs. MacKenzie will do. I've never heard of an establishment where the housekeeper was also the mistress's personal ladies' maid. Can you imagine Mrs. Astor or Mrs. Vanderbilt allowing a situation like that? It's not the way things are done, and every lady in that Four Hundred knows it. There's certain rules to running a household that can't be changed." Cook shook out that day's *Herald,* flipping greasily through the pages until she reached the society section. She gulped down news of the city's social elite with as much gusto as she did her first early-morning bowl of hot, milky coffee.

"Are they here for tea?" Colleen looked up anxiously at the big clock that hung on the wall opposite the scrubbed pine worktable.

"Tray's all laid out in the pantry, and the kettle's about to come to the boil," Cook said, never lifting her eyes from the newspaper. "Just pour boiling water in the pot, swish it around a little, pour it out, spoon in the China leaves, add more water, and take the tray up. Try to get it to the parlor while it's still hot."

No matter how many times Colleen prepared the afternoon tea tray, Cook gave her the same directions, as if a girl who had drunk hundreds of cups of tea in her life wouldn't know how to scald the pot properly. Cook didn't believe anyone was capable of doing anything in the kitchen without her supervision. For all her gruff ways, though, she was nearly as kind to the maids as Mrs. Dailey had been.

"I'm off then." Colleen balanced the heavy tray against her shoulder, fragrant tea steaming against her cheek.

"Brigid will have the bread sliced and the butter and jam laid out when you get back. And there's a nice chocolate cake I baked while you were out this morning," Cook said.

One foot faltered as Colleen turned toward the narrow, un-carpeted wooden stairs. Cook knew she'd left the house. Had she mentioned it to one of the other servants? Had someone else seen her in the cobbled yard? Been looking through one of the front basement windows that showed a passerby's feet but precious little else until you leaned over and stared upward through the security grate? Should she say something to Miss Prudence? Warn her?

She could feel beads of perspiration dribbling down the side of her face. Vapor from the hot tea and the sweat of fear. *Jesus, Mary, and Joseph,* she whispered. Phrases from the Hail Mary punctuated her steps until she finally reached the parlor door. She felt like a lamb on its way to slaughter.

"Just put the tray down on the table, Colleen," Mrs. MacKenzie said as she had directed dozens of times before. "We'll serve ourselves."

"Yes, madam."

"And you might check to see if Miss Prudence is coming down. We won't wait for her, though."

Colleen thought there was a tight, expectant air about Victoria MacKenzie and her brother. Both of them looked at her as if in anticipation of something, even while dismissing her. She tried to think of a task she might have left undone, but she'd been too well trained to have forgotten anything. Eventually, since Cook had noted her absence this morning, someone would say something. Probably Mrs. Barstow.

The door to the housekeeper's parlor had been open when Colleen passed by with the tea tray, the room empty. Strange. It was unlike the housekeeper to leave her parlor door unlocked when she wasn't there. By this time in the afternoon both Mrs. Barstow and Mr. Jackson would be walking together along the hall from their parlors toward the servants' dining room, heads together discussing the day's successes and failures. Minor infractions were usually dealt with over afternoon tea; corrections made in public had a way of not being repeated. But the housekeeper's parlor and the hallway had been empty. Had there been the sound of two voices behind Mr. Jackson's closed door?

What was it Colleen's mother said you heard when someone close to you was about to die? A howling scream, a wail borne on the wind. The banshee, come to warn that Death was on its way. The skin at the nape of Colleen's neck twitched and itched as though a scaly hand had run ragged fingernails over it. She clutched the rosary in her pocket and hurried up the staircase to the second floor.

Miss Prudence came toward her, smiling the way she hadn't smiled in months. One hand triumphantly raised a key above her head, then quickly tucked it into a handkerchief. "I'll put these back in my room and go down to tea right away, Colleen. I suppose Mrs. MacKenzie sent you to look for me."

"Yes, miss," she replied, giving over the envelope with Mr. Hunter's note, "but she also said they wouldn't wait."

"I won't mind having tea with the witch and her brother today. In fact, I think I'll rather enjoy it."

Miss Prudence was in and out of her bedroom again before Colleen had recovered from hearing Mrs. MacKenzie's stepdaughter call her father's widow a witch.

"Run along to your own tea, Colleen. You've more than earned it."

There hadn't been time to tell her what Mr. Hunter had said about another attempt to harm her. And Miss Prudence looked so happy with what she'd been able to do with the keys. Colleen would confess the entire conversation when she came upstairs again to dress Miss Prudence for dinner. Mr. Hunter had said nothing was likely to happen for a while.

As she pushed open the door to the servants' staircase, the odd twitching and itching of the skin at the nape of Colleen's neck started up again, but this time there was also a burning sensation that made her rub furiously as if to put out a fire. The stairway was well lit; she could see all the way to the turn where the last few steps reached the basement rooms below. From the servants' hall echoed half a dozen voices and the sounds of food being served, chairs adjusted under the long table. Cook's distinctive bark ordered someone to bring more hot water.

She paused for a moment, fighting off the sense of doom that suddenly swept over her, distracting herself from her fear by identifying the voices raised in conversation. James Kincaid in from the stable, German Clara, Frank the bootboy whose speech cracked alarmingly whenever he opened his mouth, Brigid the kitchen maid, Brian the footman who also helped out with whatever needed doing, Mrs. Barstow arguing with Cook about something. She didn't hear Mr. Jackson's voice, but he often sat in glowering silence at the head of the table. It was all so very ordinary. She'd say an extra decade of the rosary before she fell asleep tonight and beg forgiveness for giving in to superstition. The Church taught that there were no such creatures as banshees.

Halfway down the staircase Colleen heard the door to the first floor open softly, then a quick patter of footsteps on the stairs behind her. Before she could turn to see who was there, something round and hard like a knuckled fist struck her in the small of the back. Her left foot skidded out from under her as though she'd slid on a patch of slick ice. Both arms shot out, but there was no banister to grab hold of and break her fall. She felt herself tumbling forward, head striking repeatedly against the steps and the walls as she twisted and somersaulted faster and faster downward. Someone screamed.

Chairs scraped, footfalls hammered against the stone floor, cups slammed into saucers, alarmed voices called out, demanding to know what was happening.

Sprawled at the foot of the staircase, arms and legs crooked at impossible angles, blood streaming into her eyes and blinding her, Colleen knew the Church was wrong.

There *were* such creatures as banshees, and one of them had wailed her death.

Chapter 15

Colleen lay atop the long table in the servants' hall until Dr. Worthington could be located and summoned to the MacKenzie mansion. Cook washed the blood from the maid's face, tears streaming down her cheeks as she repeatedly wrung out the cloth in warm water that quickly turned red again every time the basin was emptied and refilled.

James Kincaid straightened Colleen's limbs and ran his hands over them with the gentle, expert attention he gave the horses in his care.

"I don't know how it's possible," he said, covering her from feet to chin under a warm blanket, "but I don't think anything's broken. I can't feel a fracture, and there's no sign of bone breaking through the skin. She'll have internal injuries, though. Bound to. And that's what may do her in."

Upstairs a battle raged. Victoria was insisting that the girl be bundled into one of the carriages and taken to Bellevue Hospital, where there was an Emergency Pavilion for accident cases like this. Openly defying her stepmother, Prudence refused to allow Colleen to be moved from where she lay until the doctor had examined her. She sent Frank the bootboy on a fast run to

Dr. Worthington's home and office only a few blocks away, following him out into the hallway to slip a whole greenback into his hand and whisper instructions to then run on to the Fifth Avenue Hotel and bring back a gentleman named Geoffrey Hunter.

"I really don't think it necessary for the girl to be seen by the physician who cared for your father, Prudence. Bellevue is a public hospital; she'll be well looked after there. Dr. Worthington may refuse to treat her, and he'd certainly be within his rights to do so," Victoria persisted.

"He won't refuse. When my father was alive, it was understood that every person living in his home would receive the best possible care should he fall ill or be injured. Dr. Worthington has treated many of our servants in the past; he won't turn us down now." Prudence was determined that no one but Dr. Worthington would treat Colleen.

"Jackson, tell James to ready the small carriage. I'm sure Dr. Worthington will see the sense of taking her to Bellevue," Victoria continued to argue. "Mrs. Barstow can accompany her as far as the Emergency Pavilion, but no farther. She's needed here."

"Yes, madam." Jackson's odd-colored eyes were muddied, as though the yellowish brown of the pupils had spilled over into the white of the sclera. He held himself rigidly straight, but the fingers of his hands twitched in tiny, repeated, and uncontrollable spasms. He glanced at Mrs. Barstow, standing beside him. Her face had paled at Victoria's order; she looked as though the last place in the world she wanted to be was riding in a carriage cradling Colleen's body in her arms.

It was useless to argue with her stepmother. Prudence swept past her, past the butler and the housekeeper, out the parlor door. Without thinking, she walked as quickly as she could down the hallway and pushed open the door that gave onto the servants' stairway to the basement. Halfway down she realized what she had done and came to a dead stop. Her hands reached out on either side to flatten themselves against the walls and steady her. Whatever had caused Colleen to lose her footing might still be on the stairs. She inched her way toward the basement, skirts brushing the stairs behind her as she continued to push against the walls. She took a deep breath when she reached the bottom, and stood looking upward for a moment, wondering on which step Colleen's fall had begun.

"She's not come around yet, Miss Prudence." Cook's face contracted with the effort not to weep; her work-worn hands stroked Colleen's hair gently.

"Dr. Worthington is on his way. He'll know what to do." It was the only comfort Prudence could offer. Colleen was as pale as a corpse laid out for washing; only the slight rise and fall of her chest assured those watching over her that she was still alive.

"Kincaid, Mrs. MacKenzie wants the small carriage hitched and waiting in front of the stables. As soon as the doctor comes, if he does, you're to drive Colleen to Bellevue." Jackson's voice was harsh and overly loud.

"Bellevue Hospital?"

"Is there another Bellevue? Hurry up, man."

"She can't just be laid out on the seat, Mr. Jackson. Unconscious like this, she'll roll off and that'll surely be the death of her."

"Mrs. Barstow will ride with her to the Emergency Pavilion. On Mrs. MacKenzie's orders." Jackson stood over Colleen for a moment, listening to the ragged, shallow breathing. "Let me know the moment it looks like she's coming around." Then he turned like a soldier executing an about-face and disappeared down the narrow corridor that led to his office and the wine cellar.

"Colleen is not going anywhere unless Dr. Worthington orders it, Kincaid," Prudence said reassuringly. "You can hitch up the horses, but there's no need to worry. I won't allow anything or anyone to harm her." It was frightening to see Colleen lie so still, so far away from everything going on around her.

"Will the doctor come soon, miss?" Brigid's small voice quavered; big tears rolled down her fourteen-year-old cheeks.

"As fast as Frank's feet can get to him." Prudence looked at the cups and saucers and sandwich plates that had been hastily removed from the table where Colleen lay. The servants' tea was scattered over every available surface, mute evidence of the haste with which they had left the table and run to the stairway when they heard her cry out and fall. "I think it might be a good idea to straighten up a bit while we're waiting. And perhaps Cook can organize some more hot tea. We could all use a cup."

It wasn't much, but it was something to do, something to get everybody moving again, a semblance of normality to take the place of what was so very disturbingly not normal.

"Did anyone wipe down the stairs after Colleen fell?" Prudence asked Brian the footman. He served at table, answered the front door sometimes for Jackson, and did every other job the butler gave him. An even dispositioned young man of twenty, he was clearly determined to please, set on working his way up the service ladder.

"I did, miss. There was some blood on the steps. You have to get blood up right away or it stains all the way into the wood."

"Would you show me?"

Brian led the way to the foot of the staircase and pointed upward. "There's nothing to see, miss. I took a damp mop to the stairs."

"Was there anything slippery on the stairs, Brian? A spill perhaps?"

"I wasn't looking for anything but the blood, miss. And there wasn't very much of that." He screwed up his face in concentration. "I was wondering if Colleen might have got something on the bottom of her boot and not realized it. Then if she was in a hurry coming down the stairs . . ."

"They're very steep, aren't they?"

"We're all told to be careful, miss."

"Where is the mop you used?"

"In the bucket, miss. There hasn't been time to rinse it out. Do you want to see that, too?" The tone of his voice told her how odd he thought her questions were.

"Yes. But we'll keep this between us, shall we?"

"Of course, miss. Whatever you say, miss."

The bucket had been placed just inside the scullery, mop handle leaning against the wall.

"Thank you, Brian. You'd best get yourself a cup of tea while you can, before the doctor arrives."

Prudence watched him walk back into the servants' hall, then she closed the scullery door and took out a handkerchief. There was barely an inch of dirty water in the bottom of the bucket, but what she wanted, if it was there, would be clinging to the cotton strands of the mop. She held the mop upright over the bucket until the last drops of water had fallen, then squeezed the mop head between the folds of her handkerchief until finally her fingers felt what she had been afraid she would find. Grease, some kind of slippery grease had adhered to the mop head and now stained the handkerchief.

Colleen's fall had not been an accident.

As she stood looking up at the narrow staircase, Prudence pictured Colleen rushing to get downstairs, not worrying about anything being on the steps because Mrs. Barstow was so strict that there was no danger of a spill not being promptly wiped up.

Behind her came a dark, featureless form, whoever had greased the step, making sure his quarry's foot would slip. Had that been enough? Or had an arm shot out to land a heavy blow against the girl's back?

There would be no proof unless Colleen regained consciousness and could tell them what had happened, but Prudence was certain the fall had been a deliberate attempt to kill her.

"She may not regain consciousness," Peter Worthington said quietly. He had examined Colleen, approved of the care she had been given before he arrived, and gone back upstairs to the parlor to report his findings to Mrs. MacKenzie. "Unconscious-ness this deep is never a good sign. There will have been serious damage to the brain as well as to other internal organs. We learned during the war that the gravest injuries were often those we could not see. I'm sorry, Mrs. MacKenzie, but I'm afraid there's noth-ing I can do for her. She'll need good nursing until the end, and I believe I can say that she is unaware of her own suffering. We can't hope for anything more than that."

"Then Bellevue Hospital would seem to be the best place for her, wouldn't you agree?" Victoria reached for the bellpull to summon Jackson.

"I'm afraid I don't. Bellevue is very good at setting broken bones and stitching up wounds, but Colleen just needs a clean and quiet bed where she can sleep out her last hours."

"I don't want her in the house," snapped Victoria. "It will be upsetting to the rest of the servants."

"If I may, Mrs. MacKenzie," Geoffrey Hunter volunteered. Thanks to Frank the bootboy's fast young legs, Hunter had in-tercepted Dr. Worthington just as he was getting out of his car-riage. Their explanation for Hunter's presence was simple and logical. He and Worthington had been having dinner together when the doctor was summoned, and since Hunter had been Charles Linwood's closest friend, he had naturally been con-cerned for Prudence's welfare. He had asked to come along, and Dr. Worthington had willingly agreed.

Prudence had insisted on escorting both men to the servants' hall herself, creating the opportunity to exchange a few private words. A plan had been hatched in those moments, groundwork laid, and Victoria defeated before she knew who her opponents were. Now they were ready to put that plan into action.

"I may be able to be of some small service in this matter," Hunter said.

Victoria hesitated, looked to her brother for support. Don-ald Morley had taken an immediate jealous dislike to the fellow who would have been Charles Linwood's best man had he lived. Hunter was everything Morley was not: tall, handsome, attractive to women, as muscular around the shoulders as an athlete, but with the self-assured grace of a gentleman born. He had interfered at Linwood's funeral, and now here he was again, taking Prudence's side when he had no right to speak. Donald wanted to tell him baldly that they didn't require his services, but Worthington was nodding his head encouragingly; it wouldn't be wise to ruffle the doctor's feathers. "What did you have in mind, Mr. Hunter?" He saw Victoria's eyes squeeze in annoyance; he'd explain it to her later.

"I know of a boardinghouse whose landlady takes in older lodgers in need of special care. Most of them either have no remaining family or require the kind of attention that can't easily be given in a household full of young children. Colleen could be made quite comfortable there, for the little time remaining to her."

"That sounds very odd," Prudence said.

"The war disrupted so many families that new ways of seeing to the sick and the elderly have had to be found," explained Peter Worthington. "Geoffrey's suggestion would seem to solve the problem. I've sent the occasional patient to this woman myself."

"I'm not sure," objected Prudence.

"It's settled," decided Victoria abruptly. "There's no point arguing the matter, Prudence. I've made up my mind."

Kathleen Dailey tucked the still-unresponsive Colleen into a soft, clean bed in the small first-floor room adjacent to her own. "There's a door between the two rooms that I can leave open during the night. I'll hear and wake up if she so much as turns over. Poor child. She was so young and so lonely when she first came to work in the kitchen. I was housekeeper then, and it didn't take long to see that she'd make a fine parlor maid.

Intelligent. A very sweet disposition. I was sorry to have to leave her to the likes of Mrs. Barstow, but then it wasn't my choice, was it?"

"Do you know where her family lives, Mrs. Dailey? They should be told." Geoffrey had held Colleen in his arms all the way from Manhattan to Brooklyn.

"The only thing I remember her telling me is that they were crammed into a couple of small rooms in one of those tenements down by the river where the factories used to be. It's where the Irish first came after the Famine, but worse now with so many people displaced off their land by the war and trying to find work in the cities. Some newspaper reporter called it Hell's Kitchen, and the name stuck. You could look for days or weeks even, and unless you knew where to go, you'd never find them. I wish I could be of more help, Mr. Hunter."

"Miss Sarah would have made a point of finding out, but she was long gone when Colleen came. Maybe Miss Prudence could find something in her room." It was the best Cameron could suggest. As butler, he should have made it his business to know all about every member of the staff, but he hadn't. He'd always supposed there would be more time for things like that, but there hadn't been.

"She looked before I left, Mr. Cameron." Geoffrey handed him a small suitcase that contained all of Colleen Riordan's worldly possessions. From his coat pocket he pulled out a wooden rosary and a well-worn prayerbook. "Miss MacKenzie especially asked me to be sure the rosary would be placed in her hand."

"I'll do that now, sir." Mrs. Dailey made the sign of the cross with Colleen's rosary, kissed the crucifix, and threaded the beads around the maid's limp fingers. "Mr. Reilly has gone for a priest from Saint Anne's. Perhaps you and Mr. Cameron could wait for me in the parlor. I'll see to a few things for her, then I'll be out."

She waited until Mr. Hunter and Cameron had crossed the hallway into the parlor before turning back to her patient.

"There must be more we can do, Mr. Hunter." Concern was written all across Ian Cameron's face.

Geoffrey looked carefully at the man Prudence had described as her second father. Tall, straight, every silver hair in place, dark gray eyes alert and watchful, he was a handsome man in his sixties who must have been every housemaid's dream when he was younger. He looked like an Anglican bishop, steeped in aristocratic dignity and a touch of holiness.

"I took that card Mrs. Dailey gave me to Billy McGlory's place."

"Did you now?" Kathleen Dailey had come into the room so quietly that neither man heard her. Both stood up, waiting politely for her to seat herself. "And what did that boyo have to say for himself?"

"All I can tell you is that Mrs. MacKenzie came into possession of information that would have ruined the Judge and forever tainted Prudence as the child of a man destroyed by scandal."

"So he married her to keep her quiet. Men can be such fools." Mrs. Dailey flicked imaginary dust from her black silk skirt. "Present company excepted, of course."

"Unfortunately, marriage isn't a crime," Cameron said.

"But blackmail is." *If we could prove it,* Geoffrey added silently to himself.

"She won't have left anything incriminating unburned. Many's the time I came into the library after the Judge died to find Mrs. MacKenzie standing before the fireplace feeding in papers with both hands. She never spared me a word of explanation, just a dark look because I'd interrupted her. Nothing but ashes left in the grate when she finished. I stirred them around with the poker once or twice. Here and there maybe a corner of something that hadn't burned through, but nothing with any writing on it. I would have told Miss Prudence, but there didn't seem any point to it. And she was his widow; she had a right to decide what should survive him and what shouldn't." Cameron shook his head at the memory of the flames that had consumed what remained of a life.

"All those lovely letters Miss Sarah wrote to the Judge and he to her. I know he meant them for Miss Prudence. He'd bundled them up very neatly, and he told me once, when I came to ask him something, he told me that he hoped Miss Prudence would someday find herself a husband as good as Miss Sarah had been a wife. He had tears in his eyes. I saw him put those letters into one of his desk drawers and lock it. I suppose they're all gone now." All housekeepers were called Mrs. even when, like Kathleen Dailey, they'd never married. Part of her still yearned for the romantic love that long years in household service had denied her.

Geoffrey looked from one devoted face to the other, assessing strength of character as well as the multitude of wrinkles. They had both worked hard all of their lives, and now, thanks to the generosity of the man they had served, both had come to a place that should be free of care. Except that the Judge would not stay in his grave. And his daughter Prudence needed them.

"Roscoe Conkling said something," Geoffrey began. Even as he said it, he wasn't sure he would continue.

"I think you'd better tell us, Mr. Hunter." Cameron reached out a hand to Kathleen Dailey.

"He said he thought Thomas Pickering MacKenzie had been murdered."

The Judge's former housekeeper let out the breath she had been holding. "That's why she had to get me out of the house so quickly. She couldn't have done it with me keeping an eye on her and watching out for him. I'm only surprised she waited as long as she did. The witch."

"We'll have to prove it, won't we, Mr. Hunter? She's not perfect. She must have made a mistake somewhere. We'll have to find that mistake and use it against her." Cameron might have been a New York City detective summarizing a case.

Mrs. Dailey got up and walked into the room where Colleen lay. She stood for a moment by the bed, listening to the girl's shallow breathing. When she returned to the parlor there were two red spots of pure Irish anger in her cheeks.

"She's tried to kill Colleen." It wasn't a question. "The girl knows something, and the witch decided it was too dangerous to let her go. Servants talk about their employers; they've precious little else in their lives. So Colleen's mouth had to be closed before she could say anything."

"That may be jumping to a conclusion that isn't supported by facts or evidence," Geoffrey Hunter cautioned.

"Tell us what to do, Mr. Hunter. We'll find your evidence for you."

Mrs. Dailey's smile was as thin lipped as determination and purposeful resolve could make it. She'd smile that smile at the foot of the scaffold the day Victoria MacKenzie was hanged.

CHAPTER 16

September 14, 1875

My most darling Prudence,

If you are reading this, it is because your dear father has decided that you are now of an age to need a mother's particular guidance. I left that time to his discretion, and also left to his good judgment whether or not he wished to read the missives I have penned to my only daughter.

He would not let me speak of my leaving; he could not bear it. So when I had written as much as my poor strength allowed, I bundled together my letters to you and placed them in the topmost drawer of the rosewood chest in which I have always kept my most intimate garments. He will have found the packet there himself, for I know my husband well. Thomas would not allow anyone's hands but his to touch what has lain next to my skin. Finding these letters has undoubtedly caused him pain, but that could not be helped.

A year may have passed before he opened the drawer. Perhaps two. But I see him in my mind's eye deciding finally that he must sort through what I have left behind. The jewelry is uppermost in his mind, for every piece goes to you, and many of them are too valuable to be left in an empty room. He must take them to the bank vault to keep them safe for you. When he sorts through the jewel boxes, he finds these letters. I sense his bewilderment and his hesitation. The note I have placed securely beneath the ribbon that ties them together is clear. He will have followed my instructions because he has loved me so well and so deeply that every wish of mine was granted.

And so here we are, my dear child, you and I together, mother and daughter. You are of an age that I trusted him to choose as appropriate. The letters are numbered. I think they are best read in order, though not all at once.

Imagine that we are sitting on the veranda of the Staten Island house together, I on my chaise longue, you in the white wicker swing that hangs from the ceiling. Mrs. Dailey has brought us cool lemonade and fresh baked petits fours. We sit in silence for a while, content to let the summer breeze waft over us.

Then one of us speaks, one of us asks a question. The other smiles, considers it, frames a careful, honest answer. And so we pass the afternoon as happier mothers and daughters will do, in deep and private conversation, touching on matters privy to women, laughing softly, sipping our lemonade, licking the thick, sugary, pastel icing from the petits fours.

Prudence laid the letter on her dressing table, very gently placing on top of it the silver-backed hairbrush that had been her mother's. The Judge had given it to her on her twelfth birthday. She sat looking at herself in the mirror, searching for features that were like Sarah's, wondering as she had so many times if she really did look like her. People always said a daughter resembled her mother, whether she actually did or not. It was a polite fiction no one questioned.

She held up a tinted photo of Sarah taken shortly after her marriage, when she was close to Prudence's own age. It was a studio portrait of a winsome and reflective young woman posed against a velvet drape. Dressed in a light-colored, tight-bodiced afternoon dress decorated with loops of black braid, falls of frothy lace falling from funnel sleeves, Sarah held a white lily in her hands, a broad gold wedding band clearly visible. Her hair was parted in the center, smoothed back over her ears, gathered into heavy ringlets that seemed to be tilting her head under their weight. She looked straight into the camera lens, pale eyes drinking in the photographer's lights, delicate mouth curved in the barest suggestion of a smile, a lady keeping her thoughts to herself.

I have her eyes, Prudence decided, *all shades of gray, depending on the time of day. Sometimes with hints of green when it's late at night or I'm very angry. Her hair, too, not light enough to be blond, but such a pale shade of brown that there's no good way to describe it.* Sarah's face was a perfect oval, small chin, high cheekbones, unfurrowed brow. Prudence's chin was more determined, the oval squared off at the jaw when she set herself to do something she knew Victoria would oppose. She did look like her mother; she really did. And if Sarah had been strong enough to fight the consumption to her last breath, then Prudence came by *her* strength naturally. Sarah had not known the meaning of the word *surrender. Neither,* vowed Prudence, *neither will I.*

She opened *Uncle Tom's Cabin* and took out the pages of the notebook she had found and hidden in the only way she thought safe. The house was quiet, the servants gone to bed, Victoria in her room suffering a vicious headache from the strain of this afternoon's accident. She had declared Colleen to be an impossibly careless girl who had no thought for her employer's delicate sensibilities. She would certainly not be taken back if by some miracle she managed to survive. Donald, presumably annoyed by the disruption of his comfortable routine, had gone out for a late supper, telling Jackson not to wait up. Which meant he wouldn't return until morning.

Prudence wedged a chair beneath her bedroom doorknob and put the pages of the notebook in order. She had inked a number on each of them before cutting away the binding, wondering even as she did so why it seemed necessary to take such extraordinary precautions. She had always disliked everything about Victoria and despised Donald, but until this afternoon she had not had a visceral, physical fear of either of them. That changed when Colleen plummeted down the servants' staircase to land in a bloody, twisted heap at the bottom. Pushed. Unless or until there was evidence to disprove it, Prudence would believe that Colleen had been the victim of deliberate violence.

Prudence herself was valuable to Victoria only if she were alive, and that, she believed, was the real reason behind the laudanum. Not to make it easier to bear her grief, but to ensure that she remained in the passive half light of a drugged euphoria where Victoria could control her. Unfortunately, anyone in whom Prudence confided, anyone who was seen to be loyal to her, was expendable. She was sure that was the word Victoria would use. Expendable.

Every time she tried to reassure herself, she felt a presence at her back, a warning draft that skipped up her spine and set her to shivering. Like now. She reminded herself that she was the daughter of two strong parents, and she let her thoughts dwell briefly on Colleen, lying in a bed fighting for her life. She had to believe that Colleen's will was intact, though her body had been badly battered. Geoffrey had managed to remove Colleen from danger, and as long as Victoria and Donald believed she was dying or dead, no further harm would come to her.

Dead. They had to convince Victoria that the maid had died. And soon, Prudence thought, before Victoria could become suspicious and demand the address of the place where Colleen had presumably been taken. Victoria didn't leave loose ends untied; Prudence's determined opposition to taking Colleen to Bellevue had caught her stepmother off guard, but that wouldn't last. She would want to assure herself that whomever she had persuaded to push Colleen down the stairs had succeeded in killing her. Somehow, once she was certain Victoria had been fooled, Prudence would find her way to Mrs. Dailey's Brooklyn boardinghouse; she wouldn't remain cooped up in this mansion that she had begun to think of as a prison.

Circumstances were changing Prudence MacKenzie; she caught herself standing aside watching the girl she had been and the woman she was becoming. She liked what she saw.

She was important enough for someone to want to harm her. What an odd thought. She knew she had not imagined the prodding point of a cane against her legs as she stood on a busy and dangerous street corner. Nor had she been mistaken when she'd touched the valve that regulated the gas flow to the wall light by her bedroom door and felt it wobble in its seating. With a few twists she'd been able to tighten it, turn on the fixture, and smell no leakage. Both gaslights, she reminded herself, both gaslights had been tampered with.

She'd known fear and panic on Fifth Avenue, and she'd spent all of Saturday night waiting for the smell of escaping gas. But except for this dread of some unknown evil she believed emanated from her stepmother and her stepmother's brother, Prudence was less frightened of life and loss than she could remember ever having been before.

Everything changed when Colleen fell. Was pushed. Prudence saw the incidents with the hansom cab and the slowly escaping gas not as attempts to kill her, but as warnings. She was getting too close to someone's truth. Her visit to Dr. Worthington had stirred up the embers of a case that had never been anything but cold. She wondered if she and Geoffrey had been followed to Warneke and Sons. Colleen was nearly killed on the same day she had taken a message from Prudence to Geoffrey Hunter. If the girl had secrets, the former Pinkerton would get them out of her. Everyone knew they excelled at interrogation.

She had told Colleen to be careful, that they were being watched, but she had not been able then to imagine the consequences of the threads she was following, the knots she was determined to unravel. There was an excitement to puzzling out the truth of people and events; it reminded her of the evenings she had spent dissecting case histories with her father. What else was she to do with the skills those hours had taught her? Her next challenge was the notebook written in code that she had found in the attic.

She had stared at its pages repeatedly since she'd pried it out of the secret drawer of the rolltop desk. Every mark on every page had been made by her father. Of that she had no doubt. But the combination of numbers and letters was indecipherable, though she thought she had finally detected a pattern. What the notebook contained seemed to be the briefest possible record of every major case Thomas MacKenzie had argued or adjudicated once he rose to the bench. Initials instead of names. Dates expressed in numerals. Other sets of numbers that repeated themselves so often, she was sure they were codes for a type of crime and the verdict, perhaps also a fine or length of imprisonment.

She had no idea why this record of defendants and cases was important, only the conviction that her father would not have gone to such trouble to conceal it unless there was some great secret hidden away for no one else but his daughter to find.

Prudence brought the oil lamp from her bedside to the dressing table, where the notebook pages could lie in a pool of bright yellow light between it and the lamp by which she had examined her face. She turned up the flow from the reservoir; the kerosene sputtered slightly and the flame flickered. There was a moment's dizziness as she bent too near the clear glass chimney. She held her breath, waved away the sudden updraft of smoke and odor of burning oil. She could feel the heat on her cheeks, but she had to have light, had to be able to make out the faintest marks on the papers before her. Something was hidden there, some message she had to find and decipher.

The first few pages looked as though the Judge had not worked out his code before penning the lines that were frequently scratched through and rewritten. The sets of numbers Prudence thought must be dates were frequently blacked out or rearranged, page after page of blotches until finally her father seemed to have settled on a pattern that pleased him. Clearly a pattern, but one of which she could make no sense. What she took to be numbers indicating months, days, and years did not fall into recognizable sets of dates when she tried to separate them or match one against another.

She wrote out a string of numbers from one to thirty-one, another set from one to twelve, and a third set from the year the Judge had begun to practice law. Over and over she replaced a number he had written with one from her list, crumpling and throwing into the fireplace one sheet of letter paper after another. Nothing made any sense at all. No matter how many times she tried, she could not make a set of numbers unscramble itself into a recognizable date that fit logically into what she knew had to be a chronology of cases. She only gave up when her eyes began to tear from working too long and too close to the kerosene lamps.

When she looked at herself in the mirror again, she saw a smoke- and ink-smudged face staring back at her, bleary features around which hung wandering wisps of pale brown hair floating in the updraft from the gas lamps. The last thing in the world she wanted to do was admit defeat, but this code had purely done her in. Mr. Hunter would have to find some ancient expert from the war days who could crack it. Prudence could do no more.

Wearily, she gathered the sheets of paper on which her father had recorded his secrets, scattered them once again between the pages of *Uncle Tom's Cabin,* and replaced the volume in her bookshelf. She stirred the fire to reduce to ash every bit of paper she had burned, then turned off the lamp on her dressing table, placed the other lamp beside her bed, and lowered the flame until there was only the faintest hint of light in the room. It felt safe to open the drapes in the near darkness; she would not be outlined in the window to anyone who happened to be passing by in the street below. Fifth Avenue was usually deserted this late at night except for the occasional carriage returning homeward from a restaurant or a private ball.

The sight of the empty street awoke a feeling of bittersweet nostalgia, a calming prelude to dreams. *Say good night to the world,* her father had said when he came into this very room to tuck her in. *Say good night to Mama, Prudence. She's watching over you from heaven.* She had believed, when he twitched back the drape for a moment and moonlight flooded across her bed, that her absent mother was indeed hovering beside her bed. Even now she had a sense of Sarah in the darkness that she never had in daylight. Only now Sarah was not alone. The Judge stood behind her, one hand resting on his wife's shoulder.

Donald Morley hadn't set foot inside Billy McGlory's Armory Hall since the day Victoria married the Judge. She had warned him off in terms he didn't care to dispute. The day he paid his fifteen cents and walked into the Irishman's saloon was the day he'd never get another penny from her, the day she'd throw his clothes out into the street and lock her doors against him. She meant every word of it. Victoria didn't make idle threats, just promises she always kept. He'd never in his life be able to have things as soft on his own as he did feeding off his sister's teat, and he knew it. He wasn't as smart as she was. He was bigger, stronger, and he could beat a man to death with his bare fists if he had a mind to, but he couldn't come up with the kinds of schemes that were second nature to Victoria, the very best of which had been her capture of the Judge.

"We need to retire," she'd told Donald. "You're too stupid and I'm getting too tired to keep on the way we've been doing. It's time to get out of the game for good, before one or the other of us makes the mistake that'll end it in a way we don't want."

"What's that?" he'd asked curiously. It was the first time she'd said anything about quitting.

"In jail or hanging at the end of a rope."

"I'd rather be shot," he said thoughtfully. "But only by somebody with good aim. I don't want my throat cut. I don't like the gurgling sound."

She'd snorted at him the way she always did when she wanted to let you know what she really thought of you, but it didn't bother him. Nothing Victoria did or said could hurt because he knew deep down that nothing could ever come between them. Nothing and nobody. Which is why, when she told him that the only solution she could see was to marry some rich and re-spectable man of a certain age, he too thought it a fine idea.

It never entered his head for a moment that marriage might change her, that she might start to take respectability seriously. She'd hopped in and out of too many beds for him to suspect that the power of money would make her think seriously about turning herself into a lady. Sow's ear into silk purse. When she wanted it, Victoria was a bitch in heat; it just so happened that most of the time now she had other things on her mind. She didn't seem to miss the wild life they had led, but Donald did. He missed it dreadfully. Playing the gentleman for too long made him restless and careless. He just had to keep Victoria from finding out what he was doing.

Now he stood on the corner of Hester Street wondering if he dared take the last few steps into McGlory's concert saloon.

Other places in the city tried to compete with Billy; Donald had visited nearly every one of them. No other saloonkeeper could match McGlory's flair for balancing on the razor edge of what his customers wanted and the police would allow before shutting him down.

Donald had danced in McGlory's with men and boys of all shapes and sizes, skin tones and races. He'd fondled the Africans who waited on clients in the private booths and watched breathlessly the wrestling matches where dark oiled skin rippled in the lamplight and a tiny pouch was the only bit of clothing worn. He liked tanned white skin, too, as long as it was young and unwrinkled, blond hair that reminded him of sunlight, and blue eyes. They smelled differently, the two races, and sometimes Donald was in the mood to taste one, sometimes the other. It was like deciding whether you wanted steak or chicken for your dinner, oysters or shrimp. All of them delicious. Donald seldom hurt anyone he paid and he never wondered at the morality of the commerce. He did what he did without a care for what the preachers called sin. He'd been born without an innate sense of right and wrong; what you're born without, you can't grow.

He'd go to the Haymarket on Sixth Avenue and Twenty-ninth Street, he decided, hailing a hansom cab that had just unloaded a party of happy drunks in front of Armory Hall. It was a different crowd, but one in which he dared show his face without having to worry about Victoria finding out. She'd hammered it into him until he knew the reason he had to avoid Billy's place as well as he knew his own name. Neither one of them wanted to chance McGlory's seeing him and being reminded of what Victoria had managed to get out of him. The Irishman was notoriously unpredictable when it came to things like that. He could shrug you off or order your throat slit. Just for the hell of it.

Donald was enjoying life too much to want to chance leaving it with the taste of a knife and a fountain of his own blood cascading onto his chest. He settled himself into the cab and looked back longingly one last time at the Armory. He didn't see what difference it made now that the Judge was dead, but Victoria was peculiar in some ways.

Still, it wasn't fair that she could order him to do the things she did and then not allow him a little bit of fun afterward.

Donald never saw the man who detached himself from the shadows outside Armory Hall as soon as his hansom cab turned the corner. With a nod to one of the ex-boxers working the door, he went inside to report to McGlory that Morley had been back again. Alone, as usual.

Their man at the Haymarket would shadow him for the rest of the night.

CHAPTER 17

"There's no one I can send with a message," Prudence said. "Except perhaps for young Frank. He went to Mr. Hunter's hotel once before for me, the afternoon Colleen fell."

"Getting an answer would take time, miss." Kincaid began hitching the pair of grays to the small calèche that could be drawn by one or both of the horses. "I can get you to Mr. Conkling's and be back here before either Mrs. MacKenzie or Mr. Morley is ready to go out this morning."

"I don't want to get you into trouble," she persisted.

"The lads need their exercise, Miss Prudence. I always take them around Central Park a time or two early every morning anyway. To get them ready for the day, so to speak. Nobody from the house has ever questioned me on it. So we'll slip you into the calèche from the stable side with no one the wiser if you don't mind crouching down a bit until we're out of sight."

"I'll do that," she said, smiling enthusiastically. It was like playing hide-and-seek when she was a child. Only now she would have to be much more careful not to be found. The game had turned dangerous.

She glanced toward the kitchen window, saw no one watching, then moved quickly around to the hidden side of the calèche and climbed in.

She knew she had nothing to fear from Donald Morley; she'd awakened in the wee hours of the morning to hear him stumble up the stairs. Most likely he'd not be out of his bed until well into the afternoon. She'd primed German Clara to inform Victoria that Miss Prudence was indisposed and would keep to her room. With any luck at all, the lie wouldn't be discovered. She'd have to figure out some way to deal with the consequences if Victoria decided to pay a visit to her stepdaughter, but she pushed that out of her mind.

The pages of the notebook she had found in the rolltop desk were burning a hole in her skirt pocket. She had tried to decipher them herself, then sent Colleen to Geoffrey Hunter's hotel suite with the message that she needed to meet with him. That was the afternoon Colleen had been pushed down the stairs. Even in the confusion of getting her safely out of the house, Prudence had not dared try to pass the pages to Hunter. Last night, after rereading her mother's letters, she had tried one final time to decipher the Judge's code, finally admitting defeat.

It was time to ask for help, time also to see with her own eyes how Colleen was faring.

Time to take another chance.

"Mr. Hunter is on his way," Josiah had told Prudence thirty minutes ago, putting down the receiver of the telephone that was changing the world of business as much as the advent of electricity. Voices over wires and instant light. What would be next? Horseless carriages? "Mr. Conkling is just finishing a brief."

"I don't mind waiting. There's no need to interrupt him until Mr. Hunter gets here." Prudence had waited patiently in the outer office, studying the notebook pages yet again, wondering why Conkling's devoted secretary seemed so distracted, so pale and drawn, as if he hadn't slept well in days. When Conkling brought out the finished brief and then ushered her into a seat beside his desk, she understood.

The ex-senator, as famed for his obsession with physical fitness as he was for his lawyering skills and his love affairs, was plainly suffering from fever, the skin above his full, bushy black beard as red as though he had overexerted himself in the hot sun of summer. His breath was raspy, short, every inhalation an effort; she detected a foulness to it that smelled like the pus of a lanced boil. The rigid military posture on which he prided himself had deserted him. He sat at his desk with rounded back and hunched shoulders.

"You'll need to lean on Geoffrey in the days to come, my dear," he mumbled.

"Should you be in the office, Mr. Conkling? You don't sound well."

"Not to worry. Josiah is pouring all kinds of concoctions down me. One of them is bound to work."

"Perhaps if you saw a doctor?"

"They're quacks, all of them," Conkling complained, making an obvious effort to appear better than he felt. "Now tell me what this is that Josiah says you've found."

Prudence laid the notebook pages on Roscoe's desk, fanning them out so he could see the Judge's distinctive ink and style of handwriting. She tapped a gloved forefinger on the pages. "I can't make heads or tails of it. I'm completely stymied. What do you think?"

Even at a glance, even through the haze of fever, Roscoe could tell that the jumble of letters and numbers couldn't be read in the normal way of things. "I'd rather wait for Geoffrey, if you don't mind. He's had more experience with this sort of thing than I have. Code, is it?"

"Yes, and I have no idea how to break it."

"Break what, Miss MacKenzie?"

Geoffrey Hunter breezed into Conkling's office just as Josiah appeared with a tray of translucent china cups, hot water, cream, sugar, and a pot of freshly made coffee. He placed a small silver dish of his own delicious chocolates on his employer's desk; he was that worried about him. As unobtrusive as a shadow, he faded into a corner of the office, stenographer's pad in one hand, sharpened pencil in the other.

"Before you answer my question, Miss MacKenzie, I think you should decide which of us will tell Mr. Conkling about the gas."

"What gas?" Roscoe asked.

"Colleen wasn't supposed to say anything," Prudence said.

"So she told me. Being a smart girl, and one who has a care for her mistress's safety, she knew her only choice was to disobey."

"What gas?" Roscoe repeated.

"Friday night, six days ago, there was a gas leak in my bedroom. Fortunately, something woke me up and I smelled it. I was able to open the window. Other than a fierce headache, no damage was done." Prudence raised her head defiantly, knowing she was in for a scolding for trying to keep the incident a secret.

Conkling's fever-flushed skin paled. "You could have been killed, Prudence."

"Colleen very nearly was killed."

"Who did it, Geoffrey? Do you know?" Conkling expected miracles from the man Charles Linwood had believed could solve any case, no matter how difficult.

"My money is on Donald Morley," Hunter said.

"Donald doesn't have the brains to conceive of either of the two attempts that have been made on me," Prudence said. She blushed scarlet as she realized what she had just revealed.

"Colleen told me about the gas," Geoffrey said. "I think you'd better tell us about the other one."

Josiah sat so far forward in his chair, he was in danger of

falling out of it. His pencil skittered across the page of the stenographer's notebook.

"It came to nothing," Prudence said. She sighed deeply and squared her shoulders. "At times I believe I really felt something; then I decide I must have been imagining it."

"You won't make a good lawyer unless you can marshal your facts," Conkling chided.

"It was after I'd left Dr. Worthington's office and was walking down Fifth Avenue on my way here. That was a week ago today." She described the feeling of being viciously prodded in the knees by something that felt like a cane or the pointed end of an umbrella, recounted in vivid terms the near fall, even cited what the woman beside her had said about lacing her stays too tightly.

"So when you looked around, you saw nothing?" Geoffrey asked.

"Nothing. And no one I recognized."

"Donald Morley," Geoffrey said through clenched teeth. "He's the only one who could have followed you from the house to Dr. Worthington's office without being missed. I know how those crowds on Fifth Avenue can be. He could easily have slipped away before you turned around."

"I think you're wrong about Donald. I don't like him, I don't trust him, and I'm afraid of him. There, I've said it. But he's a brute, Mr. Hunter, and a stupid one to boot. Whoever tried to push me in front of a hansom cab and gas me in my sleep had to think through his plans before putting them into action. Donald isn't capable of anything nearly that involved."

"You can't go back to that house, Prudence," Conkling declared. "I won't allow it."

"Victoria is my guardian; I'm sure she'll have something to say about that."

"You want to go back, don't you?"

"I don't understand everything that has happened, but I do know there are mysteries I have to solve, and only one place where I can find the clues Mr. Hunter tells me we need to prove my stepmother guilty of moral turpitude. I'm only valuable if I'm alive, Mr. Conkling. You've told me so yourself. So I wasn't pushed in front of a hansom cab until there was a crowd around to save me, and not enough gas was released into my room to do more than give me a pounding headache. Don't you see? I'm being warned off. Nothing more than that. Someone wants me to stop asking questions, someone is afraid of what Maurice Warneke and Dr. Worthington might tell me. I'm safer than my father was or Charles. I'm worth a great deal of money alive. I have no value at all as a corpse."

The skritch of Josiah's pencil was the only sound in the silent room until Hunter stood up and walked to the window overlooking Wall Street. He stood there for what seemed forever to Prudence, then he turned around and retook his seat by Conkling's desk.

"I heard something about a code we have to break. Tell me about it, Miss MacKenzie," he said.

"I found a small notebook hidden in a secret drawer of a rolltop desk belonging to my father. It had been stored in the attic for years, though I don't think I could tell you exactly how many."

"How did you find this secret drawer? And how did you know to look for it?" Except for one piercing glance at Conkling, Hunter concentrated all of his attention on Prudence.

"I remembered playing under it as a child. I could see my father's feet. He showed me where the drawer was and how to open it. He told me I could put my jacks there for whenever I wanted to play with them while he was working."

"Do you think it was your father who hid the notebook?"

"It had to have been. He and I were the only two who knew about the hidden drawer. He had to have concealed it so I would find it. I and no one else. I think he slipped it into its hiding place recently, Mr. Hunter. Perhaps when he knew he was dying. Until then he must have kept it on his person."

"Could there be other secret places in the house, Miss MacKenzie? In the Judge's study, perhaps?"

"I'm sure there are. I just haven't found them yet."

Hunter picked up the notebook pages that looked absurdly small in his large hand. The entire notebook could easily have fit in one of the inside pockets of a man's jacket.

"I think it's a record of all the important cases my father argued as a lawyer or presided over when he became a judge. There are sets of numbers that must be dates, clusters of letters that represent names, and a mixture of the two to indicate the type of crime, the verdicts, and the sentences. I tried the simplest, most logical substitution I could think of, but it doesn't work. No matter how many variations I attempted, the numbers and the letters wouldn't unscramble themselves."

Hunter listened to her with undivided attention, nodding his head as she explained her reasoning. "I doubt I could have done any better, Miss MacKenzie, and I've seen dozens of different codes. You're undoubtedly right about the information on these pages, right too about the Judge hiding the notebook recently. He's using a different pen on the last few pages. Look."

Geoffrey laid six pages side by side on Roscoe's desk. Josiah handed him a magnifying glass. The handwriting seemed to leap off the paper, and now it was obvious that different writing instruments had been used. "Here, on the first pages, he's using a dip pen; you can see where excess ink has accumulated at the tip of the nib. I'll have to leave this part to the experts, but I think it likely the formula for the ink he's using changes over time. Look at the last page now. Do you see the difference?"

"He bought himself a Waterman fountain pen with a gold nib. I read the advertisement in one of his legal directories. We laughed about it together because he knew it was bound to leak, but it was too beautiful to resist. That was only a year or so before he died. He and I had begun to work together in the evenings again, in his study. He was turning down invitations, for health reasons, he said, encouraging Donald to take his place as Victoria's escort. They were out of the house several evenings a week."

"Did you ever write with the Waterman? Josiah has been after me to buy the latest model, but I don't want ink all over my fingers." Conkling's breathing became labored as he leaned over the notebook pages, magnifying glass in hand. It eased when he straightened, and some of the flush faded from his face.

"Many times. There's a ladies' model, you know, much smaller than the business version. Father hinted he would be giving me one for my birthday if I liked his. Which I did. I became very adept with the dropper that's used to fill the reservoir."

Hunter laid out more of the tightly written pages, examining them with a second magnifying glass that Josiah brought from his desk in the outer office. He settled on several pages from near the beginning and then the last page, arranging the rest of them in a neat pile held in place by a crystal paperweight bearing the seal of the United States Senate.

"Miss MacKenzie, look at these pages and tell me what you see." Suppressed excitement twitched at the corners of Geoffrey Hunter's smile.

Prudence took her time before answering, moving her glass back and forth between the pages. When she looked up, they were all staring at her. Hunter looked triumphant, as if a prize pupil were about to perform, while Josiah and Roscoe appeared puzzled and not a little put out. They'd examined the same pages but had noted nothing unusual.

"The entries on these earlier pages were written with a dip pen, but the underlining was added later. I recognize the kind of stroke the Waterman creates. Sometime after he began to use the fountain pen and when he hid the notebook, the Judge went back through what he'd written and underlined some of the entries. The important ones. The ones he wanted me to notice. They tell a story, if we could decipher them."

"Josiah, will you send someone down to Trinity Church to see if Danny Dennis and his hansom cab are available?"

"I'll go myself, Mr. Hunter. He won't ask questions if it's me, and he'll come right away."

"There's someone I'd like you to meet, Miss MacKenzie. I think he may be the only man in New York City who can break your father's code. And then afterward, if you want, I can take you to see Colleen. Mrs. Dailey's boardinghouse is only a few blocks away from my codebreaker."

"I'd like that very much, Mr. Hunter."

Conkling sat down heavily in his chair. "I have to be in court again tomorrow, Geoffrey, so I'll leave Prudence in your capable hands. I'm afraid I'll need Josiah to put together the papers for the morning."

Prudence stepped to Roscoe's side, leaning over to kiss him lightly on the cheek. "You are very kind and quite right to think of my reputation, Mr. Conkling, but I'm sure Mr. Hunter and I will manage very well without a chaperone." She smiled as she said it, but Roscoe's skin was hot to the touch; she could feel the burn of his fever lingering on her lips. "We won't leave until Josiah returns. And then I think I shall encourage him to order you to bed."

"There's nothing wrong with me. I have work to do."

"You may think you're successfully fighting off a chill from your famous walk up Broadway, but if you don't rest it's bound to develop into something far more serious."

"I have a case to plead."

"Will you at least forego Delmonico's for one night?"

"Going to bed early is for old men."

"I rest my case." Prudence smiled as she said it, but she knew he could read the worry in her eyes.

"I'll have him out of here and in his bed within the hour, Miss MacKenzie," Josiah said from the doorway. "There's to be no arguing, Mr. Conkling. It won't do your client any good if you collapse in court." He gathered up the notebook pages, put them into a sturdy brown envelope, and handed it to the Judge's daughter. "Danny is waiting downstairs. He says you can have him and Mr. Washington for as long as you need them."

"Mr. Washington?"

"The horse." With a last glance back at Conkling, Geoffrey ushered Prudence out of the lawyer's office.

"Wait," she said. "Is he really all right, Josiah?"

"No. He's not. He knows it and so do I, but we keep up the pretense."

"What can I do? Shall I send Dr. Worthington to him?"

"He's already been. Mr. Conkling is not the most cooperative of patients."

"He has amazing recuperative powers. My father said he never missed a day in the Senate or in court."

"You don't want to keep Danny and Mr. Washington waiting, miss."

Impulsively, she raised herself on tiptoe and kissed Josiah Gregory's clean-shaven cheek. "Promise you'll send a messenger if he worsens."

He nodded, too touched by her kindness and too genuinely frightened to be able to say a word.

By the time Danny Dennis's hansom cab was making its way across the Brooklyn Bridge, Hunter and Prudence had thoroughly reviewed what they had learned at the Dakota and at Billy McGlory's concert saloon, trying to fit what they had found out about Victoria into the discovery of the Judge's secret notebook. It was the first opportunity they had had to talk since the afternoon of Colleen's fall. By unspoken agreement, neither mentioned the attempts to intimidate Prudence.

"He wanted me to know," she said quietly. "After everything he did to conceal it, my father then took precautions to make sure I would find out he had been accepting bribes for years. Why? There's only one answer, Mr. Hunter. Only one answer that makes any sense at all."

When she looked at him again, it was with the steely determination he'd only seen once before, across a gun barrel at the Battle of Ball's Bluff, Virginia, six months into the war. He'd fired first, but he'd never forgotten that look.

"I couldn't get Dr. Worthington to confirm it, but she was killing him, Mr. Hunter. I said it before, but if anything, I'm more sure of it than ever. She was killing him, and he knew it."

"More than that, Miss MacKenzie."

"The codicil to the will," Prudence said. "He added it without her knowledge because he realized she wouldn't be satisfied with his death, with half a fortune. She would want it all. So he made sure I was worth much more to her alive than dead. But I don't think even he realized how evil she was. He never imagined she would kill Charles also. I don't know how she managed it; I just know with every fiber of my being that somehow she did. And now Colleen has paid a terrible price for Victoria's greed."

"Conkling is right, you know. It's not safe for you to return to that house."

"Victoria thinks she can't possibly be connected to Charles's death, but she must believe Colleen saw or heard something when my father lay dying. She was in and out of the room all the time changing linens and carrying up trays. Nobody stops to think that servants hear whatever is being said until later, until it's too late to take back the words. If she believed Colleen had figured out what was done, my stepmother would also worry that she was about to sell whatever information she had. Victoria's mind works that way; she wouldn't be able to conceive of anything else."

"Did she know you'd been in the attic and in your father's rooms?"

"She saw me in the hallway, closing the door to my father's bedroom. She made a remark about someone being careless with her keys. I told her I'd found the door open and that it was the first time I'd been in there since his death."

"Do you think she believed you?"

"I wanted to think so. Then. Now I'm not sure."

"Someone had to unlock those rooms for cleaning."

"Clara does the cleaning, but Mrs. Barstow would have unlocked and then relocked them. She'd never trust her keys to Clara."

"Is it always Mrs. Barstow who unlocks those rooms? Are you sure?"

"Let me think." Prudence closed her eyes, trying to visualize the second-floor hallway. Waxed wooden floors laid with oriental runners, gaslights interspersed with landscape paintings at regular intervals along the walls, narrow tables holding decorative Chinese vases. Mirrors above the tables. She saw German Clara approaching the Judge's suite, watched her turn and stand for a moment with broom in hand, dusting cloths draped over her arm. Another maid appeared, said something, took a ring of keys from her apron pocket. It was Colleen, Colleen taking Mrs. Barstow's place on a cold winter's morning when the housekeeper's knees were swollen and painful. Victoria had already left the house, she remembered, else Colleen would never have been given the keys. Prudence wondered how many times the housekeeper had sent Colleen in her place to unlock those upstairs rooms. "No, it hasn't always been Mrs. Barstow. She has bad knees that bother her in cold weather. I saw Colleen with the housekeeper's keys at least once. There may have been other times as well."

"It's what Victoria believes that's important."

"My poor father. He cared so much for his honor and for mine. He allowed himself to be trapped into a loveless marriage to save me from disgrace and ruin. He knew what it would mean for me if what he had done became common knowledge, if he were removed from the bench and not allowed to practice law anymore. No decent home would be open to either of us, and no son would be allowed to marry me. He might have felt he would have to take his own life rather than live it as an outcast. And if the daughter of a crooked judge shared his shame, then how much worse if she were also the child of a suicide. Once Victoria had her claws in him, there was no escape."

"None."

"Do you think your cryptographer will be able to decode the notebook pages?"

"I'll let you decide that for yourself. We're here."

Benjamin Truitt and his widowed daughter, Lydia, lived in a narrow, three-story brownstone within walking distance of the part of the Hudson River called the Narrows. A park stretched from the street down to the shore, tall trees just beginning to leaf out, patches of daffodils and dandelions dotting the green grass with yellow stars. Which Benjamin Truitt hadn't been able to see for years. He was blind.

"My father will be so happy you're here again, Mr. Hunter," Lydia Truitt said. She ushered them toward the many-windowed back parlor where Benjamin spent most of every spring day enjoying the feel of the sun on his face. He was always chilled. The shell whose concussive blast took his sight in the early days of the war had also deprived his frail body of its ability to regulate heat and cold. "I hope the code you're bringing him this time is more challenging than the last one."

"It once took him a day and a half to break what the Pinkerton Detective Agency gave up on after three of their best operatives worked on it for a month," Geoffrey explained to Prudence.

"Don't tell tales on me, Geoffrey," came a strong voice from the end of the hallway.

"He has ears like a fox," Lydia whispered.

"Like a bat," the voice corrected. "Though I'll admit the fox is better looking."

The man who stood up to greet them was small, slender, bent with the pain of shattered bones badly knit together, but his thick red hair was as bright and full as a much younger man's.

He looked, Prudence thought irreverently, like a caricature of an Irish leprechaun. Without the freckles. And wearing smoked glasses to hide the blankness of eyes that could not see.

"We'll have tea, Lydia. And some of those cookies you baked this morning."

"How are you, Ben?" Geoffrey held both the codebreaker's hands in his own, bending his head to hear a whispered question. "He'd like permission to touch your face. Just briefly."

It felt, Prudence thought, as though a butterfly wing had brushed her cheek, that quickly and lightly did Ben's crooked forefinger touch her skin. She closed her eyes and sensed something passing across her lids, her nose, her lips. Passing, but not touching, as if it were enough for the blind man to allow his hand to hover an inch above what he was examining.

"Thank you," he breathed. "You're a very beautiful young woman, Miss Prudence. You don't mind if I call you that, do you?"

"Not at all." She suddenly remembered that in the coach, when they were talking about her father, Mr. Hunter had also called her by her name. Inadvertently, of course. He hadn't noticed he'd done it. She felt warmth in her cheeks and quickly ducked her head.

"I'm not a very good baker," Lydia said, pouring tea and handing around a plate of sugar cookies, "but Father insists these are worth eating."

"What have you brought me, Geoffrey? Something out of the ordinary, I hope."

"I'm going to let Prudence tell you, Ben. She found the documents and she's done at least as well as I could have to parse out what the subject matter must be."

"I found a leather-bound notebook hidden in a secret drawer of a desk that belonged to my father," Prudence began. "The entries are all in his handwriting. I think, no, I'm sure they represent a record he kept of the cases he argued when he was practicing law and the trials on which he sat as the presiding judge. But the groupings of letters and numbers don't make sense. I've tried every substitution I could manage, but nothing has worked."

"Read them to me, Lydia."

For the next half hour, Lydia painstakingly read each entry letter by letter, numeral by numeral, including any spaces between. Benjamin nodded from time to time, sipped his tea, chewed thoughtfully on half a dozen sugar cookies. When his daughter finished reading the last page, she poured a healthy dollop of whiskey into his cup and offered the bottle around the table. Only Geoffrey accepted.

"I don't see the pattern yet," Benjamin said.

"Perhaps there isn't one."

"There's always a pattern, my dear Prudence. Man can't help himself. He seeks to impose order on chaos and to understand the incomprehensible."

Lydia fastened a sheet of exceptionally thick paper to a metal slate with four rows of precisely spaced rectangles cut through the metal. She picked up a sharply pointed stylus whose round wooden handle fit snugly into the palm of her hand. As Prudence and Geoffrey watched, she punched holes through the rectangles, quick taps with the stylus that sounded like heavy drops of rain against a windowpane.

"She's creating a Braille copy for me to read with my fingertips," Benjamin explained. The tiny pops were background to his description of what the Braille system of raised dots had come to mean to so many blind persons. "Even with a memory sharpened by years of training my mind to picture what my eyes can't see, there are times when I need the absolute certainty of what Lydia copies for me in Braille. It's demanding work, but she's very good at it. Changing the position of even one of the raised dots can alter the meaning of a word."

"You said you hadn't discerned a pattern in what your daughter read to you." Prudence could hardly take her eyes off Lydia's precise tapping.

"There are patterns. But on a first reading I couldn't make sense of them."

"What will you do?"

"Very much what other cryptographers *don't* do, Miss Prudence. I shall let my brain work independently of every other sense. I'll suspend the coded pages in mental midair, if you can imagine such a thing, and fix my attention on them."

"It looks like sleeping," Lydia commented, never breaking the even tap tapping of the steel stylus.

"And sometimes it is," agreed her father. "But most often it's akin to mesmerism, although the more modern term is *hypnosis*. To put it as simply as possible, I put myself into a trance and live there with the code I'm trying to break. Associations and suggestions occur to me that otherwise wouldn't. I then examine them in a normal waking state, and almost always find the first clue that allows me to break the code. If I still had my sight, I'd be limited by what I could see. I'd spend hours poring over lines and squiggles, trying to force them into logical forms and patterns."

"That's what I was doing with the substitutions I tried."

"Exactly. That's a useful exercise if the code is simple, but for anything complex, disassociation from method can sometimes bring surprisingly useful results."

"And if the code is a substitution based on certain portions or words in an already existing text?" Geoffrey shook his head, remembering a code that had been based on a wildly popular book by Mark Twain, *The Adventures of Tom Sawyer*.

"I know the one you're thinking of," Ben said. "And I can tell you now the clue that broke that code was a mental picture that came entirely unbidden when I'm sure Lydia thought I was asleep in my chair."

"Tom whitewashing the fence?"

"Too obvious, Geoff. Our code creator thought the scene where Tom redeems the Bible verse tickets was the dullest in the book, and therefore the least likely to stick in anyone's brain. But Twain has a rhythm to what he writes, and it was the rhythm that came through the substitutions. I saw Tom Sawyer standing in front of the Sunday School superintendent as clear as if I were there myself."

"Why would someone writing in code pick a book that's so popular? Why not something obscure that few people have heard of? Wouldn't that make the cracking much more difficult?"

"It would, Miss Prudence. But your code writer needs a book that's not likely to draw attention to itself by its rarity. It also has to be readily available wherever the recipient of the messages happens to be. What Lydia read to me doesn't fit the kind of rhythm I can usually sense when a book passage is used."

The blind man reached out with unerring accuracy and lightly touched Prudence's hand. "Don't worry, Miss Prudence. Your father wanted you to know what he'd written, and now so do I."

"She's no better, Miss Prudence, but she's no worse either. That's something to be grateful for."

"It's good of you to take her in, Mrs. Dailey."

"Colleen was always a sweet, hardworking child. I remember when her mother brought her to the kitchen door. You couldn't hardly tell which of the two of them was going to break down crying first."

"I'll sit here by her for a while, if I may."

"You drink that cup of tea I brought you, miss. No matter how bad things are, they always look better over a nice cup of hot tea. Call out if anything happens. We'll hear you in the parlor."

"How much longer can she remain like this?"

"I don't know, Miss Prudence. The doctor shrugged his shoulders when I asked. She swallows water and the broth I spoon into her mouth, but that's the best that can be done."

Mrs. Dailey eased the door not quite closed, whispered a quick prayer to Saint Jude, and rejoined Cameron and Geoffrey Hunter in the parlor.

"I didn't want to leave Kathleen alone with Colleen in such a bad way," Ian Cameron was saying. His arm crept around Mrs. Dailey's still-slender waist when she sat down next to him on the silk upholstered sofa.

"I told him to go ahead, that I'd be fine here. Every single one of the boarders has volunteered to help. We held a meeting. You have an army of five former butlers and four retired housekeepers at your disposal, Mr. Hunter. They may not be young and limber anymore, but there's nothing they don't know about ferreting out secrets. The stories they can tell! Not naming any names, of course, but we all know who the other person is talking about."

"I need information about Victoria MacKenzie. McGlory knew her as Ronnie, short for Veronica, she told him. He recognized Donald Morley in the wedding photo, but not the name. Apparently, she was always accompanied by her brother when she came to Armory Hall. Which she did only until she'd gotten the information she wanted out of McGlory."

"She used him."

"But he let her get away with it, Ian. That doesn't sound very much like the Billy McGlory we've all heard about." Mrs. Dailey hesitated, then made up her mind. "If you're Irish, like I am, Mr. Hunter, every Irish name in the newspaper jumps out at you. You're constantly on watch for the ones who've gone bad. When I first came to this country, there were signs everywhere I looked. *No Irish Need Apply.* To make the sentiment even plainer, they'd put a *No Dogs Allowed* sign right beside it.

"So when there's an Irishman like McGlory giving all the rest of us a reputation as drunkards and criminals, you follow the stories about him. There's a terrible fascination about it because you know that as soon as you have to give your name or someone recognizes the brogue, you'll be tarred with the same

brush. I know a lot about Billy McGlory, and I've ways of finding out more. He wouldn't let Victoria MacKenzie disappear,
no matter what he claims. He set someone to keep an eye on
her, you can be sure of that. And that someone is bound to have
left a trail. Leave it to me. My army and I have more informants
than General Grant ever did."

"She's awake. Colleen is awake." Prudence stood in the
doorway, tears streaming down her face. "She's awake, and she
remembers."

CHAPTER 18

A corked brown bottle of laudanum sat on Prudence's bedside table. She had found it waiting for her yesterday evening when she returned from Mrs. Dailey's boardinghouse in Danny Dennis's hansom cab.

Jackson answered her ring, polite and distant, but with an ill-disguised curiosity in his flat yellow eyes. She had waited until Danny and Mr. Washington were out of sight before climbing the steps to her front door; when Victoria's butler looked out into the street they had vanished. It wasn't his place to question where she had gone or how she had gotten there, but the need to know was easy to read in the purse of his thin-lipped mouth.

"Mrs. MacKenzie is in the parlor, miss. She asked that you join her there as soon as you got home."

She'd answered with a nod, then gone straight up to her room. Where she'd seen the laudanum bottle and knew it had been placed there by Victoria. Knew the direction her step-mother had decided to take in their undeclared war. Knew, too, as she touched the brown bottle with one tentative finger, that if she let even a single drop of the lovely liquid trickle down her throat, she was as good as doomed. A Prudence addicted to lau-danum was a Prudence under Victoria's complete control. So strong a word as *addicted* was never used when referring to the ladies whose lives were ruled by the drug, but Prudence needed the stark truth of it to keep up her guard. Laudanum was an enemy that had to be fought every day and every moment; there was no truce with it, no halfhearted tolerance.

Prudence had taken a deep breath, then pulled the cork from the bottle and measured out a dose into the spoon left conveniently for her use. She stirred the laudanum and a small amount of water in her night glass, poured the mixture into the pot of violets sitting on her dressing table. The odor of the drug hung in the air; she left the unrinsed glass with the spoon inside it in plain view beside the recorked bottle and lay down on her bed fully clothed.

Twenty minutes later she heard a soft knock, the click of her bedroom door opening. Victoria's sweet perfume overlay the lingering scent of laudanum. She heard her name whispered, then the door closed again. She wasn't hungry; Mrs. Dailey had insisted on more tea and sandwiches before she and Geoffrey left Brooklyn. She would lie on her bed and think; let them believe downstairs that she'd sunk into a laudanum-induced slumber and slept through dinner. *Disarm your opponent by encouraging him to believe he's on the verge of winning,* the Judge had told her, the grin of Lewis Carroll's Cheshire cat lighting up his face, *then pounce when he least expects it.*

Breakfast the next morning was a silent meal, Prudence hardly raising her eyes from her coffee cup, eating the food served her with feigned indifference. Victoria chattered over her morning let-ters. Donald shoveled eggs, bacon, toast, and fried potatoes into his mouth as fast as he could chew and swallow, washing every-thing down with large gulps of heavily sugared and creamed coffee.

"I hope you're rested, my dear," Victoria purred. "I'm sure our recent contretemps upset you more than you realized. I myself had a terrible headache from it." She sliced open an invitation, clucked happily to herself, then set it aside. "We'll have to replace Colleen as soon as possible. I'll write to the agency this morning."

"Shall I deliver the letter for you?" Donald asked. The waiting rooms of domestic employment agencies were more often than not full of desperate young women hoping for an interview.

"I'll send Jackson or Mrs. Barstow," snapped Victoria. More and more lately, Donald had the self-satisfied look about him of a cat who's been too well fed.

"Will you spend a quiet day at home, Prudence? I'm sure Dr. Worthington or Mr. Hunter will let us know when poor Colleen has passed on."

"Yes, I think I shall. I'd like to finish up in my father's study."

"Have you found anything interesting?" Donald's eyes glinted for a moment with an emotion she couldn't identify.

"I haven't really looked," she answered. "I believe there are photo albums on one of the lower shelves and the desk drawers are rather full."

"I didn't mean that you should hurry yourself unduly, my dear." A slime of egg yolk had hardened into a streak of yellow across Donald's chin.

"It may take me a while to sort through whatever's there and box up what I find." She sounded disoriented and confused even to herself.

"I'll send Clara in to light the fire. You can burn what you don't intend to keep." Victoria's smug look told her there wouldn't be much to discover. "I know I was reluctant to let you do this at first, Prudence, but I think now that it might be a good thing after all. It's terribly painful, but it's also the way we let go."

What was she talking about? Not a single item of the Judge's clothing had been removed from closet or drawer. His expensive jewelry hadn't been touched. Even the massive gold watch lay where he had placed it the last time he took it off. *Donald. It was all for Donald.* A tailor would be summoned to the house. Alterations would be made. The gold timepiece would be nestled into Donald's vest pocket, its worked chain stretched across his chest. The thought of it made Prudence want to pound her fists on the table like a child having a temper tantrum.

She stood up, knocking over her half-empty coffee cup, stared at the brown stain spreading across the tablecloth. Without another word to her stepmother or the man who was planning to possess everything the Judge had once enjoyed, she left the room. *I'm walking in my sleep, I'm walking in my sleep,* she reminded herself, leaving the dining room door open after she had passed through.

"It's the laudanum," she heard Victoria hiss.

"How much?"

"I don't know. It doesn't matter. I left a bottle beside her bed, and when that one's empty, another will take its place. She'll do the rest herself."

What Colleen had remembered was the feel of a fist in the small of her back as she was propelled forward, lost her balance, and fell with terrifying speed down the narrow stairwell. Nothing to hold on to to break her fall, nothing to soften the hard edges of the steps against which she tumbled. She'd heard someone scream, and realized it was her own voice echoing down into the floor below. Then nothing. Nothing at all until she awoke in the softest bed she'd ever slept in, Miss Prudence sitting beside her, every muscle in her body aching as though some evil child had beaten her senseless with a baseball bat.

She had wept with the pain and the gentle kindness being

shown her, fallen asleep again within minutes of awakening. Asleep, not unconscious. There was a difference, Dr. Worthington had explained, not holding out much hope for natural sleep when he'd first examined Colleen. When Prudence left, Mrs. Dailey had been sitting at the maid's bedside, rosary beads slipping through her fingers as she counted off the decades, head nodding in rhythm with Colleen's breathing. She'd have a nice bowl of hot soup waiting when the child woke up.

"I'd hoped for more," Geoffrey said on the ride back across the Brooklyn Bridge. "I'd hoped that she might have glimpsed her attacker's face as she fell."

"She was certain it was a fist, though. She said she'd been punched often enough growing up to know when she was being hit."

"You were hit, Miss MacKenzie. Struck across the back of the knees hard enough to make them buckle."

"Prodded. I could feel the point of the cane or the umbrella, whichever it was. Even through my skirts."

"It's the similarity that's bothering me. An attacker grows comfortable with a certain type of assault. He does the same thing over and over again. It becomes his modus operandi and one of the tools police use to track him down."

"Are you saying that the same man who came up behind me on Fifth Avenue pushed Colleen down the stairs in my home?"

"It's possible."

"Then it can't be a stranger. It has to be someone I live with every day."

"I said once before that my money was on Donald Morley."

"Colleen was barely halfway down the stairs when she was struck. Whoever it was turned around and disappeared onto the first floor."

"Is there another staircase down into the basement?"

"No. But there is a back door that opens on to the courtyard and the stables."

"I know you believe that you're being warned off, that somehow your visits to Maurice Warneke and Dr. Worthington threaten your assailant, but his intent was clearly much more vicious where Colleen is concerned. He wanted to kill her."

"It's such a muddle, Mr. Hunter, and it's getting worse every day."

"Most cases start out simple, and end up with more twists than a hangman's rope."

"When we first talked, in Mr. Conkling's office, all I wanted was to rid myself of Victoria's hold over me. That was the simple beginning, I suppose. Then we began doubting the truth of my father's death. And Charles's. Now these attacks that seem to be coming out of nowhere."

"Pandora's box."

"That's exactly how I feel. If I'd never challenged Victoria, would all these other evils have been released out into the world?"

"You're not responsible for anyone else's actions but your own, Miss MacKenzie. You didn't cause evil to happen."

"That's something, at least."

"Stay with the simple beginning for the moment. We have to prove Victoria's direct involvement. Once we have that, everything else will fall into place."

"I'll find what we need," Prudence told him. "We already know that my father hid the notebook in a place where no one but me would think to look for it. He's left enough evidence behind for us to build a case on; he was too good a lawyer and too experienced a judge not to have figured out a way to bring Victoria to justice.

"He was passionate about the law, Mr. Hunter. You had to have known him the way I did to comprehend that. I don't pretend to understand how he could bring himself to do what he did for Billy McGlory; I can only tell you that he loved my mother more than life itself. He knew McGlory would never admit to the briberies; only by providing a list of the men who had paid the saloon keeper to have the charges against them dismissed could justice be served. Someone on that list will break, will confess to what happened. Once that information is out in the open, Victoria will be seen for the blackmailer she is. The rest of what we need has to be hidden somewhere in the house, somewhere he felt confident I would find it, but no one else. He would have known I could never surrender his study to Donald Morley without a fight, so that's where I think I'll find what else he left for me."

"I thought you'd already searched the study."

"That was a week ago, Mr. Hunter. The day after Charles's funeral. I had only just weaned myself off the laudanum, remember. For the second time. Colleen brought me two letter cases. One contained the ten letters to my mother I told you about. The other one was a jumble of odds and ends I couldn't imagine my father ever throwing together like that. He was too organized a man to have left crumpled papers and unopened envelopes lying about. When I took a close look at them, I discovered they belonged to Donald. He'd been using my father's desk, dumping his things into one of the drawers. Victoria must have cleaned it out, and he hasn't even realized that he's missing anything." She threaded the fingers of both hands together as tightly as she could. "I remember the feelings that came over me that day. I tried to recall what happened right after my father died, and I couldn't. Not the details. I was floating in a fog of laudanum then; I can't trust what little I do remember. It's been gnawing at me ever since that I didn't do a thorough search, that I let my emotions overwhelm me."

"It takes a long time for opium to work its way out of the body. Some say that once awakened, the craving never leaves you. That's what laudanum is, opium by another name."

"My father told me about the opium dens on Mott Street. He

said they were the most hellish places on earth, and that if he could, he'd deport every Chinaman who sold it."

"In one form or another, opium is everywhere. Your harmless laudanum is a prime example."

"I could weep, Mr. Hunter, except that it wouldn't change anything. I have no idea how much of what happened after my father's death is lost forever in a laudanum haze. Or dream. That's what it feels like, you know. Like a dream. Nothing is painful, nothing is important enough to grieve over. You float heavenward. For as long as you have that brown bottle in your hand, you have safety. You retreat to a place where no one can reach you."

It was on the tip of Prudence's tongue to tell him that she'd put all of that behind her, that she'd come out of the laudanum haze stronger for having had to fight its seductive power alone and in secret. *Not yet, my child. It's a battle that's never quite won, a war that never ends.* The easy release of laudanum would tempt her for the rest of her life. The victory she could and would claim would be the downfall of Victoria. *That I swear to you,* she promised her father.

Even now, sitting at the Judge's desk, the study door closed, just thinking about the cloud of laudanum in which she had floated made her yearn for the same oblivion that had cost her so many memories. Prudence could picture the small corked bottle upstairs on her bedside table, feel the weight of it in her hand, smell the alluring bitterness masked with honey when the cork was pulled out. What was it Geoffrey had said? *Once awakened, the craving never leaves you.* He was right. Geoffrey Hunter was right. Laudanum's siren call would never be entirely stilled; it was as much a part of her now as the blood that flowed through her veins.

Memories surged up as Prudence opened first one desk drawer, then another. It was as if the wood that had so often felt the touch of the Judge's hand now released something of him into his daughter. Clara had come and gone, leaving behind the small fire into which Victoria had suggested her stepdaughter toss whatever she didn't want to keep. She would have to concentrate, rein in the mind that was racing in all directions looking for clues to explain why everything had changed so completely two years ago. Three, she corrected herself. Victoria had had an intimate relationship with the Judge for at least a year before the marriage took place.

She wondered if the concierge at the Dakota, Mrs. Markham, had told them everything she knew about Victoria. Playing the stenographer, Prudence had remained mute, had allowed Geoffrey to ask all the questions. Geoffrey. When she wasn't exercising strict control over her thoughts, Prudence called him Geoffrey. She liked the sound of his name, liked the feeling of warmth that poured over her whenever she thought of him that way. She whispered it aloud. *Geoffrey.* She felt strength in the name, in the man. Something else, too, something she was reluctant to acknowledge. *Concentrate,* she admonished herself. *Concentrate.* And from somewhere far off she heard the faintest whisper of a voice. The suggestion of a chuckle. *Love is like laudanum. Once it gets hold of you, there's no getting away from it.*

Prudence emptied the contents of the desk drawers into the large wastebasket where she had nestled her cat a very long time ago. On its side, softened with layers of linen napkins filched from the dining room, the wastebasket had made a very respectable house for the long-suffering animal who loved his young mistress as faithfully as a dog. Barnaby. Barnaby the cat. She hadn't thought of him in years. She smiled to herself as she sat before the fire, the first handful of papers in her lap. She would read each of them carefully, searching for strange marks that might indicate another code, trying to imagine a giant puzzle whose many pieces she had to find.

An hour later the wastebasket was empty and she was no closer to finding anything of value than when she sat down. Almost nothing had been written by the Judge; nearly everything she had read was scrawled in Donald Morley's practically illegible hand. Unbeknownst to her, he had been using the study for weeks now, perhaps even since just after her father's death. Geoffrey had told her that Cameron remembered seeing Victoria pitching handfuls of paper into the fireplace. How she must have laughed to herself at setting Prudence the same task, but with worthless notes and scribbled lists and advertisements ripped out of the newspaper. Nothing of worth, nothing of value, nothing that would indicate a man's serious reflections.

She put the wastebasket back where it belonged and sat down at the desk. It had been as she was about to leave the attic that she had remembered the hidden drawer. Perhaps the same magic of memory could be made to work again. She tried to recall the hours spent in this room with the Judge, pictured him sitting at his desk, herself opposite, heavy law books lying open between them. *Walk backward,* she told herself, *walk backward through time.* She ran her fingers along every inch of each of the drawers, searching for a joint that was a shade too wide, for a spot in the wood that would give way beneath her fingers. Nothing. Nothing but a splinter she pulled from her finger, a drop of blood tasting of iron. It was hard to give up hope, the hardest thing she'd ever had to do.

The shelves that had been full of books last week were nearly empty. True to her word, Victoria had ordered her husband's extensive law library boxed up. Filled packing cases were stacked around the walls, each box meticulously labeled. Prudence wondered which fortunate firm or law school was supposed to be the recipient of such a fine collection. She was determined that not a single one of the Judge's books would leave the house.

Where would I hide something that I feared someone close to me would destroy? Prudence asked herself. *If I were my father, where would I put what was most valuable to me?* There was a safe in his dressing room, but that was too obvious. If Victoria didn't know or hadn't found the combination, she would have had it forced open as soon as the gate was closed on the family vault. *If I were my father, what would I do?* They'd played hiding games so often when she was a child that it grew to be second nature to try to best one another. A single concealed cache would not be enough to satisfy the Judge's obsession with security. He would create a diversion somewhere, a false place of concealment to lead a searcher away from the greater prize. And he would know that Prudence could not be fooled.

Sitting at his desk, imagining him looking for a place only she would discover, her eyes tracked the shelves that covered three walls of the room. If he had had a second safe installed, he would want it to be where he could chuckle over how well he had hidden it, where he could glance up from the documents he was studying and be reassured no one would find it. Prudence took a deep breath, lowered her head as if to read something that lay before her, then quickly raised it, allowing her eyes to track naturally before her.

Finger in her mouth, the sting of the splinter starting to ease, she walked toward the shelves directly opposite where the Judge would have sat, shelves that seemed to have been untouched, where her father had kept works of philosophy and the natural sciences, histories written in several languages, outsized books of geography whose folded map pages could be opened to four times their original size. She had found this portion of the library irresistible when she was a child, had loved running her small finger along the blue rivers and the coned mountains, sounding out the wonderfully strange names as her father described places she would then dream of in her sleep. Her favorite of the heavy geographies was still there, a compendium of the Lewis and Clark expedition that had charted the vast northwestern territories of the country nearly a hundred years ago. Many a night she had fallen asleep imagining herself to be the young Indian woman Sacagawea. She had even made up her own version of Shoshone, which the delighted Judge had pretended to understand. Such a long time ago.

The hand with the injured finger reached out for the volume that had given her so much pleasure, and the moment she felt the embossed and gilded leather cover against her skin, she knew. The Judge had often left notes for her between the pages of the book she had loved more than any other. Entrusted to Sacagawea, who, like the Judge's precious Sarah, had also died in her twenties. There was some other tantalizing tidbit of information she couldn't quite remember. Something about Sacagawea retrieving the records of the expedition when one of the boats capsized. Retrieving records, journals, and unsent letters. Prudence smiled, and sent a winged message of thanks to the father who had taught her to apply logic to the hiding games he set her. If there were a safe, he had placed the heavy geography tomes in front of it. Sacagawea on guard to help Prudence recover what might so easily have disappeared forever.

"Prudence?"

Lost in the hope of what she might have found, she hadn't heard Victoria's repeated knocking. Holding the Lewis and Clark book against her chest, knowing she dared not explore any further, she opened the study door, slipping the key into the pocket of her skirt before her stepmother could see it.

"The door was locked."

"It seems to be sticking. Perhaps Jackson could put a drop or two of oil on it."

"Mr. Hunter has called. He's in the parlor. He says he's come with bad news."

"Colleen!"

Victoria held out her hands for the book, but Prudence shook her head. Within moments she was across the hall and through the parlor door. Geoffrey turned, as did Donald Morley.

"I'm sorry to be the bearer of bad tidings, Miss MacKenzie," Geoffrey said. "It's Mr. Conkling. He collapsed after court today. He said he had a terrible pain in his head, and the next thing anyone knew he was unconscious on the floor. They've taken him to his apartment at the Hoffman House Hotel. A doctor was summoned immediately, but I've also stopped by Worthington's office. He's already on his way uptown."

"Josiah has been worried for at least a week now that something like that would happen."

"Are you talking about Mr. Conkling's secretary, Prudence? How do you know what he's been worried about?" The two red spots of anger that always gave her away burned brightly in Victoria's cheeks.

"I had some questions for Mr. Conkling, Victoria. Nothing you need concern yourself about."

"I wanted to let you know as soon as possible, Miss MacKenzie. And I'm afraid the news about your maid is not very good either. They called the priest this morning. I imagine she's gone by now."

That was the story Cameron had suggested and all had agreed upon. Colleen would be safer presumed dead than alive.

"I'm sorry to hear that. She was a good girl, very quiet. I don't think I spoke more than a few words to her or she to me the whole time she worked for us. I had the impression she was shy." That should put Victoria's suspicions to rest.

"We'll be responsible for her burial expenses, of course." Donald jingled the coins in his trousers pocket. "Modest expenses, that is."

"Dr. Worthington asked me to tell you that he would see to the arrangements. He's done it many times before. The body will be turned over to her family. He said he would send you the necessary accounting."

"The MacKenzie family will make some sort of appropriate gesture, Mr. Hunter. Flowers perhaps? Donald will see to that if you or Dr. Worthington will provide him with an address."

"I would advise against it, Mrs. MacKenzie. You don't want to give the impression that Colleen's fall was in any way connected to her employment in this household."

"I forgot, Mr. Hunter. Like Mr. Conkling, you're a lawyer, aren't you?"

"Perhaps a gift to the family of double Colleen's last week's wages? That would be more than generous and is what's generally done when a member of staff dies in service."

"I see."

"The suggestion came from Dr. Worthington."

"Donald?"

"I think the sooner we put it all behind us, the better. Tell Worthington we agree. He can send us the bill."

Brother and sister nodded, for once in complete agreement. Colleen was dead. The incident was closed, the danger averted. Dead men told no tales. The same could be said of maidservants.

"Will you stay for a cup of tea, Mr. Hunter?"

"Thank you, Mrs. MacKenzie, but I think I'd better get back to Mr. Conkling. Josiah is taking his collapse very hard. Someone will need to make sure he doesn't fall ill himself."

"I'm sure it's nothing serious. The Judge always said that his friend Roscoe would outlive him by twenty or thirty years." Victoria rang the bell. "I'll have Jackson see you out, Mr. Hunter. Did you take a cab?"

"It's waiting for me."

"I found a book my father intended to give to Mr. Conkling, Mr. Hunter." Prudence held out the Lewis and Clark history and geography. "He told me many times how much the senator admired Lewis and Clark. Will you take it to him?"

"How very kind of you to remember." Geoffrey Hunter took the heavy book and tucked it casually under his arm. He hadn't missed a beat. "I'm sure Mr. Conkling will be delighted to have it. He's likely to be laid up in bed for a week or more."

"He's such an interesting man," Victoria said. "And a very

good lawyer. My late husband said he was one of the best, that a legal document crafted by Roscoe Conkling would stand up to any kind of challenge."

"I'm sure we all hope that's true." Prudence smiled the most laudanum-addled grin she could manage. "I'm so tired and a little dizzy. I wonder if it's something I ate."

CHAPTER 19

Victoria MacKenzie had been one of the most talked-about beauties of last year's Easter Parade along Fifth Avenue. This year she was obliged to wear widow's weeds from head to foot. Swathed in heavy skirts, a stifling veil, and black gloves, she thought she looked like an enormous Black Witch moth struggling out of its cocoon.

"I don't understand why you want to bother going to church and that ridiculous parade," Donald complained. He had a vicious headache, a roiling stomach, and very little memory of the good time he must have had last night. "No one expects a recent widow to follow all of the conventions."

"You know nothing about the way society functions, Donald. Widows are watched more closely than wives, and I am most definitely expected to be at Trinity Church this morning. We have a family pew that will be glaringly empty if we're not there to fill it."

"Prudence can go with you."

"Of course she'll be there. And so will you. Propriety demands a male escort who is also a member of the immediate family. Unfortunately, you are the only one in this house who fits that description and is at least nominally vertical."

"What do you mean by that?"

"The Judge is dead, Donald. You have to take his place."

"I wish you wouldn't order me around, Victoria. I don't like it."

"Where were you last night?"

"Where I go is none of your business."

"You won't go anywhere if I cut off your funds."

"You wouldn't dare."

"I've dared a great deal in my lifetime, brother dear. Drink another cup of coffee. I sent that stupid Clara to wake up Prudence, but if she's not down here at the table in another minute, I'll go up and shake her myself."

"I think it's a bad idea to leave the laudanum bottle beside her bed, Victoria."

"After this bottle is finished, she'll have to come to me for what she won't be able to live without." Victoria licked delicately at her lower lip and smiled the loveliest smile anyone could have wished for. "She has to be made to acknowledge and welcome her dependency. It won't be easy, and it will take time, but eventually she'll do anything I ask her to do, sign any paper I put in front of her. I won't even have to threaten. The sight of that small brown bottle just out of her reach will tame Miss Prudence faster than a slaver's whip."

"She's still not down."

"Drink your coffee and try to remember what it feels like to be sober."

Victoria took the stairs to the second floor as briskly as her skirts allowed. She was impatient to be out of the house, finished with the long church service and walking among the well-dressed crowds along Fifth Avenue. *Next year,* she promised herself, *next year I won't be wearing black. One full year of mourning is enough for anyone.*

Without bothering to knock, Victoria opened Prudence's door and swept into the room with the pentup energy of a dark tornado. "Prudence! Wake up! You'll never be dressed in time! Where is that stupid girl I sent to get you up? Prudence!"

One, two, three. She didn't dare wait any longer. One hand raised to cover her eyes against the sun pouring into the room as Victoria yanked back the drapes, Prudence turned over and then lay flaccid and unresponsive in her bed, seeming to drift in and out of sleep as she moaned once against the light and burrowed deeper into the bedclothes.

She felt rather than saw Victoria storm over to the bedside table, pick up the empty bottle of laudanum, and hurl it angrily against the wall. "How much of that did you take last night?" she demanded, reaching down to shake Prudence by the shoulders.

Prudence forced herself to flop in her stepmother's grip like a rag doll being waved around by an angry child. Her neck snapped, her long light brown hair whipped from side to side, and her cheek burned where Victoria slapped it. Then it was over. She lay flat in her bed again, every sense alert to the rest of the drama being played out in her room.

"I told you to get Miss Prudence up, you stupid girl," Victoria snarled at the maid who stood thunderstruck and frightened in the doorway.

"I get coffee, madam." Clara's English was tentative under the best of circumstances, her German accent thick now with the certainty that she'd done something wrong. Again.

"Put the coffee down and go get a chair in the hallway. You'll sit outside Miss Prudence's door until we get back from church. Do you understand me?"

"Yes, madam."

"Then do it."

The door slammed shut behind Victoria. Prudence could hear the staccato rap of her heels across the corridor into her bedroom, then moments later her firm steps on the broad staircase to the main floor.

It had worked; her plan had worked. Easter Sunday was the

one day every employer made sure the household staff attended church without fail. The moral obligation to see to the spiritual welfare of their hirelings was satisfied early this year, April 1, 1888, just three weeks after the Great Blizzard. Every member of the MacKenzie staff would assemble in the servants' hall to be inspected by Mrs. Barstow and Jackson before being shepherded out the door to their respective churches. And God help the servant who couldn't recount an authentic-sounding version of the day's sermon.

The only thing Prudence hadn't anticipated was Clara being ordered to sit outside her bedroom. She waited until the front door opened and closed, then stood at the window to see Victoria and Donald handed up into the carriage while the line of household help mounted the stairs from the kitchen areaway and trudged off along Fifth Avenue. Careful not to make a sound, she retrieved the laudanum bottle from where it had bounced off the wall. There were still a few drops inside. She dipped a spoonful of water from the glass by her bedside into the bottle, swishing the liquid around until she was sure it was well mixed, then poured it into the coffee Clara had brought upstairs for her young mistress.

"Clara?" Prudence opened the bedroom door.

"Yes, miss. Do you need, miss?"

"No, nothing, thank you. But here, you can have the coffee, it's still warm. I don't want it. I'm going back to sleep." When Clara had taken the cup and saucer from her outstretched hand, Prudence yawned, smiled sleepily, and closed the bedroom door again. She wasn't sure how long she'd have to wait, but maids were always tired, they never got enough sleep, there was always too much for them to do. She'd seen Colleen struggling to stay alert as she went about her duties. Surely Clara, sitting in the stuffy hallway, believing Prudence to be asleep, and with a good few drops of laudanum in her, would doze off in ten or fifteen minutes. She stared at the ormolu clock on the mantel, willing the minute hand to move.

When Prudence finally judged it safe to open the door, she heard soft, contented snoring and saw an overworked Clara slumped in her chair, chin pillowed on her chest.

Donald's room first. He was the more likely of the two to be careless and she couldn't afford to waste time. Victoria would be drawn to the informal Easter Parade that meandered along Fifth Avenue, but Donald could just as easily refuse to accompany her. There was no predicting how long Clara would sleep. Taking off her soft slippers and sliding them into the pockets of the robe she'd put on over her nightdress, she went barefoot up the staircase to the third floor, hugging the stair rail and stepping close to the edge of each riser where the wood didn't creak.

Donald Morley hadn't bothered to lock his bedroom door. Perhaps he never did. Prudence was inside before she could give herself a chance to change her mind. Despite Brian the footman's best efforts, Donald was clearly a man who would always need to be picked up after. There was a general air of untidiness in his room that could only be achieved by someone who restlessly moved small items around from where they should be to somewhere else. A fresh cigar butt had been ground out in a crystal ashtray, a half-drunk glass of whiskey left beside it. Whiskey on Easter Sunday morning? It looked as though Donald had decided to change his cuff links at the last moment. The ebony box in which pairs of cuff links should be resting in velvet lined slots was overturned, its contents spilled haphazardly amidst a collection of odds and ends scattered atop the chest of drawers.

She went first to the two tables beside the bed that had been carefully made before someone sat on it and rumpled the dark burgundy satin coverlet. Donald had emptied the contents of his pockets into the drawers. Not once, but many times. Coins, crumpled bills, dirty handkerchiefs, bent cigars, a flurry of calling cards, several pieces of what seemed to be sausage casing, buttons, and fragments of ripped and soiled lace. She looked at each of the calling cards, but none seemed to be more significant than what any gentleman collected at every new introduction. No writing on any of them. She closed that drawer, leaving the contents as stirred together as they were when she opened it. The table on the other side of the bed held more of the same.

Nothing in the pockets of the pants and jackets hanging in orderly rows in the armoire, nothing concealed under the piles of laundered and ironed undergarments, shirts, and handkerchiefs in the chest of drawers. She got down on hands and knees to peer under the bed, ran her hands beneath the mattress and behind the headboard. Still nothing. She tried to think of where she would hide something she wanted no one else to discover, remembering the secret drawer in the rolltop desk and the many folded map pages of the Lewis and Clark tome. Standing on a chair, she pulled each picture away from the wall, feeling from one side of a frame to the other for papers that might have been glued against the backing. Nothing. It looked as though Donald had no past at all, not a photo or scrap of a letter connecting him to any life before this one. She knew that if she were forced to move from one place to another, there would certainly be things she would be so loathe to leave behind that a spot would be found for them no matter how full her suitcase.

Suitcase. There it was, shoved back against the wall on top of the tall armoire where the suits were hung and polished shoes and boots ranged in neat rows beneath. She knew as soon as she'd wrestled it down, standing on tiptoe on the chair, that she'd found what she'd been looking for. Even before she opened it, she knew.

The rectangular suitcase was small and battered, stains like dark patchwork disfiguring the leather, brass clasps and locks blackened and unpolished. She thought it might once have been a gentleman's overnight case; someone's initials had been painstakingly etched into the leather. L.W. Either someone other than Donald had owned this case when it was new or Donald Morley had once gone by a different name. Hands trembling with anticipation, fumbling at the catches, she opened the suitcase. And nearly cried out in disappointment.

More crumpled handkerchiefs. Collarless shirts and underwear gray with age and use. Neckcloths stained yellow with old sweat. Shuddering in distaste, Prudence shook each repulsive garment, then dropped it onto the bed. When the case lay empty before her, she ran her hands along its faded lining, but felt nothing suspicious or unexpected. No irregularities that would suggest a hiding place for documents or jewelry one wanted to keep from the curious eyes of servants. She bent closer, eyes concentrating on the seams, looking for a break in the stitching, a different hand with the needle, a contrasting thread color. Still nothing. Perhaps Donald was exactly what he seemed to be—a man who ate and drank to excess, whose habits of personal cleanliness left a great deal to be desired, who was happy to live off the charity of his more ambitious and talented sister.

Prudence found it when she was closing the suitcase, as her fingers brushed against a section of stitching that seemed not quite as deep as the rest. There it was. Thick thread sunk to a depth that didn't quite match if one looked carefully. The leather had been slit along the side, then glued down again. She could feel the cracked, dried-out glue with her fingernail. She would need something thin and sharp to slide between the leather covering and the body of the case. A letter opener on Donald's untidy desk. That would do, would have to do. Slowly, being careful not to leave scratches, she pried her way along the glued strip, catching in one hand the bits of dessicated adhesive that fell out as she worked. The slit was no more than eight or ten inches in length; she thought it might have begun its life as a genuine rip, enlarged by someone desperate to hide something.

Using the letter opener, she felt inside the narrow gap, her heart beating faster when the white corner of a piece of paper was teased out far enough for her to hold it in her fingers. A second piece of paper, and then a small photograph, only as large as the palm of her hand. Nothing else. She ran the letter opener from side to side, listening intently for a telltale rustle, held the leather up while she peered beneath. Nothing else. She had everything that Donald had thought to hide.

Menus. Two menus. One of them was dated April 30, 1881, and listed the luncheon choices at the Grand Central Hotel in White Sulphur Springs, West Virginia. The second, dated June 10, 1880, touted that day's evening fare and festivities aboard the Mississippi riverboat *Natchez VIII,* with an illustration of stained-glass windows depicting dancing Indians. Scribbling down names, places, and dates on the back of an envelope she found in the jumble atop Donald's small writing desk, Prudence eased the two menus back under the leather covering, then turned her attention to the photograph, the date 1881 neatly inked on the back.

She recognized Victoria and Donald immediately; both looked younger, but there was no mistaking their features. They stood on the wide veranda of a large private home or hotel, its entryway flanked by tall white columns. Between them, sitting in a chair that had wheels mounted on either side, was a handsome, elderly man wearing the mustache and closely trimmed beard popular in the South of General Robert E. Lee. For a moment, Prudence wondered if she were looking at a picture of the famous general, then she remembered that he had died five years after the war's end. Not the commander of the Confederate Army of Northern Virginia then, but clearly someone who had chosen to look as much like him as possible. An elderly, wounded veteran of that terrible war?

Making her mind up on the spot, Prudence nestled the photograph inside her bedgown, then concentrated on reclosing the leather flap she had opened, spitting repeatedly to moisten the old glue, using the letter opener to press down on the two edges she was trying to fuse together again. It might not hold under rough handling, but it would have to do. She mentally thanked the severe Mrs. Barstow for frightening the maids into dusting every surface until a white glove stroked across it came up clean. There wouldn't be telltale streaks to give her away. She pushed the small suitcase back until she felt it stop against the wall. Standing below, looking up, you couldn't be sure anything was there.

Thank you, Donald, she breathed. She was certain he had held on to the menus and the photograph for a reason, most likely to be used against the formidable Victoria. They had to be the opening wedges of a future campaign to control or bring her down. Donald thought them important enough to keep and hide; they must be keys to the past his sister was determined to hold secret. *Thank you, Donald, for being greedy, callous, and a would-be blackmailer.*

It was going to make all the difference in the world.

CHAPTER 20

Victoria's room was also unlocked, though not purposely so. Before leaving for Easter services, Prudence's stepmother had shouted again at German Clara, one arm pointing toward the spot in the hallway where the maid was to set her chair, then stormed off to the parlor. Her bedroom door stood open half an inch from its frame; she'd been too angry to realize that she hadn't turned the key in its lock. With a glance at the still peacefully snoring housemaid, Prudence slipped through the door and into Victoria's private world.

The scent was strong and cloying, a heavy attar of roses nauseating in its thickness, as if someone had mixed a concentrated flowery oil with the ether used in operating theaters. She had been in Victoria's room many times, but Prudence had never grown used to its feeling of excess. She felt smothered by the deep pink satin, the gold-leafed French furniture, the inability to take a deep breath without tasting the perfume Victoria used so liberally. Reminding herself that she might not have much time, Prudence moved as quickly and as efficiently through her stepmother's drawers and armoire as she had through Donald's. With the same result. Nothing.

Where Donald was careless and unorganized, Victoria was neat and compulsively unable to keep anything that was slightly worn or last year's fashion. Whatever had been hanging in her armoire at the time of the Judge's death was gone, replaced by a dozen black gowns, each one as close to being scandalously unmournful as the widow dared. Every outdoor dress had its own hat and flowing black veil, its own pair of polished black boots. Prudence supposed that as the year of deep mourning drew to a close, Victoria would summon dressmakers to outfit her in whatever was being worn that season. One by one the black dresses would disappear. There was no small suitcase stored atop the armoire, not even a hatbox.

The only time she allowed herself a stirring of anger was when she found some of her mother's jewelry in the midnight blue velvet jewel case she had played with as a small child. She recognized the diamond and sapphire waterfall that had hung around her mother's neck, the matching earrings that were long enough to graze her shoulders, and the twin bracelets she had twirled on her own four-year-old arms. An emerald and diamond ring her mother had tied on to her finger with silk thread, a dark pearl larger than any of the pebbles she had collected to decorate her sand castles at the beach, a rope of perfectly matched black pearls that could be twisted into a necklace of many strands or left to hang gloriously to the wearer's knees. Other pieces so familiar, they brought tears to her eyes as she touched them. Her mother's jewelry was supposed to come to her, and until it did, her father had said it would lie in the vault of one of the trust and safe deposit institutions that had begun to compete with banks for the safekeeping of their customers' stock certificates and jewels.

Mr. Conkling had alluded to this jewelry when he told her about Victoria's control of her trust, but the full force of what he said hadn't registered until now, now that she held in her hands what her mother had once worn, what should never, never have been allowed to adorn the person of her successor.

A widow couldn't wear any jewelry except her wedding ring and perhaps a mourning brooch containing a lock of the deceased's hair, but Prudence knew that Victoria had not been content to bring this jewelry from the safe deposit box to lie unworn in its blue velvet case. She had slipped the rings onto her fingers, threaded the earrings into her ears, fastened the necklaces around her throat, slid the bracelets onto her arms. Admired herself reflected in the mirrors that were everywhere in this room, twirled to catch and reflect candle and gaslight, laughed aloud at the feel of so much wealth on her skin.

She had been poor. Victoria had been born and brought up poor. Prudence knew it as surely as she knew her own name. It was the only explanation that fit, that clarified what was dark and murky in her stepmother's character, in her refusal to answer questions that might shed light on her past. Somewhere, many years ago, Victoria had taught herself to deflect inquiry, to evade polite queries so adroitly that a conversation would be long over before the other party realized she knew no more at the end of it than she had at the beginning.

"Miss Prudence? Miss Prudence?" A soft knock on her bedroom door just across the hall told Prudence that Clara had emerged from her laudanum nap. She heard the door open, Clara's soft tut-tutting at the mounded-up covers under which she believed her mistress still lay sleeping. "I get more coffee," the maid muttered. A moment later her footsteps thudded on the bare wood of the servants' stairwell. Not even in an empty house would Clara presume to descend the main staircase.

There was only one more place Prudence hadn't searched, but a quick glance told her that Victoria's Louis XV writing table was unlikely to hold any secrets. The shallow drawers contained monogrammed letter paper, envelopes, black bordered visiting cards to use in the sixth month of her widowhood when she could begin making calls again. A journal whose pages were blank. A gift from someone who hadn't known that a woman like Victoria would never confide her thoughts to paper? A gold filigreed tray containing inkpot, pens, a sand shaker, and a very sharp gold letter opener. Each item precisely positioned, like a row of military cadets.

To one side was a stack of letters to be answered, invitations Victoria was expected to decline, household bills to look over and send on to the housekeeper for verification, menus to approve. Prudence rifled through them quickly, searching for anything that did not belong. Nothing. Nothing.

The anger she had beaten back when she held her mother's jewelry in her hands and realized that Victoria had been wearing the pieces Sarah had bequeathed her daughter nearly strangled Prudence with its sudden violence. She had been so certain she would find something she could use to prove her stepmother guilty of moral turpitude, so sure that Victoria would have kept a piece of incriminating evidence from her past. But she hadn't. The only clues to what Victoria and her brother might have been and where they had come from were two menus and a photograph that Donald had hidden from his sister. Prudence felt sick to her stomach; the rage and the helplessness nauseated her, made her head throb and her hands tremble.

The last thing she did before she left Victoria's pink silk lair was to take the emerald ring from the blue velvet jewel case and slip it on to the ring finger of her right hand. It fit perfectly. When she held her hand out to admire the square-cut emerald and its two flanking diamonds, she thought there was another way in which she resembled her mother. Their hands. Sarah had bestowed pale gray eyes, soft brown hair, and long, slender fingers on her beloved daughter.

What she would do if or when Victoria missed the ring was something Prudence decided she would deal with when the moment came. The only important thing today was that she had managed to steal back from Victoria one of her mother's precious belongings. For the time being, one would have to be enough.

The hallway was empty when Prudence closed Victoria's

door behind her. She tiptoed to the servants' staircase and eased the door open. No sound of tired feet climbing the uncarpeted stairs. Clara must still be in the kitchen two floors below, grinding coffee beans and heating water. Prudence would have a few moments to study the picture she had taken from Donald's room before the maid returned.

There was an odd scent in the corridor, a lingering odor of maleness that shouldn't be there. Donald smelled of tobacco, whiskey, and bay rum cologne; this faint aroma was of strong soap and sweet Macassar oil. Donald didn't use Macassar oil to slick back his hair; Victoria refused to cover the backs and arms of every upholstered chair with linen protectors to absorb the stains. Could one of the male servants have remained at the house? Did German Clara, made fun of by the other servants for her heavy accent, have an unsuspected beau?

Smiling to herself at the thought of what might be taking place in the kitchen, Prudence opened her bedroom door.

And screamed.

The man who whipped around to face her had been standing at the foot of her bed, staring down at the mound of pillows and rolled blankets meant to trick the maid into believing her mistress was still asleep.

"What are you doing in here?" Prudence demanded.

Jackson looked from the bed to the barefoot, angry young woman clad in nightgown and robe, slippers sticking out of the robe's pockets, a huge emerald and diamond ring glittering on the hand she'd automatically raised to protect her bare throat. He took his time answering, as though he were memorizing every detail of the scene.

"I thought it might not be a good idea for you and Clara to be alone in the house, Miss Prudence," he finally said. "So I came back."

"What made you think you could come into my bedroom?" She was trembling with her father's temper, feeling the violation of Jackson's presence with every breath she took. She nearly choked on the faint but nauseating smell of the coconut and cananga oils used in the manufacture of Rowland's Macassar Oil.

"Clara was worried. I came up to check that you were all right." Jackson smiled, began moving in her direction.

Prudence would have to edge out into the hallway to avoid him, but that felt too much like retreat. This was her house. She wouldn't allow a servant to intimidate her, especially not one of Victoria's creatures.

"Does Mrs. MacKenzie know you came back? Did you tell Mr. Morley?"

"No, miss. They'd already gone."

Jackson was within arm's reach now, so close she could read menace in his odd yellow brown eyes. Avarice, too, as the eyes flickered to the emerald and diamond ring on the hand she had not lowered from her throat.

"I bring coffee, Miss Prudence," said German Clara from behind her. The maid halted in the doorway, not sure whether she should enter.

"Thank you, Clara," Prudence said. "You can put it on my dressing table. Jackson is just leaving. He came back to make sure we were safe. Wasn't that thoughtful of him?"

"Yes, miss." Clara sidled past her mistress and the butler, set down the coffee, then stood with clasped hands, waiting to be told what to do next.

"There was no need to worry, though. You didn't need to send him up to check on me."

Jackson scowled at German Clara, who looked startled, confused, and then frightened. She bobbed her head, but said nothing, even after he left and they heard the door to the servants' staircase open and close again.

Prudence understood without asking that German Clara hadn't known Jackson was in the house until she'd seen him in her mistress's bedroom.

* * *

The last person Geoffrey Hunter expected to see standing outside his rooms at the Fifth Avenue Hotel late on Easter Sunday morning was Prudence MacKenzie. Yet there she was, dressed in the drab gray outfit she had worn to the Dakota. She had learned to make herself invisible, the first lesson every Pinkerton operative was required to master.

"I hoped I'd find you in."

"Is something wrong?" A quick look in both directions assured him the hallway was empty.

"I didn't inquire at the desk. No one noticed me." She brushed past him into the parlor, striding to the windows that overlooked Fifth Avenue, pulling aside the curtains to scan the street. "I didn't think anyone would be out for the parade yet. It's still too early."

"There's coffee on the sideboard."

She removed her gloves, laid her purse on the large round table where he had eaten his breakfast, hesitated a moment, then took the pins from her hat and placed it beside the purse. Clearly a woman preparing to work.

"Colleen?" she asked.

"Is up and walking. Dennis brought me a message last night."

"Mr. Conkling?"

"Furious that he's been confined to his bed. Josiah says the pain in his head was bad enough to bring in a doctor who diagnosed exhaustion and an abscess in the right ear, both brought on by his trek through the blizzard. Mr. Conkling doesn't entirely believe him."

"I'd like that coffee you offered," Prudence said. She poured herself a cup from the silver pot on the sideboard, added cream and sugar. Brought it back to the table. "I searched Victoria's and Donald's rooms this morning. I found a menu from a hotel or resort in White Sulphur Springs, West Virginia, another from a Mississippi River steamboat, and a photograph."

Between sips of the hot coffee she told him the whole story, omitting only the odd confrontation with Jackson. The butler's explanation had been plausible and she'd soon gotten over her fright at finding him in her bedroom. Prudence didn't want to have to waste time and energy arguing with Geoffrey Hunter about her safety. Hadn't she already proved that she could take care of herself? "I don't know what I would have done if Clara hadn't proved susceptible to the laudanum. There weren't more than a couple of drops left in the bottle." She wanted desperately to ask him if the Judge had left anything for his Sacagawea in the Lewis and Clark book, but forced herself not to ask the question. Not yet.

"I know this place," Geoffrey said, smiling nostalgically as he read the copy of the Grand Central Hotel menu she had reproduced from memory. "We used to spend the hot summer months there before the war. I was just a child, but I remember it. Sometimes we stayed in one of the cottages on the grounds, other summers in the hotel itself. Everyone who was anyone in the South in those years went to White Sulphur Springs. It was the equivalent of Saratoga Springs to Yankees. Northerners," he corrected himself. "1881. Victoria married the Judge two years ago; she'd already been living at the Dakota for a year before that. The latest she could have come to New York City would be the summer of 1884, but I think it had to have been earlier than that. She knew about McGlory's troubles with the law, knew enough about how the city works to suspect he'd had to have bribed at least one judge."

Prudence's head jerked upward, a proud lift to her chin, anger in her eyes.

"I'm sorry."

"I have to learn to accept it, but I haven't yet. The very thought is painful, so I keep avoiding it. I shouldn't." *Not if I want to bring down Victoria. I have to make myself as hard and as ruthless as she is.*

"She probably came to New York fairly soon after this photograph was taken. Which could mean that whatever profitable scheme she had in mind for the elderly gentleman in the wheeled chair was unsuccessful. Either he died or his family stepped in to save him. Something happened to make her and Donald travel north."

"What about the other menu? What does that tell you?" She had sketched out a close facsimile of what she had replaced in Donald's suitcase, thanking the governess who insisted she learn to draw from life and then paint from memory every flower in her mother's Fifth Avenue garden. Tedious work she never enjoyed, but she'd developed a good eye and a modest talent that helped to pass many a rainy afternoon. What she hadn't realized until she put it to the test this morning, was that she'd also honed her memory so that all she had to do was close her eyes to recall accurately what she had seen.

"One or the other of them may have started out working the Mississippi River steamboats. Some of them are as luxurious as anything you'll find anywhere. There's a lot of gambling, and where there's gambling there's also liquor and women. You never have just the one vice, it's always a package of three."

Prudence didn't know how to phrase it delicately, so she blurted out the question while she had the courage to ask it. "Was Victoria a kept woman? Did she sell herself?"

"They call them ladies of the evening or ladies of the night. The French are more descriptive. *Les grandes horizontales.*"

"My father married a woman who gave herself to anyone who could pay her price."

"It may not have been that tawdry, Miss MacKenzie."

"It was. You know it, I know it, and there are bound to be others who know it." She had turned her mother's emerald ring so the stone was pressed against the palm of her hand where she could feel it burning her skin with a cold green fire. Now she twisted it so the emerald and the diamonds lay atop her finger, and held out her hand for him to see. "I took this from Victoria's room. It was my mother's."

"Beautiful. It's beautiful."

"My father gave it to her the day I was born. She wore it every day of her life until the end. I was lying on her bed nestled against her side the day she took it off her finger and gave it to me. She told me I was to give the ring to my father that night before I went to bed and he would put it away for me, but for the rest of the day I wore it or carried it around in my fist everywhere I went. I couldn't bear to leave it in Victoria's possession. So I took back what was mine." She lifted her chin defiantly.

"Bravo, Miss MacKenzie. I applaud your resourcefulness and your larceny."

"Not larceny, Mr. Hunter. It was never her personal property. It was always mine."

"I stand corrected."

"Please, before we go on, what did you find in the Lewis and Clark volume?"

"Nothing."

"I couldn't have been wrong. My father knew how much I loved that book, how many hours I spent poring over it, reading every word, imagining myself to be Sacagawea. If there were any place in his study he would have hidden something for me, it was there, in the folds of the map pages."

"I unfolded every one of them, Miss MacKenzie. More than once. If anything was hidden there, it's been destroyed. I'm sorry."

"I was so sure."

"Your father wasn't an obvious man."

"No. He told me that a good lawyer never argued a case the way his opponent expected."

"I have a theory about how he might have used this book." Hunter opened to a page he'd marked with a slip of paper. "Look there, in the middle of the illustration. What do you see?"

Prudence leaned over the table where the book lay. "It looks like a smudge, as if a drop of ink had been wiped off. Very faint, but still visible."

"What I think the Judge did was hide papers he knew Victoria would be looking for, perhaps duplicates of the information we found in the notebook. He made sure when he did it that the ink would be fresh enough to leave that smudge you see. Victoria would think she'd found what he was concealing from her, and she either wouldn't notice that faint stain or she'd think it was an old smear. He trusted you to remember that no ink had ever been spilled on these pages despite your childhood fascination with Sacagawea."

"Two copies of the code. One for Victoria to find and destroy, one for me. And instead of more code, smudges of ink to tell me what he'd done. He was protecting me."

"He was. He was doing everything he could to make Victoria feel safe. As long as she doesn't feel threatened, as long as she thinks she's at no risk of losing out on the Judge's fortune, you're in no danger from her."

"So she burned whatever she thought might jeopardize the future she'd made for herself."

"She did. She's gotten rid of anything that could possibly incriminate her or cast a bad light on any of the Judge's decisions."

"That means everything we need is gone."

"We have the notebook, and we have to keep looking. No matter how slim a chance may be, we have to take it. So what I want you to do is to study that book page by page the way you did as a child."

"What am I looking for?"

"Anything that's different. Anything you don't remember being there before. Words that look like a reader's notations in the margins. The faint outline of writing that's meant to be brought out with the application of lemon juice."

"It sounds fantastical."

"You had the imagination as a child to pretend to be Saca-gawea. The Judge had to find a way to get information to you that he thought would succeed. He's already deflected Victo-ria's interest by giving her something to destroy. If there are other secrets embedded in the Lewis and Clark pages, you're the only one who will be able to find them. He was a cautious man, remember. That's why he hid the notebook in the rolltop desk. He counted on what was hidden here being lost, and made sure you'd have the other copy. In gambling, it's called evening the odds."

"I'll need more coffee," Prudence said. She had been about to tell him that she suspected the Judge had had another safe in-stalled in his library, carefully hidden behind the handcrafted paneling of the bookshelves, but then she changed her mind. She'd been so sure they would find incriminating evidence in the Lewis and Clark book, but they hadn't. How many other things had she been wrong about? To be so certain and then to be shown to be mistaken was more than embarrassing. It was humiliating. She decided she would wait until she had found the safe before saying anything about it.

Watching her as she bent over the Lewis and Clark volume, Geoffrey wondered if she would trust him enough to let him put the emerald ring in his safe before she left. He decided to wait until the last moment to ask her for it.

CHAPTER 21

"I'm not in any danger, Mr. Hunter. Victoria can't harm me without losing a great deal of money, and we know she'd never do that. She's worked too hard for it."

"I'd feel better if you would let me keep your mother's ring for you."

"You're probably right, and I'm most likely being foolish not to give it to you for safekeeping."

"But you won't." They'd been arguing almost since climbing into Danny Dennis's cab.

"Victoria has taken everything from me that I valued. She may have hastened my father's death. She certainly tried to make me a prisoner in my own home. That's what I was becoming, Mr. Hunter. There's no point denying it. Eventually, if she had her way, I would turn into one of those shadow women whose families make sure they are never seen in public. She's destroyed whatever she could find that would testify to the love between my mother and father. I think that was pure jealousy because Victoria isn't the type of woman who will ever know what love is. She's incapable of loving, I'm sure she considers it a weakness to be exploited. But deep down, she's envious of anyone who *is* loved. She must hate my mother's memory very much.

"That's why I took the ring. That's why I'm keeping it close to me. Do you understand?"

"Have you ever had any dealings with someone who's desperate, Miss MacKenzie?"

"Only myself."

He didn't answer.

"I'm very much a novice at all of this, Mr. Hunter, but I have no intention of allowing Victoria to win. She doesn't know I've been systematically searching the house, and she won't find out. I've been very careful." He might see her as inexperienced and naive, but there was more to Prudence MacKenzie than appearances. She had a rapidly stiffening backbone and a core of anger she hadn't suspected was there until she had stood in her stepmother's bedroom and taken back something that was hers.

It took courage for someone like this proud young woman to reveal so much of herself. Under other circumstances she might have blundered on single-mindedly until she found answers to her questions or destroyed herself with laudanum. But the bond forged between them at Charlie's funeral had grown stronger as they delved deeper into the mystery of who Victoria MacKenzie was and what she might have done. Prudence had asked Geoffrey several times to call her by her name; he decided it was time.

"If you're determined to do this, Prudence, I want to make it as safe for you as I can."

She flushed a lovely shade of pale crimson, like the beginning wash of a sunset over water.

"Thank you, Geoffrey."

Danny Dennis thought it was about time some of the social fences came down between Mr. Hunter and Miss MacKenzie though he never let on he'd listened to a word of what passed between them. He had the gift of keeping a stolid face no matter what he heard funneled through the small trap door in the roof through which passengers gave directions and handed up their fares. It never ceased to amuse him how quickly they forgot that the driver of their hansom cab was seated just above and behind them.

The clop of Mr. Washington's hooves and the clack of the cab's wheels over the cobblestoned streets was background music to what Danny heard over the years. He could focus his hearing like a bat zoning in on the buzz of an insect. Very few of the talkative men and women who rode in his cab had any secrets left when they descended onto the street again. Eavesdropping helped pass the time.

The other thing people took for granted was that a hansom cab driver knew every street, landmark, and address in the city. The best ones, like Danny Dennis, never forgot a passenger or where they'd taken him. He hadn't driven the Judge more than a handful of times, but he decided he'd cast his mind back over those trips while he was waiting for Mr. Hunter and Miss MacKenzie to finish their business today. If something stuck out, if the Judge had gone to a place a man of his standing wouldn't normally go, Danny would remember it.

He thought Mr. Hunter handed Miss Prudence out with a new measure of gentle concern when Mr. Washington delivered them to the Brooklyn brownstone where the blind war veteran lived with his widowed daughter. Danny had asked around about Benjamin Truitt and liked what he heard.

Truitt came back from the war nearly completely blind, bones and muscles so badly shaken by the concussive force of the shell that didn't quite kill him, that for months he hadn't been able to walk without the help of his two young sons. Who died before reaching manhood in one of the cholera epidemics that carried off so many every summer. The baby, too. Followed by his wife within the year. Yet no one ever heard him rail against God or his fellow man. He never asked why such suffering should be visited on him and not on someone else. No complaints. Ever. Silence was Ben Truitt's defense against life, the silence of a withdrawal so complete that visitors who saw him in his chair often wondered if he were still breathing.

Lydia had been married and widowed in the same month, so they settled in together to live quietly in the shadow of their fates. Father and daughter. All that was left of what should have been a happy, growing family. She took back her maiden name and for years they didn't speak of those they had lost, touching the wounds ever so gently and privately to feel if they'd grown hard scabs. When they did give themselves permission to begin to remember, they also started to smile and laugh again, though neither of them would be bold or daring enough to look for other loves. They had each other and their memories. Apparently that was not quite enough happiness to tempt the Fates. The gods were no longer jealous; they left them alone.

"Now that I know the cipher your father used, Miss MacKenzie, I'm embarrassed that it took me all of four days to work my way through. It's not one that's commonly employed, but I have seen a variation of the Wildflower once before."

"The Wildflower?"

"Cryptographers are sometimes rather fanciful creatures." Ben raised a hand to his smoked glasses, reassuring himself they still sat securely on his nose. He had asked Lydia to describe his eyes to him once, long ago. After that day he was seldom if ever without the concealing protection of the dark lenses. "The man who invented this cipher named it Wildflower because if you were to map out its patterns, you might think you were looking at a sketch of a ragged petal wildflower done all in separate numbers and letters rather than the flowing lines of a typical pen and ink drawing."

"I don't think I understand."

"Nevertheless, you intuitively guessed at the general type of information the Judge was trying to conceal. You saw that pattern."

"Only because I already had some idea of what it might be. I knew my father's habit of recording his every thought and action. He bought his journals from the same stationer every year; there was an entire bookshelf of them in the small writing and smoking room just off his bedroom. All gone, of course. I'm sure those were the first things my stepmother consigned to the flames."

"Once I realized what we were dealing with I was able to dictate the several permutations to Lydia. Wildflower was so named because the cipher goes through various stages before it begins to resolve itself, rather like a plant that sprouts from a single seed. Any mistake made during any of those sequences destroys the meaning. It's actually quite a clever idea."

"The substitution values change frequently, as you would expect in any good cipher." Lydia smiled as warmly at Prudence as though they two had worked together through the long hours of Benjamin Truitt's careful reasoning. She handed her a neatly written list of dates, names, and trial results. "This is the final transcription. I went over everything twice, from beginning to end. Father never makes a mistake, but I can't say the same for the person who must take down his very rapid dictation."

"If you compare the original cipher with the permutations you'll see that the same letter or number can be represented by any one of the other twenty-five letters or nine numbers. What you tried to do in your substitutions was make the values constant; that's why the meaning remained hidden." Ben's explanation was matter of fact and without embellishment.

"Do you understand this, Geoffrey?" It was lovely to say his name out loud like that, as though it were entirely expected and completely proper.

"I pretend that I do," he said, accepting another copy of the transcription from Lydia.

"I matched the underlining, of course, since that's the part of the notebook he really wanted you to know about." She pointed to the entries that stood out from all of the others.

"The Judge threw out the first case on September 24, 1873, a

Wednesday. The defendant's name was Patrick Monoghan, the charge murder. Dismissed for insufficient evidence. The number fifty was added later, when the underlining was done." Benjamin leaned back in his chair so that his head was supported, his legs stretched out on a horsehair hassock. He looked as though he were reading off the ceiling, one finger tracing an invisible line of letters in the empty air. "The numeral fifty wasn't part of the original code."

"He wanted me to know the amount of the bribe. Fifty thousand dollars."

"I wish I could tell you more about the cases he underlined. A good many of them, I'm afraid, Miss MacKenzie. I thought to go to a newspaper office to read the back issues, but there wasn't enough time." Lydia reached out to touch Prudence's hand, thought better of the presumption, and poured tea instead.

"That's why we've got a bakery cake today. I've kept my dear daughter too busy to work her usual marvels in the kitchen. It's not nearly as good as your lemon bars, Lydia, but it isn't bad. I'll have another slice, if you don't mind cutting it for me."

"Of course not, Father." She folded his fingers around the edge of the plate and the silver fork so quickly and skillfully that you had to be paying close attention to see how she had made it possible for Ben to appear as independent as a sighted man.

"There's one notation that deserves special attention," Ben said. "It's different from all the others."

"Different in what way?" Geoffrey asked.

"It's the very last entry," explained Lydia. "Not underlined, so perhaps not one the Judge considered important."

"Lydia believes he changed his mind about this case. I agree with her."

"I don't understand, Mr. Truitt," Prudence said.

"You won't know for sure until you've found the relevant newspaper article, but I think the Judge accepted a bribe to dismiss the case, then decided he could no longer collude with whoever was paying him. There are two sets of code, the first one scratched through. Both indicate that the crime was a double murder, but whereas the first reads dismissal of all charges for insufficient evidence, the second records that the defendant was sent to Sing Sing to serve a life sentence. What's interesting to me is when a man is convicted of two murders, he always hangs. But not in this case. And it was the Judge, remember, who decided and imposed sentence."

"Mitigating circumstances?" asked Geoffrey, the lawyer.

"The defendant's age is given as nineteen."

"Younger men have been hanged. Many of them."

"You said this was the last entry?" asked Prudence. She turned to the final page of the transcription. "The date is April 1886. Two months after he married Victoria. My stepmother," she explained.

"There may not be any connection," Geoffrey warned. "Let's not speculate too soon. We need newspaper accounts for all of these entries. Now that we have court dates, initials of the defendants, and sentences imposed, it shouldn't be difficult. The *Herald* has good records of its back issues. Ned Hayes knows some of the reporters there from when he was on the force. He'll be able to persuade one of them to go into the archives for him. They call it the morgue."

"How is he?" asked Truitt.

"Not well."

"Do all of the war veterans know one another?" asked Prudence.

"Many of us met in infirmaries or hospitals. Or crammed into a railroad car making its way toward home or a cemetery. You tend to dispense with the niceties when you think you're dying." Again Ben Truitt felt for the smoked glasses hiding his eyes. "Lydia and I followed Ned's short-lived career in the police department through the newspaper. He was a Confederate officer, but he was paroled on his word of honor after he recovered from his wounds. He used to read to me; we were in the same hospital ward for months. The difference was that my injuries were easily seen; his were deeper, slashed into the soul of who he was. I doubt he'd remember me."

"Father makes personal secrecy a part of every project he accepts," explained Lydia to Prudence. "He's devised his own elaborate code system to conceal his identity."

"It amuses me."

"Protects you, you mean."

"You're frowning, Lydia. I can always tell when you try to put a note of false cheerfulness into what you say." Ben sat up as straight in his chair as a man in a witness box. "We had some disturbing encounters when I first got into this business. It seemed best to work in the shadows."

"What my father is hinting at is that attempts were made on his life. Two of them. If it hadn't been for his extraordinary hearing and my own good aim with a pistol, they might have succeeded. The United States government is not his only client, certainly not one of the best paying."

"That would be the railroads?" Geoffrey guessed.

"The railroads, of course. They hold the keys to the country's future prosperity, and they know it. The men who own and run them are more ruthless than any of the celebrated conquerors of antiquity. A man's life means less than nothing. Money and power are their meat and drink." Ben held out his empty cake plate.

"Father helps them keep their secrets from one another," Lydia explained. "At a price."

"You would have made a good Pinkerton, Ben."

"Pinkertons need eyes, Geoffrey. There were plenty of them spying for the Union during the war, but not a single one of their operatives was blind. And none since, as far as I know."

"Miss Lydia." Prudence put down her teacup, glancing hesitantly at Geoffrey for a moment. She had an idea, a scheme she'd have to broach without consulting him. "Miss Lydia, do you act as courier for your father's business?"

"I do. Not always, but often enough. Respectable women

aren't likely to be closely watched. I've learned ways to disguise myself and disappear from a street or a hotel lobby before anyone realizes I've gone. Most of the time it's a matter of picking up or leaving a package. I've been followed, but never successfully." She didn't bother to hide the pride that was evident in the quiet boast.

"Does this have to do with what we decoded?" The breaking of the code was all Ben, but over the years he had come to consider his daughter's eyes as very nearly his own, her safety as paramount. He usually preferred to know as little as possible about the context of the enigmas he was unraveling. In this case, a Judge had made a ciphered record of his cases. That was all Hunter and Miss MacKenzie had told him. He hadn't asked for any additional details.

"It does." Quickly and succinctly, Prudence told them about the Judge's second marriage, explained their suspicions, described how she had searched the house and what she had found in Donald Morley's bedroom. She handed the photograph and the copies she had made of the menus to Lydia.

"Are you having her followed?" Ben directed his question to Geoffrey.

"Lightly followed."

"What does that mean?" asked Prudence.

"I have a man watching the house. He keeps a record of where Victoria and Donald go, how long they stay, when they return. But he doesn't always or even usually follow them inside their destinations. That's the lightly part."

"You're thinking that someone needs to go to White Sulphur Springs, West Virginia, aren't you, Miss Prudence?" Lydia said. "To the Grand Central Hotel. I assume that's where the photograph was taken. It looks like the front veranda of a hotel." Still holding the copies of the menus and the photograph, she turned slightly in her chair and spoke directly to Prudence. "Your stepmother was trolling for a rich husband. An elderly rich husband who could be depended upon to trouble her very little and die conveniently soon after the wedding. Women are a great deal crueler and more clever than men ever give them credit for being." She glanced at her silent but attentive father, then turned back to Prudence. "Have you ever heard of The Lost Cause?"

"It refers to the chivalry of those who lost the recent war despite their courage and dedication to preserving a nobler way of life," Geoffrey explained. The muscles along his jawline tightened.

"I don't understand," Prudence said.

"West Virginia is at least a two-day journey, if you make all of the rail connections through Washington City," Lydia said. "Another two or three days to question the hotel staff and exchange gossip with whatever guests are willing to talk to one of us, then two days back. A week spent chasing down a photograph and a menu, with no guarantee of success. There's an easier and much faster way to find the information you need."

"Bravo, my dear. Very clever." Ben Truitt saluted his daughter with a raised teacup.

"Ned Hayes would know how to get in touch with them," Geoffrey mused. "He was one of the youngest officers ever to command troops for the Confederacy. Wounded and captured at some no-account skirmish in North Carolina. I don't think he was more than eighteen or nineteen years old at the time you met him, Ben. His mother took him south with her when he was sixteen. He did his duty as she saw it, but after his capture he never went back. I always wondered if that's what he's trying so hard to forget."

"Ned isn't the only ex-Confederate living in New York City," Lydia continued. "What you have to remember is that families were torn apart in the war. After it was all over and peace was declared, they had to mend and forgive each other as best they could. Many refused, of course, but for others it was enough to know that someone of their blood had survived, whatever side he fought on. It can't be easy, living in your conqueror's country, so a lot of these deeply wounded men and women have formed societies that meet to keep the old dreams alive and honor the memories of those who fell because of them. What I'm proposing is that you show this photograph where it's most likely to stir old memories."

"If someone recognizes the gentleman in the wheeled chair, it's possible they'll also know his story," Prudence said.

"And how it intersects with Victoria," Ben finished.

"I can't imagine they would welcome a Yankee in their midst," Prudence said.

"I was born and bred in North Carolina," Geoffrey said. "The only thing that kept me from putting on a Confederate uniform was the accident of age."

"Do you think Ned Hayes will help?"

"He will. Ned has a burning thirst for justice. That's another reason he was encouraged to leave the New York City Police Department."

"Many a loyal Confederate gave his parole rather than be sent to one of the prison camps," Ben contributed. "It's never been held against them. People will calculate how young Ned was when he fought his first battle. They'll honor that in him and overlook the rest."

Prudence took a deep breath. "I'm sorry," she apologized. "We should have told you everything from the very beginning."

"Need to know," Lydia said. "In the world of ciphers and codes it's much safer to operate with as little overall knowledge as possible. My father has always said that his life hangs from the slender strand of need to know."

"Yet one of the greatest pieces of advice ever given to a combatant is to know his enemy," Ben said. "Not always the easiest thing to do."

"My father said it applies to lawyers as well as to generals."

"And on that piece of very sage wisdom, I think we should

leave." Geoffrey gathered up the photograph and the facsimilies Prudence had made of the two menus.

"We'll keep your names out of it," Prudence promised. "No one will ever know who broke the cipher."

"Fire is a great keeper of secrets," Ben Truitt said.

Geoffrey had not mentioned their suspicions about Charles's death. As hard as it was to keep from sharing that information with these intelligent and caring people, Prudence respected his reticence. *Need to know,* she reminded herself.

Lydia kissed her new friend lightly on the cheek. "Don't fret, Miss Prudence. Geoffrey and Ned Hayes may have to take the stage for a while, but you have a role to play in this charade also. And it may be the most important one of all."

Halfway across the Brooklyn Bridge, Danny Dennis flicked his whip at a large horsefly that was about to settle on Mr. Washington's broad back. He'd remembered something about the Judge, but it didn't seem important enough to mention. Better follow up on his own first. He'd light a candle tonight on his way home. It never hurt to remind the angels that there was work to be done.

CHAPTER 22

"Has she arrived, Sister?"

"Same as every Tuesday afternoon, Mr. McGlory."

"If anyone should ask, I'm not here."

"No one ever has."

"Just the same. I'm not here."

"Would you have me lie about one of our most generous patrons?"

"I would, Sister Angelica. Except that it doesn't have to be a lie now, does it?" He turned the visitor log around so she could read the name he'd written on the line below Mrs. Barstow's signature. *Father Sean O'Loughlin.* "If anyone asks, all you have to do is point. There's only the two of us today."

"That's lying by omission, and well you know it. *Father Sean O'Loughlin!* I suppose it was bound to come to that eventually, pretending to be a priest!"

"My sainted mother, God rest her soul, wore her knees out praying for me to become a priest. And I haven't gone so far as to wear the collar." He hadn't. Glimpsed from behind, the black suit he'd put on was plain enough to pass for a priest's, and he had no intention of letting anyone see his face. He'd a scarf to wind around his neck to conceal the lack of priestly collar and a hat to pull down low.

"She should have known better," Sister Angelica snapped. Then smiled, because Mr. McGlory, for all the terrible things that were said and written about him, had never failed to answer any of the nuns' urgent requests. He gave even when they didn't ask, and all he wanted for it was to be remembered in their prayers. "Get on with you now, I've work to do."

They sat for ten minutes without saying a word, McGlory on one side of the hospital bed, Frances Barstow on the other. It was always this way at the beginning. It took time to adjust to the fact that the young woman lying still as death between them was alive, to remember that she had once been a fine dancer, a happy soul who laughed more than she cried, a creature so beautiful that many men had fallen in love with her and one of them had beaten her into insensibility.

Her baptismal name was Mary. She was Frances Barstow's younger sister and Billy McGlory's second cousin, once removed. Victoria's housekeeper called her Molly.

"How is she?" Billy asked. He always started with the same question. It was what you did in a hospital. Except that in this wing there was no hope of recovery. Hearts beat and lungs breathed, but eyes did not see and brains neither recognized nor remembered. Mostly there was silence in the long white room where beds were separated by white curtains hung from the ceiling for privacy.

"Sister Angelica says she's failing." Tears had run down Mrs. Barstow's cheeks, dried there in streaky runnels. "She hasn't much time left, and that's a blessing, I suppose. But I'll miss her, I'll miss her terribly when she goes."

"It's already been too long, Frances. She wouldn't have wanted anyone to see her like this. You know how she was, always looking at herself in the mirror."

"She was so pretty when she was little. So pretty."

"You can't blame her for what she became. She made her own choices, and I never heard her say she regretted them."

"She thought he was in love with her."

"He's dead now, so it doesn't matter. He paid."

"I never asked you about that."

"There's nothing to be said. He beat her up and then he fell off a pier. He was dead drunk, and then he was just dead."

"They say on the street that Billy McGlory always pays his debts. And always collects on what's owed him."

"It keeps things simple. People know where they stand."

Molly Barstow had been dying under the care of the Sisters of Charity for almost three years. When Frances Barstow brought her to their hospital the girl was unconscious, both her arms broken and one of her legs. She'd been beaten so badly that her body was black and blue from the neck down. She was bleeding from the ears and her skull was flattened on one side from being hit so hard and so many times. The only place he hadn't used an ax handle on her was her face. Molly had been in a coma from that day to this one.

She'd worked in McGlory's Armory Hall from the time she was seventeen until a protector set her up in her own house. When Frances asked her cousin to give her a job, too, so she could keep an eye on her sister, he did. Family was family. Billy's girls didn't have a madam because the Armory wasn't a brothel, but Frances was as close to one as made no difference. She looked out for them as best she could, and when the inevitable happened and they wept in her arms over it, she sent them to someone who usually managed to get rid of the problem without killing them. The only lady of the night she hadn't been able to save was her sister.

Billy paid for the special care Molly needed, and gave generously to the Sisters of Charity even though the nuns would have given his cousin the same devoted nursing if he hadn't donated a nickel. But Billy paid his debts. So did Frances Barstow. It was a family trait.

Frances accepted without question that Billy needed someone to be his eyes and ears in the household of a rich Judge's mistress who was going to lose her housekeeper. The Dakota had opened another world to Frances Barstow, one she never wanted to have to leave. When Victoria Morley became Victoria MacKenzie, Frances moved with her to the mansion on Fifth Avenue.

Every few weeks, without fail, Billy showed up at Molly's bedside on a Tuesday afternoon. They talked. About family. About Molly's condition. And always about what Victoria MacKenzie was saying and doing. He never told his cousin what his interest was, and Frances knew better than to ask.

The hard part about being Victoria MacKenzie's housekeeper was the discipline the mistress of the house insisted be maintained over the staff. Not that Frances hadn't had experience managing people; she had, all those soiled doves Billy had entrusted to her. But Fifth Avenue was a different place altogether. Everyone except Frances had been there for years, some of them going back to the time of the Judge's earlier marriage. The first one to go had been the housekeeper Mrs. Barstow replaced, the most recent casualty the butler who had once been the Judge's valet.

Almost three years now, and Frances Barstow had nearly forgotten the woman she had once been. She had remade herself after the housekeeper who trained her as a maid all those long years ago before Armory Hall. A strict unsmiling woman who hovered like a predatory hawk over the young girls who were in service under her. Harsh, unforgiving, cold, and never showing any weakness of her own. Frances Barstow took that housekeeper as her model and succeeded in creating a persona she now wore as effortlessly as if she had never had to learn it.

"I think Mrs. MacKenzie is beginning to make mistakes," Frances said.

"Explain."

"One of the maids was killed last week. She fell down the staircase that connects the kitchen and the servants' hall in the basement to the first floor where the family parlors are." Frances smoothed the white coverlet that barely moved, so shallow was Molly's breathing. "I don't think it was an accident. Colleen had been up and down those stairs hundreds of times. I think she knew something and had to be silenced."

"There have been two other deaths connected with that family in the past three months."

"Miss Prudence's fiancé died in the blizzard. I don't see how that could be anything but an accident. The Judge went down more slowly. I saw the decline. It was his heart giving out, they said. Maybe. The maid who died was the same one who changed his sheets and brought up his trays after the first attack left him bedridden. She was in his room more than Mrs. MacKenzie, nearly as much as Miss Prudence."

"What are you saying, Frances?"

"Only that if there was anything to know about that death, she would be the one who would know it."

"You think Victoria killed him, killed her husband?"

"I think she's an evil woman, Billy. I don't know why you sent me there, but you were right to do it." She had her own suspicions, which she was sure he would never confirm. Victoria MacKenzie had taken something personal from Billy; he was biding his time before taking it back or exacting a price Frances didn't want to know about. "If Victoria did help the Judge into his grave, and if she persuaded someone to push the maid down the stairs, then she's cleaning house, getting rid of anyone who stands in the way of what she wants. I can't imagine that she's stupid enough to go after you, if that's what you're waiting for." Molly twitched and moaned; it meant nothing, but Frances always hoped. "Her stepdaughter is next. Miss Prudence."

"What does the rest of the staff think?"

"No one will say a word if it means losing a position. Mrs. MacKenzie is the kind of employer who wouldn't think twice about letting a servant go without a reference. A maid or a manservant without a reference would never work again."

"Tell me about the maid who fell down the stairs."

"I think she was pushed, Billy, and I think it was Obediah Jackson who did it."

"Who is Obediah Jackson?"

"All I know about him is that he appeared the same day Ian Cameron was given the boot. Cameron had been the Judge's butler for years; he was supposedly like one of the family. Victoria had him out the door and Jackson in his place before any of us knew what was happening. No explanation."

"You're right. She's cleaning house." He'd never intended allowing Victoria to walk away from what she'd done to him, but he was a careful man. The reformers were howling for his blood and his livelihood; he was keeping his head down, biding his time. The longer he waited, the safer Victoria would feel, and the sweeter the taste of his revenge. He thought it might be time to set things in motion. No hurry. Nobody ever escaped from Billy McGlory.

"Miss Prudence is next. And that would be a terrible shame."

"It would be, Frances. From what I've heard of her, it would be a significant loss to at least one interesting gentleman of my recent acquaintance. Perhaps two."

"How often does Donald Morley come in?"

"He mostly goes to the Haymarket now. I have a friend there who takes care of him." T-Boy had never been in Mr. Mc-Glory's private office before. The smell and feel of the soft leather cradling his body was nearly as sweet as swamp grass in an early Louisiana spring. He was definitely going to have to go back home sometime soon.

"I need to know everything about him, T-Boy. From how he takes his coffee in the morning to what he wears to bed at night. He has a sister. I want him to tell you everything there is to know about her, too. If you have to make a choice, she's more important than he is. Do you understand?"

"My friend is good at finding things out, but if I tell him to make himself unavailable and spread the word, Morley will come back here to the Armory. It may not be until Thursday or Friday though."

"That's all right. I don't think Mr. Morley is going to give me anything to worry about for a while yet. But it's always best to be prepared."

"Yes, sir."

"As long as you know what you have to do."

Billy McGlory handed T-Boy a heavy leather wallet. T-Boy didn't dare open it right then and there, but he couldn't resist a surreptitious heft. Defnitely good money for what he would have done for free. Everybody knew that McGlory paid his debts. And collected on what was owed him. That was the part that frightened most people.

"I don't want you leaving the house again today, Prudence. What will people think?" Victoria looked to Donald for encouragement and support. He was slicing the top off his second boiled egg and reading the morning paper.

"I agree," he mumbled.

"I won't then. I'll work in my father's library." Prudence sighed, measured out eight drops of dark, bitter liquid from the laudanum bottle she'd brought with her to the breakfast table and stirred them into her coffee.

"Eight, Prudence? Is that wise?"

"This must be a weak solution, Victoria." She held the bottle out to her stepmother, as if urging her to try it for herself, her eyes wide with innocence. *Think calf,* she told herself. *Think wide eyes and a blank stare.*

Victoria waved off the proffered brown bottle.

"Jackson tells me you were out nearly all day last Thursday, and then again on Monday, but you didn't take the carriage. I don't like that, Prudence. I don't like you going out alone. It smacks of deceit. If you need air, Kincaid can drive you to Central Park, though I'd much prefer we go together."

"I'm sorry, Victoria, it won't happen again."

"Where did you go?"

"Please. Must I?"

"I insist, Prudence. Where did you go?"

She ducked her head and spoke into her crumpled napkin so the words were muffled and nearly unintelligible. "I went to visit Charles." It was the only thing she could think of that would be impossible to prove or disprove.

"Speak up. I can't hear you."

"She said she went to the cemetery where Linwood is buried." Donald laid down his newspaper.

"Is that right? Is that what you did?"

"Yes. There's a bench near the family crypt. I don't remember how long I sat there, but I couldn't seem to leave. I just wanted to be near him for a while."

"I forbid you to go there again, Prudence. Anything could happen alone in a place like that."

"I was afraid if I requested the carriage, I'd have to tell you why I wanted it. There was no one I could ask to go with me. The Linwoods went to their country house right after the funeral."

"You knew very well what I would say, didn't you? That was deliberate deceit on your part. Your father would be furious with you."

"Please, Victoria, may I be excused?"

"Something is wrong with your stays," Victoria scolded, pointing at a spot on her own perfectly smooth black silk bodice. "That German Clara *has* to be replaced."

"She does her best," Prudence said. The emerald ring she was wearing on a gold chain around her neck had worked its way out of the spot where she had tucked it into her corset. She could feel the lump of it under her black mourning dress as she pushed it back down with one impatient finger. "She didn't lace me tightly enough, that's all. Please, may I go now?"

Geoffrey had been right, of course, as he usually was. Prudence should have given him the emerald and diamond ring to lock in his safe. She had been headstrong and impulsive to insist on keeping it herself, foolish to imagine that Victoria wouldn't notice the slightest imperfection in her dress. She thought the gold chain was thin enough to be invisible under the fabric of her gown, and thank God for high necklines, but she would have to find a way to keep the ring itself more secure. As soon as possible, she'd slip out of the house and walk to the Fifth Avenue Hotel. She had done it once before, she could do it again. This time she would hand him her mother's ring without being asked for it.

"That was odd," Victoria said.

"What was odd?" Donald went back to his newspaper.

"Spending all that time in the cemetery. I think she's lying to us, Donald."

"Why would she do that?"

"I don't know. Hand me her coffee cup."

"It's empty."

"Then give me her spoon."

"Her spoon?"

"Must you always repeat everything I say?"

He rattled the paper to show his annoyance, but he also reached across the table and handed Prudence's spoon to Victoria. He always ended up doing what she told him to.

"And now here's something else that's odd," Victoria said.

"What's that?"

"Coffee on the spoon. Just coffee. I saw her stir in the laudanum, but there's no trace of it on this spoon, Donald." She put it into her mouth again to show him what she meant. "There should be at least a slight tinge of bitterness, but there isn't."

"Coffee isn't bitter, Victoria."

"Nothing completely masks the taste of laudanum, Donald. You know that as well as I do."

"What does it mean?"

"It means she's taking us on. She thinks she's being clever, but she has no idea what she's up against. She has to go. I was planning to wait a few more weeks, until she was good and surely muddled, but there's no chance of that now. She's either watered down the laudanum I've been giving her or she replaced it entirely with something else. She has to go."

"It's a good time for it." He pointed to an article in the newspaper. "It says here that Conkling's doctors are keeping him confined to his bed. His wife has come down from Utica."

"Which means he won't be around to interfere. By the time he recovers, if he recovers, Prudence MacKenzie will be long gone. There won't be anything to alarm the bank officers, and with a doctor's certification of her nervous condition, no one will ask questions."

"What about Geoffrey Hunter? He was at the church the day of Linwood's funeral, and he stuck his nose in when Colleen had her accident."

"From what I've been told when I've asked about him, he's a dilettante. No real profession. He and Linwood were at school together, so he felt an obligation to his friend's fiancée. He's supposed to have been a Pinkerton for a while, but he's one of those people who's easily bored. He'll be more than happy to find out he no longer has to worry about Prudence MacKenzie, that she's gone where proper care can be taken of her. And that will be the end of it."

"Good. I'm getting tired of always having her around."

"Patience, Donald. She'll be out of here as soon as I can arrange things with Dr. Yarborough." Victoria smiled at him. "You can have the Judge's library all to yourself."

*   *   *

"Clara, go up and tell Miss Prudence that the library is open," Victoria directed, unlocking the door with the Judge's key, still on its gold chain.

"The extra packing boxes you asked for are downstairs in the luggage room," Mrs. Barstow said. She watched the maid climb the stairs and hoped Clara had understood Mrs. MacKenzie's instructions.

"Good. They can stay there for the time being."

"If I may ask, madam, what is it we'll be using them for?" If it hadn't been for yesterday's conversation with Billy, she would never have dared pose the question.

"You'll be told when you need to know," Victoria said.

Mrs. Barstow waited for a few moments, as if expecting further orders, then excused herself. "I'll just check that the dining room has been cleared," she explained unnecessarily. Mrs. MacKenzie's silences made her nervous, as did her habit of exchanging as few words as possible with the household staff.

By the time Prudence came downstairs, German Clara trailing after her, Victoria had disappeared into her bedroom, closing and locking the door behind her. Donald had gone into the parlor to smoke his morning pipe and doze over the newspaper. He would have preferred a snooze in bed, but Victoria insisted on keeping up appearances.

The house was quiet, empty feeling, as though whoever lived there had gone away for a time. Prudence thought it had been like that ever since the Judge died, worse after Charles was lost to her. She waited until Clara started down the servants' staircase, then quickly retrieved the hidden key from its hole in the coatrack. She needed the safety of a few moments of delay for what she intended to do; she couldn't afford to have Victoria walk in on her with no warning.

Prudence locked the library door behind her, then went straight to the shelf where the Lewis and Clark book had lain atop a pile of other outsized volumes of geography and exploration.

The panel had been cut so skillfully into the grain of the wood and fitted so precisely that she had to search with her fingers to find it. Only if you already knew it was there could you see it. Remembering the mechanism of the hidden drawer in the rolltop desk, she tapped gently where she thought the spring must lie. The panel that concealed Judge MacKenzie's safe popped open without a sound. Behind it was a lock whose combination Prudence devoutly hoped was a date her father had known she would never forget.

Prudence tried her mother's birthday first, forward and backward, then the date of her death. Her father's birthday, her own. As each group of numbers failed, she grew more desperate. Her fingers slipped as she turned the dial, her mind went blank and refused to supply her with more possibilities. Finally, reduced to random twists, she was forced to admit defeat. Time was what she needed, but time was her enemy in this household. She closed the panel, checked to make sure it truly was invisible to the uninitiated eye, and slid the heavy, awkward stack of geographies in front of it, filling the rest of the shelf with smaller books.

As quietly as she could, she unlocked the library door, but did not open it. She would ask Geoffrey to put Lydia and Ben Truitt to work on reasoning out the combination to the safe. In the meantime she would have to be satisfied with knowing it existed and that she had found it.

Victoria was bound to come check on her soon. She had to be convinced by what she found that her stepdaughter was neither a threat nor even much of a challenge. Judge MacKenzie had believed that a deceptively meek appearance often won the day in the courtroom.

Or in life.

Behind the locked door of her bedroom, Victoria reread the commitment papers that would remove Prudence from her home. Permanently.

She had counseled Donald to have patience, but she understood his eagerness to be rid of the Judge's daughter. She herself was as annoyed and irritated by the girl as it was possible to get without losing her temper outright. And that was something Victoria tried very hard not to do. She had spent too many precious hours cultivating the calm demeanor of a society woman to risk it all for the indulgence of letting fly her anger. Unless Prudence provoked her beyond bearing. She felt the itch of a hard slap on the palm of her hand. She smiled, picturing the shock on her stepdaughter's face when she delivered the stinging blow. Too bad it was unlikely to happen.

She would speak to Dr. Yarborough, tell him she wanted the date of Prudence's confinement advanced. The young woman was becoming more and more demanding and unreasonable with every passing day. She would have to fabricate a few telling incidents to demonstrate how very much Prudence was in need of the serene atmosphere in which Dr. Yarborough's ladies found refuge from life's burdens. No one had to ask for laudanum at his clinic; it was liberally and frequently dispensed.

Victoria stayed in her bedroom only long enough to lull Prudence into thinking she would not be interrupted. It was important to her plan that the girl feel safe. But it was equally essential that she not be given the opportunity to slip away again. Did she really think she could fool anyone for very long with that absurd story of going to visit Charles Linwood in the cemetery?

Victoria crept noiselessly down the thickly carpeted stairs. She smelled Donald's pipe tobacco seeping under the parlor door; he'd very likely have pinpoint burns and flakes of ash strewn across his vest. She wondered if she'd ever succeed in making a gentleman of him.

The library door opened easily, its massive brass knob cool in Victoria's hand. She half expected to find a disheveled Prudence rummaging among her father's few remaining books, fruitlessly searching for some final missive he might have left her.

She needn't have been concerned.

Prudence had curled herself into the depths of a huge arm-chair. Tears had left telltale tracks down her cheeks. She looked lost, helpless, and forlorn. On her lap lay an open photo album of her childhood.

Nothing suspicious. Nothing to worry about.

Still, it would be easier for all concerned if Prudence's trip to Dr. Yarborough's clinic were made without fuss or protest.

Victoria wondered if she could manage to slip a few drops of unadulterated laudanum into her stepdaughter's afternoon tea. That's all it would take. She understood human weaknesses very well; her greatest successes had come from taking advantage of them.

CHAPTER 23

The kind of police detective Ned Hayes had been was meat and drink to reporters who had to file inches of copy every day. Flamboyant and daring, handsome and well-spoken, he was far removed from the ordinary Irish beat cop and corrupt Tammany detective. He never laid a stick across a suspect's back, never kicked out a drunk's teeth, never availed himself of the sexual favors available free of charge to the city's finest. The only rumor about him that reporters never managed to verify was whether or not Edwin "Ned" Hayes was a man of independent and substantial means. He was, of course, but that bit of information did not make it into the light of day. Nor did his war record. He'd paid good money to become a nobody before he became a copper.

By the time Detective First Class Ned Hayes saved Billy McGlory's life, he'd stepped into someone else's limelight once too often, and he was too clean for Tammany Hall to ignore. Sooner or later he'd turn his attention to the bribes that kept his brother cops fat and happy, and when he did, he'd bring the New York press and the do-gooders along with him. So while Tammany was pleased that he'd saved McGlory, whose saloon paid dearly for the privilege of staying open, the bosses decided that Hayes would have to fall.

He resigned before they fired him. Newsmen who had raised a glass or two with him in better times telegraphed their sympathy down the length of a bar or with a quick tilt of the head, but they wrote what they were told and paid to write. Roscoe Conkling sent Josiah Gregory around to offer the lawyer's services should Hayes want to sue. It would have been a helluva scrappy fight, but Ned decided to withdraw quietly and gracefully.

He made sure that Russell Coughlin, who wrote for the *New York Herald,* knew about his morphine purchases, and then denied none of the stories that made the rounds. *Ned Hayes is on the slide. The bottle. Smoking a pipe. Taking it rough. The needle. It won't be long. Too bad. He was a good man while he lasted.*

Barricaded inside the house his mother had abandoned a year into the war when she took herself and her sixteen-year-old son and only child to her family home in South Carolina, Hayes picked his way into his memories through a veil of bourbon. Soothed himself with the white powder that could be smoked, sniffed, rubbed along the gums, or cooked down to an injectable solution. When he had finished with his own life, he pored over the lives of others, reading his way book by book along the library shelves that had been impressively stocked by his bibliophile father. He did not find the answers he was looking for. Only contradictions and more questions. He drank more bourbon and resorted more frequently to the lovely powder until he became the addict everyone already believed him to be.

He was saved by the body servant who had suffered his descent with tears in his eyes and gentle remonstrances that went unheeded. Until the day Ned Hayes very nearly died when the bourbon and the morphine met in his body in epic proportions and fought over which should ultimately kill him. Tyrus Hayes, who had taken his master's last name when freedom came, reluctantly tied Master Ned to his bed, then sat down beside it to wait for consciousness and the terrible drug hunger to return.

When they did, he bathed the man he still thought of as a child in cool water every half hour, straightened his limbs after each bout of the convulsions that abraded his skin beneath the restraints. Ned railed, pleaded, threatened, and wept for release. The old man who had loved him since the day he was born stuffed cotton in his ears and didn't loosen the ropes by so much as an inch. Day after day for a week, Ned woke and slept, soiled himself and was cleansed, twisted and rubbed his limbs raw against the ropes, screamed his desperate need for the powder and the drink. It didn't matter how close he came to death, or how many times he yearned for it, Tyrus was determined that it shouldn't be granted him. Not this way.

The cure was not one that many survived, but within a month after Tyrus had tied his master to his bed, it was complete. Ned could barely stand, could not walk without support, and was thinner than the ancient ex-slave who was very nearly skin and bones. But he was free. His body was free, though his mind never would be. From that day on he measured and monitored every ounce of bourbon he swallowed, every pinch of morphine he allowed himself. If he didn't, there was a black shadow standing just over his shoulder who did. "I think that be enough for now, Master Ned," the voice would say as the callused, bony hand reached for glass or needle. And Ned would stop. Wherever he was in his memories or his suffering, he would stop.

Perversely, because heroism had never appealed to him, he allowed the stories of his addictions to continue to spread, growing more and more lurid with each telling. It came to be an undisputed fact that the once promising Ned Hayes was a drunk and a drug fiend. Since he was never seen in public, never tossed into the street from a bar or a brothel he'd set out to trash, never picked up and escorted home by policemen who would be well paid for the service, he gradually faded from discussion.

Too many men, and not a few women, disappeared into their bottles every day for Ned Hayes's case to be remarkable. He'd had his moment of notoriety when he saved Billy McGlory's life. There were some reporters who thought he was already dead. So be it.

The only spark of life Ned had shown in over a year of near sobriety had been when Geoffrey Hunter knocked on his door and asked for help in getting to Billy McGlory. Something about that visit stirred him out of his lethargy, awakened the old detective instincts. And now Hunter needed him again. It was almost enough to make him want to quit drinking altogether. Tyrus had a smile on his face nearly as broad as the one on the muzzle of that ugly white horse Danny Dennis drove around.

"I'm going to give you the story of your career," Ned told Russell Coughlin, who nearly spewed out the beer he was drinking when Hayes sat down beside him in the Easy Shamrock saloon. "But you've got to keep it under wraps until I give the word."

"Jesus, Mary, and Joseph, Detective!" Coughlin sputtered.

"I'm not in the department anymore, Russell."

"You look like hell, pardon my saying so."

"Looks can be deceiving."

Russell Coughlin could smell a story a mile away. The sweet stink of someone else's scandal was hanging all around Ned Hayes, making the reporter's fingers tingle for the pencil stub and pad of paper in the breast pocket of his threadbare tweed jacket.

Hayes handed him a list of thirty-seven names and dates. "Start with Patrick Monoghan, accused of murder in September 1873. Charges dismissed."

"What am I looking for?"

"Every man on this list has a story. You'll have to dig around in the *Herald* archives, but they'll all be there. You've got twenty-four hours to find the who, what, where, when, and why of every mother's son of them. I especially want to know if they're alive or dead, and where to find them. When you've got the information, take it to Roscoe Conkling's office in the United Bank Building down on Wall Street and Broadway. Give it to Josiah Gregory and then walk away. You'll get a call when it's time to write the story, but if what you've done leaks, you'll get nothing."

"I'm guaranteed an exclusive," Coughlin stipulated.

"How else?" Hayes smiled, the handsome man he had once been shining through and lighting up the bar stool he occupied. "One more thing. The last set of dates and initials on the list may be more important than some of the others. Follow the story to its end, whatever that is, especially if the man died in Sing Sing. Check up on his relatives, find out whatever you can about them."

"I'll do it," Coughlin said.

"No leaks. Do we have a deal?" Hayes asked.

They shook on it.

In her comfortable bed on Fifth Avenue, Victoria MacKenzie had no idea that her past life was catching up to her.

Nor had she reckoned on someone else's past crossing paths with hers.

Danny Dennis's cab waited in the alleyway behind the MacKenzie mansion.

"Kincaid said he'll give the note to a maid he called German Clara. She doesn't speak much English, but all she has to do is find and give it to Miss MacKenzie. He's waiting for her in the courtyard." Dennis paced impatiently beside the cab, acutely aware that anyone looking out one of the mansion's upper-story windows would wonder what a hansom cab was doing parked in the alley. He leaned into the cab again. "I think she's coming, Mr. Hunter. I heard a door open."

Moments later Kincaid appeared, leading a veiled figure in black past the stable block.

"You'd best be out of here," he said to Danny Dennis as he helped Prudence into the hansom and retied the curtain that had been drawn down to hide the vehicle's occupants. He glanced up at the mansion's rear facade. "I don't think anyone's spotted you."

Dennis nodded his head and clucked to Mr. Washington.

Kincaid watched the cab disappear down the alleyway and said a quick prayer of thanks that everyone in the MacKenzie household knew that German Clara didn't understand half of what was said to her. It wasn't much protection for the girl, but it was better than nothing.

"We've been invited to Mrs. Cavanaugh's Wednesday Afternoon At Home," Geoffrey Hunter explained. "Ned arranged it."

"I'm pleased to make your acquaintance, Miss MacKenzie." Ned Hayes raised his top hat and bowed as gracefully as the crowded interior of the hansom permitted.

"And I yours, Mr. Hayes. I don't think we'd have been able to get to Billy McGlory without your help."

"It's a pleasure to be able to serve so lovely a lady."

Hayes thought Geoffrey was right about the late Judge's daughter; she was indeed a rare one. Unconcerned about admitting to an association with the most notorious saloonkeeper in the city and as at ease unchaperoned in a hansom cab with two men as if she sat in her own parlor. Pale gray eyes that looked directly at you unafraid of what they would discover, a smile that came from the heart, and with it the kind of rock-solid single-minded determination you seldom saw in young society women. A rare one indeed.

"Mrs. Cavanaugh is leaving the city at the end of the week to take the waters in Saratoga Springs. She suffers cruelly from dyspepsia." Geoffrey smiled. "When you see her, I think you'll understand why."

"You'd better tell me what this is about," Prudence said, settling herself against the tufted leather of the seat. Danny Dennis was as good a driver as there was, but even he couldn't smooth out the cobblestones.

"Mrs. Cavanaugh is a widow in her early seventies," Ned began. "Her father was a banker here in New York City who took his family to White Sulphur Springs, Virginia, instead of Saratoga one year. To your Grand Central Hotel, in fact, where his daughter Laura, the present Mrs. Cavanaugh, met her husband. They married, and from what I understand she quickly became more Southern than Geoffrey or I could ever manage. To make a long story short, Colonel Cavanaugh lost everything during the war, including his life.

"Mrs. Cavanaugh's father was elderly by that time, but he was lonely, too. So he traveled down to the ruins of what had been a fine plantation and took his daughter and her three adult children North. Rescued them from penury and almost certain death from starvation and disease. The son, another Colonel Cavanaugh, had been badly wounded; he lost an arm and has to use a cane to get around. The two daughters were widows like their mother, but childless. The father was so incensed at the conditions he found them living in that he vowed his daughter and her family would never go back. So when he died, he left everything to Laura, including the house we're going to today, but with the stipulation that unless she and her heirs continued to live in it, the rest of his fortune would go to charity. Remember, he was a banker. Rich as Croesus."

"They've been in New York ever since?"

"With an occasional trip to Saratoga or White Sulphur Springs to take the waters. The father made sure the South Carolina plantation was lost to taxes long ago."

"I think I understand now," Prudence said.

"Miss Lydia was right," Geoffrey added. "The Lost Cause is alive and well in the widow Cavanaugh's parlor. Every Confederate who can prove his pedigree is welcome to her Wednesday Afternoon At Home."

"And that's where you think we'll find someone who can identify the man in the wheeled chair. Who might even have met Victoria or Donald at the Grand Central Hotel?"

"I believe it's the best chance we've got."

"I don't have a Confederate pedigree, Geoffrey," Prudence reminded him.

"You do now," he said. "We're distantly related cousins."

"Kissin' cousins, Miss MacKenzie," explained Ned Hayes. "That's what we call them down home."

She stared at him for a moment, then burst out laughing.

"I can't imitate the accent," she finally said.

"It's something you're born with, like freckles or a gap between your front teeth," Geoffrey assured her. "Not necessary for you because although male members of your family fought for the South, you've always lived in the North. The fewer lies you have to remember, the easier it is to make them believable."

To Prudence's uneducated ear, the two men now sounded exactly alike. A fellow Southerner could have told in an instant which state each man claimed as his own.

"How did you manage to get invitations, Mr. Hayes?" Prudence asked.

"Kissin' cousins, Miss MacKenzie," he answered, twinkling his blue eyes at her. "Kissin' cousins."

By the time Danny Dennis stopped his cab to let them out, Prudence was as comfortable in her new identity as she was likely to get. And relishing the challenge.

Mrs. Laura Cavanaugh's lavishly appointed home was as grand as any of the new showplaces being built along Fifth Avenue by Vanderbilts and Astors. The ceilings were high, coffered, and gilded, the windows heavily curtained and draped, the polished wood floors dotted with priceless Turkish carpets. Freshly cut spring flowers stood in Chinese porcelain vases on tables and sideboards, their light scents cutting through the fog of perfumed women and pomaded men promenading through three parlors separated one from the other by doors that slid back into the walls.

The butler who ushered them in held out a silver tray to collect their calling cards, but after that familiar beginning, this At Home was unlike any Prudence had ever attended.

A fair sprinkling of the men were in full dress Confederate uniform, though little of what they wore resembled the worn and often bloodstained uniforms of the last days of the war. These were marvels of the tailor's art, hand stitched and fitted, beribboned and hung with medals, finished off with epaulets, gold curlicues, double rows of polished brass buttons, fringed sashes, and scabbarded swords.

"They're like wax figures in an exhibition come to life," Prudence breathed.

"It's The Lost Cause being recreated in a new and better image," Geoffrey corrected her. "If these people and others like them have their way, the South will pass into history as a glorious era to be yearned for and never forgotten."

"I was there," Ned snapped. "No war is glorious."

A handsome man in his early or mid-fifties limped toward them, the left sleeve of his gray uniform pinned across his chest, his right hand wielding a gold-handled burled walnut cane.

"I'm delighted you finally decided to join us," he said to Ned Hayes, bowing stiffly and quickly to avoid the embarrassment of not having a free hand to shake.

Introductions were made. Geoffrey was apparently also a kissin' cousin, though much further removed than Ned. Prudence wondered if everyone in the South belonging to a certain social class was related. The colonel's sisters, one very thin, the other so excessively round that she tilted from side to side as she walked, escorted Prudence toward the parlor where most of the ladies had gathered around their hostess.

Mrs. Cavanaugh held court from a gold silk brocade cushioned settee meant to accomodate two people, now amply filled with her considerable bulk. She motioned to Prudence to come sit by her, a gesture not lost on the thin daughter, who set a chair close by her mother's settee. By the time Prudence finished her first cup of tea, Mrs. Cavanaugh had extracted her entire life history from her, or at least the story concocted by Geoffrey and Ned. Tiny, crustless sandwiches no wider than the width of a finger appeared and disappeared with amazing rapidity, iced cake squares came and went just as quickly. Laura Cavanaugh was past mistress of the art of speaking and eating at the same time without mangling a word or dropping a crumb.

"Ned told me you've been puzzling over something I might be able to help you with," she finally said, touching a tiny linen napkin to her lips.

It was the opening Prudence had been waiting for. She took the photograph she had found hidden in Donald's suitcase and handed it to her hostess. "It was in with my late father's personal correspondence. Just lying there in the drawer loose, like he'd thrown away the letter it came in, but maybe decided to keep the picture a little longer. When I showed it to Cousin Geoffrey, he said he thought he recognized the Grand Central Hotel veranda by the chandelier hanging over the front door. There's not another one like it anywhere; they had to reinforce the roof so they could hang it. You can just make it out right behind the man seated in the wheeled chair."

Laura Cavanaugh peered at the photograph through the lorgnette she wore pinned to her bodice. "That's Colonel Nathaniel Jamieson," she declared confidently. "He got shot off his horse right before Appomattox. He probably would have preferred to die, but he didn't. Sat in a wheelchair the rest of his life, such as it was. Lord help us, he was well past fifty years old when the war started, but he wouldn't stay home like most men of his age. I think his wife was dead by then and he had grown up children; he never did marry again."

Prudence looked politely puzzled. "I just assumed the lady standing beside him there was his wife, though much younger of course, and the other man perhaps his son." She turned the photograph over and pointed to the date written on the back. "But that doesn't make sense, does it? This says 1881, so if his wife was already dead and he didn't remarry, is this his daughter? The reason I ask is that I thought if I found out who the gentleman in the wheeled chair was, I could send the photograph to his family. Just in case." So many family mementos had been forever lost.

"That's got to be her, Mama," the thin daughter said, pointing at Victoria. "She had gall, I've got to give her that."

"I'd forget about sending this photograph anywhere but into a good, hot fire," Mrs. Cavanaugh said crisply. She passed it to the daughter whose chubby hand reached across the back of the settee. "What do you think, Bethann?"

"Well, we never did meet her, of course, but we heard all about her. There's nobody else would pose with Colonel Jamieson like that, and the date is right. I'd say she's got to be the one."

Prudence waited for Mrs. Cavanaugh to decide whether she should reveal what she knew to the stranger sitting opposite her. Both daughters looked as if they were about to burst with the effort of holding back. Prudence decided they needed a little prodding.

"I'm sure I can find an address for Colonel Jamieson or one of his children," she said. "I know I'd be forever grateful for a memento like this." Nothing too definite that she'd have to explain. Just hints at losses too painful to be discussed.

"I don't suppose it would do any harm to share what we know," Mrs. Cavanaugh mused, "Colonel Jamieson being dead and all. Nothing ever came of it, and the woman in question had the common sense to disappear."

"I don't know that that's absolutely so," corrected the thin daughter. "About her leaving on her own, I mean. We heard the hotel told her and her brother they were no longer welcome there. That's him, standing behind Colonel Jamieson."

"I am so confused," Prudence said, shaking her head. "Now I don't know what to do."

"Well, there really isn't any point in not telling because it turned out all right in the end," Mrs. Cavanaugh decided. From all around the room came the rustle of silk skirts as ladies moved closer. Nobody wanted to miss a word.

"Start with Colonel Jamieson, Mama."

"Like we told you, he was wounded at the end of the war and he never did get along with his son. They argued about everything, so the Colonel finally moved himself into Charleston. He had a house down on the Battery. The thing was, he didn't deed any of the family holdings over to his son, just left him and his daughter-in-law out there in the Low Country miles and miles away from Charleston to run the rice plantations with nothing but expectations. Nat Jamieson had been a rich man all his life, and the war didn't change that. When he got to feeling too bad, or he was tired of the same old Charleston faces all the time, he'd take himself up to White Sulphur Springs for the hot muscle cure. That's how he met Victoria Morley."

"That's her name, the lady in the photograph?" Prudence asked.

"That's her name all right, but I wouldn't exactly call her a lady."

"Seems like everyone who'd been at the Grand Central Hotel that year wrote to tell us about it," chimed in the thin daughter. "According to what we heard, Victoria Morley wanted a husband. The older and sicker, the better. As long as he was rich."

"That sounds terrible," Prudence said, trying to sound both shocked and disbelieving.

"Well, the next thing anyone knew, the Colonel's son and daughter-in-law came down on him like a pair of chicken hawks. I guess they didn't want to take a chance Miss Morley would get him to a preacher and persuade him to write them out of his will before they could snatch him away. They hustled the Colonel off to the rice plantation and the dust hadn't even settled on the road before the hotel management told the Morleys to pack their bags. The two of them had been there four or five months by then. They say she'd trolled her way through half a dozen prospects, but once she spotted the Colonel, she was dead set on reeling him in."

"Nobody ever did find out who their people were," said the thin daughter.

"Probably didn't have any," sniffed Mrs. Cavanaugh.

"Does anyone know where they went?" Prudence asked.

"North. The stationmaster said they bought tickets for Washington City and asked how much it would cost to travel on to New York City. I reckon they figured they'd about used up the ready supply of husband material in the South, not that there was a lot of it left." Mrs. Cavanaugh picked up the last small square of iced cake. "Northern gentlemen aren't any smarter about women than Southerners. Maybe she got that rich old man she was looking for after all."

"Your instinct about the moral turpitude stipulation is what's going to bring Victoria down," Geoffrey said when the three of them were back in Danny Dennis's cab. The reek of cigar smoke and bourbon clung to Hayes and Hunter; the men of The Lost Cause preferred tobacco and sippin' whiskey to tea, finger sandwiches, and cakes.

"I hope you got more damaging information than I did," Prudence responded. "All I was able to do was confirm what we already knew or suspected. The only thing new is that Victoria was nearly successful with the Confederate veteran in the wheelchair. His name was Colonel Nathaniel Jamieson, by the way. She was apparently leading him to the altar by way of a lawyer's office to rewrite his will when the man's son and daughter-in-law got suspicious and rescued him. They also made sure Victoria and Donald were unceremoniously shown the door before she could get her hooks into another of the hotel's guests. It doesn't paint her in a good light, but there's nothing strong enough to break her hold on the trusts."

"Ned and I barely got the photograph out of our pockets before someone recognized her. One of the men knew her from as far back as when she and Donald first arrived in White Sulphur Springs. This was months before they moved into the Grand Central Hotel where she met your Colonel Jamieson."

"Your stepmother wasn't nearly as careful as she needed to be," Ned added. "Though maybe she didn't have it all figured out in the early days. About where she wanted to end up and how she was going to get there, I mean."

"Donald was the one who always gave them away. He drank like a fish, played cards too well to be anything but a riverboat man, and never knew when to keep his mouth closed. Victoria was always after him not to say too much, but he didn't pay her any mind."

"I think you'd better tell her the worst of it, Geoffrey."

"Victoria got herself taken on at a sporting house. A couple of weeks after she started working there the bouncer disappeared. Just packed his bag in the night and didn't come down for breakfast. Donald replaced him."

"How did they get to the hotel?"

"That's the clever part. Victoria was popular with the sporting house clientele. She got asked for by name, and she apparently cheated the madam out of at least part of what she was supposed to turn over to her in tips. She didn't spend a dime of what she earned, saved up everything except what she had to pay for being part of the house. She bullied Donald unmercifully, snatched his pay right out of his hand half the time. In six months she managed to put away enough to rent a suite at the Grand Central Hotel for the season."

"Didn't anyone know who she was?"

"Victoria thought of everything. She timed it so her clients from the sporting house would all be gone before she made the move. And even if one or two of them did run into her at the hotel, they would have pretended not to recognize her."

"It would have worked, too, except that someone warned Colonel Jamieson's son and daughter-in-law about what was going on. I shouldn't wish Victoria on anyone," Prudence sighed, "but I'm almost sorry she failed with the colonel. She'd still be queening it over Charleston society instead of taking and ruining lives in New York City."

"Not one of the gentlemen who availed himself of her services is willing to testify to it," Geoffrey said. "I was careful not to reveal anything that could lead back to the Judge. That's why I didn't want to use the wedding picture. Cutting Victoria and Donald out of the group would have been a dead giveaway that we were hiding something, or that somebody important was involved."

"He made up some cock and bull story about a relative of ours we were afraid had run across her. I don't think anyone believed it, but at least it gave them a justification for wagging their tongues." Ned held his jacket sleeve up to his nose. "We stink, Geoff. My apologies in such close quarters, Miss MacKenzie."

"If we have no proof of moral turpitude except hearsay, we have to go in a different direction." Prudence took a deep breath, sat up straighter. "Do you think she killed my father, Mr. Hayes?"

"I don't think we'll ever know, Miss MacKenzie. And speaking as an ex-homicide detective, let me tell you why." Hayes glanced at Hunter, who nodded encouragement. Prudence was strong and resilient enough to hear the truth. "All it would have taken is an infusion of digitalis to give him a fast heartbeat. If Dr. Worthington was already treating the Judge, nobody would have suspected a thing. Increasing the effect of his heart medicine with concentrated foxglove would have brought on an attack, but the level in the medicine bottle would have been right where it was supposed to be.

"The other possibility is arsenic, not enough at one time to arouse suspicion, but over time it would have weakened him and acted on his heart. It was used so often before an Englishman developed a way to test for it that we used to call it *inheritance powder*."

"If she did do something to hasten him into his grave, Dr. Worthington would have ordered an autopsy. Thomas MacKenzie was his friend as well as his patient." Geoffrey hesitated, then decided that Ned needed to know everything. "Worthington apparently believed that Thomas was treating himself with some sort of quack remedy for old men with young wives. He said they can be dangerous."

"I challenged him on that," Prudence said. "Victoria's bedroom was at the other end of the hall from my father's and there was no sign he'd ever been in it. I don't believe the Judge ever went near her in anything like love or affection. I think the marriage was a sham from the beginning. Everything I heard today confirms it."

"There's no proof."

"You're thinking like a lawyer, Geoffrey," Ned said. "What happened to the bouncer whose job Donald so conveniently stepped into? Why would he leave without a word to anyone? It sounds as if he didn't even ask for whatever money he had coming to him. I think Victoria and Donald Morley are far more dangerous than we've assumed. I think feeding laudanum to Prudence is child's play to them. Anyone who gets in their way disappears."

"Don't go back there, Prudence," Geoffrey said. "The more we learn about your stepmother and her brother, the more dangerous it becomes for you."

"Those kind of people are like animals, Miss MacKenzie. They sense when something isn't right. You're a good actress, you proved that today, but the slightest slip will put them on their guard. They'll have to do something about you to protect themselves."

"They can't kill me," Prudence said defiantly. "Victoria would lose everything, and we know she's too greedy for that. I'm not afraid of her anymore, Geoffrey. I'm really not, Mr. Hayes. She can try to make my life miserable, but she won't break my will. Now that I know who and what she is, what I suspect she's done, she can't catch me off guard, can't make me wonder if I'm judging her unfairly. What's the worst she can do to me? Really, Geoffrey, Mr. Hayes, what can she do?"

Neither man wanted to remember women who had believed themselves to be invulnerable until they became statistics. Perhaps Prudence MacKenzie really was safe from her stepmother. Perhaps it was all over and the Judge's widow had won after all.

CHAPTER 24

Josiah welcomed Prudence to Roscoe Conkling's office with a smile on his face that stretched from ear to ear. His eyes were bright with unshed tears of joy.

"Mr. Conkling is asking for both you and Mr. Hunter, Miss MacKenzie. He's rallied. The doctor said if he continues to improve he'll issue a press statement to that effect by Saturday. Yesterday, Mrs. Conkling and their daughter were allowed in to visit for the first time since the fever climbed so high. I thought we were going to lose him, I really did."

"You kept up a very brave front, Josiah, very brave."

"I don't know what I'd do without him. We've been together for so many years."

"Do you have any idea what Mr. Conkling wants to see us about?"

"He told me to bring along the account he wrote of his walk through the blizzard. Most of it has already been published by every newspaper in town, so I don't know what he's looking for. I've got the entire file, notes and scribbles and everything he jotted down right after it happened." He bundled the files into a leather satchel. "I used the telephone to call Mr. Hunter at his hotel. He said it would be faster if he met us at Mr. Conkling's rather than coming here."

"I think we'd better go then. Jackson will have told my step-mother I've left the house. She won't be pleased."

"Is everything all right, miss?"

"I'm afraid not, but it's no secret that Mrs. MacKenzie and I have never gotten along well. If we decide to use the information that Mr. Hunter and Mr. Hayes and I discovered yester-day, things are bound to get much worse." Prudence smiled to reassure him. "Thank you for sending Danny Dennis after me. He's a formidable character. Kincaid was out and Danny re-fused to hand your note over to Jackson, which I think is the only reason I got it. Danny stood on the front stoop with one boot in the doorway until Jackson had to let him in. But he made him cool his heels in the hallway, which is where he was when I came out of my father's library. We were gone within minutes."

"Will Mrs. MacKenzie be very angry with you?"

"Danny never said a word to Jackson about who sent him, so she'll have no idea where I've gone. I imagine Victoria will be livid. I'm rather looking forward to it."

Josiah turned out the office lights and carefully locked the door behind them. Double checked it. He couldn't remember the last time he'd gotten a good night's sleep so he did every-thing twice, just in case he hadn't done it right the first time. He wasn't planning to come back to the office until tomorrow. When all of this was over and Mr. Conkling finally out of dan-ger, he'd crawl into his bed and not get out for two whole days. Now that he thought of it, since tomorrow was Friday, perhaps he'd allow himself the luxury of half a day off. He'd sit with Mr. Conkling in the morning, of course, but after that he just might go home to hot tea and his feet up.

Danny Dennis and Mr. Washington were waiting for them just outside the United Bank Building. Danny tipped his hat and

Mr. Washington stomped one foot, impatient to get on with wherever they were going.

"Mr. Hunter will be meeting us at Mr. Conkling's apartment," Josiah said to Danny as he helped Prudence climb into the hansom cab.

"And if he's late, Mr. Conkling will have to make do with me," Prudence said.

"He'll be so glad to see you, miss." Josiah settled himself in comfortably with the leather satchel at his feet. "Now, miss, what is it you and the two gentlemen discovered yesterday?"

"It's a long story, Josiah."

"And Broadway is crowded, as always."

"Have you ever heard of something called The Lost Cause?" Prudence began.

Danny clucked to Mr. Washington and the hansom cab moved off toward the Hoffman House Hotel where Roscoe Conkling was waiting impatiently for them. Since it was a warm, sunny April day Danny left the trap door in the ceiling open. He heard every word of the adventure at Mrs. Cavanaugh's At Home.

"Was he really close to dying, Josiah?" Prudence asked as the hansom cab approached the Hoffman House Hotel. Conkling's secretary had sat in stunned silence after the revelation of Mrs. Victoria MacKenzie's former profession. It was time to bring him back to the present.

"I've never heard of a temperature as high as his, Miss MacKenzie. Mr. Conkling has been out of his head off and on ever since he collapsed; I think his doctor, Dr. Barker, was ready to give up on him when the fever passed one hundred and four. He found an abscess in the right ear that he thinks was caused by the cold winds and the snow the night of the blizzard. Mr. Conkling never slowed down one iota afterward; Dr. Barker said anybody else who'd come through that experience and was that exhausted would have had the common sense to stay in bed for a day or two."

"Mr. Conkling isn't like anybody else. We all know that."

"It was a close thing, Miss MacKenzie, and he's not completely out of the woods yet."

"The fever's down, his wife and daughter have been in to see him, and he's got you bringing work over. I'd say it sounds like he really is on the mend."

"He's not coming in to the office until the doctor says he's fit," Josiah declared grimly. "I promise you I'll have the locks changed if I have to." Then he grinned. "Can't you just see him pounding on the door and yelling at me to open up or he'll have my head on a platter? I never thought I'd want to hear him shouting at me again, but after all the worrying this week I think it would be music to my ears."

"He's very lucky to have you watching out for him, Josiah."

Prudence touched one hand lightly to the little man's arm, then leaned back into her seat. She had tossed and turned all night, wondering how and when they would confront Victoria with their new knowledge of her past. It was worrisome not to be able to discuss things with Geoffrey whenever she wanted to. Until now she hadn't realized how much she'd come to depend on him, his calm steadiness and good-humored intelligence. The size and masculine strength of him, the feeling of being guarded within unbreachable walls whenever she was with him.

The only other person who had made her feel like that was her father. She still ached whenever she thought of him, despite the feet of clay he'd allowed her to discover. Every now and then an image flashed across her brain, the house on Staten Island he'd never been able to bring himself to sell, her mother lying thin and pale in her bed, the sound of persistent coughing.

"We're here, Miss MacKenzie," Josiah said.

Roscoe Conkling's apartment was as luxurious as Josiah Gregory had been able to make it. Since his employer was a big man, Josiah had scoured the city for oversized furniture that would swallow up his long frame and allow him to stretch out his legs. What was comfortable for Conkling was sometimes a difficult struggle to get out of for smaller people, but Josiah had refused to compromise. Even his bed was longer than the average; it was the only one Roscoe had ever slept in where his feet didn't start dangling over the edge sometime during the night. Everything about his rooms, from the dark maroons and forest greens of the upholstery and drapery to the masculine smells of woodsy English cologne and well-oiled leather proclaimed that a man of influence and position lived here. It was the retreat he'd been trying so hard to reach on the night of the blizzard.

Josiah had planned carefully, making sure that when he and Prudence arrived, Mrs. Conkling and their daughter Bessie would have gone downstairs for lunch and only one of the round-the-clock nurses hired by Dr. Barker would be in attendance.

"I don't like being fussed over," Roscoe declared as soon as the nurse left them alone. "I can't abide it."

"You look very well taken care of," Prudence soothed. She took the chair Josiah placed for her beside Roscoe's bed. "She's only doing what she's been told to do. You won't get well again if you don't stay in bed and rest."

"The fever's down. I'm perfectly fine."

"You're not *perfectly* fine, and even a slight fever is of concern in a man your age," Josiah scolded. "Sir."

"Where's Hunter?"

"I'm here," Geoffrey said from the doorway. He pulled a chair close to Conkling's bed and sat down, his eyes doing a quick check of the ex-senator's condition. He wasn't sure how strong Conkling really was. Roscoe always put up a good show and never admitted to weakness.

"Did you bring what I asked for?" Conkling asked his secretary.

"I did." Josiah fanned out the contents of a cardboard folder. "I brought everything."

"What is this about, Mr. Conkling?" Prudence asked.

"I've remembered something, but I'm not sure I'm recalling it correctly."

"He was delirious, Miss MacKenzie. The fever made him relive that nightmare walk up Broadway, every step of the way and every gust of wind that knocked him down."

"I wasn't delirious."

"I'd like to know what to call it when you're out of your head, raging like a crazy man, and so hot, the cloths they put on your head had to be changed every few minutes." Josiah's nod was the self-righteous bob of a man who knows what he's talking about.

"You're exaggerating."

"Ask the doctor, if you won't believe me."

"I think you are much improved, Mr. Conkling, very much improved. I haven't heard you argue so much since the last time Josiah tried to talk some common sense into you." Prudence waited until Roscoe returned her smile. "Now then, if you two will stop bickering, perhaps we can get on with the business that brought us here."

"Josiah, find those pages I wrote about stopping in front of the Astor House when William Sulzer decided he'd had enough. Those pages and the ones right after, especially the part about Grace Church."

It took him a few moments, but Josiah knew his employer's papers well; it was his job to keep everything in order so that anything Roscoe needed could be found at a moment's shouted command. "Here they are," he said, laying aside the pages that weren't wanted.

"Read them to me."

As Josiah's well-modulated voice droned on, it was as if the blizzard in all its fury came to blow itself out in Conkling's bedroom. Roscoe was as adept at recreating a scene on paper as he was in the courtroom. The biting cold and the fierce wind. The snow blowing so thickly that it whited out the street, the buildings, everything but what lay within arm's reach.

"Stop. Read that section again." Conkling pushed himself forward on his heap of pillows, his eyes bright with excitement. "That's what I thought I remembered. William Sulzer went into the Astor House, but Charles and I continued up Broadway. I remember the voices of the men inside at the bar and in the lobby as the porter opened the door for him, then the silence when it closed. Now find the paragraph about looking back just after I made it past Grace Church."

Josiah read it through twice. "I don't understand," he said.

"When I turned around, Charles had fallen behind. He was a few hundred yards away from Grace Church, and I had the notion he might have stopped there except for feeling he couldn't leave me. Then I saw someone else coming along behind Charles, and I raised my arm to the both of them. I thought at the time that Sulzer must have changed his mind and come back out of the Astor House and that Charles was waiting for him to catch up with us. I knew they wouldn't be able to hear me through all the wind howling, but I figured if I waved, they'd see I was all right and able to make it to Madison Square on my own. But that wasn't Sulzer coming through the snow behind Charles. He never left the Astor House."

"Are you sure, Roscoe?" Geoffrey had sat silent throughout the reading of Conkling's notes. He had agonized over Charles's death so often that he was nearly numb now with the repetition. Except that the ace of spades his friend had laboriously and no doubt painfully pulled from his pocket screamed out a message and a warning. It had to be something Geoffrey was supposed to recognize about the man Conkling had seen following behind them. No other conclusion made any sense.

"I forgot because Sulzer wasn't the one who told me, and I wasn't paying attention at the time. It was the next day, before we knew Charles was missing. I was on my way to court, and I overheard a conversation in the hallway. Someone was talking about having spent the night sitting in the Astor House bar with half the lawyers with offices on Wall Street because every hotel room was taken. There were cots and pallets in all the corridors by the time he got there. Don't ask me who was doing the talking, because I have no idea, but he said it was a great way to sit out the blizzard and he'd highly recommend it for the next time we have a snowstorm. He mentioned several of our colleagues by name, and I'm sure now Sulzer was one of them. So you see, if he never left the Astor bar, it had to be someone else on Broadway that night."

"Dear God in Heaven." Josiah stared at the papers in his hand as if he could will them to say something else.

"If it wasn't Mr. Sulzer, then who was it?" asked Prudence. She had gone very pale.

No one answered her.

"A heavy tree branch fell on Charles when he sat down on a bench in Union Square," she said. "It knocked him unconscious, so that he fell forward off the bench and into the snow. Where he froze to death." Her voice broke on the final word; she choked back the sob that was threatening to burst from her throat.

"His pockets were gone through and his briefcase taken," Roscoe said.

"The police decided that a street bum came along and robbed him." Josiah blinked hard and fast in concentration as he tried to picture the scene. "A street bum would have taken his coat, too."

"I don't see how we'll be able to prove anything now. It's too late," Prudence said. "Is there any way to tell the difference between an accidental blow and a deliberate one? Does it even matter? Nothing will bring him back."

"Truth matters, Prudence. Truth matters more than anything else in the world." Conkling laughed. "Listen to me, a lawyer, pontificating about truth, when what I really do is try to get my client off no matter how guilty he is. Truth doesn't matter where the law is concerned, it's all those twists and turns we can take around it."

"Roscoe," interrupted Geoffrey. "Can you describe the man you saw through the snow?"

"I assumed it was Sulzer."

"But we're certain now that it wasn't. William Sulzer is tall and thin, as I recall. I met him once in the Linwood offices. He was consulting on a case."

"Very tall, very thin," Conkling agreed, closing his eyes.

"Are you all right, sir?" Josiah asked.

"I'm picturing that moment when I turned around and waved. Don't distract me."

In the silence, Prudence reached out to touch Geoffrey's arm. What she was thinking was so illogical yet so certain in her own mind, at least, that it frightened her into seeking the support of his strength. She felt a palm cover the hand resting on his sleeve, and then the warmth of both his hands wrapped comfortingly around her own. It seemed as though they were sharing the same thought.

"Stocky," Roscoe said, eyes still closed. "The man wasn't as tall as Sulzer; he didn't have that scarecrow look about him. Even wearing a topcoat and hat, Sulzer wouldn't have been that bulky." He opened his eyes and stared at the three faces looking back at him. "Why didn't I notice it at the time? Why didn't I sense something dangerous about him? I waved and turned back around and kept on slogging my way home as though I were out to win some kind of competition. I didn't spare a second thought for Charles after that. I was too preoccupied with myself. I thought because he was young and strong that he was bound to make it."

"Donald Morley," whispered Prudence. "I don't know how he knew where Charles would be, but it had to have been Donald."

"When we went to the Dakota, nothing had been done to the apartment Victoria was supposed to move into," Geoffrey said.

"She never intended to leave the Fifth Avenue house," Prudence said. "She never meant for the wedding to take place. She planned Charles's death from the moment she heard the will read and realized that the Judge had outsmarted her. The only way she could win out over him was to make sure I did not marry. And the only way to do that was to kill the groom."

"Maurice Warneke as good as told us that Charles's death wasn't an accident."

"He also said that what the dead leave behind can bear witness for them."

"If we'll learn to listen. In this case, learn to see and believe what's right before our eyes."

"Go back to Warneke, Geoffrey," Conkling instructed. "Tell him what I've remembered. Tell him I'm willing to swear in court that someone was following Charles that afternoon. See if that will persuade him to come forward with his own suspicions."

"What about proving moral turpitude against Victoria?" Prudence asked.

"Ned Hayes thinks we have a better chance of proving blackmail," Geoffrey said. "He has a *Herald* reporter digging through the newspaper's morgue to find the stories written about those thirty-seven men whose initials the Judge underlined in his notebook. We're hoping the articles will tell us more about each man, personal details, family relationships, where he lived then, clues about how or where to find him now." Geoffrey thought he knew what else was in Ned's mind, but he wasn't ready to share it. He doubted he ever would.

"We already know they walked out of court free men," Prudence said.

"All but one. The last case he wanted you to know about, the man he sent to Sing Sing."

"If any of those men admit to being freed because of a bribe, it's bound to come out that none of them could have come up with the amount of money my father was given. Someone with deep pockets had to have bought their freedom for them. If they worked for him, McGlory's name is bound to be mentioned."

Geoffrey should have known that Prudence would go straight to the heart of the matter. She'd never met McGlory, and please God she never would. But she had his measure.

"Billy McGlory would never allow it to happen," Conkling said. "He'd make sure everyone who could testify against him would have his mouth permanently closed."

"Have you ever practiced criminal law, Mr. Conkling?" Prudence asked.

"My clients are wealthy and influential men, child. It's best not to question how they got that way."

"I'll stop by Warneke's and then I'll go find Ned," Geoffrey decided.

"Someone has to keep Victoria and Donald from suspecting that their world is about to come crashing down around their ears," Prudence said. "I'm the only one who can do that."

"Are you sure, Miss MacKenzie?" Josiah asked.

"I've told all of you a dozen times or more that I don't have anything more serious to fear from Victoria than harsh words and tight purse strings. For the sake of her standing in society, she has to keep the myth of our loving relationship as alive as I am. I'm willing to play along with her for as long as it takes."

"It might be possible to buy her off," Conkling said. "If we can't win a case against her in court, we can always try a little blackmail of our own. I don't doubt that it would be expensive, but it would get rid of her once and for all."

"Not yet," Prudence said. "I think of that as a last resort. I don't want the killers of my father and my fiancé to walk away from their crimes with fat purses."

"I agree," said Roscoe. "We should only consider it as a last resort." He was more tired than he cared to admit. The pillows behind his back were like welcoming white arms, plump and soft. His eyes were closing, his head lolling to one side.

"Danny Dennis can see me home," Prudence said. "I promise you I'll be fine, Geoffrey. Don't waste time worrying about me. You need to talk to Warneke again and catch up with Ned Hayes."

Josiah gathered up the papers scattered across Conkling's bed.

The door to Roscoe Conkling's bedroom was ajar when they left, the nurse nowhere in sight.

Mrs. Barstow followed Mrs. MacKenzie's instructions to the letter, making sure all of the household staff took advantage of the extra half day off, seeing them out of the house, locking the door behind the last one to leave.

"I'll be on my way then," she told her employer. "Unless you need me to stay?"

"No. I'd prefer that all of you, senior staff included, have some extra time to yourselves. We've been through a great deal in the past three months. Mr. Morley and I will also be going out. I want to see for myself that the area around the Judge's crypt is being kept up, and to speak to the Trinity Church sexton about it. One cannot leave these things to chance."

"Would Madam care for anything before I leave?"

"Nothing, thank you, Mrs. Barstow."

"Then I think I shall take myself off to Central Park for the afternoon. It's lovely and warm today."

"A very good idea."

She hasn't changed either her shoes or her dress, Mrs. Barstow thought as she left the upstairs parlor and descended the servants' staircase. *Why is she lying to me?*

She put her hat and gloves on, picked up her pocketbook, re-locked the kitchen door. Stood for a moment in the unaccustomed early-afternoon quiet of the rear courtyard facing the stables, then walked around the side of the house and up Fifth Avenue. A hot spot burned on the back of her black bombazine dress, as though someone had focused sun through a magnifying glass. She knew without turning around that Mrs. MacKenzie was watching her from a parlor window.

Up Fifth Avenue she went until she was certain she could no longer be seen, until the hot spot on her back cooled and she knew the watcher had turned away from the window. Two long blocks, that should be enough. She turned right at the next cross street and began to make her way toward the alley running behind the mansions facing onto Fifth Avenue. This was the world of work hidden behind the elaborate facades of the luxurious homes of the wealthy, where coachmen drove carriages and horses after depositing their passengers at their front doors. Down to the end of the block she went, into the alleyway where private sanitation companies emptied the rubbish and manure bins, past rear gates that led into secluded courtyards, into the stables and carriage houses above which the outdoor men servants had their rooms.

Family and members of the inside MacKenzie household staff rarely had reason to visit the stable area; it smelled of horses and hay, of the oil used to keep the harnesses supple, and the polish that shone the brass fittings of the carriages. Each stable was its coachman's private domain, his small kingdom, where he could be alone with the horses he loved. When Mrs. Barstow stepped through the courtyard gate and skirted the stables to reach the kitchen door, she felt oddly like a trespasser. A click of the lock and she was inside again, no one the wiser, certainly not Mrs. MacKenzie.

If asked, she couldn't have explained why she had sneaked into the house like a thief. The few extra hours the staff had been given didn't amount to a whole half day, and there wouldn't be time for her to get to the Sisters of Charity and back again without having to curtail the time she could sit by her sister's bedside. The nuns wouldn't know what to make of her, anyway, if she showed up unexpectedly.

The walk in Central Park had sounded nice, and she might

have gone, if Mrs. MacKenzie hadn't sat there in her indoor shoes and gown and blatantly lied to her. No lady could dress herself without the help of a maid; Victoria MacKenzie wasn't going anywhere. Neither, she thought, was Mr. Morley. He hadn't been in the parlor, but she'd smelled a freshly lit pipe in the hallway; he was somewhere in the house.

Victoria MacKenzie had emptied the house of its staff, then lied to get rid of her housekeeper. There would be no witnesses to whatever she was planning, something Billy would definitely want to know about. Miss Prudence? Hadn't Frances herself said that Mrs. MacKenzie was cleaning house? Hadn't she predicted that Miss Prudence would be the next to go? But where? How? That was reason enough to stay behind.

Mrs. Barstow sat at her housekeeper's desk, the door to her parlor closed, no lamps lit, nothing to break the silence of the basement rooms except the hallway clock marking the quarter hour, the half hour, then three chimes that echoed in the emptiness.

CHAPTER 25

Jackson opened the front door to Prudence, then closed and bolted it the way he did when he was locking up for the night. The snap of the double locks and the thump of the steel bar as he lowered it into its cradles on either side of the door felt out of place in the early afternoon. Ominous, as though a battle or a siege were about to take place.

Prudence expected Victoria to storm out into the hallway and demand where she had been, but her stepmother wasn't in the parlor. Neither was Donald, though the strong scent of his pipe hung in the air. The dining room had been cleared of luncheon, the table bare and shining around its centerpiece of cut spring flowers.

"Has Mrs. MacKenzie gone out?" she asked, returning to the foyer. She didn't like the idea that she might be alone in the house with Jackson. She hadn't forgotten the shock of finding him in her bedroom; something about his odd yellow eyes made her think of a carnivorous gleam seen through the bars of the Central Park Zoo.

"Mr. Morley is out, miss. But he's expected back shortly."

"Did he take the carriage?"

"Yes, miss."

"Where is everyone else? The house feels empty."

"Mrs. MacKenzie has given the staff the rest of the day off, miss. I was about to leave myself when I heard the bell."

That explained the locking up, but Prudence knew that her stepmother would never leave her alone in the house. There was too much animosity and suspicion between them. So where was she?

Victoria had to have a reason for emptying the mansion of its servants, but try as she might, Prudence couldn't find it. She had that same odd sensation of teetering on the brink of a fall that she had experienced in the crowd on Fifth Avenue. As though she were about to lose her balance and could do nothing to stop it. Until Kincaid drove Donald back, there would be nobody near her she could trust.

"If there's nothing else, miss?" Not waiting for an answer, Jackson disappeared down the hall in the direction of the servants' staircase to the lower floor.

Prudence breathed a sigh of relief, glad to see him go.

As she climbed the stairs to her bedroom, Prudence fingered the gold chain from which hung her mother's ring, nestled deeply between two stays of her corset. Just touching the tiny links gave her confidence, reminded her why she had taken the ring, and why she was going to such lengths to hide the theft from Victoria. Not theft, reclamation. She had reclaimed what belonged to her.

She should have given it to Geoffrey while they were together at Mr. Conkling's apartment, but despite promises to herself that she would hand it over for safekeeping, she hadn't been able to bring herself to part with it. And now she was glad she hadn't. *It's my armor,* she decided. *A knight never goes into battle without his armor.*

She had had an idea during the ride from Conkling's apartment, listening to the rhythmic clop of Mr. Washington's hooves on the cobbled street. What if, instead of creating a combination from family dates, her father had chosen an occasion linked to his profession? She could almost hear his voice congratulating her. She couldn't recall when he had taken his judge's oath, but the date was written on the back of the photograph he had posed for that day in his new judicial robes. A photograph that stood on her dressing table.

She glanced toward Victoria's room, half expecting her stepmother to open her door in response to Prudence's footsteps on the stairs. Nothing. The disturbing silence in the house remained unbroken. The last time it had been this quiet Prudence had entered her bedroom to find Jackson staring at the mound of pillows and blankets he thought was her. The memory made her shudder.

Still nothing. No one waited for her in the room left clean and orderly by the efficient Clara, who had somehow found the courage to bring her messages from Kincaid. The Judge smiled at her from her favorite photograph of him; she pried it out of the frame and memorized the date.

One more item to get: the key to the library that she'd hidden under her mother's pearls. She couldn't count on Victoria's having left the door unlocked and she didn't want to risk being seen reaching behind the coatrack in the downstairs hallway for the key hidden there. She lifted the lid of the velvet-lined case that contained the only piece of her mother's jewelry Victoria had allowed her to keep. The strands shone with a soft satiny glow, the diamond clasp winking in the folds of the velvet. Prudence lifted the pearls from their nest, then pried up the heavy cardboard to which the lining was glued. She reached for the key, then stared at the bottom of the jewel case, fingers poised above emptiness. The key was gone!

Surely she was mistaken. She turned the case upside down, shook out the velvet lining, uncoiled the pearl necklace, knowing even as she searched that she would not find the key tangled in its strands. Only one person could have taken it. Victoria had been suspicious the day she tried the library door and could not open it, had probably never accepted Prudence's hasty explanation that the door was sticking. Like a dog scenting a buried bone, the Judge's widow would not rest until she'd found what she was looking for. She'd known instinctively that her stepdaughter must have had a second key and was using it to lock herself into the library when she wanted to be alone there. And so she'd taken it from her, the way she'd deprived Prudence of nearly everything she cherished.

More determined than ever that she would open her father's hidden safe, Prudence crept quietly from her room and down the main staircase. Before she risked the key concealed in the frame of the coatrack, she'd make sure the library door was locked. But as she reached the bottom of the stairs, a small figure in a maid's uniform stepped into the hall from the entryway. German Clara, holding in her hand the key she must have found when Colleen's duties became hers. She put one finger to her lips to signal the need for silence, then insisted that Prudence take the key.

"Jackson," she whispered, her eyes wide and worried.

"I understand," Prudence said, "I'll lock the door behind me. He won't be able to get in. Thank you, Clara."

"I go now," the maid said.

"Enjoy your afternoon out," Prudence said.

German Clara nodded, then padded softly toward the servants' stairway.

The library door was unlocked. Prudence slipped the key into the pocket of her skirt, then turned the knob, looking around the empty hallway behind her as she stepped into the room.

Victoria was waiting for her.

"That wasn't very smart of you, Prudence, leaving the way you did this morning without a word to me of where you were going. I thought we had agreed you wouldn't do that anymore."

Be careful. You'll be worse off if you're caught in a lie than if you say nothing. She kept her lips firmly closed and waited.

"Where did you go?"

"Nowhere important."

"Jackson said a hansom cab driver brought a note that he refused to hand over to anyone but you. By the time I came downstairs you were already gone. Where did you go, Prudence?"

"I told you, it's not important."

"I think you went to see Roscoe Conkling. I think you spent the past few hours sitting by his bedside listening to lies and false accusations that I could drag him into court for making. That's where I think you've been, Prudence. And it wasn't a smart thing to do at all."

Prudence had a flash of visual memory, of the door to Roscoe's bedroom ajar as she and Geoffrey left. But neither of them had opened it. The last person through that door had been the nurse, and surely she would have closed it to give Mr. Conkling and his guests privacy.

Not if she were being paid to report who visited him and what they discussed. Not if she had been told to pay particular attention if a certain young woman or a dark-haired man came to call. When they didn't see her as they left, Prudence had assumed the woman had gone to make herself a cup of tea while her patient entertained his callers, but it hadn't been that at all. She'd been Victoria's creature, another of her informants. Prudence felt the blood drain from her face.

"I see you think you've figured something out. How clever of you."

Everything she had heard or discussed in Conkling's apartment exploded like fireworks in Prudence's brain. For the second time that day she relived Charles's walk up Broadway, his struggles through the terrible wind and the drifts of heavy snow. She watched a bulky figure follow after him, saw Conkling raise his arm to wave. Charles staggered to the bench in Union Park, took off his hat to shake the snow from the brim.

Her mind would go no further. Rage far stronger than any anger she had ever experienced blinded her to her own safety, made her forget that she had promised to lull Donald and her stepmother into a false sense of security. Charles had stood in Victoria's way, so he had had to be removed.

"I don't know how you managed it, but Charles's death wasn't an accident, was it? He was brutally attacked and left to die in the snow. How could you? How could you?" She took an angry stride toward Victoria, then realized that her stepmother was sidestepping her, that she had circled and blocked the only way out of the library. By the time Prudence understood what was happening, Victoria had locked the door to the hallway and safety. She held up a key that did not hang from a gold chain.

"I wondered why the door wouldn't open that day," she said, dangling the silver key from her fingertips. "Don't you know that every woman in the world hides things in her jewelry case? I would have expected something more imaginative from you, Prudence."

"It was Donald, Donald killed him," Prudence spat, her fingers curling into claws. Geoffrey had been right after all. She wanted to scratch out Victoria's eyes, scrape the mocking smile from her face.

"You're jumping to unwarranted conclusions, Prudence. I told you Conkling was feeding you lies." Victoria moved toward her, voice low and persuasive, the sway of her walk like the lazy hypnotic swing of a cobra's head before it strikes.

Prudence was beyond caring now. "You killed my father, too. Did you give him digitalis, Victoria? Is that how you did it? Or was Dr. Worthington right? Was it one of those quack potency concoctions that set his heart pounding too fast for his body to bear? Except that he never bought anything like that for himself. He wouldn't. He hated you. He could hardly stand to be in the same room with you. You made Donald buy it, but you were the one who fed it to him. He thought he was being given what his friend and physician had recommended, but it was an elixir of death he swallowed. Wasn't it, Victoria? Wasn't it?"

Her stepmother's arm lashed out and caught Prudence's dress at the neckline. One hard downward tug and the silk ripped, revealing the gold chain that lay against her skin. The delicate gold broke when Victoria pulled on it; pain lashed across the back of Prudence's neck. A moment later the emerald and diamond ring the Judge had given to Sarah MacKenzie when their only child was born lay in Victoria's predatory palm.

"I missed this the same day you took it. That was Sunday, Prudence, when you played your little charade so well, you fooled even me. For a while. I know when someone has been in my room. I can always tell. There's a certain disturbance in the air, and no matter how careful the intruder is, something seems not quite right. You should have looked more closely at yourself in the mirror. Silk clings to the skin; it outlines whatever lies beneath it." Victoria slipped Sarah MacKenzie's jewel onto the third finger of her right hand. "Emerald is the stone of true love. Did you know that?"

A hot wash of bile rose from Prudence's stomach and filled her mouth. She was living her worst nightmare, Victoria gloating as she laid claim to Sarah MacKenzie's most treasured possessions.

She had to get out of this room where she had once felt so safe, had to flee the house while she still could. Victoria and Donald wouldn't kill her; they needed her alive in order to enjoy the Judge's money. She had boasted that they couldn't harm her, but she had forgotten that they could reduce her to the state of an automaton through the half-sleep of laudanum, something she feared with every fiber of her body.

It was too late for subterfuge. They were no longer playing games with one another. If Victoria and Donald really wanted her gone, they wouldn't hesitate to force the laudanum down her throat. Donald would hold her down; Victoria would pinch her nostrils until she had to open her mouth to breathe. And then it would be too late. Once would be enough. The demon of addiction would hold her in its thrall again and they would watch her so closely there would never be a second chance to escape.

Victoria didn't try to stop her when Prudence ran to the door and tugged at the knob with all her strength. She pounded on the solid oak and called out as loudly as she could. She didn't dare scream Kincaid's or Clara's names, but she hoped that somewhere in this vast house someone would hear the commotion and come to find out what or who was causing it.

"It won't open. You're well and truly caught," Victoria said. "Make as much noise as you want, Prudence. It won't do you any good. The staff is enjoying an extra afternoon off, a special consideration for all of the difficult times we've been through recently. No one is here to help you."

Prudence felt her hair fall down over her shoulders, shaken loose by her struggle with the door. Tears of frustration stung her eyelids, but she wouldn't give Victoria the triumph of seeing her weep. Her only hope now was to face down her formidable stepmother. She had to concentrate on remembering that she was worth more alive than dead, had to believe that would save her, would help her endure. *Protect your secrets, my child, protect your secrets. Therein lies your strength. In the end, they will save you.*

"I wonder why you came into the library, Prudence. What did you hope to find here? Is there something I've missed?"

She didn't dare glance in the direction of the hidden safe. Victoria would know in an instant that the answer to her question lay concealed there. She would find the safe. She would hire someone to open it for her. Prudence's last hope of defeating her would go up in smoke.

"I came to be alone with the memory of my father," she said. She infused as much dignity as she could into the simple statement. Despite the ripped dress and the ruined coiffure, Prudence sensed that if she kept her wits about her, she might be a match for the woman who seemed to be holding all the winning cards.

"He was a weak man, you know. He allowed a hopeless case to bring him down."

"He loved my mother. Whatever he did was to save her."

"As I said, he was a weak man."

"I won't allow you to malign him."

"You forget yourself, Prudence. A widow has a closer tie than a daughter. Legally and in every other way that matters."

"What do you want from me?"

"Now we come to it. I prefer honesty, don't you?"

You don't know the meaning of the word, Prudence thought. But she didn't say it aloud.

"Don't you wonder where Donald is this afternoon?" Victoria asked. "I'll tell you. He's gone to a doctor's office. A particular kind of doctor whose practice specializes in treating women suffering from hysteria, melancholia, and hallucinations. Which, I regret to inform you, are exactly the symptoms you've displayed since your father's death. Dr. Yarborough has a clinic upstate where his patients find peace and tranquility."

"I won't go," Prudence said.

"You won't have a choice. Dr. Yarborough only admits women by court order, and your commitment papers are being presented to a judge this afternoon. I expect word any moment that they've been signed."

"I won't go," Prudence repeated.

"If you fight it, they'll put you into a straitjacket. I understand it's very uncomfortable. I'll pack a small bag for you. It's the least I can do." Victoria turned away from her stepdaughter, walked toward the door.

Desperate not to be locked in to await the fate that was coming her way, forgetting in her panic the key that German Clara had insisted she take, Prudence lunged at Victoria. The rustle of her skirts and her own desperation gave her away. Once again Victoria sidestepped her stepdaughter, but this time she did more than allow her to fall to the floor. She reached for the lamp on the Judge's desk and threw it as hard as she could. The chimney exploded upon impact, sending shards of glass and splashes of kerosene everywhere. Prudence's fingers touched her forehead and came away bloody.

"You need the help of a doctor skilled in the treatment of hysteria, Prudence. Anyone looking at the mess you've made of yourself would agree."

Without another word, Victoria left her. The key turned loudly in the lock. Prudence heard the tap of her stepmother's retreating footsteps, and then there was silence. She tried to stand. Blackness overtook her and she fell.

I have to get out of this room, Prudence thought, *I have to get out of this house before Donald gets back.*

How long was I unconscious? Victoria had left her alone in the library, crumpled in a bloody heap on the floor. Confident, as always, that she had the upper hand, knowing that Donald would arrive any moment with the men who would take away her annoying stepdaughter.

She underestimates me, Prudence thought, *and that's how I'll bring her down. She always thinks she's stronger and more clever than everyone else,* a voice whispered.

As she struggled to her feet, Prudence felt the sharp thrust of something metal against her leg. She slid her hand into the pocket of her skirt and folded her fingers around the key the Judge delighted in concealing from her when they'd played their hiding games.

The key the maid had insisted on giving her would be her ticket to freedom. *Thank you, Clara.* If only she could stay on her feet and keep moving.

She wiped as much of the blood from her face as she could,

remembering that she had heard Dr. Worthington explain after some childhood accident that head scrapes always bled profusely. It didn't mean there was serious injury.

She had to go now, now before she was buckled into a straitjacket and hauled off to peace and tranquility. She knew what that meant. A waking death of drugged half-sleep. In her case, once the first drops of laudanum were poured down her throat, there would be no coming back. *Breathe, breathe deeply.* Miraculously, the confusion and the pain lifted; she could stand without trembling, could hold the precious key without dropping it.

Before she inserted the key in the lock, Prudence pressed her ear to the wooden door, listening for any sound of movement on the other side. She remembered what Victoria had said about packing a bag, and knew that her best, perhaps her only chance of escape was while her stepmother remained upstairs. She unlocked the door, slipped through into the hallway, then locked it again behind her. *Think. You have to gain time, you have to send them in the wrong direction.*

The family door to the stable courtyard was at the end of the first-floor corridor. Seldom used, it was a way for the master of the house to reach the stables without having to go through the servants' hall downstairs. Prudence opened the door just a crack, enough to suggest that she'd used it to flee the house. Then she ran for the servants' staircase and the warren of storage rooms in the basement where she could hide until it was safe to slip away. She opened the door as carefully and quietly as her nerves would allow.

The staircase was dim; she didn't dare turn on the electric bulb to illuminate the descent. She felt her way downward, hearing her footsteps echo in the silence of the servantless house. She'd never been pursued before, never had to hide from people who wished her harm. She felt more alone on this empty, echoing wooden stairwell than she'd ever been in her life. This was where Colleen had been pushed, where she had been ex-pected to fall to her death.

Prudence felt a hand reach out and close firmly over her arm. She nearly screamed at the frightening force of it, then she rec-ognized the face of the man looking worriedly down at her.

"This way, Miss Prudence," James Kincaid said. He caught her at the bottom of the stairwell when she stumbled at the un-expected sight of him. "I have a message to deliver upstairs, then I'll be right back."

"It's all right, miss. You'll be safe with us. I promise." Mrs. Barstow stepped out of the shadows.

Prudence struggled against the arms reaching for her. "I have to hide until it's safe to leave this house. I have to get away." She could feel the iron control she'd tried to impose on herself slip-ping away, could hear the panic in her voice.

"You have to believe us, miss. We're on your side in this," Kincaid promised.

"Are they coming for me?" Prudence asked.

"Yes, miss. They're on their way. Mr. Morley sent me on ahead to tell Mrs. MacKenzie to get you ready. They're proba-bly right behind me."

"Go, Mr. Kincaid," Mrs. Barstow said. "Take Miss Prudence away from here. I'll deliver your message to Mrs. MacKenzie. She won't question it. That should give you enough time to get away."

"You're not supposed to be here."

"I'll tell her I broke a heel off my shoe on the way to Central Park, so I had to come back. I'm ashamed to admit that she thinks I'm her creature. She doesn't trust anyone completely, but she won't be suspicious of me. I'm sorry for that, Miss Pru-dence."

"Mr. Hunter," Prudence said. "We have to find him."

"We will, miss," Kincaid said. "I have a plan. But right now the important thing is to get you into the carriage."

"One more thing, Kincaid, then I'll be ready." She recognized the voice in her head reminding her to keep her secrets, but for the first time in her life, she ignored its warning. Prudence tore out a page from the housekeeper's small notebook that lay on the kitchen table and scribbled the address of Mrs. Dailey's boardinghouse in Brooklyn. "If it goes badly for you, Mrs. Barstow, if Mrs. MacKenzie threatens you, there's a safe place you can come to." She thrust the paper into the housekeeper's hand, closing the arthritic fingers over it. "She can be vicious when she's crossed, and unpredictable. Look what she did to me."

"You can trust me, Miss Prudence. I swear it on my sister's soul." Mrs. Barstow crossed herself. "I won't tell anyone and I won't break my word." She nodded to Kincaid. "Go quickly," she urged. "I'll be all right. It's not me they're after."

She pressed a clean linen napkin to hold against her forehead into Miss Prudence's hand. Then she slipped the tiny housekeeper's notebook into the pocket of her black dress. The piece of paper with Mrs. Dailey's address written on it fluttered to the floor. Mrs. Barstow never felt it drop from her fingers.

Kincaid hurried Prudence to the stables, picking her up in his strong arms when she tripped on the cobblestones and would have fallen. He wrapped a blanket around her, picked up the linen napkin when she dropped it. "Hold this against the cuts," he reminded her, pulling down the shades to conceal her presence inside the carriage.

"They won't know you're gone until they open the library door," he said. "Mrs. MacKenzie will wait until Dr. Yarborough and his attendants arrive before unlocking it. But we have to leave right now. We can't risk running into them."

"I don't know where Mr. Hunter is," Prudence said. "He was supposed to go back to the mortuary parlor and then look for Ned Hayes or the reporter who's searching the *Herald*'s archives for him. He could be anywhere."

"Try not to worry, Miss Prudence. I told you I had a plan."

Kincaid closed the carriage door and checked to be sure it was tightly fastened. Then he quietly led the big grays out of the courtyard and into the alleyway, leaving one of the large double doors open behind him. That was part of the plan.

Moments later, the carriage had cleared the alleyway and merged into the traffic on Fifth Avenue. Its destination was Danny Dennis and his cab stand at Broadway and Wall Street.

CHAPTER 26

"Are you sure you weren't followed?" Danny Dennis asked, unfastening Mr. Washington's nosebag. A sprinkle of oats fell to the pavement. Danny was moving as fast as he could. He didn't doubt for a moment that the whole MacKenzie affair was coming apart.

He'd been shocked at the sight of Miss Prudence's bloodied forehead and the ripped gown only partly concealed by the blanket she held around her shoulders. As Danny listened to Kincaid recount the story of what had happened that afternoon, he knew he'd have to keep a tighter rein on his temper than he'd ever had to do on Mr. Washington. The Irish were notorious in New York City for their love of the drink and the violence of their quick rages. Danny had conquered the drink, but there were days when his temper still got the better of him. Today was likely to become one of them.

Kincaid shook his head. "Nobody saw us leave. I made sure of that. This Dr. Yarborough has a judge in his pocket. The commitment papers were being signed without any kind of examination or hearing."

"This is what we're going to do." Danny Dennis

leaned into the carriage to speak to Prudence, gesturing Kincaid to join him. "Listen now. I'll locate Mr. Hunter, and I may need the help of some of the other hansom drivers to find him, so it'll be up to Mr. Kincaid here to get you safely out to Brooklyn, Miss MacKenzie."

"I need to speak to Mr. Hunter. He's as good a lawyer as he was a Pinkerton. He has to block that court order, Mr. Dennis. I have no legal rights until he does."

"We can't risk your staying in Manhattan any longer than it takes to get you to the bridge, Miss Prudence. I'll find him for you and I'll tell him everything. You have my word on that." Danny thought she looked as battered and exhausted as a bare knuckles boxer after a bad fight. No wonder she wasn't arguing with him.

She'd told him and Kincaid what had gone on in the library, everything she could remember. He hoped she hadn't held anything back. Mr. Hunter had to know everything or he'd be working with one hand tied behind his back. He knew Miss Prudence sometimes liked to play her cards as close to her vest as her father had done. If you could say such a thing about a lady. But now wasn't the time to keep quiet about anything.

Danny crossed himself as the MacKenzie carriage rolled away. James Kincaid was a good man and a fine coachman. He knew his horses and he wasn't afraid of pushing them to their limits if he had to. Danny had had a quiet word with the two hansom drivers who pulled their cabs out into the stream of vehicles surrounding Miss Prudence's carriage. They'd follow along as far as the Brooklyn Bridge, just in case.

It never hurt to stack your deck.

"Where in the world is Jackson?" complained Donald Morley. "I had to use my key to let myself in."

Two heavily muscled men in the white uniform of hospital orderlies stood beside him, one of them holding a straitjacket, the other a sheaf of documents for Mrs. MacKenzie to sign. Dr. Yarborough was a stickler for having all the required forms properly filled out.

"They've all gone." Victoria set down the small overnight case she'd packed for her stepdaughter. The less this removal looked like a kidnapping, the better. "I'm afraid I couldn't persuade your patient to take her laudanum. She became hysterical. I had to lock her in the library, but she may be dangerous. I heard glass breaking in there."

"We don't take any chances," the attendant holding the straitjacket said.

"Where is Dr. Yarborough? Didn't he come with you?"

"He's sent instructions up to the clinic, Mrs. MacKenzie, and he said to tell you he'll be there as soon as he can get away."

Victoria signed the papers she was handed, a cluck of annoyance sounding deep in her throat. For the kind of money she was paying that quack, the least he could do was show up in person. She handed Donald the key to the library. "Show them where it is," she ordered. "She's made so much trouble for me this afternoon that I don't want to see her again."

"We'll have her in the jacket and calmed down in no time," one of the attendants assured her. "We have laudanum with us. On Dr. Yarborough's orders. It'll make the trip upstate easier on her."

"She won't take it. She'll fight you."

"She'll be in the straitjacket, ma'am. She won't have a choice."

"She's not there, Victoria. The room's empty." Morley's voice cracked as Victoria swept past him angrily.

"Must I do everything myself? Can't you do one single thing right for a change?"

One of the white-suited attendants stood guard in the library doorway while the other continued to search the room for the patient who had disappeared. The smell of kerosene from the broken lamp was strong; fragments of glass crunched beneath Victoria's shoes.

"She must be here. The door was locked and I had the key. Both keys. She couldn't have gotten out."

"I've checked the windows, ma'am. They're all locked. She didn't leave that way."

"There must be another key. Someone else in this house must have another key," raged Victoria. She tugged on the bellpull, than realized there was no one downstairs except Mrs. Barstow to answer it. "She had to have had help. Someone must have heard her and let her out."

"Do you want us to search the house, Mrs. MacKenzie?" the man with the straitjacket offered. He thought he'd seen a door to the back courtyard of the house standing slightly open at the end of the hall. He hadn't thought anything about it until now. "She might still be on the grounds. Is there a garden outside?"

"I want answers, not guesses," Victoria snapped, "and I want them right now." She circled the room slowly, examining every shelf, looking for whatever it was she was sure she had missed. There were only two possibilities. Either Prudence had been helped by one of the servants who had disobeyed her orders, or another key had been hidden somewhere inside the library. And if that were so, then what else remained hidden? What else had the Judge kept from her?

"Victoria?" Donald took a tentative step toward his sister. You never could tell what she'd say or do when she was in one of her moods.

"Go out to the stable and bring Kincaid in here. I want to know what he's been doing."

"He brought you my message, Victoria."

"I know that, you idiot. He might have heard her. He might have been the one to let her out."

"Did you ring, Mrs. MacKenzie?"

"Is Kincaid downstairs?"

"He left to go back to get Mr. Morley right after I brought you his message, madam." Mrs. Barstow shook her head. "He must have misunderstood you, sir," she said to Donald. "I'm sure he told me you expected him to deliver a message and that you were waiting for some papers to be delivered. But he was definitely supposed to go back for you. He'll be mortified, sir, if he got it wrong."

"Did you come up here to the library again, Mrs. Barstow?"

"No, Mrs. MacKenzie, I didn't. Just that one time. I thought I'd have a quiet cup of tea in my parlor, but I did see the strangest thing when I glanced out the window."

"What was that?"

"Well, it was so odd that I hesitate to say." She was dragging it out as long as she could. Every moment of delay counted. "As I said, I was making myself a cup of tea and I glanced out the window. I thought I saw Miss Prudence stumbling across the courtyard and then out through the carriage gates. It was so strange that I put the kettle down and went outside to see for myself what was going on. There was a young woman lurching along the alleyway, not toward Fifth Avenue, but in the other direction. It couldn't possibly have been Miss Prudence."

"Go after her," Victoria ordered.

Dr. Yarborough's two orderlies ran out the front door to the carriage waiting at the curb. One of them climbed in, the other hoisted himself up beside the driver, who whipped up the horses and turned the vehicle away from Fifth Avenue.

Watching from the open doorway of the MacKenzie mansion, Morley wondered how many of Yarborough's patients made a run for it. They'd catch her. She didn't stand a chance alone and on foot. Stupid of her to run away from Fifth Avenue where the crowds were. It just showed she wasn't thinking clearly. He went back inside to tell Victoria that they'd have her straitjacketed and dosed within minutes. Nothing to worry about.

* * *

"Mr. Jackson. What are you doing here?"

"I could ask you the same question, Mrs. Barstow." He stood foursquare in front of her in the main hallway. She'd nearly cried out when she saw him.

"I broke my heel on the way to Central Park."

"Who's there?" Donald Morley stepped into the hallway from the parlor. "Jackson, is that you?"

"Yes, sir." What was going on? He'd counted on no one being home except the Judge's daughter.

"You can join the search now that you're back."

"Sir?"

"Come in here. Mrs. MacKenzie will explain it to you. Tea, Mrs. Barstow?"

"I'll have it for you in a few minutes, sir." She edged past Jackson.

He glanced toward the stairway to the second floor, and then followed Morley into the parlor.

"Miss Prudence has been unwell," Victoria began. "I'm sure you're aware of that, Jackson."

It would have been inappropriate to comment, so he didn't. This was not the time for a misstep.

"We decided she needed to be under a doctor's care. Unfortunately, she suffered a complete breakdown this afternoon, resulting in hysteria. Somehow she managed to get out of the house without my knowing it. Mrs. Barstow was the last one to see her. I regret to say that she was fleeing the doctor's attendants. They've gone after her, of course. A very sad situation, but one I'm sure will be remedied when they catch up with her. Which they will."

"I suggested to Jackson that he join the search. He knows the neighborhood far better than Dr. Yarborough's orderlies."

"I'll be glad to help, sir, in any way I can."

Victoria looked at him, a frown creasing her forehead, her mouth pursed as if she'd bitten into something spoiled or sour.

She didn't trust him. There was too much about Jackson that was murky, contradictory. He had served them well enough, and been paid outlandish sums for some of what he'd done, but that didn't make him anything more than a hireling. He should disappear when he'd outlived his usefulness. Which Victoria thought was probably sometime in the very near future.

The problem with people like Jackson was that they were unpredictable. Eventually they began thinking for themselves and then spiraled out of control. It was a short step from conspiring to torment someone to taking that same person's life. The next logical thing to do in a mind twisted by the delight of inflicting pain. Donald was like that. Victoria rode him mercilessly to keep him in line. If Jackson took that final step, if he killed Prudence either accidentally or because the act gave him pleasure, it would be the end and the ruination of everything Victoria had been working for. She could almost feel him tugging to break free and she wondered what past crime was eating at his self-control.

She caught Donald's eye; he had a speculative look that was easy to read. Jackson's days were numbered.

The only sound in the kitchen was the whistle of water coming to a boil in the kettle. Mrs. Barstow had taken a plate of sliced cake from the pantry, a small platter of sandwiches from the cold larder. No matter what was going on in the house, Mr. Morley was never off his feed.

She sensed Jackson's presence in the doorway, but kept her back turned to him. The sooner she got the tea tray ready, the sooner she could carry it upstairs. He'd be gone on the search for Miss Prudence by the time she got back, and not a moment too soon. Something about the way the butler looked at her in the hallway had jarred her already unsettled nerves. She wasn't afraid of him, but there were times when he reminded her of Billy, cold as ice when he wanted to be. Unforgiving, too.

"What is this, Mrs. Barstow?" Jackson scooped up a piece

of crumpled paper from the clean floor, read it, then held it out to her.

"I'm sure I don't know," she answered, pretending to barely glance at it. "I've a tea tray to prepare. I'll thank you to get out of my way." Jesus, Mary, and Joseph, it was the page Miss Prudence had torn from her housekeeper's notebook. How had it gotten on the floor? Could she grab it out of his hand and tell him it was no business of his?

"Whose address is it?"

"I told you I don't know what you're talking about."

"It's a page from your housekeeper's notebook, isn't it?" Jackson seized Mrs. Barstow's arm, spun her around until he could hold her tightly against his body. He plunged his hand into the side pocket of her skirt, brought out the small notebook, let her go. "Here," he said, opening it to where a page had been ripped out. He flung the notebook to the floor, held what she was denying any knowledge of where she could read it. "You helped Prudence MacKenzie get away, didn't you? She couldn't have done it by herself. I want to know if this is where the Judge's daughter thinks she can hide. You're going to tell me."

Mrs. Barstow blanched and made a futile grab for the bit of paper. He struck her across the face with the back of his hand, an angry, savage growl drowning out the steaming kettle. The housekeeper fell against the cook's table, one hand upraised to ward off the next blow.

"I'm going to ask you one more time, and then I'm going to beat it out of you," he said. "You'll tell me, in the end. But I'll break your arms and knock the teeth out of your jaws before I'm done with you."

She held out for as long as she could, until her sister's voice in her head told her that nothing was worth the punishment Frances was taking. The men always won, and the young miss she was protecting had had a decent head start, would be safe among friends. What was the point of refusing to speak now?

So Mrs. Barstow mumbled Mrs. Dailey's name, nodded when Jackson asked one final time if that was where Prudence MacKenzie had gone, and confirmed that she hadn't left the house on foot. Kincaid had been driving her. Jackson let her sink to the floor, where she lay in such pain as she had never imagined possible. Until finally the red heat of agony ebbed and a cool, welcoming darkness enveloped her.

He dragged the housekeeper's lifeless body to the stables, placed it in an empty stall, and covered it with hay. It would be hours before Kincaid returned from Brooklyn, if he did come back tonight. Even if Victoria MacKenzie didn't fire him as soon as he got the grays safely back in their boxes, James Kincaid wouldn't stay, not with Miss Prudence dead.

As she soon would be.

Before he set out after the Judge's daughter, Jackson cleaned the blood from the kitchen floor and turned off the gas under the kettle.

Chapter 27

"She's safe, Mr. Hunter. You have my word on that," Danny Dennis said. "James Kincaid is driving Miss Prudence out to Brooklyn. He won't leave her and he won't let anything happen to her."

He'd found Geoffrey Hunter coming out of Warneke and Sons and told him everything he knew. "Mrs. MacKenzie and Mr. Morley are still inside the house."

"Are you sure?"

"Your man out front sent word by a runner," Dennis said. "He won't leave unless one of them does, but he wanted you to know what was going on. The boy says the men looking for Miss Prudence know what they're doing. He thinks they're both ex-fighters. Bare knuckle boxers."

"We have to make sure the hunt is called off," Hunter said. "If Yarborough's orderlies scour the neighborhood and come up with nothing, they'll suspect Mrs. Barstow deliberately misled them. Do you know where this doctor's offices are?"

"About ten minutes from here."

"Let's go. And if Mr. Washington makes it in less time you can give him an extra nosebag of oats tonight. On me."

* * *

"Miss MacKenzie is a patient of mine. You have no right to interfere with her treatment." Dr. Stanley Yarborough almost never had to deal with angry relatives, though he wasn't certain to which branch of the MacKenzie family his uninvited visitor belonged.

"I'm Prudence MacKenzie's attorney, Doctor."

"You'll find the paperwork in order."

"Need I remind you that you're talking about the daughter of one of this city's most respected jurists? Judge MacKenzie is deceased, but the members of the legal profession who knew and respected him are legion. My client does not feel the need to be treated at one of your clincs. I'm sure you understand that mistakes are sometimes made. It's best to undo them before the damage becomes permanent."

"That's not the way we do things in medicine, Mr. Hunter."

"Which is why you lose more patients than I do clients."

"I don't have to put up with insults. I must ask you to leave." Yarborough reached for the bell that would summon his nurse.

"When malfeasance and moral turpitude are proved against my client's stepmother, you'll fall with her, Doctor. You and the highly profitable empire of laudanum addicts you've created. I hope for your sake that every single file on every single patient can stand up to the kind of scrutiny the Judge's friends will consider it their duty to impose. I don't think you'll make it out of the courts unscathed. Or with your fortune anywhere near intact, especially after you make restitution and pay your legal fees. Did you know that lawyers are more expensive than physicians?"

"What are you asking me to do?"

"Three things. Dispatch someone to cancel the search and bring back your orderlies right away. Then send a special delivery telegram to Mrs. Victoria MacKenzie informing her that her stepdaughter has been found and is now under your care. She should have it within the next thirty minutes."

"And the third condition?"

"Petition the judge to void the order of commitment. Then turn the MacKenzie file over to me. Every signed form, every note you made. The originals."

"In return for which?"

"I leave your office and you'll never see me again."

This time, when Yarborough reached for the bell to summon his nurse, Geoffrey Hunter did not stop him.

"They've found her," Victoria said, waving a telegram in her hand. "This just came from Dr. Yarborough. Prudence is on her way to his clinic upstate. The commitment papers have been sealed by the court, so no one will ever find her. All we have left are the loose ends to tie up."

"Conkling's nurse won't say anything," Donald said. The money Victoria had given him to bribe the woman was burning a hole in his pocket. He decided he'd go to the Haymarket again tonight. He'd found entertainment there that was nearly as satisfying as what Billy McGlory offered.

"What did you do, Donald?" Victoria knew that look and it worried her. It meant he'd stepped outside the limits she'd drawn for him. Just when things were beginning to fall into place. Such a fool. If he weren't her brother, she would have gotten rid of him long ago.

"She can't be identified," he said smugly, "even if somebody goes to the morgue looking for her. I made sure of that."

"It wasn't necessary."

"She knew too much. She heard the whole miserable Charles Linwood story the way Conkling told it to Prudence."

"And Geoffrey Hunter. And Josiah Gregory."

"Gregory is next." Donald jingled the coins in his pockets, ran his fingers along the edges of the bills folded neatly together. "He lives alone in an apartment a child could break into. I'll take care of him tonight." *On my way to the Haymarket.*

"Then we leave New York for at least six months. Europe, I

think. By the time we get back, no one will remember Judge Thomas MacKenzie or his daughter. Society rolls over anyone who can't keep up with it."

"What about Hunter?"

"Nothing. The rumor I heard about him being an ex-Pinkerton is true, which means he could be dangerous. It's best to leave him alone. Conkling or the Linwood firm will find him another case to work on. As long as there are no new threats to counter or deaths to investigate, he'll soon lose interest in the MacKenzie mystery."

"Are you sure?"

"I know men, Donald. Just be certain that when you deal with Josiah Gregory, the police will conclude he was the victim of an interrupted burglary. No clues that could lead to inconvenient questions."

"And Conkling?"

"You leave him to me. Roscoe has a weakness for a certain type of woman, and he's more interested in his legal cases than acting as unpaid trustee for Prudence MacKenzie, no matter how much he professes to care for her. He won't protest when I tell him I've chosen someone else to hold the estate's paperwork. I'm her guardian, remember? Conkling likes the spotlight and those enormous fees he demands. Just taking care of Jay Gould's affairs should keep him busy enough to forget all about our little laudanum addict."

"How many of his patients does Dr. Yarborough cure?"

"None. Once a patient crosses his threshold, she's a resident for however long it profits her family to keep her there. I think Prudence can look forward to a good many peaceful years rocking away her afternoons on Dr. Yarborough's veranda. Mornings in the warm baths of hydrotherapy, afternoons in the embrace of morpheus. Such an enviable and uneventful existence, don't you think?"

"When are the servants due back?"

"Not until later this evening. I'm making an early night of it."

"No celebrating?"

"Have you forgotten I'm a widow?"

"Well, I'm not."

"Just be careful. We're very close to the finish line now. When I pay off Jackson there won't be any more loose ends that need tying up."

"Is it safe to let him go?"

"Jackson isn't the kind of man who's destined to lead a long life. He'll always be in trouble. Someone else will eventually kill him for us." Victoria waved down Donald's objection. She looked pointedly at the belly straining against his waistcoat. "He's not a Josiah Gregory. He'd be a hard man to take down. Jackson would fight back, and he might win. It's not worth the risk."

"The housekeeper?"

"I have a bad feeling about her. As if I've seen her or known her in other circumstances, but I can't remember what they were. I'll give her a good reference and a bonus when we close up the house. She'll find herself another position, and that will be that. Is there anything else you need reassurance about?"

"Nothing more, Victoria. You've thought of everything."

But she only imagined she had.

Mrs. Dailey's boardinghouse sat silent and nearly empty. She had served an elaborate full tea an hour later than usual this afternoon, then shooed her lodgers out to walk it off and watch the sunset from the shore. What she really wanted was to spend some time alone with Miss Prudence and Ian Cameron, just the three of them together again, reminiscing perhaps about the Judge and the life they enjoyed before the witch ruined it.

James Kincaid refused to leave until Geoffrey Hunter arrived, so the grays had been taken down the street to a stable where they would be fed, watered, and curried before the return trip to Brooklyn. Whenever that was. He sat with Colleen until she dozed off, then joined the others briefly in the parlor before excusing himself to stroll down to join the boarders. He'd seldom seen faces as alight with joy as Kathleen Dailey's and Ian Cameron's. He'd keep an eye on the house from the shoreline, but everything looked luminous and peaceful in the red-gold glow of the setting sun.

It would be dark in an hour or so; Kincaid hoped Hunter would have arrived by then. The grays and the caleche had to be back in the MacKenzie stable tonight or Mrs. MacKenzie would report them stolen. He needed to work on the story he would have to tell. Nothing too elaborate, nothing that would trip him up. Fortunately, New York City had so many traffic mishaps in a single day that he could take his pick. Maybe he'd get the stable owner to replace a few of the spokes on one of the caleche's wheels. That should do it.

Mrs. Dailey allowed the young miss half an hour in the parlor, no more. She looked wan and unsteady in her chair, the events of the day finally catching up to her. Kathleen put her into her own bed in the room next to Colleen, a cold compress on her head, the boardinghouse cat curled up and purring at her side. She shouldn't be allowed to fall asleep for a few more hours yet, in case of a concussion, so Ian Cameron sat beside her, reading aloud from the evening newspaper.

Kathleen Dailey listened to the drone of Cameron's voice as she carried what was left of the crustless ham and cucumber sandwiches, current scones, whipped cream, tiny frosted cakes, chocolate bonbons, and marrons glacés into the kitchen, wrapping them carefully and placing the neatly labeled packages into the ice box. She hated leaving Miss Prudence for even a moment, but there was always someone who wanted a nibble before going up to bed and if she didn't get the leftovers on ice, they'd spoil.

She'd need to send someone to the corner for another bottle of cream for the boarders who liked a cup of hot chocolate in the evening. The last of what the milkman delivered this morning had gone into a blancmange for Colleen, whose appetite was still not what it should be. She'd mention that to the doctor the next time he came.

She didn't hear the kitchen door open behind her, bent over the bread safe as she was, tut-tutting to herself over what remained of the perfect loaves she'd baked early this morning. A shame to waste the lovely brown crust, but you couldn't serve proper tea sandwiches unless you cut it off. Mrs. Dailey decided she'd put the crusts aside for an eggy bread pudding with raisins and a nice whiskey hard sauce. Humming busily to herself, she never felt the blow that knocked her to the floor, never heard the footsteps making their way toward the bedroom where Colleen lay weak and defenseless.

But Ian Cameron did. He heard the sound of a body collapsing, then the hard rap of a man's boots against the wooden floor of the hallway. He motioned to a wide-eyed Prudence to stay silent, not to make a sound, then he crossed into Colleen's room and picked up the baseball bat he'd kept close at hand ever since she'd been brought to the boardinghouse. Now he took up his position behind the bedroom door; he'd allow the intruder to enter the room, but he wouldn't get far. And when Ian swung his bat, he'd do it with all of his aging force.

Jackson had hailed a hansom cab on Fifth Avenue, but he had given the driver a false address two blocks away from Mrs. Dailey's. Not until the man drove off did he take the first steps of the short walk toward the hiding place of the young woman he'd come to kill. He planned to survive his revenge; he wanted no one to be able to link him to the body in the MacKenzie stables or what was left of Prudence MacKenzie when he finished with her.

Jackson had falsified his letters of reference, lied about his past employment, and gotten taken on as underbutler in the MacKenzie household because he'd been recognized as a person who could be paid to remove obstacles. Only a year before, hotheaded and crazed by jealousy, he'd killed his wife and her lover, the child who might or might not be his nestling in the

Jezebel's womb. And then he'd left, dragging coals from the fireplace to smolder through the wood floor of his house and burn it to the ground. Presumed dead, since no one suspected that the body of the man lying alongside his wife was not him. He'd bought false identity papers in Chicago and settled in to enjoy the rest of his life. Until he read in the *Tribune* that the man suspected of killing him, held, then released for lack of evidence, had been arrested, tried, convicted, and sentenced to life in Sing Sing. He'd come back, but it was too late. Artie of the laughing eyes and dancing boxer's feet was dead.

"Don't worry," he'd told his big brother a few months before. "The fix is in. Get the hell out of town before somebody finds out you're not the dead guy." He'd punched Jackson a light one on his upper arm, held him tightly the way brothers do, then sent him on his way.

And Jackson, told not to worry, didn't. Fixes were the way of the world. You paid a guy, he did you a favor. You were in each other's pockets.

There was a man on Hester Street everybody was afraid of because he said he always paid his debts. And collected what was owed him. Jackson admired that. He decided he'd be another one who got what he'd been promised. The judge who welshed on his part of the bargain had to go, but so did the woman who convinced her new husband not to take any more bribes. Too dangerous for someone busily climbing the social ladder. That's what the word on the street was. The street was right more often than not.

It could get complicated if you tried to sort it all out and decide who deserved what. So Jackson didn't. He thought about what needed to be done until he felt good about it, and then he got to work. He'd finish it this evening, as the sun was going down on Artie's birthday. He should have been twenty today, but nineteen years was all his brother got. So the Judge's daughter wouldn't have more than that, either. Jackson thought of it as collecting on a debt.

The blow that landed across the back of his head did credit to Mr. Cameron's Scots ancestors who roared into battle wielding heavy two-handed claymores capable of unhorsing a man in full armor. Jackson's skull cracked along a thin line, while the brain inside the protective cage of bone banged from side to side, bruising itself, beginning to bleed from vessels damaged by the bony surface that was supposed to protect them.

Jackson swung around on feet that seemed rooted to the floor, raised his hands to the clamor in his head that was deafening him, saw the tall, dignified, silver-haired man with upraised bat ready to strike again, and lunged at him, scrabbling to wrench the bat out of Mr. Cameron's hands.

A woman screamed and then began shouting for help. She sounded young. Jackson let loose the bat and fumbled at his belt for the knife he'd sharpened in the MacKenzie kitchen. Blood was streaming into his eyes, blinding him. He staggered in the direction of the voice, but when his knees hit the bed frame and he reached down for her, she was gone. And it wasn't Miss Prudence, his injured brain realized. It was the maid, Colleen, the dead maid who'd rolled and tumbled down the servants' staircase and into a coma.

"Run," he heard Cameron shout. "Run. Get Kincaid. Get help."

He ought to have figured on the coachman being here, but there'd been no grays, no carriage parked outside to warn him.

"This way, Colleen," he heard someone cry. "Get behind me."

Even through the fog of pain and the veil of blood, he knew who it was. He'd come all this way to find her, and now she stood within arm's reach, swaying on her feet but glaring at him, daring him to come any closer. He wondered what made her so brave, and then he saw the pistol in her hand, a ladylike Remington derringer with fancy scrolled grip and deadly barrel pointed straight at him.

"I should have realized it was you," she said. "Donald Morley wasn't clever enough to think of all the elaborate statagems that had us fooled."

She knew. She understood it all. It was his hand that had pushed her toward the hansom cab, his fingers that had rigged the gas lamps in her bedroom. Victoria had had nothing to do with her stepdaughter's close brushes with death. Laudanum had been her weapon, addiction her overriding goal.

Jackson's pale yellowish brown eyes fixed themselves on Prudence, glazed over with the icy determination of his hatred. It was time.

He had to kill her. Artie was counting on him.

The bullet pierced his shoulder. The knife fell from his useless hand and clattered on the floor.

"It's over, Jackson," Prudence MacKenzie said. "It's over now."

He howled and swung from side to side like the injured animal he was; then he barreled past the startled Cameron and disappeared out the kitchen door.

"Let him go," Prudence said. "Where's Mrs. Dailey?"

Cameron found her crumpled on the kitchen floor, struggling to get to her knees.

"Are you all right?" he asked, bending over to help her into a sitting position. "Kathleen, can you hear me?"

"There's a block of ice in the ice box. Chip off a few pieces and hand them to me in a towel," she directed. "I'm fine. Did he get to Colleen?"

"He was after Miss Prudence. He didn't lay a hand on either one of them."

"Holy Mother of God."

"Colleen is whimpering and shaking, but she's safe. No harm done. I hit him over the head with the baseball bat hard enough to take out any other man. That one's got a skull like iron. Miss Prudence shot him."

"I'll go see to her."

"No, you won't, Kathleen. I'll help you up into a chair, but there you'll sit until Mr. Kincaid gets here. Miss Prudence has gone out onto the porch to wave at him. He'll have heard the shot and known what it was."

"I wish you'd swung the bat harder," Mrs. Dailey said. "God save me, I wish you'd swung it harder." She made the sign of the cross on forehead, breast, and shoulders, then lowered her head into her hands and gave over to quiet sobbing.

Jackson lurched his way along the shore, rallying when the cool salt air and an occasional spray from the river washed across his face. He was afraid to slow down, terrified that if he stopped, he would not be able to get his feet to move again. Down the shore road, across the park toward Fourth Avenue. Then right in front of him, looming large in all of its cantilevered glory, rose the Brooklyn Bridge. He had to get back to Manhattan, to Little Five Points where he'd grown up, where he knew the streets and the neighborhood, where he could lose himself in the crowds. Where he could find somebody to help and hide him until he could try again.

His head felt as though a company of miners were banging against it with sharp pickaxes. There wasn't a hansom cab in sight, but the bridge rose up against the blue and crimson of the sunset sky. On either side of the roadway along which traveled hundreds of horse-drawn vehicles every day stretched the pedestrian walkways used by workers who couldn't afford any transportation but their own feet.

He'd find a cab on the other side of the bridge. All he had to do was walk across the East River, holding on to the railing when the dizziness threatened to overwhelm him. Fresh air and exercise would restore him; by the time he reached the other side he'd be himself again. What was it that had happened? Why was his head hurting so much? Jackson couldn't remember. No matter. One foot in front of the other. Lift it up, place it down, lift it up, place it down.

At the last possible moment he hesitated, leaning against the bridge railing, staring across to Manhattan outlined against a fiery orb. If he took the carriageway instead of the walkway, he might be able to stop an empty cab. The city was so far away, his head hurt so much he couldn't think, and his legs were going weak on him. He wasn't sure he'd be able to make it on foot after all.

Danny Dennis made the turn off the bridge at nearly the same moment Prudence MacKenzie fired the loaded derringer she'd found under Mrs. Dailey's pillow. He was driving too fast to pay much attention to the man staggering through the park toward the roadway. The drink was a terrible curse, especially for the Irish. He hoped the poor bastard made it home in one piece. Danny hadn't taken a drop in years, not since the night he'd been so far gone he'd put Mr. Washington up without removing his head harness and blinders or checking for feed and fresh water.

Kincaid burst out of Mrs. Dailey's front door as soon as he recognized Danny's hansom cab. "They're all right," he yelled, running toward them, "but the bastard got away. It was Jackson."

"You go ahead, Mr. Hunter. Find out what he's talking about." Danny knew right away that the figure tottering his way toward the Brooklyn Bridge wasn't your ordinary drunk.

"I'm coming with you," Hunter said.

"Miss Prudence needs you," Kincaid said. "I'll go with Danny. We'll get him, Mr. Hunter. You've got my word on that."

"We're both coming." Somehow Prudence had made it down Mrs. Dailey's walkway and out onto the sidewalk. She stood there swaying from side to side, the gun she had used to shoot Jackson still clutched in her hand. Nobody inside the house had been able to persuade her to surrender it.

"Prudence, give me the gun," Geoffrey said.

"No. I'm not finished with it. I'm not finished with him, either."

"Kincaid and Danny will take of Jackson. You need to tell me

everything that's happened, and you need to give me the gun."
He very slowly reached out, and when she made no move to
raise the derringer and point it at him, eased it from her grip,
handing it off to Kincaid.

Prudence stared at him as though realizing for the first time
what she had done, then she said his name. "Geoffrey?"

He caught her in his arms as she collapsed. "I guess you are
going without me," he said. "Good luck. And don't come back
without him."

By the time he reached Mrs. Dailey's front porch with Prudence in his arms, Ian Cameron had come out to help. He
stepped back when he saw the look in Mr. Hunter's eyes and let
the former Pinkerton carry Miss Prudence into the house by
himself.

James Kincaid leaped onto the hansom cab and held on
tightly as Danny pulled Mr. Washington into a tight turn, then
set him off at a fast trot back in the direction from which they'd
come.

"What happened?"

Kincaid repeated what he'd been told, described what he'd
seen. "She shot him," he marveled. "Took aim and got him right
in the shoulder."

"She should have killed him," Danny said. "In self-defense."

"She said it wasn't the smart thing to do. Dead men can't talk."

"She said that?"

"Her exact words." Kincaid pointed. "There he is. On the
bridge."

"We've got him," Danny said. "Now all we have to do is run
him down."

A quarter of the way across the bridge Jackson heard the clip
clop of a trotting horse behind him. It hurt to turn his head, but
he did it. An enormous white horse grinned ugly yellow teeth
at him, the driver flicking a whip through the air inches above
the animal's back. Jackson raised an arm to wave him down.

Hansom cabs weren't supposed to stop on the bridge, but a fare was a fare. If the cab were empty, it would stop. He could climb in, sink back against the cushioned seat, and try to concentrate on what had gone wrong.

Someone had struck at him with a fire iron or a piece of fire-wood. No. He remembered now; it was a baseball bat, wielded by an aristocratic-looking old man. Cameron, who'd trained him when he was an underbutler. He'd taken the first few steps into the room where someone lay sleeping. Then a loud crack-ing sound; the worst pain in his head he had ever felt; another, sharper pain in his shoulder, darkness, confusion. Running. He had raced out of the house, down paved sidewalks, across grassy fields. Running and stumbling, getting up every time he fell be-cause he had to. Running onto the bridge.

Why wasn't the hansom cab slowing down? Would it go right past him? Was the driver afraid he couldn't pay? Jackson ignored the entrances to the railed-off pedestrian footpath, stum-bling unsteadily along the farthest edge of the carriageway, fling-ing up first one arm then the other, as if he were warding off a host of stinging flies. If he lost his footing he'd veer out under the oncoming vehicles.

None of the passengers in carriages or hansom cabs paid him any attention. A few drivers flicked their whips in his direction, others shouted to him to get on to the footpath where it was safe. But no one stopped. Drunks could be dangerous; best stay out of their way. He'd eventually fall down and sleep it off.

Danny Dennis drove with two whips mounted beside his seat. One of them was short, light, meant more for the cracking sound it made than actual contact; the other was a vicious in-strument that could strip the skin from a horse's back or send him flying along the roadway so fast that his hoofs struck sparks from the cobblestones. Coachmen who traveled empty, danger-ous roads at night kept the long, heavy whip handy to deal with human predators. Now Danny settled the wrapped leather handle into his right hand, let Mr. Washington's reins lie loosely coiled around his left fist, and urged the horse on with the clucks and clicks that only they two understood.

Kincaid held on to his seat and said nothing. It wasn't his cab. One driver didn't second-guess another, never interfered with a decision. The job was dangerous enough without distractions and arguments. He knew what Dennis was planning to do, and he approved.

If Jackson reacted to the sight of the whip raised over his head the way most highwaymen did, he'd throw his hands in the air and give himself up. A man's face could be sliced to ribbons by the steel tip that was sharper and more deadly than a knife. It was no longer Danny Dennis's intention to kill Jackson, not even to maim him, though he was fully prepared to use the whip if he had to. His first thought had been to run him down, but knowing that Miss Prudence and Colleen were all right had cooled him off. Bringing Jackson to justice and watching the hangman fit the noose aound his neck would be far more satisfying. He was sure that was what Mr. Hunter and Miss Prudence expected him to do.

Mr. Washington edged closer and closer to the railing, the bulk of the empty hansom cab rocking from side to side behind him. The oddly flailing human kept looking over his shoulder as he ran. He had gone from confused to frightened to terrified, and his face was so contorted that he hardly looked like a man anymore. His fear sweat filled the air with the acrid stench common to all hunted creatures just before they were brought down.

For a moment they were neck and neck, the running, staggering man and the evenly trotting horse. Jackson looked to his left and saw to his horror a steel-tipped whip outlined against the sunset sky. He flung up an arm, but at the last moment he overbalanced. His feet slipped on the smooth roadway of the bridge, he turned to grab the harness of the huge horse beside him, then felt his knees buckle as his legs collapsed and he was dragged against the railing. A flash of bright light told him that the hansom cab had flung him loose and passed him; he shouted with relief.

A private carriage swerved to miss him. Desperate, he made a grab for the horse's bit, thinking to bring it to a halt and beg for assistance. But the animal snorted with the pain of the metal viciously jerked against its tender mouth and reared in its traces, dragging Jackson under dancing, destructive hooves. He felt the carriage stop, the driver descend to the roadway, heard voices explaining, arguing, coming to an agreement. He smelled horse and blood, felt the excruciating pain of broken bones and ligaments ripped from their moorings, lost consciousness as hands reached down to carry him to safety.

He sensed a rough woolen blanket being wrapped around him, his body settled hurridly into a cab, the sound of leather curtains unfurling and being secured, a door slamming.

By the time Danny Dennis and James Kincaid reached the Emergency Pavilion of Bellevue Hospital, Jackson had regained and lost consciousness more times than he could count. A crowd of familiar faces hovered over him. They seemed to have a lot to say, none of which he wanted to hear. It was too late to be called to account, too late to pay with anything but his own death for the lives he had taken. He'd never regretted them, never wasted a moment's energy or thought on his victims. Even now, he brushed them away with supreme indifference.

He'd made mistakes with Prudence MacKenzie because he'd wanted so badly to get it right, to give Artie a birthday gift like none other he'd ever gotten in his short life. So he'd played with her, tortured and teased her like a cat with a mouse, and none of it had worked. He should have pushed her harder on Fifth Avenue, should have allowed the gas to pour into her bedroom instead of trickle, should have killed both of them in the empty house when he had the chance. She and German Clara both. But he hadn't. He'd tried too hard to make it perfect for Artie, and he'd ended up giving him nothing at all. He'd explain it when he saw him. His brother would probably laugh and tell him it didn't matter. Artie never took anything seriously.

He wasn't supposed to be here at Bellevue. This was where Mrs. MacKenzie had ordered the maid Colleen taken. After she'd told him what she wanted done with her. So long ago. So very long ago.

"We've lost him," the doctor on duty told the cabby and his friend who had brought in the accident victim. "Given the extent and the type of his injuries, it's probably for the best."

"He has no family, no resources," Danny Dennis said.

"We'll bury him as a pauper then," the doctor decided. "I don't suppose you know his name?"

"No idea," Kincaid replied.

CHAPTER 28

"We'll tell them tomorrow, Mr. Washington. Now that we're certain."

Danny Dennis often preferred a talk with his horse to the chatter of his fellow humans. Tonight, when he and Kincaid returned to Mrs. Dailey's from Bellevue, there had been so many questions and exclamations that his head soon ached with the noise and clamor of it.

They'd told Mr. Hunter and Miss Prudence everything, except for one small detail they thought might trouble her. Jackson would lie in an unmarked pauper's grave, in the potter's field on Hart Island. And good riddance to him.

The stable was clean and warm, quiet except for James Kincaid's rhythmic snoring and the occasional stomp of a hoof. They'd agreed that it was too late and too dark to drive back to Manhattan; there was plenty of room where the grays had been boarded for another horse and two tired drivers.

Danny couldn't sleep. He'd finally remembered where he had taken Judge MacKenzie one afternoon nearly a year ago, and he'd gone back there himself. To the premises of the Peerless Safe Company, where a check of their ledgers confirmed that they had constructed a most unusual type of safe for the Judge. They wouldn't tell him where in the house they'd built it, nor how it was concealed, but their records were excellent. If the Judge's daughter would present herself at their offices with suitable proof of her rights of inheritance, they would provide her with details of its exact location and the combination.

He'd intended to tell Josiah Gregory first, so Conkling's secretary could supply Miss Prudence with the papers she'd need, but then all holy hell broke loose and there hadn't been either time or opportunity. With all that had happened today, he thought the young miss needed to hear some good news. And tomorrow Mr. Hunter was planning to confront Mrs. MacKenzie and Mr. Morley. She'd definitely need strengthening.

He'd overheard her telling Mr. Hunter what she had expected to find that was still missing. Letters, she'd said. A lifetime of love poured into letters the Judge had written her mother, the woman whose mortal illness he'd tried to stave off by selling his integrity. Danny could hear in her voice how badly she wanted to find those letters and how certain she had been that her father would have found a safe place for them.

And he had, Danny believed. A very *safe* place.

Danny Dennis stretched out in the hay he'd piled in front of Mr. Washington's stall. He had no doubt whatsoever that he'd ferreted out one of the last missing pieces of what he'd come to think of as the MacKenzie mystery. He wasn't a former Pinkerton like Mr. Hunter, but he was the next best thing.

"I still don't understand why you had to bring Yarborough into it," Donald Morley complained. "We could have handled Prudence ourselves, Victoria." It had turned out all right in the end, but his way would have been so much easier. He could feel the parlor walls closing in on him.

"I don't want her in the house."

"Why not? That's where people expect her to be. The grief-stricken orphan being looked after by her loving stepmother and her uncle by marriage. She wouldn't have been that much trouble."

"She got entirely too close to Conkling and that ex-Pinkerton who works with him. It's better for us if she's in a place where there's no chance she can contact either of them. Pinkertons are always a concern. I can smell one from a hundred yards away."

"What do they smell like?"

"Trouble. They stink like trouble."

"I still don't like it."

"I'm going to explain this to you one more time, Donald. As long as Prudence stays in the city, Hunter will come sniffing around her. You know I'm right about that. He'll give up once he gets used to the idea that she's gone. He won't know where to look, and I have no intention of telling him. We'll close down the house except for a few servants and go to Europe. He'll lose interest in a matter of months."

"I hope you're right."

"Have I ever been wrong?"

"I recall a certain wheelchair-bound Confederate colonel from Charleston, South Carolina. You let him get away from you."

"I underestimated how fast a Southern gentleman's family can move when they sense someone poaching on their private preserve. That never happened again."

"Maybe not."

"We'll make one visit to Pinestone Manor before we leave. To make sure Dr. Yarborough is carrying out the orders I've given him."

"Is he really a doctor?"

"I didn't ask to see his credentials."

"Both of us don't need to go."

"So far today you've contradicted everything I've said. Every single thing."

"Then cut me loose."

"Don't come home until you're in a better mood, Donald. And watch yourself, wherever you go."

"My dear sister." Morley raised one of her delicate hands to his lips and bowed over it as gallantly as a suitor. He'd picked and poked at her deliberately, impatient to be off to the Haymarket. Or perhaps he'd chance Billy McGlory's Armory Hall, which was where he really wanted to go. What were the odds McGlory would be down on the floor? Or that he'd recognize Donald after all this time? There was also the matter of Josiah Gregory to see to. Victoria's way of dealing with potentially dangerous obstacles was too slow and uncertain for his liking. He much preferred the more direct method. He was very good at it. He hadn't been caught yet, and he didn't intend to be. "Don't wait up for me."

"I never do."

Russell Coughlin hadn't turned everything he found over to Ned Hayes. That last case, the one he'd been told to pay particular attention to, might turn out to be a gold mine. If he read it right, the fix had been in, but the judge didn't come through, and a good-looking, nineteen-year-old kid who claimed he was innocent died a few months after arriving in Sing Sing. Reformers were screaming their heads off about alleged prison abuses.

It was a great story. Coughlin was thinking of writing a book about it.

"The morgue doesn't always have every issue of the paper," he told Hayes. "It's supposed to, but you know how it is. Somebody comes looking for something, walks off with that day's rag under his coat because he's in a hurry and can't be bothered to copy down the information he needs. Sometimes the missing edition turns up, sometimes it doesn't. From what I've read, you've got enough without it."

Ned Hayes didn't like it, but he didn't have any choice in the matter. He promised Coughlin he'd let him know when he could break the bribery story, then took the clippings the reporter had given him to Billy McGlory. Hayes had a bad feeling about Victoria MacKenzie. She needed to be stopped. Fast. And Billy was the man to do it.

Artie Sloan was younger and handsomer than his only brother. He had the face of an angel, an easygoing disposition, and a way with the ladies that was guaranteed to get him into trouble. He drifted into Billy McGlory's orbit when he was still wearing short pants, and never saw any reason to leave it. The pay was good, the work easy, the drink cheap, and the women always available. Artie had no ambitions in life; he was happy enough drifting along. Maybe something better would come his way, maybe not.

Artie didn't think much of it when Jack killed his wife and her lover. They had it coming, and in his world there was only one punishment. The best thing about the way his older brother handled the whole business was setting fire to the house. Sheer genius. The coppers decided that the husband had killed his missus because she had been unfaithful, then burned the house down, getting caught in the conflagration before he could escape. Served him right, they said. Then the neighbors started talking. They remembered seeing two men go into the house that night. Where was the other body?

When one of the detectives from Mulberry Street picked up Artie for questioning, he'd thought McGlory's accountant had forgotten to pay the weekly vig and the detective had been sent to hassle him to make the point that coppers could be mean when they got grouchy. They accused him of an adulterous relationship with his sister-in-law and the murder of the brother who'd confronted him. The woman, too. He couldn't tell them Jack was alive; they'd want to know who the dead man was, and that would put his brother's neck in a noose.

So Artie trusted in Mr. McGlory's well-oiled system to solve his problem and told Jack to take the next train to Chicago and stay out of sight. Which he did, changing his name to Obediah

Jackson. Jackson was easy to remember, and Obediah was biblical. It meant servant of God.

The accused had worn a new suit and tie the day he came up before Judge MacKenzie, knowing there might be reporters in the courtroom. Billy liked his men to look their best. Artie wondered if the judge was sick; he looked terrible. He didn't worry even when he was bound over for trial; appearances mattered. He'd be out before morning.

It didn't happen. Artie stood trial, was convicted of the heinous crime of fratricide and the incidental slaying of his sister-in-law, and sentenced to life at hard labor in Sing Sing. His lawyer told him not to be concerned; he was working on it. Nothing like this had happened since the deal was first struck with Judge MacKenzie; nobody could explain what had gone wrong.

If Artie had told the lawyer the truth, things might have turned out differently. But he didn't. He couldn't take the chance that Jack would be charged with murder, and he knew for a fact that people were looking out for him. He just had to be patient.

So Artie Sloan went up the Hudson River to Sing Sing. It was the worst place he could have been sent. He couldn't keep his mouth shut, so they put him in the dark cell for a hundred days. By the time he came into the light again, his mind had failed; he'd found refuge from the unbearable in madness. He declined rapidly after that and died before his twentieth birthday.

The only thing the reporter who wrote the Artie Sloan stories had not known was that the kid really was innocent. The brother he was supposed to have killed was alive and well in Chicago, where an out-of-date New York newspaper his landlady had put aside to clean the windows with tore the heart out of him.

"It's coming apart, Billy." Ned Hayes tossed a packet of newspaper clippings onto McGlory's desk. They were alone in the luxurious second-floor office and parlor where he and Geoffrey Hunter had first pursued the tenuous connection between Victoria MacKenzie and the owner of Armory Hall. A bottle of champagne stood in a silver ice bucket, a crystal glass of the golden liquid fizzing at each man's elbow.

"You better tell me what this is about, Ned." McGlory nudged the stack of clippings with one manicured forefinger, sliding them around in front of him until he saw an artist's caricature of Patrick Monoghan grinning up at Judge MacKenzie after his murder charge was dismissed. Dismissed for insufficient evidence, absence of key witnesses, and a laundry list of other failures of the prosecution to prove its case.

"The Judge didn't trust her. How could he? Victoria blackmailed him into marriage by threatening to ruin his daughter's life. You gave her that ammunition when you dropped Patrick Monoghan's name; it was the first, but not the only case the Judge threw for you. He needed the money that initial time, and later on he was in too deep to be able to get out. Victoria knew there had to be others besides Monoghan, so she set out to find enough of them to hog-tie her prize bull. I don't know how many she eventually identified. Five, six? Maybe more. She's the only one who can tell us.

"But the Judge would always be smarter than she was. He kept a notebook and hid it in a place no one but his daughter would know to look. Thirty-seven names, Billy, every one of them duly recorded by the city's newspapers. Somewhere among those thirty-seven names is the man who's going to send you back to prison. One of them will squeal until his curly tail falls off. He'll make a deal. Or maybe it'll be Victoria herself. She can testify in court against you, and I'll bet any jury in the land would believe her."

"They know to keep their mouths shut." McGlory emptied his champagne glass, poured himself more of the imported French wine. "You know how the system works, Ned."

"I do. But there's one small detail I'm not sure you know. And that's going to make all the difference."

"I don't think so."

"Victoria will sell out to save her own skin."

"It's not a crime to marry a wealthy, older man. As for blackmail, I doubt that can be proved if the only document you have is a marriage license."

"She got impatient, Billy. She killed him. The doctor who signed the Judge's death certificate is having second thoughts, and the undertaker who put him in his coffin will also urge an exhumation. Whatever Victoria used on him will still be there; it's only been a little over three months. She doesn't have any family behind her to buy off a conviction, so she'll have to work out her own deal. You're a big fish, Billy, maybe the biggest one in town. The politician who brings you down can write his own ticket. He'll have every reformer and do-gooder in the city organizing their supporters behind him. All he has to do is prove you bought Judge MacKenzie once, just once. Victoria can give him that proof, and don't doubt for a minute she will." Ned Hayes wasn't smiling now. "I'm sorry, Billy, but I thought you should know what's going to come at you."

"So Judge MacKenzie's widow walks free and I go inside. That hardly seems fair. Murder wins out over a bribe?"

"That's the way it looks to me."

"How long do I have?"

"Not long enough. The way I think it will go down is that Conkling or some other lawyer will represent the Judge's daughter and go after the exhumation order. The district attorney will indict Mrs. MacKenzie, and she'll have her own mouthpiece working out a plea bargain before the story hits the papers. You'll go down on her word, and once you take that first step, the rats will start coming out of the woodwork. Everybody will be jockeying for a piece of Billy McGlory's empire. That's the way I see it happening."

"Very tight, very simple."

"I'm sorry, Billy."

"I pay my debts, Ned."

"I know."

"I also collect on what's owed me." And Victoria MacKenzie owed more than Ned Hayes suspected.

"I know that, too."

"As long as you understand how things work. A man who doesn't act on the information he gets is a fool. Nobody's ever said Billy McGlory is a fool."

"I hope nobody ever will."

"Drink up, Ned."

"What am I drinking to?"

"Good health to old friends and bad cess to new enemies."

It was the only way. Geoffrey Hunter hadn't agreed; he'd asked Ned to stay away from McGlory, at least until Hunter had talked to Warneke again. Ned had nodded, but promised nothing, and in the end he'd known it would be folly to wait. Victoria MacKenzie might have stepped up into another social class entirely, but she'd gotten there at the cost of at least two men's lives. The law would never touch her, so someone else would have to bring her and her brother to justice. An eye for an eye. A life for a life. Simple. Final. Debt paid.

Ned was sorry to have to deceive Hunter, but he had no second thoughts about turning Victoria MacKenzie and Donald Morley over to McGlory's tender mercies. Someone had to sweep the streets.

Donald Morley staggered out of the Haymarket just before he would have been thrown out. He'd long ago lost count of his drinks, and there'd been more than one partner in the dark cubicle rented out to customers by the half hour. One of his pants pockets was turned out, the other just as empty. The skin of his face felt as though someone had rubbed sandpaper across every part of it. He gingerly stroked the tenderest spots and wondered which of his favorites he'd spent time with tonight. They'd all blurred together after a while.

Inside the Haymarket the music blared and beat on, cigar and cigarette smoke hung low above the tables, and the mingled stench of cheap perfumes and shaving lotions, raw whiskey, sweaty sex, and vomit made it hard to breathe. When you ran out of money, you were invited to leave or were tossed out into the street, whichever you seemed to deserve at the time. Just as well. The shock of cool and relatively clear night air was clearing his head and soothing all the sore places on his body. Early April was still cold once the sun went down; he thought it must be well past midnight.

Victoria would be fast asleep in her bed when he got home, but no matter, he'd had enough experience sneaking in with his shoes in his hand to manage it one more time. There was something he had to do, but he couldn't remember what it was. Somebody who hadn't been home when he'd gone after him on his way to the Haymarket earlier in the evening, somebody he needed to deal with tonight if he could figure out who it was. He stopped for a moment, ran a hand inside one of his boots, straightened when he felt the handle of the thin bladed knife in its sheath. Knives were his favorite weapons, as exciting to hold and use as a child's best-loved toy.

Donald had defied Victoria tonight, but he was confident she'd never find out. The thought of Prudence in a straitjacket had aroused him in a way he knew the denizens of the Haymarket wouldn't be able to assuage. So earlier in the evening, before he'd made his way uptown to the Haymarket, he'd slipped into Billy McGlory's Armory Hall, unnoticed, he thought, eased his way up the stairs to the second floor and into one of the private, curtained cubicles. Where he'd waited.

The danger of being spotted by McGlory had been worth it. The young man who'd pleasured him for the one sublime hour

that was all Donald could afford was rapturously adept. Innocent and soiled at the same time, with lips that coaxed the last
drop of sensual delight from his client. T-Boy. That was his name.
Afterward, they'd lain together in a tumble of arms and legs,
drinking out of one another's glasses, laughing, whispering, and
nibbling their way down from the heights to placid satiety. He
remembered telling T-Boy things he shouldn't have, boasting
about the most successful schemes he and Victoria had pulled
off, the grandest being the Judge, of course. Gulling the great
and feared Billy McGlory himself. Had he told all? He couldn't
recall, but he had the uneasy feeling that he might have described
the sudden flash of inspiration he'd had when that Sulzer fellow walked into the Astor House and began regaling everyone
there with the tale of Conkling and Linwood still outside in the
blizzard, determinedly slogging their way up Broadway.

They hadn't always been lucky, Donald and Victoria, but
that afternoon, trapped in the Astor House bar by the storm
raging outside, Donald Morley had felt the hand of fate on his
shoulder. For the first time in his life he made a decision without consulting Victoria. And acted on it. Linwood had never
suspected a thing, though he had looked behind him once. Stupid fool. Victoria had never intended allowing Linwood to live
long enough to assume control of Prudence's fortune, but neither had she been able to work out exactly how to kill him.
Donald solved that problem; she'd looked at him without the
usual scorn in her eyes that made him squirm. He'd rendered
her speechless. For once in his life, he'd held the winning hand.

Donald hated to leave T-Boy, but he'd had no choice. He
was short on money, and he had a job to do. Josiah Gregory
had to be eliminated, the killing made to look like an interrupted robbery. So he'd left Armory Hall as surreptiously as
he'd entered it, nearly sober by the time he got to Gregory's
dark and empty apartment. He'd waited, but not too long. The
arousal T-Boy had momentarily satisfied crept over him again
like an itch that gets worse the more you scratch it. He'd taken

Gregory's poorly hidden stash of money, locked the apartment door behind him, and left. Gone to spend the secretary's money at the Haymarket, confident that the killing could be done another night. There was always time for murder.

He had to piss. He had a feeling he'd piss more than once on his way home tonight. Whiskey did something to his insides that set everything free. And then there were all the beer chasers he'd poured down his gullet. He stepped over to the gutter, but there was a pile of reeking horse manure stinking up the street. Weaving back and forth like he was, he'd probably step in the damn stuff. So he backed up, turned around, and leaned one arm against the first building his feet carried him to. With the other hand he fumbled at the buttons on his trousers, determined not to ruin another pair of pants, especially these. The way the waistband was sewn held his gut in and minimized the belly he'd grown since Victoria had started them both living the good life again.

He'd just gotten a decent stream going when he heard a soft footfall behind him. Damn, he couldn't let go, couldn't turn around. Maybe whoever it was would keep on walking. He could still make out the Haymarket's door in the light from the streetlamps. The bouncer whose name he never remembered was pacing up and down rubbing his hands together. This close there wouldn't be any danger. Still, it might be a good idea to make his way back and wait for a hansom cab with the bouncer for company. Nothing left for a tip, but he was good for it. Damn. He'd already pissed out a river and couldn't seem to stop.

The knife took him under the ribs, under and across and into the heart in one swift upward thrust. The lungs were punctured for good measure, and because the knifer was exceptionally careful when he killed, he sliced the liver into two neat pieces. He held Donald Morley up until the blood stopped pumping, then he eased him to the pavement and rolled him against the wall into the puddle of piss. The body looked like another drunk sleeping it off where he fell. The knifer tweaked Donald's coat over his exposed and shriveled private parts, then strode off down the street into the darkness. The Haymarket bouncer never heard a thing, noticed nothing except a customer who was pissing against the brick one minute and gone the next.

Victoria sat in the parlor until nearly eleven, not because she thought Donald would make it home before dawn, but because she was too angry to go to bed.

Cook had sent up a late and very ample cold supper, so that, at least, had been all right. Everything else had rubbed her wrong.

Neither Jackson nor Mrs. Barstow had come back this evening. And Kincaid wasn't in his usual place in the stables, either. Questions hung in the air between servants and mistress, but the staff could not ask and their employer would not have answered.

Victoria couldn't imagine what had kept Mrs. Barstow. She supposed that Kincaid might have gone off in search of one of those disgusting smelling liniments he was always rubbing into the horses' knobby forelegs, and then met up with some fellow drivers. They were worse than old women the way they gossiped. She'd have a few words to say to the three of them in the morning.

One niggling worry refused to go away. That was Billy Mc-Glory. He lurked at the edge of her consciousness like a spider in the farthest corner of a seldom-used room. She had stolen something from him and gotten away with it, yet she knew, she had heard it said many times, that McGlory always paid his debts and collected on what was owed him.

Information and intimidation were at the heart of the empire of illegal activities over which he presided, but he had let her go free without any restraints or further contact. The seeming generosity bothered her; it was unlike him to give anything away, especially a judge with the power to keep skilled killers on the right side of prison bars. She was almost certain that once she claimed Judge MacKenzie for her own and persuaded him that he was certain to be caught if he continued taking Billy's bribes, McGlory had cut him loose. He didn't like sharing with anyone and he didn't trust even the hint of a partnership.

Blackmail was always tricky; victims tended to be unstable creatures to begin with, obsessed with keeping hidden the secrets that made them vulnerable. They could be dangerous, unpredictable, as volatile as a poorly mixed explosive. She'd taken the Judge from his blackmailer, and in so doing, blackmailed McGlory, too. Some people would say she'd written and signed her own death warrant, but here she was, three years after she began this scam, a free woman with more money than she could spend in a lifetime.

There had been a few weeks of uneasiness after the Judge's death, when she feared McGlory would come after her. After all, she'd stolen his crooked judge, then eased that judge into eternity when she no longer needed him, after he'd agreed to her demands. She remembered the exaltation she had felt seeing him sign the precious codicil to the rewritten will in Roscoe Conkling's office. The realization that now she was done with Thomas MacKenzie; he'd signed his own death warrant.

She was a little surprised that he succumbed so quickly, and worried that she'd wrongly estimated the strength of what she was giving him. But nothing happened. Dr. Worthington signed the death certificate. No one suspected a thing. Even the nosy Irish girl who'd been constantly underfoot in the sickroom obliged her by dying. After so many years of mischance, Victoria's fortunes had taken a decided turn for the better.

No stranger approached her in the street and no threat was ever delivered in the mail. She decided that when McGlory cut the Judge loose, he must have let her go also. The reformers were after him like ticks on a dog; he had to watch what he did, and who he did it to. Lucky Victoria had slipped past the dangerous time; all she had to do now was hang on.

Why was she so edgy tonight?

Still restless even after she'd taken a warm bath and finally gotten into bed, she heard the longcase clock in the downstairs hallway strike midnight then one A.M. By that time she'd allowed herself a generous dose of laudanum from the bottle left standing beside Prudence's empty bed. They were right, everyone who said the magical elixir could soothe away a day's troubles. Two or three additional swallows, no more. Just enough to smooth the rough edges of her anxiety and stop her eyelids from twitching.

The last thing she heard was soft footfalls that stopped at her door. Damn Donald! She was just drifting off and in no mood to hear him ramble on drunkenly about his evening at the Haymarket. She took a deep breath and let herself sink under the warm laudanum blanket. Her brother could wait until morning; everything could wait until then.

Victoria's visitor carried with him in his pocket a small bottle of unadulterated tincture of opium, the base ingredient of the laudanum so popular in the treatment of everything from hysteria to loose bowels. He had mixed the tincture with honey and a sweet liqueur, but the taste was still distinctively bitter, making it difficult to swallow. Unless the lady had done some of his work for him, he would have to restrain her with what he carried in a black leather bag not unlike the ones doctors used. His directions had been unequivocally precise. The death must be believed to be accidental, a consequence of profound melancholia brought on by her widowhood. Therefore no marks on the body.

She might not have drunk enough of the laudanum from the bottle on her bedside table for the effect to be much more sleep inducing than hot milk with a dash of sherry. There was no way to know for sure. Unfortunate, but he had come prepared for all possibilities. With a touch as gentle as that of a skilled nurse, he looped velvet lined restraints around her wrists and ankles, tethering her legs to the bedposts, carefully replacing each limb under the bedclothes as he worked. When he had finished, he spread a towel under her chin to protect the embroidered silk coverlet, then cradled her against his chest the way a mother does the baby she is about to feed. He laid a napkin near her mouth in case she should attempt to cry out, then unstoppered the tincture of opium and poured the first few drops between her lips.

Victoria's eyes opened in shock and disgust as soon as the bitter-tasting liquid pooled on her tongue. She tried to raise a hand to wipe it from her mouth, but found she could not. It was as if her legs and arms no longer belonged to her, were mysteriously unresponsive to her commands. In her panic she did not at first feel the man's arm around her, nor see his face bent solicitously over her own. When the napkin was jammed into her mouth to muffle her outcry she bit down hard, but succeeded only in grinding her teeth together through the linen. Tears sprang into her eyes and she shook her head vigorously to stop them. There had never been a situation, no matter how apparently hopeless, that Victoria had not managed to escape and even turn to her advantage. She simply had to get control of herself, still the frantic beating of her heart, and figure out what in God's name was happening. What was being done to her?

McGlory. The name came without conscious thought or invitation. Someone had dragged her name into a threat against McGlory, and this was his answer. She looked up into the soft brown eyes of the handsome young man who was holding her, and read in them the whole story of her doom.

"It's best to let me finish the job without fighting it," he said. He smiled at her, brushed a wisp of hair from her forehead, eased a portion of the napkin from her mouth. "What happens is that you fall asleep. There's no pain, nothing to fear. Just a longer and a better sleep than you've ever had before. You won't be alone, I promise. I'll stay with you throughout." He picked up the brown bottle she'd brought from Prudence's room. "We'll start with a bit more of this, I think. It's easier to get down. Then you won't mind the other so much."

It happened so quickly she had no defense against it. The laudanum bottle slipped under the napkin as he jerked it from her mouth, the liquid poured into her throat, and to keep from choking, she swallowed it. By the time she realized what he had done, the napkin filled her mouth again and she could feel a warm, heavy languor beginning to weigh down her body and numb her brain.

"There we are. See how easy that was. Now we'll wait just a bit and do it again." He sometimes thought of himself as a priest of sorts, sitting quietly beside a dying man or woman to ease the pain of this life and smooth the path to the next. Not that he believed there was another life. He just referred to it to ease the fears of his travelers. He liked that word better than any of the others that might describe the service he performed.

"Time for another dose," he said cheerfully. The lady's mouth was slack, but her eyes told him she still understood what was happening. Quickly then, and back into her mouth went the napkin. Probably for the last time. He thought she was ready for the pure tincture of opium, which he'd have to ease down her throat more slowly than the laudanum. It was thicker, especially mixed with the honey, harder to swallow. But it did the job more quickly and more surely. She'd be gone before that clock downstairs struck the hour again.

And so would he.

CHAPTER 29

Roscoe Conkling died a week after Victoria MacKenzie and Donald Morley were buried in Woodlawn Cemetery. The former senator had been pronounced well on the road to recovery just eleven days earlier.

Before the press could write that Conkling was on his feet again, he suffered a relapse. His fever spiked, his mind wandered in delirium; the doctors drilled a hole into his skull to relieve the increasing pressure on his brain. He survived the operation, regained consciousness, tore the bandages from his head, and had to be forcibly anesthetized to keep him in his bed.

On and on it went, day after interminable day, pain, fever, delirium, then spells of terrible coughing from lungs that were filling up with fluid. Finally, the great heart that was the essence of Roscoe Conkling failed; he lapsed into a coma from which death was a welcome release for those who were caring for him. His body was transported home to Utica.

No one mourned him more deeply or more sincerely than Josiah Gregory, who sat for hours at Conkling's desk, moving crystal paperweights around aimlessly, drinking cup after cup of the strong coffee that had fueled Roscoe's tremendous energy. When the time came, he removed a copy of Conkling's will from the safe in which it had been locked, and gave it to Geoffrey Hunter.

"This concerns you more than anyone else," he said. He wore a black armband on his coat sleeve and had hung a large black crepe ribbon on the office door.

"I'll miss him," Geoffrey said. "He saw something in me that I'm not sure I would have found without his conviction it was there." He wasn't sure he wanted to read the will with Josiah's sad eyes looking on. He was afraid he knew what Conkling had done. When the grieving secretary handed him his employer's silver letter opener, he knew he had no choice.

"You can skip over the family bequests," Josiah urged. "Everything that isn't a part of his practice goes to Mrs. Conkling, with an additional bequest to Miss Bessie."

Geoffrey's eyes skimmed quickly down to the signatures at the bottom of the last page. "He wrote it himself."

"Which makes it unbreakable. Mr. Conkling was a much more private person than people thought. He liked to keep what really mattered to him close to his heart." Josiah smiled as if remembering one of Roscoe's well-hidden tender moments. "I'll leave you to read the rest of the will in private." The door to the outer office closed quietly behind him.

Conkling had left his law practice and its client list, the remainder of the fully paid up five-year lease on the office space, all of its furnishings, and his private law library to his great and good friend Geoffrey Hunter, with the request that Josiah Gregory be given the opportunity to serve him as well as he had served Roscoe. If Josiah, now a respectably rich recipient of the ex-senator's generosity, cared to continue in his current position.

Geoffrey read through the remainder of the will. As Josiah had said, it was simple, straightforward, and not the least surprising. Julia Conkling, who had made a life for herself in Utica, would not contest any of its provisions.

Tucked into the folder containing the will was an envelope with Geoffrey's name on it and the word *private* written in Roscoe's distinctive script. In the lower left-hand corner was a date. *April 5, 1888.* The day that Geoffrey and Prudence had sat in Roscoe's bedroom while Josiah read aloud the recounting of the famous walk up Broadway the night of the blizzard. Phrases leaped out at him as he unfolded the letter addressed to *My dear Geoff.* He smiled, remembering that Roscoe rarely shortened anyone's name, usually only when he was attempting to hide some strong emotion. He read on.

> *Brevity is not one of my talents, but I'm afraid that I'm not quite up to par at the moment. Suffice it to say that if you are reading this note, I did not survive the blizzard after all. Josiah will have given you a copy of my will; Julia's lawyer has the original and will undoubtedly be contacting you.*
>
> *And now to you, my dear boy. Pinkerton knew it all along; you were one of his best operatives. That's why he quarreled with you so frequently; Allan knew his time was nearly up and yours was just beginning. Jealousy can twist even the best of men. You were wise to get out when you did. The work you've done for me and for others here in New York has more than proved your worth.*
>
> *But you cannot continue indefinitely living in a hotel suite and taking only the occasional commission that strikes your fancy. A man has to devote himself to a cause, or he ends up cursing himself for the waste of his life. I wouldn't presume to tell you what that cause should be, but I do presume to leave you an office to which to come every morning and a factotum par excellence. I speak of*

Josiah, of course. Whether it's the law or detecting that calls you, and I feel it must be one of the two, you could do much worse than to have him at your back.

Prudence. The Judge loved her too much, educated her as if she were not a woman, and left her alone in this world long before she was ready to make her own way. He thought to protect her in marriage; perhaps it is better this way though it cannot justify Linwood's death. She has a fine mind and she is one of the bravest souls I've ever met. You will need to be her true friend for many years to come.

The letter ended abruptly, a large, untidy *R* tilting its way across the bottom of the page. As if Conkling had used up the last reserves of the energy for which he had been so celebrated.

"We'll need to get the lettering on the door changed, Josiah," Geoffrey said, walking from the inner to the outer office. "You'll have to order new stationery, too."

"How shall it read, sir?" There was a lift to Gregory's voice, a hint of the firmness with which he had ordered Roscoe's professional life.

"Hunter and Associates, Investigative Law."

"And Associates?"

"And Associates."

"I'll order the smallest amount of stationery possible." Josiah wondered how long it would take Miss Prudence to demand and get equal billing.

Face your enemies and your worst fears. Go back to the place where you were defeated. Stare down the nightmares and the memories until you overpower them. Bring nothing of the hurtful past into the new future you make for yourself.

Prudence had always welcomed the Judge's reassuring voice,

but now another man had slipped into her thoughts and she wasn't making any effort to keep him out. Not since Geoffrey Hunter had caught her in his arms and carried her into Mrs. Dailey's boardinghouse. They had been through so much together. Jackson shot and running away. Kincaid and Danny Dennis hurtling toward the Brooklyn Bridge, Mr. Washington's hooves beating a metallic tattoo on the cobblestones. A whirl of bright blue sky overhead when she began to fall. Geoffrey's fathomless dark eyes and the anxious look on his face as he reached for her. The kaleidoscopic sounds and images had replayed themselves in Prudence's mind until gradually the derringer's sharp blast faded, the white horse ran in silence, and Geoffrey smiled. Strong, muscled arms held her; she was safe.

Until she returned to the house on Fifth Avenue. Then the fight to regain her sense of self began anew. With it came the recurring temptation to surrender to the peaceful oblivion of laudanum. She could taste its bitterness, feel the rush of letting go that came with the first swallow. Sometimes, when the craving ambushed her, she wondered how much longer she could hold out. Thankfully, each attack was weaker than its predecessor.

Face your enemies and your worst fears.

She had freed herself from the bondage of physical dependence, but she needed a talisman against a moment of weakness. She found it in the emerald and diamond ring that celebrated her birth, that Victoria had ripped from her neck in this very library. Gift of her father to her mother. While she wore it, it was as though both parents girded her with their strength.

She was fortunate, Prudence thought as she paced the Turkish carpet, surrounded by the hundreds of books her father had collected, now restored to their shelves. She had no memories to face down of how Victoria and Donald met their ends. Geoffrey and Ned Hayes had spared her the sight of Victoria dead in her pink silk sheets, and stood in for her at the identification of

Donald's pallid corpse laid out on one of Bellevue's mortuary slabs.

When propriety demanded she attend the burial in Woodlawn Cemetery, Geoffrey shook hands and received condolences on her behalf, murmuring the sad tale of Mrs. MacKenzie's accidental overdose. It happened so often that no one questioned the account. Prudence said nothing and kept her mourning veil firmly in place to hide the tight smile she could not always bite back.

Between them, Mrs. Dailey and Cameron purged every trace of both Morleys from the MacKenzie mansion. Mrs. Dailey found a new housekeeper to replace the murdered Frances Barstow, but Cameron would allow no one to occupy the position he had held for so long. Miss Prudence would need him more than ever, he explained to the disappointed Kathleen Dailey; reluctantly she agreed. Besides, he reminded her, she had the injured Colleen to nurse back to health. The girl would have to keep to her bed for at least another three weeks; recovery from a fall down a flight of stairs didn't happen overnight. Prudence welcomed his return.

Go back to the place where you were defeated. She had done that. She had relived Victoria's sudden attack, the sound and feel of glass shattering against her head, the horror of being locked in to await her fate. *Stare down the nightmares until you overpower them.* She had sat alone for hours in her father's chair, fingers digging into the leather. Remembering. Rejecting. Defeating. One by one the nightmare memories drifted away and disappeared like smoke on the wind. The Judge's library became her precious sanctuary once more. The hard-won battle with the horrors of what Victoria had attempted to do to her was over. She had emerged triumphant.

Bring nothing of the hurtful past into the new future you make for yourself.

One demon remained to be exorcised.

Prudence knew the household staff was worried about her. She had grown thinner and more silent by the day, and she had to remind herself to smile her thanks for the many small services done without her asking for them. Geoffrey had stopped by several times; she'd seen the worried frown cross his handsome face when he thought she wasn't looking. The last time he was here, she'd asked him not to come again for a while.

"How long?"

"I don't know." It was true. She didn't know how long it would take to find herself again, but she sensed she could not hurry the search.

Jackson had deserved the full measure of his end, as had Victoria and Donald. All three of them had blood on their hands. But Frances Barstow had not earned death at the hands of a madman. Kincaid maintained that the housekeeper stayed behind to divert Dr. Yarborough's attendants from finding Prudence. Which meant she had died so that Prudence might live.

The guilt was strangling her.

Stare down the memories until you overpower them. She turned her inner eye to the kitchen one floor below where she sat, to the stone floor where Mrs. Barstow must have lain while Jackson kicked her ribs into shattered pieces of bone, where she had taken her last breath in unimaginable pain. Kincaid found her body in the stable where Jackson had concealed it; he told the whole story of that dreadful afternoon to Geoffrey, who understood that Prudence would need to look once more on the face of the woman who had first betrayed and then rescued her. Maurice Warneke had kept the body in his cooling room.

On Geoffrey's instructions, Warneke had done nothing to reconstruct Frances Barstow's face. Prudence had to see for herself the damage done by the man she had shot. Whatever Mrs. Barstow had done in her life to earn a stay in purgatory had been forgiven by what she endured before she died. There was a hard lesson to be learned from Frances Barstow. Prudence thought she might never understand all of it. But what she felt as she forced herself to remember was a gradual easing of the pain of guilt, a sense that someone who had much to be forgiven could also bestow the gift of exoneration.

Prudence would never forget these last few weeks; for years to come she would wake up trembling and drenched in sweat. But the ghosts would one by one absent themselves, would find their own peace and cease haunting her.

The fire German Clara had lit spit and crackled, sending sparks against the screen, embers that beat against the worked iron until they fell, spent, to the floor of the brick fireplace. Prudence watched them burn themselves out, saw their bright red light turn into gray ash.

She stood up, shook out her skirts, ran her fingers through the heavy weight of her upswept hair, loosened a few pins. Delighted in the feeling of release and freedom as the curls cascaded against her neck.

The maid had brought a carafe of coffee and a plate of Cook's best currant scones to tempt her mistress's appetite. Split, toasted, and liberally buttered, the scones filled the air with the rich smell of fresh baking. The aroma of the coffee reminded her of every morning's new beginning. She couldn't remember the last time she'd relished the food set out for her.

Prudence took a bite of scone, then pushed open the heavy library drapes, drawn tightly closed against light and air. Yards and yards of green velvet rolled back from windows that cried out to be opened to the fresh, fragrant air of springtime.

She wondered where Geoffrey was at this moment and whether he would call on her today, then realized he would continue to respect her request to stay away. Until she told him otherwise.

There were decisions to be made, work to be done. They had talked about a new venture, an exciting opportunity to be developed in Roscoe Conkling's old offices. Not your ordinary law practice. Not even your predictable private investigation firm. Something that combined the best of both.

Her eyes drifted to the new telephone standing on what had been the Judge's desk. Now hers. Prudence smiled when she heard Geoffrey's voice. It was as though he were standing right beside her.

"I'm ready," she said. "I'm ready."

Hunter and MacKenzie, Investigative Law. Equal partners. Prudence liked the sound of it.

ACKNOWLEDGMENTS

Working with the support and encouragement of other writers is the greatest motivation an author can have. Thanks to Alexis Powers and to all of my fellow Writers Workshop members who listen to and validate each other's work with respect and enthusiasm.

Special thanks to Louise Boost, Joyce Sanford, and Betty Barry, who have made my Tuesday mornings some of the best hours of the week. Nothing escapes their critical eyes and ears, and every suggestion is made with only one goal in mind: to tell a better story.

Jessica Faust, agent extraordinaire, has been a fierce advocate of this book. Her suggestions, analytical approach to revisions, and unflagging enthusiam were of immeasurable help. Thank you, Jessica!

My editor, John Scognamiglio, knows exactly where to apply the editor's touch. No question ever goes ignored or unanswered; he is the gentlemanly soul of courtesy.

Whenever I've floundered, my husband has been there to throw me the lifeline of confidence and love. His belief in me has never faltered.

Although this is a work of fiction, the Great Blizzard of March 1888 was real. New York's former senator did make a three-mile trek up Broadway through blinding snow and howling-winds that resulted in his death. The newspapers of the time carried stories, sketches, and photographs of the devastation caused by the sudden and unexpected storm. Everyone who survived the blizzard was eager to tell his story.

To this mystery writer, it seemed the perfect time and place to attempt to hide a murder.

Heiress Prudence MacKenzie is a valuable partner to attorney Geoffrey Hunter, despite the fact that women are not admitted to the bar in New York's Gilded Age. And though their office is a comfortable distance from the violence that haunts the city's slums, the firm of Hunter and MacKenzie is about to come dangerously close to an unstoppable killer. . . .

The murders in Whitechapel are shocking enough to make news worldwide, and in the autumn of 1888, Geoffrey and Prudence find the stories in the *New York Herald* quite unsettling. But London is not the only city to be terrorized by a mad butcher.

Nora Kenny makes the occasional journey on the Staten Island Ferry to work in Prudence's Fifth Avenue house, just as her mother once served Prudence's mother. As little girls, they played freely together, before retreating into their respective social classes. Still, they remain fond of each other. But when Nora slips away to Saint Anselm's one chilly Saturday to confess her sins and never returns, Prudence is alarmed. And when Nora's body is discovered in a local park, Prudence is devastated.

Nora will not be the only young woman to fall victim, but the police are uncertain what they are dealing with. Has the Ripper sailed across the Atlantic to find a new hunting ground? Is some disturbed soul copying his crimes? A former Pinkerton agent, Geoffrey intends to step in where the New York Metropolitan Police seem to be failing, and Prudence is just as determined to protect the poor, vulnerable females being targeted. But a killer with a disordered mind and an incomprehensible motive may prove too elusive for even this experienced pair to outwit.

Please turn the page for an exciting sneak peek of
Rosemary Simpson's next Gilded Age Mystery

LIES THAT COMFORT AND BETRAY

coming soon wherever print and e-books are sold!

CHAPTER 1

"Jack the Ripper's killed number seven. An Irish girl this time, younger than the others. Only twenty-five. The detective in charge had photographs taken of the scene and the victim. I don't think I'll buy a newspaper next week." Josiah Gregory rattled the pages of the *New York Herald* of November 10, 1888. The shocking story of the mutilation of Mary Jane Kelly was graphic and unsettling.

"Have you ever been to London, Josiah?" Geoffrey Hunter set down the *New York Times*, which was running the same story, but in far less detail; its readership preferred to be informed and only inadvertently titillated. The lead story in the column cabled by their London correspondent was the partisan wrangling of the Parnell Commission. Politics as usual first, then the Ripper.

"I haven't, sir. Mr. Conkling went, of course. Twice. Once in 1875, then again two years later. He was a great one for seeing everything there was to be seen, but I doubt he ventured into Whitechapel."

"You still miss him, don't you, Josiah?"

"Every day. I always will. You can't spend that much of your life with someone and not regret his absence. I was the senator's personal secretary from his first swearing in at the House of Representatives in Washington until he died. Almost twenty-nine years."

"You could retire, if that would suit you."

"And do what with myself, Mr. Hunter? I'd rather stay on here with you. I'm used to working, and I'm used to this office."

"What else does the *Herald* say about Mary Jane Kelly?"

"So much that I'd be careful not to leave the paper lying around where Miss Prudence might pick it up. The Kelly woman was a lady of the evening like all the others the Ripper's killed, but this time he did more damage to the corpse. The doctor on the scene is quoted as saying it was worse than anything he's experienced in dissecting rooms. The Ripper cut the body open and took out all of the organs. He sliced her face so badly it didn't look like a face anymore and nearly severed her head when he slit the throat. Then he hacked off all of her private parts. That's the short version, Mr. Hunter, and about all I care to read." Josiah folded the newspaper four times into a neat rectangle that he handed to his employer. "As I say, it's nothing Miss Prudence should see."

"I've already read the story, Josiah." The young woman standing in the doorway to Geoffrey Hunter's office was tall and slender, dressed in black, but without the long, heavy veils of full mourning. It had been more than ten months since her father's death, nearly eight since her fiancé had been murdered in the worst blizzard the northeastern seaboard had ever known. "You shouldn't leave the outer office unattended if you don't want intruders coming in unchallenged." Prudence MacKenzie smiled to take the sting out of her words, and was immediately transformed from a pretty girl into the kind of delicate beauty men instinctively want to possess and protect.

"Let me take that," Hunter said, standing to reach for a rectangular package secured in brown paper and tied with butcher's twine. "What is this, Prudence?"

"It's the Hunter and MacKenzie stationery," she said. "I decided I couldn't wait for delivery. I went by the printer's on my way here." Using the scissors Josiah handed her, Prudence cut through the string and then the sturdy wrapping. "What do you think?"

The letter paper was a heavy, off-white bond, the firm's name engraved across the top of each sheet in a thick calligraphic script. *Hunter and MacKenzie, Investigative Law.*

Josiah Gregory ran his fingers lightly over the lettering. "Mr. Conkling would have liked this," he said. "It's what he hoped for when he made out his will that last time."

Like Prudence's fiancé, Roscoe Conkling had been among the 200 New York City casualties of the Great White Blizzard, though it had taken almost a month before the damage done to his body during a long walk up Broadway at the height of the storm finally killed him. When he knew without a doubt that he would not survive, the former senator from New York deeded his office and his law practice to Geoffrey Hunter and wrote a letter in which he urged him to follow a profession that would give meaning to his life. Josiah Gregory, now a man of independent means through his longtime employer's generosity, had been an unexpected and invaluable bonus.

"I'll put this away." Josiah gathered up the new stationery, the wrapping paper, the twine, and the scissors. Moving quickly and quietly, with a deft neatness that defined his every movement and gesture, he retreated to his desk in the outer office. He'd give Miss Prudence and Mr. Hunter a few minutes to themselves before he brought in the coffee tray. November was always cold and damp; nothing made a New York winter bearable like strong, sweet coffee with a good dollop of heavy cream.

"I did read the article about the Ripper's latest atrocity."

Prudence unfolded the newspaper Josiah had placed on Geoffrey's desk, settling herself in one of the client chairs to look at the headline. "I cannot imagine what kind of monster would do something like this, not once, but seven separate times. They're calling him a lunatic and a homicidal maniac. For once I don't think the press is exaggerating. He has to be insane, Geoffrey. It's the only explanation that makes any sense. Thank God it's not happening here."

"We've had our share of killers. No country or society is immune from violence. Think about what we did to one another not very long ago. The war's been over for twenty-three years, but for some people it's as though it were still being fought."

Matthew Brady's photographs of Union and Confederate dead on shell pocked battlefields had horrified and saddened a nation torn in two by irreconcilable beliefs and a warrior culture that enshrined blood sacrifice. Death had ridden the land for four long years, and when it was finally over, greed galloped in like a fifth horsemen of the Apocalypse.

There were more enormously wealthy men in America now than ever before, but there were also legions of hopelessly poor and homeless men, women, and children. Armies of exploited workers whose wages barely staved off starvation. Violence was commonplace in big city slums, but few of New York City's killings could match what Jack the Ripper was doing in the far away London cesspit of Whitechapel.

"How could he do what they say he's done? Especially this latest killing, this Mary Jane Kelly. The reporter writes that he carved her up as casually as a butcher does the carcass of a sheep hanging from a hook in a slaughterhouse. I don't think I'll ever be able to understand the man who did that."

"Would you be able to defend him, Prudence?"

"Women haven't been admitted to the bar in New York, Geoffrey. It's only been a few months since New York University finally allowed three women to enroll in their law courses.

Whether they'll graduate with anything equivalent to a law degree is another matter entirely."

"You didn't answer my question."

"I'm not sure I can. My father taught me everything he knew about the law. Even though the lessons took place at home, I learned as much if not more than any intern in any law firm in the city. The Judge made sure of that. But since the bar is closed to women in this state, your question is moot."

"There was a killer in Austin, Texas, three years ago. He murdered eight people, seven of them women, mostly in service. Chopped them to death with an axe."

"Did someone defend him?"

"I don't think the murders have ever been solved."

"Like Jack the Ripper."

"One theory is that when a murderer leaves the area where he committed his crimes, he doesn't stop killing; he starts again in a different place. The Ripper is still somewhere in London; there's no telling how many more women he'll kill before something or someone forces him to leave."

"For an ex-Pinkerton, you don't sound very optimistic that the Austin killer or the Ripper will ever be caught."

"I'm not. You can trace a *crime passionel* to a spurned lover, and a murder committed in the course of a burglary to the man who's foolish enough to pawn what he's stolen. You can even link a poisoner to the victim. But if someone kills for the sheer pleasure of killing, and there's no personal link to his prey, then he'll only be caught by accident, by some small, fortuitous mistake he doesn't realize he's made."

"At least we don't have a Ripper in New York City." Prudence refolded the newspaper, placed it headline down on her partner's desk.

"Not yet. It's only a matter of time before someone decides that London shouldn't have all the glory."

"Surely not."

"Sooner or later we'll have an American Ripper, Prudence. For all we know he's already at work; the newspapers just haven't discovered him yet."

"Can you manage, girl?" Brian Kenny handed his daughter a heavy wicker basket containing the freshly butchered bodies of four of his wife's finest stewing hens. Wrapped in saltwater soaked toweling, they'd keep nicely until she could hand them over to the MacKenzie cook in the house on Fifth Avenue. "Mind you keep the lid on tight, now. Mrs. Hearne is that careful about what she puts in her soup pot."

Nora Kenny drew her small, slender self up to her full height of just over five feet. She'd bundled her black hair into a fisherman's knit cap for the cold, windy ride from Staten Island to Manhattan, but there was nothing she could do to keep the red from her cheeks. Chapped skin and lips were the price you paid in November for having a fair Irish complexion. "I'll be fine, Da. I've carried baskets heavier than this one many a time."

"Don't forget it's Sunday tomorrow. You don't want to miss Mass."

"I'll go to Saint Anselm's with Colleen." Nora had become good friends with Miss Prudence's maid, sharing a room with her whenever she worked at the Fifth Avenue house.

"One of your brothers will be here to meet the ferry next Saturday. Mind you're on time to catch it. Your ma will worry me to death if you don't."

She could feel a blush deepening the scarlet of her already cold reddened cheeks. It was always like that when she had something to hide.

"Go on then. The ferry's about to pull out."

A surge of passengers crowded across the dock toward the new paddle wheeler named the *Robert Garrett*. Nora slung the handle of the wicker basket over one arm, picked up her carpetbag with her free hand, and smiled up at her da. She was his only girl in a family of ten children, six of them still living, thank God. He worried about her more than he did any of the five lads. He'd been reluctant to let her go by herself to help get Miss Prudence's Fifth Avenue house ready for the Thanksgiving and Christmas holidays, but she'd reminded him of how welcome the extra wages would be and he'd given in. Brian had a terrible soft spot for his Nora.

As soon as the *Robert Garrett* pulled away from Staten Island into the choppy waters of the Hudson River, Nora found herself a comfortable seat in the portside saloon, the basket containing the plucked fowl sitting in an empty seat beside her, carpetbag at her feet. From this side of the ferry she could look out the windows that ran all along its side and see the enormous Statue of Liberty that had gone up on Bedloe's Island two years before. The weather on the day of the dedication had been bad enough to force cancellation of the planned fireworks. Nora remembered how disappointed they'd all been, crowded onto the family's two fishing boats to catch a glimpse of President Grover Cleveland, then forced to return to Staten Island in thick fog and heavy rain without having spied a single dignitary. The mist swirling up from the river today reminded her of that late October day in 1886. She and Tim Fahey had just begun walking out.

The ferry wasn't as crowded today as she'd thought it might be. Most of the seats were taken, but there were none of the weekday crowds pressed against the rails. Nora let her thoughts fly ahead to the mansion on Fifth Avenue where she'd be spending the coming week. She and her mother had both worked for the MacKenzie family since the Judge first built the Staten Island summer house named Windscape where he hoped his wife would recover from the tuberculosis. She didn't, of course. No one ever did, though sometimes the invalid coughed out bits of his lungs for years until the final hemorrhage.

Nora came to Windscape as a three-year-old, tied by a long rope looped around her waist and fastened to one of the thick wooden legs of the kitchen table so she wouldn't wander and get into mischief. Agnes Kenny kept a watchful eye on her daughter as she peeled potatoes, polished silverware, or baked the Irish soda bread that Sarah McKenzie loved to nibble with her afternoon cup of tea. The child was four when she was first let loose to play with Miss Prudence, the two of them a lively, mischievous pair whose antics brought a smile and occasionally a laugh to Miss Sarah's lips. Then a cough. Laughter always exacted a price. Nora remembered the sound of that coughing, how it echoed through the rooms, getting worse and worse until Miss Prudence's mother stopped coughing and the house became empty and silent.

Once they'd grown out of childhood, which happened early in their young lives, Miss Prudence and Nora seldom met, though Nora continued to accompany her mother whenever Agnes went to Windscape to cook or to clean. The Judge never spoke of selling the house, but he was seldom there. When the summer air in the city was brutally hot and hard to breathe, Judge MacKenzie brought his daughter across the river to the white painted house on the hill, but the young miss was never alone. There was always a nurse or governess or tutor beside her; she'd grown beyond the free, open play of the early years. She was being groomed to take her mother's place in a society from which Nora would forever be excluded.

That was the way of the world, her mother told her, reading the sadness in her daughter's expressive blue eyes. Miss Prudence didn't mean anything by it. She'd just moved deeper into the world she'd been born to, leaving her childhood playmate behind. Where she belonged. It was all about knowing your place and keeping to it. That was why her parents approved of Tim Fahey, why they'd pushed her in his direction and encouraged the engagement even when Nora herself was sure it was no longer what she wanted. Her ma said there wasn't a finer young man on Staten Island than Tim, and that Nora and Tim fit together as well as they did because they were so much alike. They lived in the same world.

She smiled at her da's caution to remember to go to Mass tomorrow. One of the reasons she was taking this early ferry was so she could stop by Saint Anselm's for Saturday confession on her way to Miss Prudence's house. She'd already confessed this particular sin to Father Devlin on the island more times than she cared to think about. She was sure he hadn't recognized her yet through the screen, but eventually he would and then there'd be hell to pay. Priests weren't allowed to reveal what they were told in confession, but she couldn't afford to take any chances.

She could walk in off the street to Saint Anselm's and be just another blue eyed, black haired Irish girl. Lost in the crowd. She'd been to Mass there many times with Colleen, but she didn't know any of the priests personally and they didn't know her. She'd whisper her sin through the grille, bow her head for absolution, gabble her penance at the altar rail, and be on her way. Ten or fifteen minutes at most. The hens wouldn't mind.

The other stop she had to make was more important. She decided to go there first, just in case it took longer than she had planned for. If she didn't make it to Saint Anselm's before confessions ended for the day she'd have to lie to her mother about receiving Communion on Sunday because you couldn't go to the altar with a mortal sin on your soul.

Then it would be back to Father Devlin again when she got home because she knew she wasn't going to stop. She was caught already, so what could it matter?

Unless something happened in the meantime. Unless she was wrong.

She'd told so many lies by now that a few more wouldn't trouble her conscience at all.

CHAPTER 2

Weekly confessions at Saint Anselm's started at midafternoon during the winter months. The November sun usually set by five o'clock and even with snow on the ground to reflect the light from streetlamps, it was dark as well as cold. People wanted to get home.

This Saturday only one of the three priests assigned to the parish was on duty. Father Gerard Mahoney, Saint Anselm's sixty-year-old pastor, was confined to his bed with a mustard plaster on his chest. Father Kearns, the assistant pastor, had been called to the bedside of a dying child.

"I'll manage," Father Mark Brennan assured both his colleagues.

"Give them all five Our Fathers, five Hail Marys, and five Glory Bes," coughed Father Mahoney. "The faster you get them in and out, the more they'll thank you for it." The pastor had been known to say an entire Mass from *Introíbo ad altáre Dei* to *Ite, Missa Est* in twenty minutes flat.

It wasn't Father Brennan's way to rush his flock along like sheep being herded to the shearing pen. He scrupulously matched each sin to its appropriate penance, not forgetting to accuse himself of the sin of pride for lacking humility in the doing of God's holy work.

The line outside his confessional box was long, stretching halfway down a side aisle. He took his time with each sinner, and as a result many would-be receivers of the sacrament gave up and went home, especially once four-thirty had come and gone. Parishioners popped their heads through the massive wooden central doors, took a look at the length of the line, lingered a moment to gauge how quickly, in this case how slowly, people were entering and emerging from the curtained side boxes. They dipped their fingers into the holy water font, made a sketchy sign of the cross, and were out again before their coats had finished steaming in the indoor air. They wished Father Brennan would learn to speed things up. This wasn't the old country; everyone in America was in a hurry.

It occurred to Nora Kenny that she ought to step out of line and be on her way to the MacKenzie mansion, but once she made up her mind, she seldom changed it. Both the Kenny parents and all of the lads were like that, too. Obstinate, mulish, as immovable in their determination as an Irishman could be. And proud of it.

She reminded herself of the other reason she wouldn't give up today. Agnes Kenny expected all of her children to walk to the communion rail every Sunday, and God help the one who didn't. So if Nora was to allay any suspicions her mother might have about her recent excuses to slip away from the house on her own, she had to receive Communion next Sunday. Today was her last chance to confess to a priest who could be counted on not to recognize her. She hoped the hens weren't warming up too much. She couldn't smell them, so they must be all right.

When it was finally her turn, Nora stepped into the confessional, knelt, and made the sign of the cross. "Bless me, Father, for I have sinned. It's been one week since my last confession."

It wasn't as dark as in the church on Staten Island; Nora could see more than just a shadow on the other side of the curtained grille. This priest was young and handsome, his hair nearly as dark as hers, the hand he raised in the blessing long fingered and finely sculpted. She wondered if he would look in her direction; most priests faced forward and only leaned sideways a bit toward the penitent.

She started with the venial sins, the way she always did, hoping that when she slipped in the great big embarrassing mortal sin of committing impure acts he might be busy with his own prayers and not notice. But he did.

"Did you commit the sin of impurity with yourself or with another?"

The question shocked her. The priest on Staten Island had never asked Nora Kenny for details. "With another, Father."

"Are either of you married?"

"No, Father."

"How many times did you commit this sin of impurity since your last confession?"

"Twice, Father." She could feel the sweat beading on her forehead. Her voice was shaky, and she thought she might cry. *Why couldn't he just give her a penance and absolution and be done with it?*

"Have you thought that a child might be conceived?"

She didn't answer, afraid her voice might penetrate the long dark red curtain that fell over the backs of her legs. Unwilling to risk losing the little control remaining to her.

She heard a deep sigh and knew he was finally finished.

"For your penance I want you to kneel before Our Lady's statue while you say five decades of the rosary. Ask Our Blessed Mother for the grace to stay chaste."

She was sure tears were making tracks down her cheeks.

"Now make a good Act of Contrition and tell Our Lady how sorry you are to have sinned against purity."

Just before Nora lowered her face into her cupped hands to whisper the Act of Contrition, she felt his eyes on her. Dark brown eyes in a stern face. One glimpse through the fan of her fingers, but it was enough. This was the kind of priest everyone tried to avoid, the kind who took things too seriously and could make life miserable. She supposed she deserved it, though. She'd tried to avoid Father Devlin and this was the punishment she got.

She asked a man leaving the church ahead of her what time it was. Quarter past five. Just enough time to drop the hens at the MacKenzie house and get herself back to Saint Anselm's by six to say her five decades of the rosary. She'd learned in First Holy Communion class that you had to do your penance to make the absolution stick. The nun teaching them hadn't used those exact words, but that was the gist of it. If she ran both ways and didn't stop for a gossip when she gave Cook the hens, she could just make it.

There would still be time afterwards to complete her other errand, the one she couldn't tell anyone about. Seven o'clock. That's when her things would be ready and she could pick them up.

It was early dusk. The lamplights hissed softly in the cold evening air. Nora was surprised how easy it was to navigate the sidewalk despite the heavy basket bumping against her hip. There was no smell of dead hen coming from it, and when she reached a hand in, the cloths in which they were wrapped were still damp and cool. Almost as good as keeping them on ice, she thought. She passed few women as she walked; it was mostly men striding along in a hurry to get out of the cold, faces muffled in wool scarves, gloved hands carrying parcels or leather briefcases. Horses clopped by, nostrils breathing out steam, drivers hunched over to catch a draft of warmth from their broad backs. She'd give anything to be in one of those hansom cabs, but even if she had the money, no one would stop for a girl out all alone after dark.

Nora breathed a sigh of relief when she recognized the MacKenzie mansion, a thick blanket of green ivy climbing over its deep redbrick facade. Quick now, down the areaway steps to the kitchen door.

But when she hauled on the bellpull, she heard no sound of

ringing inside. No footsteps tapped their way to the door. She didn't have time to stand there and try to figure out where everybody was.

She thought about pounding on the door and calling out, but what if a policeman were passing by and heard her? He'd haul her off without waiting to listen to an explanation and then she'd really be in trouble. She yanked on the bellpull one more time, then set down her basket, turned on her heels, and sped up the concrete steps to the street. Moments later she was back on Fifth Avenue, dodging and ducking her way toward Saint Anselm's.

She didn't expect to be climbing the broad stone steps of the church alone. She had looked forward to the comfort of light streaming out into the darkness as the doors opened and closed behind parishioners stopping by for a quick prayer or to light a candle on their way home from work. Catholic churches were never entirely empty.

But the wide steps were barren and Saint Anselm's had the look of a church settling into locked emptiness for the night.

Nora scurried through the vestibule, her shoes clattering on the stone floor. It was warmer inside the church itself, with a comforting fustiness hanging in the air, as though the people who had stood in the aisle waiting to go to confession had left bits of themselves behind—the smell of damp wool and wet leather shoes, that tangy scent of unwashed winter clothing and skin, the tobacco smoked by the men, the cheap scent worn by the women. It reminded her of going into the parlor at home before her mother readied up the coal stove and sent the wonderful smells of supper wafting through the rooms.

The church was dim because no one had turned on the huge, newly electrified chandeliers hanging from the ceiling. Banks of votive candles flickered at the side altars and the blood red sanctuary lamp burned steadily beside the tabernacle to remind her that Christ was present. God was here.

Nora genuflected, made the sign of the cross, and crept into a pew close to the side altar where a larger than life Virgin Mary in blue robes and white veil looked down at her. The kneeler boomed against the floor as she pulled it out and it slipped from her cold fingers. She glanced around guiltily. No one had heard. There was no one kneeling behind or to either side of her. No matter. She needed to get started on the five decades of the rosary she had to say.

She heard a sound like a key turning in a lock, but muffled, as if it came from the vestibule. Not a lock, but the click of one of the switches that turned on the electric lights? She waited for brightness to flood down, and looked up to see the chandeliers come ablaze, but the dimness all around her did not change. She clung more tightly to the rosary beads she'd wound around her fingers, feeling the sharpness of the small silver crucifix digging into the palm of her hand. She'd never been by herself inside a church before. No matter that the sanctuary lamp proclaimed the presence of Christ, Nora felt very alone and now very frightened.

She made her mind up quickly. Intention was all important when it came to sin, and she'd intended to say her rosary at the Virgin's feet. She'd kneel beside her bed in Colleen's room tonight instead and tag on an extra decade for the absence of a statue.

Nora got to her feet and scrambled out into the aisle, shoving the rosary beads into her coat pocket, pulling out the warm mittens her mother had knitted for her. She bobbed awkwardly in the general direction of the altar, then turned and fled toward the vestibule, pushing open the swinging doors with both outstretched arms, feet flying across the stone floor. Her hands flattened themselves against the outer doors and her body followed, pushing desperately to make them open. Nothing. They didn't yield to her pounding fists or to the sobs that burst from her throat. Why were the doors locked? Why hadn't someone looked into the church to make sure it was empty before closing up for the night?

She turned to go back the way she had come. There was a small side door opening onto a narrow alley that ran the length of the church. She'd seen people ducking out that way after Mass when they were in a hurry and didn't want to have to stop and talk to the priest standing outside on the main steps.

But the door she had just run through wouldn't budge. She didn't remember hearing it happen, but somehow it must have locked itself behind her. She was trapped in the vestibule.

The only thing she could do was make so much noise that a passerby would hear something odd and stop at the rectory next door to tell the housekeeper or one of the priests. Nora pounded until her arms went numb and then flamed in pain; she yelled and screamed until her throat closed up and nothing came out but a hoarse croak. Finally, all strength and hope gone, she slid down onto the stone floor, back propped against the wooden door, legs stretched out in front of her, bruised hands lying slack and useless in her lap, too spent and tired even to cry.

She wondered if anyone would be surprised that she hadn't kept her seven o'clock appointment. No matter. As soon as the church was unlocked tomorrow morning she'd be on her way. Colleen would scold her for not showing up when she was supposed to, and then together they'd have a good laugh about it.

When she began to tremble with the cold, Nora crawled to the lost and found chest against the side wall and pulled out coats, scarves, and sweaters that smelled of dust and other people. She made a nest on the floor and curled up into the bits of clothing, singing and humming to herself to keep up her courage. She thought about the soup her mother made from hens like the ones she'd left in the MacKenzie areaway. Hot chicken broth with lovely chunks of meat and vegetables floating around in it. She could taste it on her tongue, feel the heat in her empty belly. And how nice it would be to close icy fingers around the warmth of the bowl.

Nora fell asleep, a ragamuffin huddled into lost and forgotten garments so worn that no one had bothered to retrieve them.

She was deep in her dreams when the man who had locked Saint Anselm's doors came to stand over her. The picture of innocence, someone else might have thought.

He knew better.

Connect with

Visit us online at
KensingtonBooks.com
to read more from your favorite authors, see books
by series, view reading group guides, and more.

Join us on social media

for sneak peeks, chances to win books and prize packs,
and to share your thoughts with other readers.

facebook.com/kensingtonpublishing
twitter.com/kensingtonbooks

Tell us what you think!
To share your thoughts, submit a review,
or sign up for our eNewsletters, please visit:
KensingtonBooks.com/TellUs.